BEFORE THE ROOSTER CROWS TWICE

A NOVEL

Inspired by True Events

C. ARDEN MICHAELS

Big Red House Publishing
San Diego, California

Dedicated to
my entire family and dear friend and mentor, David,
without whom this book would not have been written.

And to Michael ~

Life is a lightning flash
Sparking tough and easy times.
Approach each with God's love and grace – giving thanks always
And you will weather any storm.

Forgive those who wrong you
Although they will be hard to forget.
Forgiving is for ridding your life of binding strongholds.
Make sure you are also asking God to forgive you as well.

Embrace the skills and abilities God has gifted you
Without complaining that they are not enough or what you expected.
He loves you. And everything has its purpose.
Learn something and grow stronger from every experience -
no matter how small.

Remember: God, family, everything else – in that order.
You will understand why.

Sign the mark you leave in life – with love.
You have already succeeded with my heart.

I love you so much.

My sails are filled with wind now
And my bow is in line with the sea.
The anchor's been lifted
And the strong current has grabbed hold -
Carrying this weary vessel to Thee.

~C. Arden Michaels
for John, 1953-2012

BEFORE THE ROOSTER CROWS TWICE

Chapter 1

BROAD IS THE ROAD

"It's Friday the thirteenth, a full moon, *and* Mercury is in retrograde!" Robbie bellowed. Heavy chunks of his raven hair violently shifted back and forth as the harsh, warm desert wind blew through the passenger window.

The mid-June temperatures were reaching more than one hundred degrees. It was the first time Robbie, Stuart, and Sarah had been on a long road trip together. They tried to avoid having to turn on the gas-sucking air conditioner, which could have easily overheated Sarah's little convertible. Instead, they kept the canvas top up to block the scorching summer sun.

Robbie's fear-peddling outburst startled the others, but they were not surprised by his typical display of social awkwardness. He attempted to excuse that part of his personality with charisma. His random, ill-chosen statements paired well with his egotism. Sarah noticed, but she was too entranced by the man's charm and handsome, chiseled features. These characteristics had been pleasant distractions ever since the day they met, four months prior.

"Good grief!" Sarah scoffed and giggled. "You're not going to dwell on *that* this weekend, are you?"

Stuart – who had been relegated to the back seat – piped up in agreement, "Robbie, you really don't believe that crap, right?"

They anticipated the next few days to be filled with fun. It was the end of the work week. The last thing either of Robbie's friends wanted to talk about was astrometry or astrology. Their friendships had become strained over the last several months. The vacation to Roka Valley was an attempt to make amends with lots of laughter, affection, and booze.

"There could be good or bad consequences from this trifecta," Robbie said.

"You think we'll be eaten by coyotes?" Stuart mocked.

"No, Stuart. I'm guessing a werewolf will get us," Sarah laughed sarcastically.

"You really shouldn't joke about superstitions and cosmic occurrences. This is a rare event. The full moon falling on a Friday the thirteenth won't happen for several years. Mercury in retrograde, alone, is known to cause chaos, breakups, or communication breakdowns," Robbie explained. "I know *you* believe what I'm saying, Sarah." He stared at the side of her face, waiting for a show of concern.

The two had spent moments together talking about the zodiac signs, their compatibilities, and speculation about the future from a new age perspective. Robbie took it more seriously than Sarah. She was in awe of the constellations, but he was fascinated with the perversion of them in the form of astrology. Sarah would often read her horoscope for relationship guidance and owned a book describing the traits of each sign. She was not nearly as educated on the subject as her dark-haired friend. It gave them something to talk about – that and the undeniable physical attraction between them.

Whether there was truth to any outcome resulting from the coincidental lineup of the moon and day – or an optical illusion of a planet traveling backward in space – Sarah and Stuart ignored Robbie's warning.

She typically perked up her ears whenever Robbie had something arousing to say about fortune-telling. Not today, though. They were well into this journey, and she was not about to turn back because of superstitions.

"I'm hungry," she said, switching topics. Sarah was clever and savvy at manipulating conversations about subjects that pleased her. She was an exotic woman with long, wavy, blonde hair and emerald-green eyes – the kind that hypnotized men. With a fit body like a twenty-five-year-old and the face to match, Sarah attracted males of all ages. She did not appear to be in her mid-forties. She was sleek and sultry. Her features hinted of European descent, but she was a true American.

The guys kept Sarah around to make themselves look good. Ultimately, Robbie was mystified by her. He was lost, but not taken. He would be doomed if he ever succumbed to that beauty. Protecting his fragile ego was a top priority. Acting like an ass and teasing her was his favorite way of communicating. "I've got something for you to eat," Robbie replied with a devious smirk.

Sarah peered at him annoyed, acknowledging his double entendre. He raised one eyebrow in silent reciprocation. She looked him over and then slipped into a daydream. Robbie's appearance was inviting. His long-sleeved, white shirt and loose-fitting jeans were rugged and manly. He was far from being a conformist and never wore appropriate attire for any occasion, or the weather. Despite being overdressed for the desert, some-how, he remained cool under all that material.

Sarah appreciated his well-kept style and freshly showered body. The scent of desert wildflowers gently made its way through the open window. It brushed past Robbie's tanned skin, delighting her senses as it blended with the smell of his aftershave and shampoo. The memory of the two of them – together – flashed through her mind. She tried desperately to focus on the road.

"Did you want to eat something or not?" Robbie interrupted Sarah's fantasy.

"Huh? Oh – yeah," she replied, remembering her pangs of hunger.

"I have chips in my bag, if you want."

"Sure. I have snacks, too," she said, looking over her shoulder at Stuart to imply he search her luggage.

"What do you need, Sweetie?" Stuart gently chimed in.

"I brought a jar of salted peanuts. It's back there somewhere."

"Hang on," he mumbled while fumbling for the nuts.

"Boy, you are hungry!" Robbie exclaimed, throwing a bag of potato chips in her lap. "By the way, did you know your lips look fuller from this angle? It must be your incessant need for food." The random dig came out of nowhere, hitting Sarah where she was most sensitive.

She was humble and insecure when it came to her looks. She hated the shape of her mouth, especially her profile, but it was a mouth most women would kill for. Her lips were beautifully rounded, and Robbie loved kissing them.

But his remark was meant to sting.

Where did that mean comment come from? Sarah wondered. She surmised that calling upon Stuart to retrieve an alternative snack ticked Robbie off, as expressed in his snarky words. "What's wrong with my lips?" she asked sheepishly.

"Oh, nothing. They just look bigger than usual, that's all," Robbie responded.

Sarah wanted to say something hurtful back, but remained quiet. She grabbed the nuts from Stuart. Just then, an elderly woman drove by, turned into their lane, and slowed down in front of their car. Sarah hit the brakes, which threw all three forward until their seatbelts locked up.

"Oh, my God!" Robbie barked, slamming his palms into the dashboard. "I hate old people!"

After gasping from the surprise, Sarah remembered that Robbie had expressed his distaste of the elderly before. In the back, Stuart – who was composing himself – shook his head from side to side in disgust. Both he and Sarah were not completely shocked at Robbie's statement. They knew the man did not accept much of society. He was somewhat disconnected, finding fault with just about everything and everyone around him. Stuart and Sarah prepared themselves for another eruption.

"Old farts should be rounded up and burned when they reach fifty-five," said Robbie, right on cue.

Sarah quickly turned toward him – holding back the strong desire to slap his face – and said, "Really? Just fifty-five? Ya know, Robbie, you'll be old someday, too. I wonder who will take care of *you*. I know! Her name is Karma." Her sarcasm came promptly. Sarah knew fifty-five was only ten years away from her own age.

"Ha! Very funny," Robbie said with a smug grin. "Whatever. I'm not going to be on Earth that long anyway."

Sarah snickered at his statement, but wondered why he thought of an early demise. She brushed it off and kept driving. Nothing mattered much to Robbie, including living or dying. He was all about shock and awe. He wanted to get her goat and reveled in making her wonder about his mental state. She was very fond of the elderly, and he was highly aware of it. She knew full well that he wanted to hurt her by digging at her weaknesses. As to why he did it – was a mystery.

"I crack myself up," Robbie boasted, running his fingers through his shiny black hair.

"You're so arrogant," Stuart spouted in Sarah's defense.

The statement from the back seat caught Sarah off guard. She smiled inside and stayed focused on the road. She was pleased that Stuart finally said something about his friend's behavior. Stuart typically kept to himself, but there were rare occasions that brought about a stirring within him. He was mostly a spectator during his time in the car. He was smart, analytical – the strong, silent type. However, the move to call out Robbie for his attitude was somewhat of a shocker.

"That was harsh!" Robbie said, peering over his left shoulder. "But, say what you want. I'm thick-skinned."

Truthfully, Robbie was not at all thick-skinned. He was sensitive and vulnerable, never showing those traits to others. Sarah could see inside of him. She did not want to hurt him in retaliation, but nevertheless, she knew there were times that Robbie needed to be taken down a peg or two; and this was one of them.

Sarah felt contentment as she looked at her confidant in the rearview mirror, upon which a necklace with a gold cross hung. It swayed to-and-fro with the breeze. The metal reflected the golden color of the sun, casting glimmering darts of light onto Sarah's face.

Stuart's sandy-blonde mop of curls got messy from the fast-moving air that swirled around the car's interior. His disheveled look made him appear down-to-earth. His fair locks softened the sharper, technical aspect of his personality. Stuart was a stable force in Sarah's life. Although they had only known each other since February, she trusted him the most. They could talk for hours, sharing dreams. They understood what the other was saying before even finishing a sentence. If only she could have experienced the same quality of communication with Robbie, things would have been less difficult.

Long Beach was already hours behind them. The trio headed toward the sleepy desert area of Roka Valley – their desolate destination. They still needed to stop for a tire check and gas-tank refill. Sarah noticed there were no other food items in Robbie's bag, aside from the chips he gave her. She fully expected, that at any given moment, her passengers would cry out to stop and get something to eat. But the car fell silent for a good hour after their embarrassing exchange.

The desert lent itself to reflection and deep thinking. *Why am I here with this pair of misfit men?* Sarah wondered. Albeit quite the misfit herself, Sarah felt as though she was brought into their *tribe* for a reason. Maybe it was to fix them. She often fell into relationships with men who needed some adjusting. They were either non-committal or uncomfortable with themselves. Both issues often led to mistreatment. She never understood why she stayed with guys like that. It must have been their sex appeal and seductive techniques. Being a giver, empath, and real good listener, it was easy for men to want more of Sarah. They jumped on those qualities, like kids in a bounce house, but committing to her was another story. *My face must scream* – come walk all over me. *How stupid can I be?* she silently lamented.

The experiences of failed relationships had deepened the soft creases in Sarah's forehead. Permanent lines were now hidden under long strands of hair that flowed over to one side of her face. Sarah still possessed a wholesome, tantalizing, demure appearance. She was as timid as a mouse on the outside, a great companion, and a devoted lover. After men discovered her hidden *inner* strength, they ran. She could see their weaknesses, and it scared them silly.

Robbie ran. At least his brain did. He acted as though he wanted Sarah around him, but showed no concern for whether she remained in or out of his life. He protected his heart, and it started right from the moment they met. Yet for some strange reason, Sarah was intrigued by his pompous attitude. He was the negative to her positive.

Don't these men know that it just can't end well when they act foolishly? she continued to ponder. *They might get what they want if they just went about things the right way. Women need to understand and respect themselves, too, and not just take it as it comes. In the end, they* both *lose respect for the other.* The inaudible conversation was frustrating for Sarah. She had a captive audience. Anything she spoke aloud would be heard. But her mouth never opened to tell both of them a woman's perspective on love. She did not want to come across as a lecturer or mother figure, so she kept quiet. Instead, Sarah just rolled her eyes, inhaled a long, deep breath, and stared at the horizon.

The sun beat down on the tiny car, and the smell of the hot leather seats mixed with Robbie's freshly washed hair. She was reminded, over and over again, of his presence and what they had once shared. It was a cruel tease.

When the silent hour was up, Robbie was ready for round two. "You know what else I can't stand? Kids!"

Sarah and Stuart quickly acknowledged his announcement with a glance toward each other in the mirror.

"The brats shouldn't be heard until they're eighteen," he snarled. "I don't believe they have much significance till then."

Sarah burned with resentment. She said nothing, and neither did Stuart. They had heard enough. She was not caving in to Robbie's cocky quips with a response. In her opinion, Robbie was only confirming that he did not know how to love anyone, except himself. She knew he was trying to rile her up by making preposterous statements. He knew Sarah wanted to have children and was running out of time. His nasty remark was a way of making it very clear that she would not be having *little ones* with *him*.

Sarah was piecing together his crass words and actions. The stupid comments, arrogant attitude, and even grabbing the front seat ahead of Stuart – who was two inches taller – were all parts of Robbie's controlling behavior. It did not help that a large amount of testosterone oozed from his pores. He expected privileges and made sure they favored him, especially at the expense of others – including his friends.

In contrast, Stuart was so good-natured. "By the way, it's really cozy over here," he blurted out.

"Hey, you know the best part about being in the back seat, Stuart?" said Sarah. "You've got all the goods. Can you dig out that CD you made for me?"

Both Sarah and Stuart loved food, wine, and culture. He was the only person the adventuresome lady had ever met that enjoyed relaxing to the sound of Spanish guitar.

Robbie could not relate. "Oh, dear God! If I have to listen to *that*, I'm getting a full hour of heavy metal, later!" he demanded.

Nothing made sense to Sarah. She was annoyed by his criticism. The man ran hot and cold, wanting her to like him, but making her hate him. In addition to his immaturity, he was seven years her junior. She worried that if they ever became a real couple, he would grow tired of her and find someone his own age, or younger. He was a free spirit that blew with the wind. Sarah was like a little bee flying against him, getting swept up and carried away.

"I need alcohol, you guys," Stuart interrupted as he rummaged through the CDs. "Robbie, where is that liquor store we always go to?"

"As I recall, having come out here with you a billion times, there's a convenience store and gas station coming up," Robbie responded. "Do you remember passing a sign that read, *Roka Valley - 80 miles,* a few moments ago? The store is about thirty minutes from that sign."

"That's too long to wait!" said Stuart. He held up the CD for the taking.

Robbie ripped the disc from Stuart's fingers so quickly that his hand hit Sarah's dangling crucifix. It poked him in the skin. "Ow!" Robbie winced and rubbed his injury. "Are you actually going to play boring, foreign instrumentals in this small little space?" he snapped. "And can you get rid of this stupid necklace? I don't know why people carry those meaningless symbols around anyway. It's not like your life is going to be saved if a cross hangs in your car. When death comes a knocking, it comes a knocking."

Sarah felt judged and thusly timid. A weird feeling came over her. "But Stuart and I like this music," Sarah whimpered, "and that's my father's cross."

"You're not a Christian, are you?" Robbie probed.

"U – um . . . ," Sarah stumbled.

"Because, if you are, we've totally corrupted you!" he laughed and glanced at Stuart. "You definitely haven't acted like one. We may have to rethink our plans for including you in a lot of good times."

Sarah was embarrassed. "N–no – I don't believe in Jesus – anymore," she continued to stutter. "I mean, He was a good man. My parents were big on religion, but I'm over it now." She did not want the guys thinking that she was a *do-gooder* or a *Bible beater* – negative terms she had heard people use toward Christians. And she definitely did not want to be excluded in any fun. "I can take the cross down if it bothers you, Robbie."

"No. I didn't know it was your dad's. At least leave it up to remember *him*," Robbie sneered. "It's good you're not religious, because we have plenty to tempt you with."

"Let her enjoy the music, Rob," Stuart changed the subject. "I put that CD together a few weeks ago. You might like it; it's cool!"

Robbie's temper flared. "For crying out loud, play it then!" he demanded, shoving the disc into the player. He asserted a façade of machismo toward things he viewed as the farthest from manly – certain music and religion.

An icy chill ran through Sarah's veins, like a frigid breeze across a lake. Robbie's dramatic reaction made her uncomfortable. She tried to ignore it and enjoy the dulcet music.

They all listened while gazing out their respective windows at the undulating hills of sand and azure-colored sky. The deep – almost spiritual – guitar strumming gave the scenery a richer purpose as they journeyed on. It sounded like the score of a dramatic film.

The group was soothed for twenty minutes or so, and Robbie found himself tapping his fingers on his knees to the beat. He was starting to like and admire Sarah's taste in music. She exchanged a grin with her partner in the back seat.

Stuart's memory was triggered when he saw her smile. "Oh, for crying out loud; how could I have forgotten? The desert must have put a spell on me!" he frantically yelled. "I made a fantastic concoction of rums and juices." Stuart rescued a container from a soft-sided cooler bag – hidden under a mound of beach towels – and started chugging.

Sarah watched her tousled-haired friend swallow down his libation. A sweet flow of contentment passed through her. She found herself reminiscing about her nights out with the two men – nights filled with excessive drinking, dancing, and loving. She was captivated by Stuart's eyes. Like the bluest of oceans, they were the icing on the cake to this perfect dessert of a man. She saw him as sincere and kind. Unlike Robbie, Stuart had a compassionate soul.

Sarah's gut was calling out. She wanted to say something sappy, but knew if she did, it would be met with sarcasm. Whenever the men realized they had let their guards down, they countered with harshness. At the same time, her tongue ached from holding back salty comments about Robbie's change of heart for the music. Ultimately, she could not contain herself. "I see you're enjoying yourself, Rob," Sarah's voice boomed through the tunes, the wind, and Stuart's sloppy slurping.

Robbie rolled his eyes. "It's better than silence."

"I feel good being with you guys on this trip. I really think we met for a reason."

They stopped what they were doing and turned to listen intently to Sarah.

"I don't know what that reason may be. But I feel some of my most joyous times have been with the two of you." Her hands shook nervously

– anticipating a response. Sarah popped a few peanuts from the jar she had wedged between her legs.

In a way, the two men were protectors – from her perspective. They kept her close, observed her moves, and analyzed her every word. It seemed as though they needed her. Yet there was something untouchable about them. She was a flickering flame to a slow, consuming darkness – a ground wire to their electrically-charged lives.

"You're like the perfect girlfriend," Robbie stated unexpectedly. He reached over and plucked the jar of nuts from inside her thighs, caressing and tingling her skin in the process. His body language was confusing at times. He flirted, then retreated.

The mental rollercoaster he made Sarah ride was frustratingly magnetic. She wanted to play along, but dared not, to avoid her own heart from getting pummeled. He poured a handful of nuts into his palm and returned the jar to the inside of her legs.

"Thanks," she said with a sensual glance. Sarah had no doubt she was the *perfect girlfriend*, or at least the best one either of them would ever find. "What made you say that?" she inquired.

"You like everything we like. You're a bud. It's all good!" Robbie's somewhat endearing words blanketed the ugly comments he had spoken earlier as well as some of the issues they had before starting their trip.

Sarah grinned half-heartedly. She felt herself being snared back into his mental lair. *If I am the* perfect girlfriend*, then why am I not* your *girlfriend?* Sarah wondered. Whatever the reason for Robbie's indifference, she liked the compliment.

As the three friends entered a more remote area of the desert, Robbie brought the light-hearted moment to a screeching halt. "Enough of this sap! I need to bang my head," he announced, motioning for Stuart to pass him his heavy metal CD.

Sarah wanted to kick herself for the soft, girly words she had told her companions. She had hoped that neither of the guys would be dismissive, but there was no such luck. Her kind remarks yielded a disappointing outcome. The head banging was about to begin.

Chapter 2

WATER INTO WINE

Whether it was the extreme heat or an epiphany that brought clarity to Sarah, she finally realized they were in the middle of nowhere. Before, she was only going through the motions of driving from one place to another. She looked out at the hills, cacti, and sand. The friends were adventuring deeper into uncivilized territory, and the reality of being far away from home made her feel vulnerable.

"Don't forget to stop for beer!" Stuart's voice boomed from the backseat as he guzzled the last bit of his alcoholic mixture. "If I don't have brew, my weekend's shot to hell."

Ahh, the need for beer. Another macho request from my boys, Sarah mused. She giggled under her breath and peered off to a butte in the distance. Its rocky formation captured her interest. It was mysterious and virile, perhaps symbolic of the men she was with.

Stuart capped his empty vessel and buried it under a mountain of crushed ice in the small cooler behind Sarah's seat. He grabbed a handful of the white granules. Between the sweltering air temperature and the warmth of his body, the ice quickly turned into liquid, but not before he rubbed the frozen bits across his forehead and down the back of his neck.

It was soothing and quickly rid his skin of the sweat. Stuart closed his eyes in satisfaction. The remaining water dripped down the back of his hand and forearm, evaporating before reaching his elbow.

Robbie's metal CD still blared loudly in the car, filling every nook and cranny – as well as their brains – with nerve-wracking, repetitive beats. Sarah hoped that when it became Stuart's turn, he would change the mood back to instrumental bliss.

The long-awaited gas station and grocery store was just on the horizon.

"Why didn't you bring beer from home?" Sarah yelled over the head-banging noise.

"I buy on the fly. Preparation is not my strong point," Stuart chuckled. "I bring what's important." He was referring to the alcohol he had already downed – and himself.

Sarah smiled at Stuart's irresponsible comment. There was an unspoken expectation that each person would carry their own weight by bringing food and drinks. She brought a few sandwiches, sodas, the jar of peanuts, and a big bag of trail mix to last her the weekend. The guys figured that either Sarah or other women at the camp would have food if they found that the desert grocery store was closed.

"Robbie, you think you could turn your music down? I'm getting a wicked headache," Stuart moaned.

"Fine," Robbie grumbled, lowering the volume.

"Thank you," Sarah whispered.

Griffin's Grocery & Gas Stop was finally within sight – and it was open. Located about forty minutes from their destination, it was the last place to stock up on supplies such as fuel, food, and alcohol. Sarah pulled up to the pump and shut off the engine. Stuart handed her his credit card and winked. The guys hastily got out. One shoved the nozzle into the gas tank. The other filled the tires with air, before they both bolted into the store.

After paying at the pump, Sarah took time to park closer to the building. By the time she found a spot and went inside, the men had vanished. The two made a beeline to the liquor section and grabbed a case of beer, four bottles of wine, tequila, brandy, some cold cuts, bread, and a huge bag of chips.

Sarah laughed when she found them and saw their shopping cart loaded with alcohol. However, their upbeat, jolly demeanors were quickly doused when she noticed the newspaper headline on a stand at the end of the liquor aisle. *"Oil Tycoon Dies in Plane Crash,"* she read out loud and then picked up the paper to check out the story. "Oh, my God! I know this guy. This is so sad."

"Sarah, don't be so depressing!" Stuart interrupted and then shouted Jesus' name. "We want to have fun and not have to think of morose news." Stuart ripped the newspaper from her hand and threw it back on the rack, practically tearing the pages. He continued looking at the wine selection, shaking his head in frustration as he combed the aisle.

Sarah was shocked and taken aback by Stuart's choice of words. His anger made her want to withdraw, but she resisted the feeling of passivity and spoke up. "Sorry, to be such a drag," she said sarcastically, "but I interviewed and photographed this guy when I lived in Connecticut. He was nice to me. Am I not supposed to care when I find out that someone I know and liked is dead?"

Stuart stopped in his tracks and turned to face her with a stern look in his eyes. "I really don't care," he growled. "Did you forget that this is a fun weekend getaway, Sarah? No reading the news!"

Robbie ignored them and pretended to be interested in several bottles of cabernet sauvignon.

Sarah felt overwhelmingly dismissed. Stuart's sudden, escalated demeanor was confusing. She wondered why acknowledging an incident – whether negative or positive – had any bearing on *his* mood. *Where was the sweet guy that had been in the back seat of my car?* she wondered. A wave of anger made its way to the surface of her lips. "What the hell is wrong with you guys?" she barked.

Robbie remained quiet and picked up a bottle of wine to read its flavor content. His ears turned in to the conversation, catching every word. He almost spoke out in support of Stuart, but this time, he let his friend put Sarah in the place they both wanted her to be. She was to speak positively, or shut up.

"Don't make us regret having you drive us out here," Stuart retorted.

Sarah was beside herself with shock at the condescending statement. *Wow. Just wow. The irony,* she thought. The two men grumbled and griped at times – especially Robbie – but when someone else wanted to air any grievances, it was not allowed. Sarah was used to seeing sadness, death, and despair. As a photographer, it was part of her job. She could not understand his reaction.

The men continued to look at wine.

Sarah glanced at the tossed newspaper. With a tear in her eye, she let out a long sigh and took a moment to reminisce about the tycoon. *The man deserved to be remembered by those who knew him or knew of him. Everyone deserves as much,* she thought.

Stuart observed Sarah's somber face. He started to feel an ounce of regret for his actions. But he did not apologize. Instead, he tried gentle intimidation. "Good thoughts, ok? We're on this trip to have fun. Please remember that."

Sarah fell into a daze as she gazed down the aisles of the small store. They all strolled up to the registers and silently paid for their items.

As the three walked outside toward the car, their steps were several feet apart from one another. Robbie took in his surroundings. Stuart stopped to look at the sand and rocks, also. As he absorbed the beauty of the scenery, he was awestruck. Sarah noticed, but said nothing. He did not deserve her kindness at that moment. She looked out at the desert and breathed in to catch a whiff of cactus and old tumbleweeds. Even the sand seemed to have a scent. It smelled like stones found up the beach – away from the water – sundried and cold.

Sarah pressed the unlock button on her key fob while her eyes remained fixed on the distant hills. Robbie and Stuart put their items in the trunk. Then – as if supernaturally synched up – they all got into the car. On to Roka Valley.

Less than fifteen minutes into the ride, Stuart reached for his colorful, empty, aluminum drinking vessel. "Oh, I think it's time for a little *Happy Jesus*, my lifeline to Heaven," he proclaimed, raising his cup.

"Yes! *Happy Jesus!*" Robbie emphatically agreed.

"What are you doing back there?" Sarah inquired, eyeing Stuart's makeshift bar.

The former contentious conversation at the grocery store was washed away with the introduction of booze.

"I don't tell all my secrets," Stuart smiled, passing her the cup. "Here, little darling. Take a long, hard swig of that."

"What's in this *Happy Jesus?*" Sarah asked while keeping an eye on the road. "And what's with the name?"

"Oh, wouldn't you like to know? Let's just say I turn the water into wine," Stuart mocked. "It tastes a little like Sangria, only better."

Sarah laughed, nearly choking on the liquid. She quickly discerned that there was more brandy in the mixture than regular wine. It was a strong concoction. She knew in her heart that drinking while driving could land her in jail, but she might be considered a better *perfect girlfriend* if she followed their rules. Adoration was her goal that weekend – and she was willing to get it at all costs.

After making its way to Robbie and Stuart, the beverage returned to Sarah's mouth. She swigged. It was biting yet cool going down. It refreshed her burning body. Drinking had recently become an everyday occurrence in Sarah's world. Doing it in the car was commonplace. It was normal for them to bring along bottles filled with liquor on many of their outings, especially when they hit the beach. She did not care what the consequences were. It was fun, exciting – and dangerous. Getting drunk was their escape. Problems or issues they tried to leave behind, were ditched together. Indulging had become their lifestyle.

"How much longer?" Sarah whined.

"About twenty-five minutes before we reach the campsite," said Stuart. "I'm off to beddy-bye. Please, play me some of that Spanish guitar. It is my turn, after all."

"Thank you," Sarah whispered under her breath. She did not want to get too excited about the return of her music. Robbie might start acting like a fool again.

The head-banging compilation was gently replaced with Stuart's CD.

"You're going to sleep for barely half an hour?" Sarah asked.

The liquor from his flask, the hum of the car's engine, and the re-introduction of his favorite music had taken effect, causing Stuart to tire. He had gotten little to no sleep the night before, anticipating the trip. By the end of Sarah's question, he had already fallen asleep.

"I don't know where I'm going, and I know nothing about this place," Sarah pleaded to Robbie, who was also getting very heavy-eyed. "Please, stay awake." Sarah had no idea what to expect. She had only done a little research on Roka Valley. All she learned was that there was a ghost town near the Colorado River – and they were headed for it.

"Quit your worrying. This is our sixth time out here. You're going to have a blast. There will be vast open desert, a cool flowing river, and lots of booze," Robbie reassured her.

Sarah glanced in the rear-view mirror at Stuart. His eyes twitched. She had reservations about going to Roka Valley in the days leading up to their departure. Although she was not too concerned about the drive to a desolate place with a winding river running through it, her real fear was of being thrust into a crowd of unknowns with nowhere to escape.

"I can already smell the hamburgers and hotdogs!" Robbie exclaimed. He stuck his tanned face out the window into the warm breeze.

The scent of grilled food drifted through the air. It was inviting to the eager partyers. Most likely the aroma was coming from some other place, or maybe it was conjured up in their imaginations. Sarah stepped on the gas and flashed Robbie a big grin.

"You go, girl!" he exclaimed.

Sarah's change of attitude allowed him to feel uninhibited. While Stuart was napping, Robbie moved in for a little display of affection to see what he could get in return. He stretched his upper body and nuzzled an area of delicate skin behind her ear.

Sarah winced as his nose tickled her neck. "What was that about?" she snickered. Her words instantly killed the moment.

"I'm buzzed," Robbie said. He passed off his advance as an intoxicated flirtation, quickly withdrew, and followed up with a gentle squeeze of her thigh.

Sarah looked back at Stuart to see if he had seen Robbie's moves, but he was fast asleep.

Chapter 3

TILL DEATH DO US PART

Little did she know, Sarah's trip to the desert was months – if not years – in the making. Many things that had taken place in her life were patches in a carefully crafted and quilted future.

Prior to moving to Long Beach, California, Sarah lived on the East Coast in Bristol, Connecticut, where she worked as a professional photographer. There, she met a man whom she nicknamed, *Alley Cat*. He was drop-dead gorgeous, with light brown hair and cheek dimples that showed prominently when he smiled. Standing at about six foot three with bulging upper body muscles and massive broad shoulders, he looked like Adonis. He was sweet at times, but complex at others. Sarah fell in love with his thick, muscular arms, strong legs, and unstoppable charisma. Of course, charm always did her in. By Sarah's definition, Richard Foster was her soulmate.

The first three years of their relationship were romantic yet tumultuous. They fought incessantly. The quarrels led to more than their fair share of breakups. When Richard decided he had enough or needed a change of scenery, he just stopped calling Sarah. He would be gone for days – sometimes weeks – leaving her to believe that he would not return.

Oftentimes, he secretly left the state, most likely to hook up with other women. But Richard always came back to Sarah, and she welcomed him, reluctantly. He understood she was a solid foundation for him, a stark contrast to his promiscuous, alley-cat lifestyle. Toward the end, it took pleading and much persuasion on his part to win Sarah. She had her limits.

The two finally separated after Richard made one drastic mistake. He insisted she get rid of her little, rescued dog. Sarah's attention was constantly on Em, who had a terminal health condition. Richard had no use for a sick pet. He felt slighted when Sarah doted over the white and tan terrier mix. Em was her baby. They were inseparable.

Despite the valid reason for being hurt, Sarah was not about to let Richard call the shots regarding the innocent pooch. She decided she could not stay with a man who did not love what she loved. The choice to break up with him was simple, especially after the long emotional ride he had put her through. Richard had to go.

Unbeknownst to his family, Richard had inner struggles. His entire relationship with Sarah, from beginning to end, was filled with mind games and mental abuse. Because of his manic-depression, he was notorious for gas-lighting and ghosting others. She needed to get out and away from the toxicity even though she was madly in love. Em was a catalyst to the final breakup, a blessing in disguise. In a way, the dog and the girl had rescued each other.

Bristol was home to just over sixty thousand people. Due to the jobs that Richard and Sarah held, many of the residents knew the couple or had heard of them. Whenever the two bumped into each other in public, crowds stopped and stared, waiting for reconciliation. The ex-lovers enjoyed the recognition they commanded. Despite having separated, their passion still burned. They delighted and played into the hands of their viewers, chatting it up and exchanging sensual glances. But it was all for show.

At the end of their interludes, they returned quietly to their respective corners until the next chance meeting. Indeed, Sarah and the tall, dimple-faced, business mogul made a compelling and sexy combination. The community of gossipers was captivated. But before they could meet again, the show came to a tragic end.

As a top executive insurance broker for a large company, Richard's work afforded him opportunities to travel, both for business and pleasure. The Big Apple was – by far – his favorite place to go. "I get lost in the rigid concrete of the city," he would tell Sarah. "That's where I feel most at home."

She hated hearing that. Sarah interpreted it to mean that Richard wanted his life to be cold and emotionless, most likely without her in it.

It was when he was on his way back from a company dinner in Manhattan that their lives changed. Richard's rental car veered off the road, hit a guard rail, and careened over an embankment. The vehicle flipped twice before landing on its roof, killing him instantly.

Most of their mutual friends learned about his death by word of mouth, social media, or from a member of Richard's family. It was shocking when Sarah received the news, via a flippant text message from a friend, *Hey, I think your ex died in a car wreck.* At first, it did not register as truth. Sarah had to read the message repeatedly. After beating his family to a phone call, it was confirmed.

It was never determined if Richard had been drinking that fateful night. If his depression hit, he would have cared less about driving back to his hotel room intoxicated. Autopsy results were kept under wraps, thanks to his protective family. Sarah did not hound them for answers. He was gone, and that was that.

A big part of Sarah died with Richard. Although their personalities and outlooks on life were wildly different, she still loved the non-committal man who had captivated her soul. Her heart yearned for him, even though her devotion and staying power had ceased.

Sarah struggled with the decision of attending Richard's funeral. If she did not go, she might regret passing on the opportunity to connect with him one last time. Seeing his family would be tough. She cried for a week straight, worrying and floundering. Funerals brought her down. Since she had not attended her parents' tribute, she was hesitant about going to *his*. She figured if she went, it would not be solely for her own closure. His mother deserved the respect of the one woman in her son's life who came the closest to becoming a daughter-in-law.

On the other hand, if Sarah went to the ceremony, she would be placing herself inside the corral of women Richard had attracted since their breakup. She was sure many would be there, displaying their shallow concerns and desires to be seen or acknowledged by his family. They would claim him as theirs.

But Richard belonged to Sarah alone, both spiritually and mentally. There was only one lover he would want at his funeral – the selfless girl to whom he vowed never to commit. She went.

Chapter 4

ASLEEP IN THE DUST.

Sarah needed to get away from all the memories that Bristol held. She felt it was time for a fresh start. With Richard no longer holding her soul there, she could break free and begin a new life with Em in another city, far away. Destination: Long Beach, California.

The light from the West Coast called Sarah. She answered. The combination of warm weather and ocean views seduced the photographer. To her, it was the remedy to get out from under the dark cloud that had formed over her life. Once her decision had been made, she found an apartment online, paid the deposit and first month's rent, and looked forward to the change.

The Golden State was a place where dreams came true – or so she heard. Long Beach was a busy city filled with industry and imports. It was also near where her parents had enjoyed their honeymoon. The couple spent a week on Catalina Island back in the '40s. Sadly, Sarah's mother and father died in a freak boating accident when they renewed their vows there in 1985. Their bodies were never recovered. In her wallet, Sarah carried an old, sepia photograph of them standing together on one of the island's beautiful beaches. After settling into her new home, she promised herself that she would pay a visit to Catalina, in their honor.

With a packed convertible and her little dog in tow, Sarah hit the road for California.

Richard's funeral would take place about twelve miles away from Bristol, at his parents' ranch home in Waterbury. The city was slightly larger, made up of mom-and-pop establishments. Richard's family real estate business was a longstanding example. His mother, Brooke, begged Sarah to come the night before the burial so they all could spend time with her and reflect. She obliged, since she was going to be passing through the area anyway.

Richard's mother, father, and siblings greeted Sarah and little Em as soon as she pulled up the driveway. Two golden retrievers joined them and ran out to say *hello*. The house looked the same as the last time she was there, except for a few trees in the front yard that had grown a bit taller and fuller. Everyone welcomed her with open arms.

"Oh Sarah! We've missed you so much," cried Brooke. She invited her son's beloved inside, and they all gathered around the large kitchen table to chat about their lost family member.

The Fosters were very close-knit. It was rare if they did not hold several parties a year as an excuse to get everyone together in one place. They enjoyed it immensely. Sarah did, too. She had never experienced such family cohesiveness.

While seated at the table, Brooke could not keep it together. Sarah's face held so many memories for her. She studied it, imagining her son kissing his lover's lips and caressing her youthful cheeks. She recalled the last time Richard and Sarah had visited; their hands were held tightly together as they stood on the doorstep in the rain. They had arrived unannounced for Brooke's surprise birthday party. Her eyes welled up as she connected with her departed son – through Sarah.

One after another, the stories they told brought laughter, frustration, and many tears. It felt good to reminisce. But soon, Sarah grew tired and mournful. She excused herself from the gathering and kissed everyone *good night*. She scooped Em up in her arms, patted the dog's two furry playmates, and made her way to the spare bedroom, where she and Richard slept whenever they visited.

Sarah threw off her clothes and crawled under the sheets. Em curled up next to her fatigued owner, who tried desperately to fall asleep. Nervousness about attending the funeral kept Sarah from resting. In addition, she did not feel alone. The blanket on the bed still smelled like Richard. She played some soothing ocean sounds on her phone, drew the plush fabric to her face, and took in a deep breath. "Good night, my Richard," Sarah whispered. She envisioned her head lying on his upper body with her nose buried in his chest hair.

Morning came, and the house guests gathered at the kitchen table over coffee and pancakes, a family favorite cooked up by Richard's father, Fred. Everyone called them *Freddie Foster's Famous Flyin' Flippin' Flappers*. No one ever left the table without downing a massive stack. The joke was usually about who was going to order the most as they watched Fred flip them out of the griddle – high in the air – and onto their plates.

This morning was different. All was quiet, except for the clanging of dishes that were passed around and the sound of juice and coffee being poured. The pancakes did not fly. The impending funeral – only hours away – caused the group to go silent. Everyone was in a pensive mood.

After they finished eating, members of the entire family marched like robots to their respective bedrooms to find something to wear. They silently exchanged turns in the two bathrooms, showering their tense bodies, and brushing their teeth. When they were all ready to leave, everyone filed into several different cars and drove to the church.

Sarah was surprised by the number of friends and acquaintances at the event. Apparently, Richard had touched many people's lives in some form or another. Numerous men and women had traveled from other states to pay their respects. She observed each face, wondering if the people had ever gotten the chance to truly know the man. *He's dead. What does it matter anymore?* Sarah consoled herself.

The ceremony was long, followed by a very emotional burial in the local cemetery. The heaviness of the day was drowning Sarah. She just wanted to be respectful, make her rounds, and get out. But there were more surprises to come for the forlorn ex-lover.

Sarah lingered in the graveyard to reflect. Most guests had gone home, except for some stragglers who decided to have tea with Brooke. No one else was there. She stopped at Richard's plot to cry. Her tears fell on the new mound of packed dirt. The afternoon sun lit up the petals of a white rose someone had placed on top of the headstone. A gentle breeze of serenity swirled around her.

She sat down on top of the dirt with her legs crossed and pictured Richard there; her head bent toward the etched marble. "Why was our love so difficult? Why could you not give in to it?" she pleaded, burying her head inside her palms. "I loved you so much and still do." Sarah's rosy cheeks were swollen and glossed over by the stream of tears. "Maybe this would never have happened if you were with me. Maybe you would never have gone to New York. I miss you!"

A startling voice spoke out from behind her, "You know – he loved you." The man's words shocked her, as if the tip of a battery had been placed on her tongue. They did not feel good, but they did not feel bad either. "Whenever he visited us, Sarah . . . ."

She cried louder, interrupting his words – words she was not sure she wanted to hear. She remained with her back to the voice and continued to sob.

The man's broad, strong hands reached down to grip Sarah's shoulders. He pulled her up slowly and twisted her body around to face him. It was Richard's brother Alex, who had left the burial during the placement of the casket. He returned to visit the site after everyone left, hoping to get some quiet time with his dead sibling. To Alex, the vision of Sarah perched on his brother's grave was surreal and beautiful. With sincerity, he spoke the perfect words she needed to hear, "Richard told me you were his soulmate."

Sarah's legs nearly buckled underneath her. She asked Alex to repeat what he said.

"Every time he visited us, he brought your name up in the conversation," he continued. "Richard told us about trying to win you back, but that you refused. He said, 'Sarah is my soulmate – what am I to do without her?' "

Tears flowed down her face as she hung her head in sorrow.

"Sarah," Alex said, gently pulling her chin up so she could look him in the eyes, "he bought you an engagement ring."

"Engagement ring?!" Sarah gasped.

"My brother gave it to me to hold onto until he was ready to put it on your finger. I just never knew when that was going to be." As he spoke the words, Alex gazed at her shocked and swollen face.

The news rang, like old-fashioned church bells clanging in a steeple on Christmas Day. They were being rung by the devil. Sarah experienced a sudden yet brief burst of excitement, as if it were Richard proposing. But reality struck, and her elation turned into anger. She was heartbroken and furious, although oddly content. Yes, it was closure, but it was so painful. "Why are you telling me this?"

"I know it was a struggle to make it work with my difficult brother. Mom and Dad had no clue what was going on in his head. But I could see how he treated you. He may have never been able to show his true love, but you deserve to know he loved you as best as he could." Alex pulled a velvet box out of his jacket pocket. It creaked as he opened it slowly, revealing a diamond ring. "Take it," he said.

Sarah said nothing, only stared at Alex's face. Confused and torn, she threw her arms around him and sobbed. She believed Richard's life was no different than his untimely death. It was an unsolved mystery.

Alex reached into his other pocket and withdrew a small piece of paper. "I think this will come in handy," he told her. "He'll help you get settled into your new place. This was a very good friend of Richard's, but he never made it to the funeral. I guess they had a falling out somewhere along the way."

Sarah looked down at his hand. Scribbled on the paper, in black ink, was the name of Richard's long-time school friend – *Stuart Savoy*.

Chapter 5

INVITATION OF THE BROKEN-HEARTED

Sarah had no intention of calling Richard's friend. After her encounter with Alex at the gravesite, she had crumpled up the paper with Stuart Savoy's number on it and tossed *it* – and the boxed ring –into her purse. The note made its way to the bottom and remained there for weeks, along with gum wrappers and old tissues.

Sarah had kept a secret from Alex as they stood over Richard in the cemetery that day. She knew of Stuart Savoy already, but the two had never met. Richard had mentioned his name many times during their relationship. In fact, it was Stuart who had encouraged Richard to go on trips just to hook up with strange women. Atlantic City, Miami, and Jamaica were some of their favorite destinations. *Some friend,* Sarah thought. *I wonder why he didn't show up to Richard's funeral?*

The idea of reaching out to Stuart haunted her. It was because of Alex that she kept the idea fresh in her mind. She felt somewhat of an obligation to him, given that he was Richard's brother. On the other hand, she could not stand the thought of being pushed to do anything. *Call a stranger? That would take a leap of faith,* Sarah imagined. She thought of what her introduction might sound like. "Hey, is this Stuart? Yeah, um – I'm your dead friend's ex-girlfriend from Bristol. You know – the one you always steered Richard away from? Wanna get together?" She laughed out loud and rolled her eyes.

Lacking confidence, Sarah could not think of any intelligent ice breakers. Animosity was not the prevailing tone she wanted coming through in her conversation with him. She just wanted to get settled in to her new, furnished place without the distraction of the past getting in the way.

The time it took to travel across the country and unpack a few boxes went by quickly. Before Sarah knew it, three weeks had passed. Trips to the neighborhood grocery store, local veterinarian's office for Em's medications, bank, and post office helped her to memorize her way around the community. The only things missing – were friends.

Solitude and loneliness got the best of Sarah. The apartment was way too quiet, and she was getting depressed. She had only met one of her neighbors and that was by accident when she went out to get her mail. She spent most of her time filling the photography jobs that she had been contracted to do. Thankfully, they were all local.

Sarah had trouble sleeping at night and soon became very acquainted with the designs of the plaster on her bedroom ceiling. She imagined what was on the other side, *Is it the universe, the meaning of life, or just the sky in its simplest form? What have I done? I just moved my entire life across the country, only to be alone.* The ceiling never replied.

She thought about praying for company and comfort, but she had no faith in God anymore. Any kind of relationship she had started with Him, as a kid, dwindled after her parents died. Richard's death was the final straw. She had no reason or time to love a God whom she no longer felt loved *her*.

When Sarah was growing up, her parents introduced her to God in the typical fashion. They took her to church, prayed at the dinner table, and would read the Bible together. It was her father that raised her to respect and be kind to others and to know that there was a Savior who died for her sins. But she never really got to know Jesus. Worshiping was just one of those grueling family pastimes that took her away from other, more exciting things. There was more she had to learn, but life got in the way, and the world led her down a different road. When God took her loved ones away, she stopped believing that He existed – or at least that is what she told herself. She rebelled after the loss of family, Richard, a love life, and having to deal with the burden of a sick dog.

It was time for Sarah to find a friend. Otherwise, being exclusively in her own company would drive her mad. *Maybe Alex was right,* she wondered. *Having someone around might help me cope.*

It was not an easy transition to start her life over at her age. Things that were familiar were gone. The unknown was a challenge. Yet underneath her insecure exterior were guts and fortitude. She had to embrace her new life and was determined to get it together.

One afternoon, Sarah finally reached a point of courage. "Oh, to hell with it!" she exclaimed. "I'm going to call this Stuart guy, for Pete's sake. What's the worst that could happen?"

Sarah needed to mentally and physically prepare. She wanted to feel good about herself and sound confident over the phone. She showered, dried her hair, and put on make-up. Rather than wear dress clothes, she threw on a fluffy, white robe. She looked sexy – like Marilyn Monroe.

Em ran into the room and jumped up on the bed to see what all the fuss was about. Her eyes widened, as if she knew Sarah would soon be retrieving Stuart's number.

"Are you here for moral support, Em?" Sarah laughed at the dog. "I'm a nervous wreck. This must be what *men* go through when they get around to calling a woman." She caressed Em, who was wagging her tail and panting with excitement. "I could text him, but I'm old school. Gotta get on the phone." *How hard could this be?* Sarah wondered. *It's not like I'm interested in Stuart, romantically.*

The anxiety was building. She pushed the negative thoughts of Stuart out of her head and tried to forgive him. After all, it was not completely his fault that Richard was unfaithful. Even though Stuart was an encourager and enabler, Richard was responsible for Richard.

Sarah wanted something to calm her nerves. "Wait here!" she told Em. "I'll be right back." She jaunted off to the kitchen to make a snack and pour a full glass of red wine, then headed back into the bedroom. "I sure am hungry. There's not much in this place, Emmy. Just your favorite – peanut butter."

The dog cocked its head to one side and waited for an offering of sticky fingers to lick. Sarah sipped the wine, took a few bites of her sandwich, and let Em clean off the oily remnants before she set everything down on the nightstand and wiped her hands.

Sarah opened her laptop and started a search of Stuart. There might be some information she could find on him before making the cold call. Richard had shared group photos from high school with her, so she knew he was particularly handsome. The keyboard clicked feverishly as she spelled out S-t-u-a-r-t S-a-v-o-y. She scrolled up and down a few pages for several minutes hoping to find something; she came up empty. Stuart was clean as a whistle. Her search was complete.

An intuitive little Em looked at Sarah and then her mother's purse, which hung on the bedroom door handle. The dog wagged its tail, jumped up and down, and barked at Sarah to retrieve it. The whole scene did not go unnoticed. "Nothing gets past you, now does it Em?" Sarah spoke to her furry friend. "I see you staring at my purse." Em let out another yap in response, and Sarah offered her another dollop of peanut butter. "Oh, alright," Sarah grumbled and slithered off the bed to unhook the bag from the knob.

The wine had not kicked in. Sarah was still nervous. She reached into the purse cautiously, slowly stirring up other notes. Of course, Alex's paper felt like all the rest of the pieces. She got frustrated and turned the entire bag upside down, dumping its contents on the floor. There it was. The note had rolled off to one side of the pile, along with the box carrying Richard's engagement ring, which distracted her.

She took the ring out and studied it, admiring its beauty. It was a simple band with a small, heart-shaped diamond. She slipped it on. It fit. Wearing it made her cry, as she envisioned Richard placing it on the ring finger of her left hand. "I can't do this. Not now," Sarah proclaimed. She wiped her eyes and composed herself. The ring was put in the box and inside the nightstand drawer.

Sarah's attention was brought back to the pile of papers on the floor. Part of the note from Alex had peeled open, revealing Stuart's name in big, black letters. She grabbed her glass of wine and stared. *Just call already!* Sarah thought as she gulped several mouthfuls of the alcohol and picked up her phone.

After slowly depressing nine buttons, she looked at the tenth. It was a seven. Sarah let out a deep and shaky sigh. *Beep.* The phone sounded off when she hit the last digit. At that exact moment, Em yelped to vocalize her satisfaction of the completed task. Sarah was startled and lost grip of the phone. As she tried to catch it, her fingers hit the *send* button. She noticed the call had engaged and quickly reached out to stop it. "Em! What the hell?" she questioned the now silent dog, who had dug its way under the blanket on the bed, fearing a scolding. "I wasn't ready!"

"Ready for what?" said a faint, raspy voice on the other end of the phone.

Sarah picked up the device from the carpet. "Hi," she giggled with embarrassment.

"Yes?"

"Sorry. Is this Stuart? M-my name is Sarah," she stuttered. "I'm your dead . . . I mean I-I'm Richard's ex-girlfriend from Bristol."

There was silence for the longest five seconds as Stuart processed her misspoken words. Awkwardness set in. Sarah wanted to hang up.

The voice replied, "Yes, this is Stuart. Hi Sarah, I've heard much about you from my 'dead' friend, Richard."

"I'm sorry, I didn't mean to say that," she whimpered. "I have been struggling to call you. I wasn't sure I should reach out at all."

"No worries," he comforted her. "To what do I owe this call?"

Sarah let out a sigh of relief and told him how she received his number. The two made small talk and exchanged stories of their mutual friend. Tears flowed down her cheeks as she reminisced about her deceased lover. "Why weren't you there – at the funeral?" she asked with slight reservation.

"We had a fight," Stuart responded. "It was partly over you, actually – if you must know."

"What do you mean?"

"He hated not being able to give you the life you wanted. We were both running from committed relationships. It was when he bought an engagement ring that I got upset with him. Richard wanted to please you, but he didn't know how."

Sarah stopped her sobbing and listened intently to his words.

Stuart continued, "Maybe for some selfish reason, I wanted him to remain single. I'll admit, I tested his love for you by taking him around other women – loose women – who enticed him. He loved you immensely. It doesn't make sense, I know. His promiscuity was like punishment to you for wanting to tie him down. I knew he had no strength. However, when he went after a gal I was dating, I couldn't take it anymore. Between that and him wanting to propose to you, I blew up at him and told him we were through being friends."

"Whoa! That's too much for me. I don't want to hear any more," Sarah insisted. Richard was dead and so was their story. The confusion was making her nauseous and resentful toward her ex – and Stuart. She needed to move on.

"Fine. I understand," responded Stuart. "But I may need to get it off my chest in the future. Not being at my best friend's funeral has been killing me. Maybe I can cry on your shoulder, someday."

"It would be nice to get to know you," said Sarah.

"Hey, join me and some friends for Valentine's Day, next week. We're calling our gathering *The Long Beach Lonely Hearts Club*."

"What's that all about?"

"It's a chance for us lonely, lust-driven singles to get together and rant," Stuart joked. "You'll be the newest inductee. That is – if you are single?"

"Maybe," Sarah snickered.

Stuart cut the conversation short. "Meet us at the Olive Pit at six," he said. "It's a casual restaurant slash pizzeria near me."

"What should I wear?" she asked.

"Black."

Chapter 6

THE GATHERING

Valentine's Day had come quickly. Sarah had scheduled a magazine photo shoot with local models for the day. Most of her time was spent down at the docks. She was now running late for her evening with Stuart and his friends.

She rushed home to take a quick shower. There was not enough time to wash her hair so she gathered up her golden locks into a tousled heap on her head. The natural look worked beautifully.

Sarah rummaged through her clothes for a decent, hip outfit that was casual yet impressive. She peered into the mirrored closet door and noticed a tiny stretch of grey peeking through the strands of blonde. Sarah shifted some loose hairs around, pinned them down to cover the streak, and laughed it off. She knew she was starting to age; however, tonight she was determined to feel young.

Suddenly, Em started to cough. Sarah looked at her pooch, anticipating vomit to follow. The little dog suffered from a collapsed trachea. It was as thin as a coffee stirrer. Despite all the steroids and suppressants the vet had prescribed, her chronic illness got worse every year. It was starting to put a strain on her heart and lungs. Sarah hoped this momentary coughing bout would pass. After about forty-five seconds of hacking, Em finally quit and laid her head down on the bed.

The hangers clacked back and forth, rubbing on the wooden closet rod. "Found it!" exclaimed Sarah as she pulled out a cute black-and-white button-down dress. "Perfect. This will satisfy Stuart's 'black' attire requirement." She held the garment up to herself in the full-length mirror. Realizing it may be too short to wear on its own, she chose a pair of skin-tight, white jeans from the dresser to wear underneath it. Sarah dropped to the bed and shimmied into the peg-leg pants. Snap!

She steamed the dress and threw it on while it was still warm, hurriedly fastening each button. Her skin tingled from the heat. She smiled, looking at herself fully dressed and thought of her meeting with Stuart. The outfit was svelte. She hoped he would notice.

She decided to text him about her shoes. *Hey there, Stuart – it's Sarah. Can I wear sandals to this restaurant?* Sarah was able to make a footwear decision on her own, but including Stuart was somewhat flirtatious and subtly seductive. The crafty move would make him visualize her getting dressed. Aside from that, she was more comfortable in flats rather than having to balance on a pair of stilettos and was hoping he would vote in favor of them.

His return text came through within minutes and read, *I prefer heels.*

Sarah was disappointed, but snickered when Stuart responded so quickly. She wondered if that meant he was interested in her. A rush came over her body. She began fantasizing about a man she had never met face-to-face. "I wonder if Stuart is still as hot as he was in Richard's photos, Em?"

The dog just blinked and wagged its tail. Sarah got down on her knees to pull out various spikes and three-inch wedges from the closet. The shoes tumbled out onto the bedroom carpet.

"Will he think I'm cute? Is it wrong that I'm having these thoughts for *Alley Cat's* friend, Emmy?" Sarah knew the dog had no answers, but she was having fun thinking out loud.

Another text came through on the phone, startling her. *But that'll do,* it read.

Sarah grinned and found a pair of low, strappy sandals. She tossed the rejected, high-heeled shoes back into the closet, avoiding any attempt at organization.

Even though she was feeling better about her outfit, Sarah still was a bit apprehensive. After all, she was meeting a host of new people, and she did not know what to expect. Either they would be casual, or stuck-up and stuffy. "I can't stress about it, Em," Sarah spoke softly; her body trembled with trepidation. "Hopefully, they'll all be nice people, my lovey." She kissed the little dog *goodbye,* squirted her neck and clothes with perfume, got into her car, and drove off.

The holiday drew plenty of traffic on the roads. Unfortunately, Sarah got caught right in the middle of it. She was twenty minutes late to the restaurant. The group had already reserved a table.

It was a chilly night. Sarah grabbed a sweater from the backseat of her car and draped it over one shoulder as she strolled into the open-air eatery. It was typical of her to arrive fashionably late, although she did not want to make a dramatic entrance. In fact, Sarah despised walking into a crowded restaurant alone, unless she had a camera wrapped around her neck for a photo assignment. She was too full of insecurities. Nevertheless, wherever she went, all eyes were on her as she entered a room. Her face and figure were still captivating.

The search for Stuart was on. Sarah sauntered around the chairs and ducked under several tall, propane heaters. Her eyes darted from table to table, hoping he would reveal himself.

There he was, sitting at a table with three people. He was handsome, just as she remembered from the photos. His hair was a little shaggier and the lines on his face were more pronounced. She made immediate eye contact with him. A dainty wave of her hand gestured to him that she was the woman he was waiting for. He nodded, acknowledging her arrival. As she walked closer, the others looked her over from head to toe.

"Hi there, Sarah!" Stuart shouted.

"Hi, Stuart. It's so good to finally meet you," she said nervously and offered her hand for a shake.

The excited man immediately got up out of his seat. The chair's feet scraped along the ceramic floor tiles, making a shrill sound. They both laughed out loud. "Hey, you knew Richard! That alone deserves a hug, rather than a handshake," he said sincerely.

Sarah was delighted and felt right at home in Stuart's embrace. One by one, the faces of his friends came into view. She scanned the entire scene and noticed the table was filled with several wine bottles. The group was not made up of lightweight drinkers.

"Happy Valentine's Day!" they all shouted and raised their glasses in salutation.

Sarah returned the sentiment by lifting her empty hand in the air. She appreciated the toast and perceived it as a sign of acceptance.

"Sarah, meet Jenny, Mark and Amy," Stuart listed his friends in counterclockwise order. He stood up tall at the helm of the table – like the proud captain of a ship – and signaled to a passing waitress to bring another bottle of merlot. Stuart wanted his new friend to catch up with the intoxicated level of the group.

They all smiled in her direction and welcomed her as a member of their *crew*. Sarah's pent-up anxiety finally drained out of her body. She sat down and waited for the wine to be poured. Along with bottles and various glasses, the patio table was filled with pizza trays. Some still contained a slice or two with toppings of pepperoni and mushrooms.

Amy was the first of the friends to offer hospitality. "Sarah, honey, relax a bit. You need a drink and some food," she said.

"Thanks, I think I will partake." Sarah was distracted when she noticed an empty chair next to her. On the table in front of it was a beer with a fresh, frothy head. The beverage had not been there long. *Whomever that belongs to, I bet they'll be coming soon,* she wondered and turned back to face the group.

Amidst the friends' chatter about trivial topics, Sarah covertly studied Stuart's face while he sipped his wine. It was in her nature as a professional photographer to scrutinize people without being noticed. She could see the once, young teenager in his eyes. Although his skin showed minor signs of sun damage and stress, he was still gorgeous with sandy blonde hair and a California tan.

"So, Stuart, why did you tell me to wear black? What's the significance?" Sarah questioned.

"Why not? This is a gathering of lonely losers. Some of us are horny as hell and mourning the fact that we have no one to sleep with."

Everyone at the table laughed. Sarah had never heard of celebrating involuntary celibacy. That was certainly what it sounded like and a different way to spend Valentine's Day.

"Mark and Amy are together," explained Stuart. "They decided to crash our singles party tonight. And Jenny is between boyfriends."

"Why did you think I was single?" Sarah probed.

"I didn't," Stuart said with a smug grin. "But I know now!"

Sarah squinted and smiled. She realized Stuart was fishing. After hearing his comment, she suspected he might be interested in something more than just a friendship.

"Well, who do we have here?" boomed a deep, boisterous voice from behind her. A man wearing loose-fitting jeans, which made a whooshing sound as he walked, bounded to the table with cockiness.

Sarah remained still and did not turn around.

He was direct and to the point – not subtle with introductions – but clever at manipulation. He was about to get what he wanted – a chance to size up Sarah's face and body. "Stand up so I can see what kind of outfit you got on, stranger," the incomer blurted out.

Warmth came over her. This man carried the scent of the forest with him. The smell of grass, wood, and a hint of vanilla aroused Sarah's senses. Her left eyebrow raised with intrigue. She stood up from the table and turned to look at her admirer. "I'm S-Sarah," she said. His ruggedly, attractive face captivated her, instantly. "A-And you are?" Sarah attempted a handshake.

The long sleeves of the man's white flannel shirt were rolled up midway, revealing his strong, hairy forearms and rugged hands. He reached out slowly. She imagined hearing the sultry, sexy bowing of violins. Upon contact, she felt an instant surge of electricity. His palm was dry – the opposite of hers, which was moist with nervous sweat.

Her vulnerability excited him. He held Sarah's hand with a firm grip, until he noticed his drink on the table. Letting go of her, he reached down to pick up the mug. Several drops spilled when he drew it to his face. "Welcome, Sarah. I'm Robbie. The smart one." He flashed her an egotistical smile just before burying his upper lip into the head of his beer. "Nice outfit," he added, swallowing hard.

"Thank you," Sarah replied. "I guess I'm the newest member of *the club*."

Robbie set his drink down. He rubbed the mixture of Sarah's perspiration and the condensation from the cold glass between his two hands, diabolically. At the same time, he stared at her sensually, roving her entire body with his eyes. The corner of his mouth turned up in a devilish grin.

"I guess you are," Robbie agreed, throwing a devious glance toward Stuart, who was engrossed in the pair's flirtatious exchange.

The competition had begun. It was easy to tell right out of the gate that Robbie was a strong alpha male – a self-proclaimed one to boot. His chest puffed up. He was putting on a show for Sarah – *and* Stuart. There was not a chance that either man would give in to the other without a fight. A fist-to-fist combat between them was not on the docket. Instead, their battle for Sarah's affection would be strategic.

A chill ran up Sarah's spine. Her body tingled. She was instantly spellbound. There was something about this Robbie character; he was different than all the rest. She sensed it. His mystique left her wanting more.

Stuart was challenged. He was very aware of Robbie's antics when it came to attracting beautiful women. He knew he must step things up a notch if he wanted to win Sarah over from his controlling, game-play-ing friend.

Sarah had not forgotten about Stuart, but the man with the beer-froth mustache was winning her immediate attention. Robbie licked his upper lip, suggestively. They both sat down at the table and began sharing background information about themselves.

"Photographer with a home office, moved from Connecticut, got a sick dog named Em, had an ex-boyfriend that died, both parents, too – there really isn't more to tell," she spilled.

"That's a lot to handle, right there," Robbie said. "I'm a scientist. I work with food in a lab, along with Stuart and Amy. That's how we met. But I've been at the company longer, so I have seniority. By the way, what's your sign?"

Stuart rolled his eyes after hearing him brag.

Robbie's intention to impress Sarah only went so far. She was captivated by his physique and charm, not his prideful proclamation. *What's with the question from the 1970s? My sign?* Sarah giggled to herself. "I'm a Virgo, why?" she responded.

"Interesting," Robbie said. "Well, well. The dark meets the light. We're in trouble. I'm a Scorpio."

Trouble? Sarah wondered until her thoughts were interrupted by the waitress who returned with a carafe of water and another bottle of merlot.

"I'm a Leo, if anyone cares," Stuart piped up.

"Oh, my – we are going to have some fun," Robbie remarked, watching Sarah take the first sip of her freshly poured wine.

"So, what's it like working from home?" Stuart interrupted. "And how is your poor little dog?"

"My dog Em is the coolest. I love her to pieces. And I really enjoy what I do," she replied. "I just don't get a chance to meet a ton of people other than my subjects, which can sometimes be animals."

"They are better than people anyway," interjected Jenny. The short, petite brunette was a drinking buddy of Stuart's who currently lived in Malibu. She ran a dog grooming business. Her visits with the boys were seldom, ever since she and Stuart ended their short affair years ago. Sarah's inception into the group intimidated her. Although they were no longer a couple, Jenny made sure Stuart kept his thoughts on *her*. She diverted his attention from the new girl by playfully nibbling on his ear and then pouring him a glass of wine.

Sarah noted Jenny's jealous move and filed it away. She knew it was going to be a challenge to get all of these professional men and women to fully accept her, but she was up for it. She craved the connection and comradery of Stuart's friends. Yet for the moment, it was only the attention of Robbie and Stuart that Sarah sought.

The two scientists were handsome, funny, and very educated. Sarah knew she would get into hot water if she allowed herself to entertain anything beyond a simple attraction. She tried to focus on the moment and enjoy the coming-together of strangers. The men carried a vibe of strength, power, and assertiveness. She began to fear that their sexy faces and traits might lead her down the road of temptation. Together, both men made the perfect man. *Which one do I want?* Sarah pondered as she sat between the two males and sipped her drink. *I wonder if one will try and seduce me.* There was a burning inside her that was gravitating toward *trouble.*

What was meant to be a good time with new friends was turning out to be so much more. It was happening very quickly for Sarah. Something uncontrollable washed over her. The unexplored territory of deciding between two men titillated her. She had not felt this way since she first laid eyes on Richard. The feeling of infatuation and butterflies had been far removed and long overdue to return.

As the events of the night unfolded, Robbie's competitiveness increased. "You're quite a sexy woman, you know that?" he whispered.

Sarah blushed and was slightly embarrassed. "I'm not sure I knew that," she teased.

"Oh, yes," he reaffirmed.

Sarah leaned closer to Robbie so no one could see or hear her. "You have intrigued me, as well," she whispered back.

As he continued to flirt, Robbie's right leg kept touching Sarah's. Sometimes it was just a soft and gentle nudge, but at other times he knocked her knee roughly. The contact was intentional; Robbie was staking claim of Sarah. "I should model for you. You can take some pictures of me – in compromising positions," Robbie quipped, "or how 'bout just naked?"

"I'm not *that* kind of a photographer," Sarah giggled, "but I'd love to take your picture."

That was the *in* Robbie was waiting for. The next meetup was not set in stone, but some sort of future interlude was established. In his mind, they now had plans for a photo shoot.

Stuart overheard the last part of their exchange and decided that he needed to step up *his* game. His only weapon, this time, in the fight for the new woman was alcohol – so he kept buying more.

But it was not long before the night neared its end, leaving Sarah to think about sobering up. The free wine was having an impact on her libido. "I'm drinking water for the next hour," she announced, "otherwise one of you will have to drive me home."

"Sweet Sarah, I know all there is to know about the effects certain food and liquids have on the body," he said, caressing her arm. "Some foods are absorbed into the bloodstream much faster than others. Some take time, so you might not feel their effects until you have consumed too much. But drink your water, if you will. We got your back."

"I'll bet your knowledge grows even more when you're naked," she joked.

That lit the wick under Robbie, and he was set afire, knowing that Sarah could spew out dirty-minded comments. His eyes gleamed, captivating her and sending her into a hypnotic state, from which she could not turn.

What did I just say? Sarah questioned herself. She felt embarrassed and looked over her right shoulder for Stuart, hoping he could save the conversation from going off the rails.

He had gone to the restroom and stopped to talk to other friends who were seated at the bar inside. Sarah felt vulnerable to the hunting tiger in wait.

"Did you know, Sarah, that doves mate for life?" said Robbie.

"I didn't know that."

"Just thought that was a cool factoid you might like to hear. The dove is my favorite bird."

The comment had nothing to do with any other subject they had discussed. Sarah was perplexed. *Is Robbie trying to tell me that he believes in committed relationships, or does he just want me to think that? Slick. Very slick,* she thought.

Stuart finally strutted back to their table, holding a drink. "Did you miss me?" he asked while seizing Sarah's waist and twisting her around to face him.

"Yes, we sure did. Glad you're back," Sarah smiled and chugged a cup of water.

Stuart had more class. He was not about to make any more moves on Sarah. He would take his time and allow things to develop, organically. The competition was still on, but his personality was not as aggressive as his counterpart, who continued to flirt with kisses on the back of Sarah's hands.

The bartender shouted, "Ok everyone, it's midnight! Closing time. Thanks for coming."

Mark and Amy, who had been quiet most of the night, gathered their belongings and pulled Sarah aside. "We didn't get a chance to chat with you tonight," said Amy.

"You were pretty busy with Rob. Be careful," Mark joked.

"I'm so sorry. It was great meeting you and hopefully we can hang out again."

"Oh, I know we will," said Amy.

"Are you ok to drive?" asked Mark.

"Sure, she is!" Jenny blurted out. "She drank a ton of water."

Sarah felt fine, but a little awkward when Jenny interrupted the conversation with her jealousy. She knew a sober Sarah would be less inclined to go home with Stuart. With all the attention coming from every side, Sarah felt like a daisy being plucked of its petals. It was dizzying.

"I'll walk you to your car, Sarah," said Stuart over his shoulder as he hugged his friends.

She nodded and turned to say a *goodbye* to Robbie. He had just finished gulping down his last beer.

"Hey, give me your number so we can set up that photo shoot!" Robbie winked.

"I've got it, Rob. I can give it to you later," Stuart intervened. "If that's ok with you, Sarah."

"Sure, that's totally fine."

Stuart squeezed her gently. "Ooh, you smell good," he added. "See you soon."

"Thank you," Sarah said, slowly releasing herself from his grip.

"I'll get your number from Stuart, later. No problem." Robbie leaned in to kiss Sarah on the cheek.

She smiled gently. Robbie's face was warm and slightly stubbled. The scent of the forest had returned to envelope her. She closed her eyes and breathed in the air surrounding them.

The two men walked Sarah to her car and watched her drive off. They proceeded to make the short trek to Stuart's place on foot and barely said a word to each other. It was just understood that Robbie would crash at his friend's place after drinking too much. Each man grinned as they thought about the prospect of getting Sarah to themselves. This night, the memory of her smile was the only thing either of them would be taking to bed.

Chapter 7

DIVINATION

It was a gloomy Saturday morning, and the smell of dewy tree leaves filtered through the partially opened window in Sarah's bedroom. The sun usually peeked through the clouds by noon, but until then, the cool breeze kept the temperature lower in the apartment.

The air was heavy and weighed on Em's little lungs, making it tough for her to breathe. She started coughing. The loud, hacking sounds from her furry bedfellow awakened Sarah from a deep sleep. "Oh, is the marine layer getting to you, baby doll?" she greeted Em with a gravelly voice. Sarah stretched out her arms and yawned.

Em looked at her owner with watery eyes and let out one big cough, before laying her head back down on the blanket. Sarah peered over the soft mound of her pillow and grinned. She was relieved, not having to get up to fetch Em's suppressant. Sarah did not want to excite the dog with a pat on the head, but she reached out and touched her anyway, only to be met with a wet tongue, licking the underside of her wrist.

"You are the love of my life, Emmy," Sarah whispered sweetly through happy tears, "the only one I trust with all my heart." There was not much Sarah could do to help Em get better. She knew she would someday face the inevitable. For now, she gave her friend all the love she could and enjoyed their time together.

Memories from the previous evening crept into Sarah's mind. She thought about Stuart buying drinks and Robbie caressing her. Feeling infatuated over two men was a new experience for Sarah. She felt alive and loved the unfamiliar emotions. *Why did Richard's death lead me to a man that just so happened to be living in the same city that I moved to?* she wondered. *Everything happens for a reason. What is the reason?*

Em interrupted Sarah's thoughts. She started coughing again. This time, it was more severe. The dog could not stop, causing her to vomit on the bed sheets. Sarah threw the soiled linens in a laundry basket and walked swiftly to the kitchen to grab the dog's medicine and a syringe. By the time she returned to her bedroom, Em was in distress and struggled to breathe. After scrambling to unlock the top of the bottle, Sarah stuck the syringe into the container and siphoned out five cubic centimeters of suppressant. The dog did not mind taking her meds, so it was easy for Sarah to squirt the red liquid into her throat. Within a few minutes, Em was calm.

"I'm sorry you have to go through this," Sarah told her. "Do you need to go pee, sweetie?" She scooped the dog up into her arms, took her outside into the cool morning air, and set her down.

After doing her business, Em ran back inside and returned to the bed. Sarah shut the door, grabbed a top sheet from the closet, and threw it over the mattress. She plucked up her down comforter, which had been tossed to the side, and snuggled up next to Em. She was not ready to start her day – just yet. Em rolled over for a belly-scratching and then fell asleep. Oh, how Sarah wished she could laze around with her and not think about work; but deadlines beckoned.

Sarah quietly slid off the bed and shuffled to the bathroom to get ready for the day. She turned on the shower, adjusted the temperature to her liking, and stepped inside. As the water flowed over her, thoughts of the men flooded her mind – specifically those of Robbie.

Fantasizing about future get-togethers excited her – museum visits, shopping, hanging out at the beach, dinners, and dancing. Daydreams shot through her head faster than fireworks on the Fourth of July. She imagined kissing him, feeling his hands caressing her arms, and his legs brushing against hers as they did the night before.

Suddenly, she realized where her mind was going. "Get out of my head!" her voice echoed through the empty bathroom. Shower time was over.

Keeping her focus on work was difficult. Sarah had several projects waiting for her. The last thing she needed was a man to distract her from productivity. As her own boss, she had to make sure she remained diligent. She wanted to stop thinking about Robbie and Stuart, but her thoughts were not within her control. The two men kept popping in and out.

It was already eight o'clock. One of the magazines, for which she freelanced, operated on the weekend and needed an answer by nine-thirty. She still had to go through hundreds of photos of the models she had taken at the docks. Sarah sat down at her computer and started sifting through the myriad of pictures, gazing at the women in the photos. Their unique features were captured flawlessly in the midday light. Sarah envied their youth and beauty. Their smooth skin glistened in the sunshine, reflecting off the water – their long, silky hair was highlighted to perfection. The scene of the boats docked at the port was a great backdrop for the shoot. She felt insecure as she studied the models. They were living exciting lives. Sarah struggled to keep her *own* life youthful and fresh.

Buzz. Buzz. A text alert came through on her cell phone. *Buzz. Buzz.* Then another. Before the screen faded to black, she caught a glimpse of the messages. They were from Stuart.

"Aaah!" Sarah screamed. With childlike excitement, she lunged at the device.

The message read, *Hey, I'm trying to gather a group together to go dancing on Friday. You on board?*

Sarah knew these men were a distraction and thought seriously about bowing out of the invitation. But hanging out with them again was too enticing. She did not want to miss the fun so she responded with an enthusiastic text, *Absolutely! What time?*

Everyone will just meet at my apartment an hour before heading to the club. How about 8? read Stuart's message.

It was the sense of involvement that made Sarah happy. She had become a part of something and it felt good. Not thirty seconds went by before she sent her response, *Great, I'll be there with bells on. I hope everyone I met can come!*

Stuart texted his address.

Then, she immediately remembered the photos that were due. "Damn! I need to get these to the magazine!" The phone was muted to avoid any more distractions and Sarah jumped back into her work.

The magazine just needed a few shots. Sarah was a great photographer and knew what her clients were looking for. Instead of reviewing every image, she was able to find a dozen perfect pictures. A photo file was put together, attached to a short email, and sent off before nine-thirty. She could rest easy; the job was complete.

Other inquiries were in the queue, but adrenaline pumped through Sarah's veins after receiving Stuart's texts. Thinking about the next get-together was exciting. Her focus on work was waning. Nevertheless, the hours passed and Sarah continued responding to emails of a dozen or so prospects. While she sat at her desk typing, she pondered, *What did Robbie mean when he said,* "We're in trouble?"

Sarah brought an astrology book with her from Bristol. It was thrown on the closet shelf when she unpacked her things. She jumped up from her desk to fetch it and thumbed through the pages, until she found information on Scorpio, Leo, and Virgo. A friend gave her *Sign to Sign* years ago to help with relationships, especially Richard's. She was more interested in reading it now.

There was a section that talked about romantic involvement between the signs, starting with each of their personality traits. Sarah read aloud, *"Virgo is analytical, a deep thinker, supportive of others, and possesses a need to be loved.* Spot on! *One aspect is always jumping to conclusions,"* she continued. "Ok, maybe I tend to do that. Let's check out Scorpio – *egotistical, sex-driven, power hungry, controlling, secretive* – that seems to fit Robbie's bill and I don't even know him yet."

Sarah continued to gather information. Predicting compatibility fascinated her. She was hooked and wanted to learn more about whether it could work out between the two of them.

"And Stuart! What about Stuart?" she exclaimed while flipping through the pages in search of Leo's description. *"Gatherer of friends,"* she read. "Wow! And *Virgo and Leo are two signs that are quite fond of each other. Leos are loyal, passionate, and spontaneous.* Now, how's the sex?"

Just then, Em walked into the room and jumped up on her mommy's chair.

"Get this, Em – *there's enough sexual tension between Virgo and Scorpio to keep things hot,"* she read loudly and pulled forward to the edge of the seat to make room for the little dog. "So, he must know how our signs work together. Ha ha," Sarah chuckled when she realized that must have been what Robbie was referring to when he joked about them being *in trouble.* "Ooh la la!"

Em barked and delighted in Sarah's silly sounds.

"As for Virgo and Leo? *Leo is dominating and adventurous in the bedroom and will bring vitality to his relationship with Virgo.* How exciting!" Sarah said, waving her hands. She continued reading until the time display on her computer screen caught her attention. "Yikes, it's afternoon, already!" Beams of orange and gold light streamed through her office window, warming her face.

Sarah hit the power button on her tabletop stereo, and 80s music began to play. The upbeat rhythm awakened her soul and took her back to her school days. Sarah could not resist the melody. She got out of her chair and danced around the room, imagining the hands of both Stuart and Robbie on her waist. As they swung her, Sarah closed her eyes and escaped into another world – one where she experienced unbridled pleasures. About five songs played before she grew exhausted and plopped down on the daybed next to her desk.

"Oh, no! I wonder if anyone has tried to reach me!" She remembered her phone had been on *silent mode* since the morning. To her surprise, about a dozen texts – from numbers she did not know – were on the display. They were all connected to a thread that Stuart had written that morning about getting together Friday night. *Why am I seeing all these? Stuart texted me only,* Sarah thought. She finally realized the shocking mistake. Stuart had sent a group text. That meant everyone saw what she had written earlier. "Oh, grief! I sounded like an idiot – desperate to see Robbie."

Another message came through. *Sorry, we can't make it. Amy has to work late on Friday, and then we're off to Vegas.* Sarah assumed that text must have been from Mark. She saved the number in her phone as *Mark and Amy* and continued to wait for more messages. Each unknown person – aside from Stuart and one other – claimed to have plans or were out of town on Friday.

I'll bring beer! read another.

Stuart chimed in. *Rob, make sure it's the kind of beer I like.*

Sarah beamed as she read it. She logged Robbie's number and started to type out a comment, but erased it.

I know you are typing something back. Just send it, Robbie's text read.

Sarah's eyes bugged out. A fear of being watched came over her. *Could he really see that I was about to text something? He must be teasing – and guessing,* she surmised. *There is no way he could know.* She searched her thoughts for something clever to say. But only a simple response came to mind. *Make sure it's light beer,* she wrote.

Robbie answered, *Perfect. What kind do you like, Sarah?*

She hesitated. *You decide :)*

The ice had been broken. Sarah could not concentrate. The conversation may have been simple, but her adrenaline increased, like the crescendo of a teapot whistle, ready to blow.

Chapter 8

DANCE OF THE MERRYMAKERS

Friday night was going to be an experience some women only dreamed of. It would be filled with young men, alcohol, and forbidden desires. Sarah was living out a fantasy that was spinning itself into a webbed reality.

The hot water from the shower stimulated her blood. It opened up her senses, but muddied her mind with dirty thoughts. She looked down at her slightly bronzed body and was pleased. She was sun-speckled and a bit weathered, but her tanned skin made her feel sexy. The scent of her shampoo and conditioner – peach, pineapple, and white-tea – would hopefully linger when she met up with the guys later. As she rinsed the remnants, the cascading waterfall of suds slithered down the curves of her entire body, tingling her. Sarah lathered up a washcloth. Her eyes closed as she breathed in the soothing aroma of coconut and plumeria shower gel. The creamy, tropical redolence reminded her of a shell-covered beach in Fiji she had once visited on a photo shoot. So many wonderful fragrances surrounded her.

She lost grip of the sudsy rag. It slapped against the bottom of the porcelain tub, splattering bubbles all over the sides. Her eyes opened. Staring at the mound at her feet, she watched the foam float away with spurts of water that pulsated from the shower head. Then, they entered – Robbie and Stuart. She fantasized about both men. They were welcomed guests in a forbidden world. In her mind, her body was an unchartered island, where three lovers had found themselves as castaways. Resting her head against the tiled wall, Sarah allowed the water to run over her face as she composed herself.

What if I'm seduced? she wondered.

She prepared to shave her legs. Guilt tapped her on the shoulder. Sarah knew that the best decision would be to steer clear of fooling around with the guys. Shaving her legs meant that she would allow them to be touched. A struggle of morality ensued. It was a battle between good – and naughty. The best thing to do would be to say *no* to any advances. But she secretly wanted to feel desired. She yearned for a sexual encounter with Robbie and possibly even Stuart – or both at the same time. The longings clouded her better judgment. She shaved her legs.

The devil reveled in Sarah's delight of her seemingly, happy life. Everything on the outside was pleasing – the job, new place to live, and perfect climate of the West Coast. On top of it all, Sarah now held the attention of two very fit, handsome, sexually-driven men. It was all hers for the taking. What could be wrong with that?

Sarah lightly slapped her cheek to wake up from the daydream. Ignoring the urge to question her scruples, she dried her hair and continued getting ready for her night out. She carefully crafted a sexy look with a white miniskirt and tight, tailored top. A pair of four-inch black-and-white pumps emphasized her legs. Between the outfit and the high heels, Sarah was sure to turn on every man at the club. But two men in particular were all she cared about.

She gathered up her soft locks into a loose, tousled bun, again. The style seemed to work. It was innocent, but only in appearance. Her full-length mirror returned the compliment of a ready and willing woman. A typically insecure Sarah felt confident and excited to begin the night. She kissed Em *goodbye* and shut the door behind her.

As she headed to Stuart's place, her mind was lost in a whirlwind of emotions, distractions, and temptations. A darker dimension manipulated her integrity. A smile stretched across her face and Sarah let out a burst of laughter. Her concern for this mysterious entanglement grew less and less. Instead, she basked in the glory of her new life, and no one could stop her.

Stuart's address was programmed into her phone's navigational app. It brought her to the right place. As soon as she pulled into the parking lot, she noticed a car with a bumper sticker on the back that read, *You Are What You Eat*. She wondered if that was Robbie's vehicle. Butterflies filled her gut. She felt flush at the thought of him and Stuart being mere feet away. She composed her nerves and summoned the universe to help her remain calm. "Make me look good, please," she whispered.

After fidgeting with her clothes, she bolted out of the car and scurried up the sidewalk in her heels. Sarah looked down at her phone one last time to make sure she had the right apartment number. With a gentle knock, she alerted them to her arrival.

"Come in!"

When Sarah opened the door, a dashing Robbie stood before her, dressed in his signature white shirt and loose-fitting jeans. "Hey, sistah," he said and swooped in to kiss her on the cheek. "Damn, you smell awesome!"

"Girl, you look fantastic!" Stuart cut in for a hug. "Mmm . . . yeah, fresh!"

Sarah was overwhelmed with the attention – and loved it. The three immediately swirled around the kitchen island, where Stuart had prepared shots of tequila. He handed one to Sarah. The mood was just right. The apartment was dimly lit with recessed lights over the counters. A low, lulling melody played from a stereo in the corner of the dining room.

That sounds a lot like classical guitar, Sarah thought. Her head cocked to one side as she tried to make out the tune. She enjoyed the exotic strumming from Spain. As it turned out, it was Stuart's favorite. He played it whenever he wanted to relax. But after they drank a few shots, the mood changed.

Robbie noticed Sarah was getting turned on by Stuart's choice of music. "Well, this isn't what I want to hear this weekend!" exclaimed Robbie as he briskly walked over to the stereo.

"You can keep it on anytime for me, Stuart."

"You like Spanish guitar, Sarah?" Stuart asked.

She nodded affirmatively.

"That's incredible! None of my other friends like it."

"Not tonight!" Robbie said, reaching for the stereo remote.

The competition between the two men had apparently picked up where it left off at the restaurant. Robbie was not about to let Stuart win Sarah over with anything – especially music. He surfed the local stations to find something he wanted. Sweet air was soon cut with noisy dance tunes. The heavy, thumping drumbeat blared from the speakers. They immediately agreed that it was the more appropriate choice. Robbie bobbed his head back and forth. Stuart made a face of approval. And Sarah giggled in delight of the threesome's musical entanglement. The night was off to a good start.

As Robbie passed Sarah on his way to pick up another shot from the tabletop, he grazed her waist with his hand. Their eyes met for only seconds. It was a tease that left her mentally pouncing forward to catch him and pull him in for a longer stare. She resisted the temptation and smiled humbly. Her sheepish innocence was a trait that would soon bring out Robbie's inner wolf.

"Is anyone else coming?" Sarah asked.

"No. No one else is coming," Robbie and Stuart said simultaneously.

Sarah instantly felt the nerves in her arms perk up. *They answered pretty quickly,* she thought. *Did they want me alone?* She forced down another shot to deal with the onset of fear. She grimaced from the taste of the straight tequila. These guys were strangers. It dawned on her that there would be no other woman around to come to her rescue, if she needed it.

"I'm ok with it just being the three of us," Stuart reassured her. "I don't have enough room in my truck for more than two passengers anyway."

"Oh! We are all going in one car?" replied Sarah.

"Yes, it's going to be tight," Robbie said, "but it's better that way."

"Ready?" asked Stuart as he put away the alcohol and rinsed the shot glasses. "Are you all fine with going to the club?"

"What are the options?" Robbie said while giving Sarah the once-over. "Honey, you look good."

Sarah blushed and tilted her head, flashing her innocent smile.

"Mmm, mmm, mmm." Robbie clapped his hands and sashayed to the door before Stuart was able to answer his question. "Let's just stick with the original plan," he said.

Sarah did not care where they went as long as she was in present company. Stuart locked up the apartment, and the group headed toward his truck. They could see the potential of being caught in a trap of lust – and they willingly went along with it. Robbie motioned for Sarah to get in the vehicle, first, so she would be in the middle. It was like a fantasy come true to be sandwiched between two sun-kissed pillars of strength.

They agreed to continue listening to the same style of music, so Sarah poked at the stereo to find a station. The pumping sounds filled their minds with thoughts of the dance-consuming night ahead. No one paid any attention, or seemed to care that Stuart was going to drive, intoxicated. He started the engine and took off down the road.

When the three arrived at Club Je'Nack, their adrenaline levels – fueled by the tequila – skyrocketed. The place was fancier than Sarah had imagined. There were bouncers and security guards in front of the doors. Limos dropped off elite guests, one after the other. After waiting in line, Robbie pulled out enough cash to pay for both his and Sarah's cover charges. Stuart trailed behind and paid his own way. The deliberate move by Robbie was a padlock, engaging Sarah at his side. He marked his territory.

The heavy, booming bass from the huge speakers caused the entire room to vibrate in a rhythmic beat. The sound was tribal to Sarah, whose chest was rattling from the rapid, metronome-like ticking of continuous reverberation. It aroused her and so did the hypnotizing strobe lights.

"Three whiskey shots," Stuart blurted out to the bartender.

"Oh geez, that's too strong!" Sarah gasped. Her words were lost in the noise of the club.

Stuart wanted his friends to hold their buzz and knew whisky would do the trick. He bought the round. It was his way of showing approval for Robbie's payment of Sarah's cover. He had his own strategy for a future claim on her.

Sarah looked at the libation sitting on the bar. She hated hard liquor. It had been difficult enough to swig the tequila shots at Stuart's apartment. Wine or well drinks would have been better. Reluctantly, Sarah picked up the miniature glass that was pushed toward her. *It's going to burn like hell,* she thought. Braving forward, her lips met the rim of the glass. She frowned as she thought of the bitter, biting fluid scratching its way down the back of her throat – like a drowning cat. The spirit was sipped in tiny, cautious intervals.

"Throw that head back, and swig it ALL down, girl!" shouted Robbie. "Be a woman!"

Sarah thought she *was* being a woman. The idea of slinging back whisky shots – preceded by the tequila from earlier – made her feel more like a sailor than the demure female she was. But she wanted to impress the guys. If she came across as wimpy, neither one of them would find her attractive. As Sarah would soon find out, Robbie was a master at pushing people into doing things they did not typically do. He guilted them into submission.

Sarah plugged her nose with one hand and tossed the whisky back with the other. She realized it was not the taste that made her wince; it was the sting. The drinks kept coming. Stuart ordered the first round of many gin and tonics, which she could tolerate. The three of them grabbed their glasses and headed for a high-top table on the side of the dance floor. The DJ played a wide variety of dance music. It was a never-ending compilation; one song flowed into another, keeping the same beat underneath.

There was unspoken communication between Stuart, Robbie, and Sarah. They stared into each other's eyes. It was time to dance. Without hesitation, they darted onto the wooden floor, like captive animals being let out of a cage. Rock star moves, sexual glares, and wild passions exuded from their bodies. A feeling of elation swept through Sarah's entire being, as if she were covered in chocolate. The three bobbed their heads and jumped up and down until sweat dripped from their foreheads.

They were free.

Sarah was renewed, living out a fantasy that was impossible to describe, even to herself. She twisted and twirled around Robbie, landing in the arms of Stuart to be dipped. She looked at the other women on the dance floor with their monogamous dates. Envy and the desire to be her in that moment, were emotions written on their faces. She pitied them.

The drums pounded louder and louder through the speakers.

Robbie grinned with approval of Sarah's dance moves. He grabbed her around the waist and pulled her in close. Stuart moved to the side and danced alone. Robbie bent down to nuzzle Sarah's neck and inhale the scent of her moist yet sweetly showered skin. The alcohol, blinding lights, and deafening music encouraged her to stay in his grip.

Stuart was not to be excluded. Sarah slithered out of Robbie's clutch, but hung onto a belt loop of his jeans as she turned to face her other partner. Raising her forearm up and across Stuart's left shoulder, she swayed her right hip toward his groin. They both smiled at each other and looked down to admire their gyrating bodies.

Robbie saw what Sarah was doing and reeled her in. He then swung her out toward the edge of the dance floor, away from Stuart. She laughed and threw her head back.

The night flowed along, like a silk dress caught in a light breeze. Nothing could break into the zone in which these three were living. Hours went by, more drinks were consumed, and the sexual pull of a toxic chemistry, increased.

During a song she did not recognize, Sarah excused herself to go to the restroom. The fun ended abruptly, but the guys knew it was temporary. Robbie and Stuart were too pumped from the alcohol and the music to worry about whether or not Sarah would have her game on when she returned. They would take her back to the dance floor, no matter what.

The loud, unfamiliar beat followed Sarah. Her head was spinning. She stumbled into a stall and two-stepped around the interior, trying to get her skirt down. She narrowly missed the toilet bowl when she emptied her bladder. Only a portion of the alcoholic poison escaped.

While getting redressed, Sarah sensed something strange in the room. There was a dark energy circling around her. This force made her feel loved, comforted, and extremely randy. She closed her eyes and envisioned Robbie and Stuart kissing her on the dance floor. They took turns having their way with her against the throbbing speakers. When they were done, the presence offered its shoulder for Sarah to rest her head.

In a flash, the vision was over, and her mind went blank. Sarah opened her eyes. Breathless, she finished up and walked out of the stall, expecting to see someone; but the room was empty. Whomever or whatever the visitor was, it had vanished. Sarah was too intoxicated to make sense of it. It was the influence of alcohol that allowed her to feel its existence. She did not imagine the event. It was real. The presence fed her with thoughts of lust and a need for sex.

Sarah washed her hands. She was refreshed and ready to get back on the dance floor –and into the arms of Robbie. He ran to meet her when she exited the bathroom. Although he could have grabbed any one of the other beautiful women at the bar – he wanted Sarah. Their faces met. For a moment, it seemed like just the two of them were in the room. A good mix of music began to play. Robbie clutched Sarah's waist and swung her in the air. His face lit up as he carried her to the wooden floor. Their feet never stopped moving. He pushed and pulled her, grinning from ear to ear with each tug.

Sarah unpinned her hair, allowing the mane to flow down and spiral around her shoulders. She was a dream. It excited Robbie. He let her know, by pulling her close to his hard body. She was turned on and felt confident that she had seduced him with such little effort. It could not have been a more perfect night. Her energy surged, and her loins were on fire. He bent down and kissed Sarah, passionately.

Meanwhile, Stuart was dancing with a cute brunette on the other side of the club. He glanced for a brief moment at Sarah and Robbie in their seductive interlude. The sight stung a little. He took mental snapshots to recall later, during his morning hangover. His plan for winning Sarah over was not going to happen tonight, so he turned around to face the dark-haired stranger. For now, he would satisfy his needs with the temporary companion.

"Last call for alcohol!" the DJ disrupted.

As Club Je'Nack started to shut down, Robbie made sure that Sarah was his for the night. He did not need any more drinks and wanted to leave before everyone else fled the bar. "Ready to blow this joint?" he said to Sarah after he pulled his mouth away from hers.

"Sure. Where's Stuart?"

Robbie did not like the idea of Sarah being concerned for Stuart's whereabouts. He appeased her, though, by containing his jealousy and agreeing to search for him. He took her hand, and they walked off the dance floor to scan the room for their messy-haired friend. Sarah tried to let go and look for Stuart on her own, but Robbie tightened his grip and pulled her close. "Stay with me. We will find him, together," he demanded. "You don't want to get lost in here." He stared deeply into Sarah's eyes with the hypnotic trance of a Scorpio and kissed her again.

She was duped into seeing two sides to this man. One was cocky, devious, and arrogant. The other was seemingly caring and protective. Sarah was falling for both.

As the pair made their way through the jungle of people, they saw Stuart at the bar, paying the tab. The dark-haired stranger he had met was nowhere in sight.

"Stuart!" Sarah shouted with excitement at the top of her lungs.

He turned to see the beautiful, glowing woman – smiling from ear to ear – having found her other man. She released her hand from Robbie's clutch and ran to meet him.

"Did you two have fun?" Stuart asked, glancing at Robbie.

"Yes, a ton!" replied Sarah. "We missed dancing with you."

Robbie did not share her sentiment. He was thrilled that Stuart was out of the picture while he and Sarah made out on the dance floor. He was in his own, self-gratifying world and determined to conquer Sarah's undivided affection.

"Let's go you guys," Stuart insisted. "We're paid up. I want to get out of here before the cops check everyone at the door." He motioned with his hand for them to leave. Even if he could not control Sarah, Stuart *could* control the drive home.

Chapter 9

THE PERFECT STORM

Along with the smell of booze and sweat, laughter filled the cab of Stuart's truck. The three friends experienced an awesome evening, and there was more to come.

"It would have been hilarious if we had left without finding Stuart!" Robbie joked to Sarah.

"Yeah, real funny," Stuart responded. "The only thing is – you would've gotten nowhere. The keys were in my pocket!"

Sarah giggled at their exchange. Hearing their deep voices, after being in such a noisy club, was a relief – and a turn-on. She was happy. Her virtue had been pushed down into the deep pockets of her soul and was replaced with a vibrant sex drive. Perspiration glistened off her freshly shaven thighs, which were lit by the overhead streetlights. As Robbie shifted and positioned himself on the seat, he could not help but stare at them. His eyes met hers in approval. A sinister smile drew across his tanned, rugged face.

Sarah's entire body was electrified, watching him gaze at her with desire. She returned his stare with a lustful invitation. "Are you in?" Sarah asked playfully.

"Not yet," Robbie said and reached out to shut the door, "but I plan to be."

Sarah laughed with a deep growl. She understood the implication of his response. Robbie took note of her reaction. He leaned into her, letting out his own rich, baritone-like moan.

The cool, California breeze blew through the opened windows of the vehicle, bringing relief to their hot bodies. Robbie shoved his hip into Sarah's side. His well-manicured right hand held the vinyl grip above the passenger window. Sarah took note of his strength, by the muscle he flexed under his sleeve.

The smell of Robbie's alcohol-tainted breath wafted past Sarah's nose. It enthralled her while he nuzzled her neck. He gently brushed away a few locks of her hair, which still draped beautifully around her shoulders. The glow of the streetlights danced upon each strand. He gnashed his teeth against her skin. She could feel their sharp enamel edges. Sarah's perfume was enhanced by her perspiration and body heat, and Robbie thought it dangerous. But he felt no fear.

Because they had been wrapped up in a world of their own, Robbie and Sarah finally realized the engine had never started. Stuart was sitting behind the wheel the whole time, just staring at the vehicle's instrument panel.

"Are you ok, Stuey?" Sarah asked, swinging her arm around his shoulders. She locked the driver's side door to keep him from falling out.

"I like that nickname," Stuart smiled and snapped back from the trance. "Yeah, *Stuey* is ok. By the way, there shouldn't be any cops on the route I'll be driving out of here."

The three were still intoxicated, but taking a taxi was out of the question. These macho men thought they were in control of everything. Stuart had no clue if there would be any cops on their way home. By reassuring Sarah of their safe path, he was comforting himself, as well.

She thought back on the night and how much she loved being with the guys. Stuart was so mellow, when he wanted to be. Robbie, on the other hand, was dark and deceptive – an emotional risk for her. But he was bold, fun, and sexy. Together, they had all the characteristics she wanted in a man – a blend of thunder and lightning, rain and wind – a perfect storm.

After several minutes, Stuart finally started the vehicle. He clung to the steering wheel and took to the road. There were only a few other cars on their path, but they were all moving at a snail's pace. Stuart shouted the Lord's name in vain and used several profane words to describe the drivers that were in his way.

"Chill, dude," Robbie laughed. "Don't go all road rage with us in the car."

"Maybe they saw a patrol car or something," she said softly to try and calm his demeanor.

Instantly, they passed a police car and gasped. To their good fortune, the officer was not paying attention and their vehicle sailed by with no incident. They were safe from the potential threat of jail time. Perhaps it was supernatural intervention, or simply good luck.

"Well, that was a close call, Stu," said Robbie.

"I never get caught," he boasted.

They all quietly snickered and breathed a sigh of relief when they made it back to Stuart's apartment, safely. Sarah should have been thankful for arriving alive, but she was too buzzed and preoccupied with a strong desire for Robbie to take the time to count her blessings. Maybe the old Sarah would have been grateful, but the new Sarah took it all for granted. There was an external force that kept her out of harm's way and another contrasting force pulling her into it.

The group stumbled out of the truck and up the sidewalk to Stuart's door.

"There's not a chance in hell I'm tempting fate and risking getting caught by that cop. I'm not driving home now," Robbie proclaimed.

"You two can stay at my place," Stuart insisted. "Crash on the floor, the couch, my bed – wherever you like."

"Is your bed king-sized?" Sarah quipped.

"In fact, it is," Stuart smiled devilishly and tried to unlock the door.

Sarah laughed. She did not expect her flirtatious, rhetorical question to be answered. No one addressed the open-ended invitation for group sleep on Stuart's big mattress. His comment just faded away.

As they leaned on each other, Robbie and Sarah swayed on the porch. They waited for Stuart, who fidgeted with the knob for nearly a minute. Finally, he realized he had been trying to open the door with his truck key. He found the right one, and the three friends practically fell into the foyer.

An awkward feeling came over all of them. Neither of the men knew what to do with Sarah, and she felt unsure of where to sleep. They all froze where they stood, staring into the darkened apartment.

Then, Stuart broke the silence, "Do you guys feel like a drink?"

"Oh, hell no! No way!" Robbie and Sarah simultaneously and vehemently declined his offer, even though there was enough *free* liquor in the place to set it on fire.

"Hey man, good night. Thanks for letting us crash at your place, Stu." Robbie's abrupt, decisive words were a lit torch in the darkness.

Sarah was stunned and speechless. She felt his body nudge her closer to the interior of the room. It was clear what he was doing, and she felt out of control.

"We can sleep out here on your couch," Robbie continued.

The game was over.

Stuart swallowed hard. He was defeated – again. His friend had stolen the prize. He turned on the kitchen lights and went to his bedroom to retrieve pillows and a blanket for his house guests.

Sarah just stared at Robbie, who was taking off his shoes and making himself at home. Everything was happening so fast. *What* was *happening?* she wondered.

"Well, there. Good night, you two." Stuart tossed the bedding on the large pit-sofa. He could not help imagining his friends rolling around on his furniture. It was silly for him to feel jealousy, though. He had no deep emotional attachments to Sarah thus far, but he still held out hope for a chance with her, at some point. The lights were shut off, and he hobbled to his bedroom, alone, leaving the couple together in the dark.

Robbie and Sarah found themselves facing each other. The streetlights beamed slightly through the window blinds, casting a diffused, white glow across parts of their bodies. Only a few inches of their faces were illuminated by the dim light. The moment sent a shudder through Sarah's spine. There were no smiles exchanged, just longing stares filled with built-up sexual tension. They studied each other intently. Their senses were heightened.

A window in the kitchen had been left open, and the din of a thousand crickets filled the apartment. Their song added a mysterious element to the aura. It sounded like an orchestra attempting to imitate the rhythm of beating hearts.

Robbie took a few steps toward Sarah. He wrapped his hands around the back of her head and pulled her face to his. Her entire body tingled as he leaned in to kiss her. It was warm and sweet.

"Robbie . . . ," she whispered.

He could feel Sarah's resistance, but his mouth interrupted her next word, and her body fell limp to the seduction. His thick, muscular arms cradled the wounded bird.

Dark desires were winning, but conflict was stabbing her in the gut. *How far am I going to allow Robbie to take me?* she feared. The thought of Stuart popped into her head. *Is he watching? Is he waiting? Can he hear our* *passionate breathi*ng? *Am I doing the right thing? I want to be with him, too.* The fantasy of having both men was rare and exciting, but if she went any further with Robbie, she might lose Stuart's friendship. At the same time, she might lose herself.

Robbie's hands roved Sarah's body. He gently tugged at her blouse to suggest removing it and rolled the buttons between his large fingers. He slowly bent her backward toward the overstuffed sofa, where they had strategically positioned themselves. Her warm skin beckoned him.

Sarah was caught in an undertow of euphoria. It drew her in deeper, nearly suffocating her. She felt totally at his mercy while being seduced by his intense kisses. But the moment was cut short. "I can't hurt Stuart by doing this."

Robbie immediately recoiled and said sternly, "Would you rather be banging *him*?"

Sarah felt a chill. The stench of jealousy turned her on, but the question was embarrassing. "I want you, Robbie. I'm just so confused."

"Stuart will be alright. He's dead asleep, I can assure you. Booze does that to him." Robbie ignored her concern and went in for another kiss.

The alcohol had not rendered Sarah completely devoid of coherency. She understood what was going on and the consequences of her actions. But the lust was so powerful. It enveloped the room – and her. She felt the sharp pain of guilt, again.

It was all so weird. Decadent. Immoral. Unhealthy.

Suddenly, the eerie presence – Sarah encountered in the bathroom at Club Je'Nack – returned. It enticed her to continue, kindling a fire within her. She did not fear it for some reason, but it bewildered her. It approved of what she was doing. *This shouldn't be happening,* Sarah thought to herself. *Something is off.* A shroud of darkness fell over her, comforting her, and providing warmth. It disguised itself as a blanket of possibility. The presence was there to tempt.

That is when Stuart entered her mind again. She pictured him behind her while Robbie fervently kissed her from the front. Sarah's deviant thoughts enticed her to caress Robbie's waist.

He immediately interpreted the gesture as a green light to continue. His hands groped every part of her trembling body before unbuttoning her tight, tailored blouse. Robbie pushed the material off her left shoulder while guiding her down onto the sofa.

"I can't," she whispered in protest, yet she did not stop him.

"Yes, you can."

Devils ran like laughing imps around Robbie and Sarah – and angels watched. She could not see any of them, but Sarah could feel them in the form of guilt. It was like a fury of waves crashing upon her. She struggled for air. The heat was too intense between her and Robbie. She gripped hunks of his thick hair at both sides of his scalp in a moment of passion. She wanted to remain wholesome, yet she hated the notion. She fought off the good and the bad while provoking both to stay.

Robbie missed one button. As he forced her blouse off her other shoulder, the button popped off and bounced onto Stuart's glass coffee table, making a *tink tink* sound. It rolled onto the floor. The alarming noise triggered Sarah's decision to stop. She guided his chin up to her face with her hand to prevent him from going further.

Robbie rolled his eyes and let out a loud sigh. He tugged the garment up around Sarah's shoulders and rested back against the sofa. He had enough resistance.

Sarah did not want to admit it, but she was relieved. All her tense muscles finally relaxed – as well as her brain. She pulled herself into Robbie's body and drifted to sleep; however, her slumber was brief. A whirlwind of thoughts kept her awake. *Did I just create a mess? What is happening to me? I've never felt like this.*

It was nearing sunrise, and despite dealing with a hangover, Stuart would be up early for his workout. Sarah wanted the scene to appear innocent as though nothing had happened. She gently moved away from Robbie and crawled onto the other side of the couch. It was cold, and he had the blanket. She embraced a pillow for warmth and watched him sleep. She wondered if he would be upset with her for leading him on. Her actions were unintentional, but she was aware that she probably appeared to him as a tease.

Sarah fastened the buttons on her shirt until she reached the spot where one had popped off. Fortunately, the empty space did not expose her too much. She pulled the fabric up to make it appear undamaged, dropped her head on the pillow, and napped.

It was not long before Stuart's two feet landed on the floor next to his bed with a thud.

A startled Sarah awakened, but lied motionless. She hoped Robbie would remain asleep so she could have a moment to redeem herself with Stuart. It was to be made very clear that nothing happened with his best friend.

Stuart made his way to the bathroom and stood at the toilet for one full minute. That was not long enough for Sarah, who was anticipating a certain amount of awkwardness, once he came out. She took a deep breath when he scuffled into the living room. With one eye peering from behind a corner of the pillow, she watched him walk bare-footed across the floor and into the kitchen.

"Good morning, Sarah. How did you sleep?"

The jig was up.

"Hi –Stuart," she whispered, trying not to wake the creature that slept on the cushions nearby. "Oh, I was able to cat nap here and there."

"Can I make you a smoothie? I only have cranberry juice, two bananas, and some protein powder."

"Whatever you have is fine with me." Sarah wanted to appear cool and collected. But she was worried that Stuart was going to mention her sharing the couch with Robbie.

He did not – at least not in the way she expected. He knew better than to cross that line, but he assumed some things. "You could have stayed in *my* bed if it was more comfortable for you."

Did he know that I stopped Robbie's advances? Sarah wondered. *Or is he just being polite?*

Stuart would have loved for her to snuggle up to him on his big mattress. He desired to be close to a woman. Even if nothing sexual happened, spooning beautiful Sarah would have been the perfect nightcap to such an awesome evening.

"Thank you for the option. I wish you would have insisted on it," Sarah said playfully.

There was no competing with Robbie that night. Stuart was fully aware of his friend's power of persuasion. But he had no plan to stop trying to impress Sarah. He filled the blender and turned it on. The whirring sound was loud enough to wake the neighbors. He poured the mixture into two glasses and handed one to her. "Cheers!" he toasted.

"Thank you, Stuey. Cheers."

As the two stood in the kitchen, slurping their drinks, they turned to see Robbie sitting upright on the edge of the sofa. His hair was in disarray and his bare chest exposed. As he rubbed his face and head, he looked at Sarah and just snickered.

She peered over the edge of her glass, trying to figure out his feelings and why he laughed. Stuart observed the silent exchange. He quickly looked away, pretending to clean out the blender.

"Ohh, I gotta go home. I'll see you two later," Robbie moaned.

Sarah expected him to motion her over to the couch – or better yet – ask her to walk with him to his car. She had hoped he would have something nice to say while being discreet in the presence of Stuart. There were no flirtatious comments or gestures as he had exhibited the entire night. She returned his sentiment with the same uncaring, nonchalant tone, "See ya."

Stuart knew what had happened. He had seen it so many times before. Robbie's love-them-and-leave-them attitude was nothing new. Yet he did not have the nerve to tell his buddy that giving women the cold shoulder was wrong. Stuart liked playing, too. He could drop a woman as fast as he picked her up. The only difference was that Stuart was *sometimes* a bit more sincere and sensitive to a female's feelings than Robbie. He was about to prove that again.

"Well, what do we have here?" Robbie reached down to tie his shoes and found the button that had popped off Sarah's blouse. He walked past Stuart to where she was standing and plunked it down inside her trembling hand for all to see. "Princess, you may want to sew this back onto your shirt. See you later, guys," he said and walked out the door. It was more important to impress Stuart with his conquest, than consider her heart.

The small amount of dignity Sarah had been clinging to was smashed. Robbie's words felt like drops of whiskey – in her eyes. Dumbfounded and embarrassed, she downed the smoothie, rinsed out her glass, and briskly walked into the living room to find her shoes.

"Are you leaving, too?" Stuart asked awkwardly. "Come work out with me." He attempted to make Sarah feel more comfortable.

"Yes – no! I've got to get a ton of stuff done at home today – bills, laundry, you know," Sarah bumbled and slipped into her black-and-white stilettos.

Stuart kissed her sweetly on the cheek and they embraced. "I'll text you at some point this week." Although it was not Stuart's place to talk about his friend so soon, he had his suspicions that Sarah was keen on the aloof man. He did not know what to say to her, but felt she needed some kind of solace to ease her worry. "Robbie can be . . . ."

"Yeah, talk soon," Sarah interrupted and walked out the door. She just wanted to get home. More precisely, she wanted to run and hide.

The leather seats in her car were cold and uncomforting. She started up the engine and sat still for a moment to shake off the night – and morning. The drive home to Em would not be quick enough.

Chapter 10

LIKE CRIMSON

Grumbling under her breath, Sarah fumbled with the keys to her front door. The hangover from the night was kicking in. The sting of the morning sun brought tears to her eyes. She squinted the salty fluid out onto her cheekbones and wiped it away, pressing hard with both hands.

Finally, the door opened. She dropped onto her sofa and breathed a sigh of relief to be home. Snapping out of a momentary daydream, the sound of unconditional love awakened her spirit. The panting of her little dog was a song to Sarah's ears. "Emmy, my love!" She lit up. Her furry friend pranced out from the bedroom, was plucked up, and taken outside to pee.

When they returned, Sarah placed the pup on her lap and folded her slender arms around her. The smell of Em's warm, soft fur was comforting and reminded her of a childhood teddy bear. Em provided consolation for Robbie's cold attitude. "It's just as much my fault, I guess," she said aloud. "People get drunk and carried away. But Robbie should know that it was way too soon to rush things. He shouldn't be upset with me, right Em?"

The dog just looked at Sarah with big eyes and rested her head on her momma's legs.

The tired woman felt guilt, frustration, pain, and wondered if the two men were just out to get their jollies with her. She did not want to make too much of something that would never materialize. Yet she still had empathy for the loneliness of both Robbie and Stuart.

Sarah shoved her face into the fur on the dog's neck and rocked back and forth. The movement helped soothe her aching body and throbbing head.

Buzz. Buzz. A text message distracted her. She swiftly grabbed the device and looked at the screen. "Robbie?"

Shopping later? I need new curtains, he wrote.

"Curtains? What the heck?" she laughed. Her mood lifted, but she needed rest. Her head filled with the weight of last night's memories. She was tickled to get an invitation from Robbie, but also frustrated by how their time together ended. She wanted him to go, but wished he would stay. Quite the fickle mess, Sarah had a choice to either let go of inhibitions and reservations, or completely walk away from this *bad boy. Do I really want to get involved with him?* she wondered.

Her fingers typed out a response – as if something else was answering for her. *Sure. What time?*

Sarah anticipated spending an exciting day with Robbie. At least it would be interesting. She was worried her emotions would show on her sleeve – expecting a serious relationship all in the same day. *Try to have a good time,* Sarah thought to herself. *Think before you do anything stupid.*

Sarah rarely thought things out when it came to men – especially ones she liked. She felt somehow controlled by Robbie. He spoke. She jumped. She should not have been so pathetically attainable, but she was playing right into his hands. Like a succulent plant, she absorbed all the seemingly sweet gestures he spit her way. His words were like drops of rain on a dry, desert floor.

Meet at my apartment – 1p? Robbie's follow-up text read.

Her rejuvenated spirit catapulted her into a frenzy of energy. She was ready for anything. *Ok! Text me your address.*

He sent it along.

She interpreted the least bit of attention from Robbie as a promise of love. The loneliness that she had felt for so long, consumed her. The hunger for the affection of a vibrant, younger man restored what she had been missing – passion.

There was no turning back now. The day's plan was set in motion. She mapped out Robbie's address which was farther away than Stuart's place. It would take about three and half hours to eat breakfast, shower, get dressed and drive to his apartment. The time would pass quickly.

Em jumped down from Sarah's lap and bit into a toy ball. She looked up at her mommy to entice her to play.

"I really don't have time for that right now, Emmy," Sarah said. "I gotta get going."

The dog pushed the ball away with her nose to show her disappointment. She dropped her head between her paws and pouted.

Men were being put at the top of Sarah's priority list. That meant Em would be spending another day alone. She gave her some medicine, in case a coughing fit occurred in her absence. The loving friend was dismissed, and she prepared to leave.

Sarah was feeling fiery and hot for an adventure with this mysterious man. She decided to wear red to get a response out of Robbie. *The color attracted bulls, so it had to work on him,* she imagined and giggled to herself. There was no telling what the hours ahead would bring, but she could only focus on how the whole encounter was making her feel. She bolted out the door.

The drive would be a scenic one. There was beauty amidst the busyness. Sarah passed Signal Hill and admired the homes that adorned its sides. From the dirty, grey freeway, she could see Mount Baldy looming in the distance. Its snowy peak distracted her during the journey to Robbie's place. She took a moment to feel grateful for choosing Long Beach as her home, but she knew there was more of the state she needed – and wanted – to see. "California is so beautiful with its versatility and depth. Look at those mountains and how refreshing they are to the soul," Sarah sighed out loud. "Just amazing – and grand."

She returned her focus to the road. It would not be long before she reached Robbie's apartment. As she watched the few cars in front of her, she stroked her hair with her right hand, pulling strays out of her face. Dragging her fingers down to the ends, she grabbed a chunk and brought it to her nose. The smell of delightfully-scented shampoo pleased her. She was clean.

Today was a fresh start with her new man. She would try and forget about the evening before, which was provoked by alcohol. Last night was unnatural. It was not raw. Today would be raw –she hoped – and real.

Chapter 11

LEAVES OF HEALING

Robbie lived in a small apartment in the Garden Grove area outside of Long Beach. The city's population was just under two hundred thousand. There were plenty of shops and malls where he and Sarah could find curtains. She thought it was a great idea for getting the two of them together and was encouraged.

When she finally reached Robbie's complex she stared at the building from across the parking lot, composed herself, and applied lip gloss. Her thoughts were flooded with rehearsed sentences of things that might be discussed – activities, friends. The beginning stage of dating was always the hardest. She was nervous.

Sarah approached the front door and knocked lightly on the wood. She looked around and tried to quickly analyze Robbie by the way he kept his porch. A collection of tiny potted plants gave her the impression that he did not want to commit to anything that would be too much work. She snickered to herself.

The sound of voices coming from inside the apartment startled her. *Who is in there with him?* she wondered. *He didn't mention anyone else joining us on our shopping spree.*

A female giggled. Sarah could see shadows through the living room window. Her body shivered and her confidence lowered. Did she arrive too early and catch him hanging out with a girlfriend? "Answer, already," Sarah whispered to herself. "What's going on?"

"Hey!" Robbie flung the door open and greeted her with a half-hearted hug.

"Hey!" Sarah mimicked. *That's it? That's all he's going to say?* she silently questioned their trite exchange and searched for more intelligent words. "Love your – foliage."

"Yeah, it's great. Glad you like my – foliage," Robbie chuckled.

There was no time for Sarah to recover from the silly statement. The female she had heard before the door opened made a quick dash across the dimly lit hallway at the back of the apartment. Discontent showed across Sarah's face, and Robbie immediately picked up on it.

"Linda! Come meet my friend, Sarah," he called to the shadow down the hall.

A blonde-haired, slightly overweight, twenty-something young woman stumbled out into the light and lunged toward her. "How are ya?" the squeaky voice rang out. "I'm Brad's girlfriend, Linda."

Confusion was now mixed with displeasure as Sarah looked the stranger over, discreetly as possible. She darted her eyes around the room for several seconds in an effort to find *Brad*. No other person was there. "Sorry, hi!" Sarah finally responded. "Nice to meet you, Linda. I'm great. Yourself?"

"Work and school – work and school. But Rob's been helping me."

"Oh, he has?" Sarah asked. *How has he been helping?* she wondered. Her face contorted like an abstract Picasso painting to try and figure out what was going on. For some reason, it mattered a tremendous amount to her that there was a woman in Robbie's apartment. She figured he enjoyed female companionship, but she did not want it infringing on her time with him. However, Sarah was relieved to hear that Linda had a boyfriend.

Robbie watched his little prey for any sign of an ensuing cat fight. He was sizing up Sarah. One wrong move and he might find her possessive, or envious – definitely not girlfriend material. But did he even want a girl-friend? He was a strategist. The man was like a snake, toying with its food before devouring it whole.

Linda dismissed herself and continued her clunky jaunt around the apartment. There were dirty dishes and school supplies strewn around the living room. Sarah dissected everything – Linda's moves, the items she picked up, the amount of wine glasses on the countertop, and Robbie's body language. She even made note of the existing curtains on the windows. They did not need replacing.

"I'll be right back," Robbie broke the silence and shuffled down the hallway.

"I'll be right here." Sarah sat down and made small talk with the third wheel. "What's your major, Linda?"

"Nursing. I'm almost finished. Just one more semester."

"That's cool! I bet you're excited about that."

"Yeah, I've learned a lot about medicine."

Who is this girl, and why is she here – roommate, friend, ex? Sarah thought. Linda was not very attractive, but Sarah still felt a little threatened by her young age. Her insecurities would show through if she did not cease feeling envious.

"Hi, crew!" shouted a man, carrying a case of beer. The door had flung open. He slammed it shut with his foot. "Oops, who are you, honey?" Brad was short and stocky, about thirty-two. His light brown, receding hairline aged him, but his strong, welcoming disposition was endearing.

"This is Sarah, babe. Robbie's friend."

"Hi, Brad."

"Hey, I got beer, dude!" Brad nodded to Sarah and yelled for Robbie to hear what he had to say. "Don't drink it!"

Robbie sauntered back from the bathroom. "Don't worry. Your beer sucks." He bent down to kiss Sarah. "Hi baby. Looks like you've met everyone now. By the way, I love the red sweater," he said with a wink.

"Hi," she replied in a breathy whisper. His *baby* comment did not go unnoticed and neither did his compliment.

"Let's eat," he said. Robbie could not remain in that state of surrender. He unlocked his hands from her shoulders and galloped over to the kitchen, where he had prepared a salad prior to her arrival.

Sarah was turned on by the kiss, but turned off by his abrupt departure from their embrace. To her, he seemed lost and searchful. What it was he was looking for – she had no clue. Robbie was clueless, too. She accepted his invitation to sit down at the table, which was very small. Linda and Brad quietly retreated to their bedroom, leaving the pair alone.

"So – where to?"

"Where to?" Sarah repeated with surprise. "A curtain shop, I would presume." She glanced again at the existing window treatments.

"Don't know of any. I think we'll shop for sheets."

"Why didn't you just say you needed sheets to begin with?" Sarah was certain that the invitation to go curtain shopping had been a ploy to get her into his apartment. She surmised that Robbie probably did not need sheets either.

"Because I didn't know I needed sheets. I just figured we'd go shopping together. Doesn't that sound nice? The curtains were insignificant." He reveled in taunting her.

"Ahh, I see," she said. Sarah was witnessing how he operated. His outward charm glossed over the feeling she had of being played. The confusion dizzied her, but a desperate need to be wanted kept her hooked. Once she finished her salad, she was ready to leave. "Let's go!"

"Ok, let's go!" Robbie eagerly replied.

Sarah no longer wanted to stay inside his apartment. It was getting late in the afternoon, and she wanted an extended outing, if possible. The more they lingered, the more Robbie would want to stay home. She would feel used if the day turned out to be just a *booty call.*

While in his car, he divulged the reason for living with the couple and how Brad was his initial roommate. "Brad's not a looker – as you can probably tell. When he finally landed a girlfriend, we were all shocked. I felt sorry for him and didn't want to lay down a bunch of restrictions. So, I told him Linda could live here – as long as she paid her way. Besides, I like having a nurse in the apartment. It makes my PTSD more manageable."

"What PTSD?" she asked. Sarah remembered the mind games and frustrating times she had endured with Richard. Was she headed into another similar relationship with Robbie?

"I was a soldier. It was around two thousand four. We ambushed a small group of guys while on a mission. The enemies, ya know?"

"Oh, wow! Then what?" Sarah was so keyed in that she could have recited his story without skipping a word.

"I was supposed to take them as prisoners. Instead, I shot 'em – all six of them. One was a teenager."

"What! That's horrifying!" she exclaimed.

"It haunts me, Sarah. I knew they would kill us if I didn't act fast."

At that moment, a car with an elderly driver rolled out in front of them.

"Crazy old farts!" Robbie shouted. "They should all be put to death."

"Huh?" Sarah was caught off guard.

"They have no place here anymore. All they do is slow down my life."

Sarah was taken aback by his quick temper – and the harmful senti-ment – especially after just mentioning being haunted by the *ambush* memory. She felt obligated to say something about both the post-traumatic stress disorder and the hatred of old people. The most relevant was addressed first. "What are you saying? They have just as much a right to be here as you do, Robbie." Her righteousness for those who could not defend themselves was heightened. "Why are you angry at seniors, for crying out loud?"

"There is no use for them. They served their time and now they can die!"

There must be a deeper, hidden purpose for his feelings, she wondered. All of what he had shared was too obscure for Sarah to hear. The only thing she could think of was that his anger stemmed from the PTSD or some other event in his past. Sarah loved old people, so his reaction to the driver hurt her. "My Nama's brilliant life of hard work and success was stripped away when she became afflicted with Dementia," Sarah cried. "It's cruel – what some people go through."

Robbie softened a bit as he watched Sarah's face fill with emotion and sadness over the mental loss of her beloved family member. "That's why they all should die younger. To avoid that horrific disease or the multitude of issues that come with aging."

"But that's not how it works. It's not for us to decide. We need to be patient with them. *Their* struggle today may be *our* fight tomorrow."

"I hear ya – but I'm not sure I buy all that."

It was sobering to see Robbie in the daylight. Sarah was not sure if everything he had just told her was meant to be confusing, endearing, or a turnoff. Strange things were festering inside the man and she wanted to know more.

They finally parked the car and walked into the mall.

While they searched bedding stores for the next hour or so, Robbie explained the ambush in detail. He told her of the moments that led up to the event and what was going through his head when he made the decision to shoot. "I saved the lives of some soldiers, but several of my friends got murdered by those assholes." His eyes glazed over and his speech became monotonous. "Their killers deserved to die a painful death. I wish I could have made them suffer more. The memory invades my dreams."

"I'm so sorry, Robbie."

"Let's keep looking for sheets – and add clothes to our list," he said as he snapped back to the present.

They found themselves walking side by side through the Domestics aisle of a department store. There was a change in Robbie's step and a lightness in his words. He was no longer in the darkness of his mind. He felt free. Even though she wanted to know more about his past, Sarah was happy to hear something less heavy.

After he was able to concentrate, new bedding was easy to find. Robbie purchased a set of sheets and wanted to keep shopping. They exhausted the remaining sunny hours of the day by browsing in various clothing stores, including ladies' shops.

Sarah stopped at a fragrance counter when she noticed a woman passing out samples. "I want to get sprayed," she giggled. "I love new perfumes."

"Go for it! I'll buy."

The lady with the tray of bottles greeted Sarah with a friendly smile and held up one of the latest scents for her to sample. Out came a spritz.

"Oh wow! This is awesome."

"Yeah, super sexy," Robbie sniffed and kissed Sarah's arm.

"What is it called?" Sarah asked the woman.

"*The Devil Inside.*"

Sarah's head jolted back with surprise. She turned to Robbie for his reaction.

"Perfect!" He grinned deviously, sprayed it lightly behind Sarah's ear, and nuzzled her neck. "Grr – I'm getting this for you."

"And I accept," Sarah smiled back.

Robbie quickly made the purchase. "My place for dinner?" he asked. He had a one-track mind. His mission was to gain Sarah's trust.

"Sure!" She was gullible to flirtation and persuasion. Sarah fell for the gift, the lunch he had prepared, the open conversations, and the attention.

"How about Chinese food?"

"That works for me."

As they got to Robbie's car, Sarah's mind raced. She realized that going back to his apartment might lead to more than just dinner. The conflict toyed with her. She wanted to stay out of his bed, but with all the shopping during the day, she convinced herself there might be a future with this guy she hardly knew. She deduced that he would not have invested a full day of sharing his past and spending money – just to have a one-night stand. Or would he?

They drove to a nearby Chinese restaurant and ordered take-out. When they arrived back at Robbie's apartment with their food, they found a note left on the counter.

> *Dude,*
> *Can you put my towels in the dryer?*
> *We're not coming back till tomorrow night.*
> *Enjoy yourselves.*
> *Brad ;)*

Sarah focused on the winky face, which indicated to her that the couple was allowing Robbie and Sarah the privacy to do whatever they wanted in the apartment.

"Cool!" exclaimed Robbie.

I bet it is, Sarah thought and unwrapped a box of beef and broccoli from the knotted plastic bag.

Robbie popped open a bottle of Pinot Noir and toasted, "Here's to a perfect day and perfect food! Mission accomplished." He clanked his glass with hers and dove into the stir fry.

Soy sauce dripped from the corner of Sarah's full, pink-toned lips, turning Robbie on. Instead of licking it off, he decided to wipe it away with his napkin. It was a sweet gesture on his part, but she longed for something more sensual. He could tell Sarah was getting close. If he gave her too much, she would only want more. Being intimate meant commitment to Sarah, and he knew well, the ways of a woman's mind. He was not ready to be with one female exclusively, yet the temptation to touch her was overwhelming. He resisted – for the moment.

The meals were devoured and the wine glasses, emptied. They got up and went into the tiny kitchen to throw away the garbage and get refills of Pinot Noir. With very little room to move around, they found themselves facing each other.

"Are you an angel?" Robbie whispered and gazed over her body. "I'm not sure which angels wear red."

Sarah giggled at his sarcasm and responded, "I just might be." Her devilish grin drew him in and he kissed her, tenderly – then forcefully. "You taste like wine," she said when they finished making out.

Robbie pulled away. "Let's watch a movie – in bed."

"Ok?" Sarah's emotions were jolted, and she clumsily followed his lead. It was obvious that if they had already known the pique of passion at the sink, there was only more of the same to come once they got horizontal. Uneasiness and confusion encroached on her heightened libido again. Come or go. Yes or no. Stay or leave. Up or down. It was nearly impossible for her to decide what to do. *What have I got to lose? I'm an angel, right?*

"Wanna smoke some pot?" Robbie said, breaking her train of thought. "It's medicinal, if that makes a difference."

Sarah fell for his manipulation. The temptation beckoned her. "Um – one little puff."

Robbie walked over to his dresser. He opened the top drawer and pulled out his nightclothes, along with a small wooden container that was stashed beneath his underwear. Sarah watched as he bent down and pulled off his blue jeans. Keeping his back turned, he changed into a shirt and boxers. Robbie's exhibitionistic nature made her giggle under her breath. She fidgeted with her fingernails.

"I'm rolling a small one for myself. If you want some, great, but you don't have to smoke it. I really wish you would join me, though."

Sarah could not see Robbie's shifty grin as he faced the dresser. His sweet request to join him worked like a charm. She could not resist. After all, she only wanted a 'little puff.'

He pulled a rolling paper out of its sleeve and then opened a small bag with buds and dark, greenish-brown, crinkled leaves. As soon as he unzipped the plastic, Sarah smelled the aroma of freshly dried pot. Robbie sprinkled the substance onto the paper and painstakingly rolled the joint between his thumbs and forefingers. Her heart pounded as he turned to face her. She followed every move of his tongue as he licked the white paper's edge, giving it a gentle sniff when the sealing was complete. "Stay with me tonight," he said.

Adrenaline shot through Sarah's veins. She could not speak or think rationally. The day's events and the barrage of his requests made her head spin.

His eyes stared deeply into hers as he lit the joint without looking down at it. He stayed focused on Sarah. His glare was hypnotic. Robbie drew in a long, heavy breath of the cannabis, tilting his head upward. Not once did he take his eyes off the woman standing in his bedroom. After he inhaled, Robbie held the smoke in his lungs. He then offered the lit marijuana cigarette to Sarah and slowly exhaled. She stared back at him while removing it from his large, strong hand. As she brought it to her lips, she sucked in a moderate amount. The herb's gripping effect caused her to cough several times. The *high* was felt immediately.

Sarah dropped into a daydream and distanced herself from the room. For a moment, she escaped to another place in time that allowed her to forget the current world. With her eyes closed, she swayed back and forth for several minutes, then wobbled to the side of Robbie's bed. She opened her eyes after she noticed a pleasant, new smell. "When did you put your sheets on the bed?" Sarah asked, looking down at the mattress.

"While you were puffing several times on the reefer," he laughed.

"Several times?"

"Yes, several times. You don't remember checking out for a few minutes?"

"No! How strange."

Robbie turned on the television and found a random R-rated movie out of his repertoire. Sarah paid no attention to the title. And she could barely hear the sound. She was just happy to be in his presence. He slowly walked toward her after shutting off the light on the nightstand. Four pillows had been piled up against the wall behind the bed. As he bent down to kiss Sarah on the mouth, he scooped up her slender body and propped her on the mound that he had crafted.

Minutes blurred into hours. By the middle of the night, Sarah found herself on her back with Robbie on top of her and her crimson clothing on the floor.

Chapter 12

SALTED WOUNDS

A beam of light from the bedroom window hit Sarah in the face, like a sucker punch. She awakened with a jolt, forgetting where she was. Robbie was on his chest, sound asleep. He was naked, with only his legs covered by the sheet.

Oh, God, what have I done? she thought as she slithered out of bed, trying to avoid the awkward exchange of *good mornings.* Sarah wanted to run out of the apartment as fast as she could – and not look back – until she could justify her actions.

Quietly slipping on her clothes and shoes, she watched for any stirring by Robbie. There was no time to stop and think about the sex, what he did to her, and what she had reciprocated. Even if Sarah stayed, she would not be able to go back to sleep. Her adrenaline had kicked up a notch and now coursed through her veins. She tip-toed out of his lair.

Knowing that her actions were rude, she decided to leave him a note. A pen and pad of paper were lying next to a small colorful box on top of Linda's school books by the kitchen countertop. She ripped out a blank sheet and scribbled a quick message.

Robbie,
I had to leave to feed my dog, Em.
I'm worried that she peed all over my apartment.
Call me later.
~Sarah

Why am I running away? she wondered and headed for the door. Her irresponsible actions would only make Robbie not want to commit to a woman even more. Although Sarah longed for the entanglement, she was embarrassed by what had transpired. She second-guessed leaving the note and glanced back to look at it.

That is when she noticed the small box, again. It compelled her to peek inside. If it was a gift for Robbie, she wanted to know. There was a drawing on the lid that resembled a 1970s hippie flower. She felt like a criminal as she pulled off the top. Thin, decorative tissue paper covered the contents. She carefully and quietly unfolded it. An aroma of grass and chocolate gently wafted by Sarah's nostrils. Immediately, she was turned on by the smell. She closed her eyes for only a moment, breathed slowly, and then looked into the box. To her amazement, there appeared to be three chocolate cookies. *Why would cookies be in a box?* Sarah wondered and drew in another sniff. *Are these edibles? Who do they belong to?*

Sarah was not too enthused about doing drugs with a guy she was dating, even if it was just weed. Those days of experimenting for fun were behind her. There was no reason to alter her reality – except maybe with alcohol. She was not afraid of smoking occasionally for fun, but she did not want to make a habit of it. And eating the drug as food was not on her bucket list. The sweets were wrapped in the manner she had found them and Sarah bolted from the apartment.

Her recollection of the last several hours grew more vivid during the drive home. Flashes of the night lit up her thoughts, like bioluminescent ocean waves. Robbie had explored her entire body. The couple's combined scents still lingered on Sarah. Part of her wanted it off. She felt free to do whatever she wanted, yet the binding of her moral compass tugged at her conscience.

Despite the internal struggle, Sarah tried to convince herself that what she did with Robbie was ok. She guessed that any passionate, sex-driven woman would die for the opportunity to be with a handsome, successful man like Robbie – better yet, *two* handsome, successful men. She had not forgotten about Stuart.

After arriving at her apartment, Sarah immediately noticed that Em did not greet her at the door. She threw her purse and keys down on the floor and walked briskly through each room. "Em! Emmy! Where are you, my love?"

Sarah searched the kitchen and dining room – to no avail. She picked up the pace, running around the whole apartment to find her friend. Finally, she discovered her in the corner of the bathroom in distress. Sarah grabbed her medicine. The liquid suppressant and steroid pill were strong, temporary remedies for the dog's disorder. At the same time, they caused serious side-effects. Em's stomach had become distended, and her heart was now enlarged. Sarah had no choice, but to give her the meds.

Em continued coughing. The serum was not working; the dog gasped for air. Sarah panicked. She had never seen Em this bad before. The situation escalated. She scooped her up and ran to her car. The veterinary hospital was only three miles away. She hoped they could help. As she drove out of the parking lot, a terrified Sarah could not remember the way.

The tiny dog was only getting a fraction of her normal air intake through her windpipe. She started to have a fit. Em's head whipped back and forth in an attempt to get oxygen. Sarah kept her eyes on her baby, barely looking at the road. Through a deluge of tears and bout of anxiety, she ran red lights and missed turns. Maybe a quick address search on her phone would help her navigate. She fumbled with her device.

"Someone, help me!" she yelled – and immediately thought of Stuart. He would assist her – if he answered her call. She knew the number by heart and dialed her trusted new friend.

Em's tongue had turned blue and hung out of her mouth. The sight put Sarah in a frenzy. She started to cry while nervously waiting for Stuart to pick up. It seemed like an eternity of rings.

Finally, he answered, "Hello?"

"Oh, Stuart! My dog is suffocating! Where is the vet clinic? I can't seem to remember. Everything looks unfamiliar!"

"Sarah! Calm down. Where are you?"

Through blurred eyes, the frenetic woman searched for the names of nearby street signs. "Stillwater, Belhurst," Sarah shouted as her vehicle breezed through an intersection. She was driving aimlessly in the right direction, but would potentially go past her destination if she did not slow down.

Stuart entered the street names into his phone app to determine her location.

"Take a deep breath, Sarah. Nothing will be accomplished if you panic. Is the name of the hospital Cali-Pet-Vet?"

"Yes, that's it!" she cried.

"You're not too far away," Stuart reassured her. He had come to her rescue.

Sarah sighed. She looked down at the old pup. Em's eyes were turning back into their sockets. The creature's plight made Sarah sick to her stomach. She felt helpless. If it took any longer, Em might lose her life.

"Turn left at the light," Stuart's voice blared through the phone, like the trumpet of an angel.

Sarah squinted hard. She was able to see the clinic through her salty tears. Her car's tires squealed as she pulled into the lot and double parked. "Thanks, Stuart. You're a godsend. I gotta go."

"Ok. I'll check on you later," he quickly stated and hung up.

Sarah whisked Em out of the car and ran through the front door of the clinic. The front office team greeted her and noticed Em's dire condition. She hurried through a quick explanation of the dog's symptoms and history before a young associate pulled the furry companion from her arms. Em was rushed to an examining room. She looked around the lobby at other pet owners clutching their four-legged family members. Others waited alone for test results.

"The doctor on call will be out with an assessment as soon as they are able to get Em stabilized," a tech told Sarah. "Please, have a seat."

"Can't I go in?"

"No, we prefer you wait out here. The animal gets too anxious when its owner is present," the person spoke to Sarah with little bedside manner.

The *animal* was family. Their choice of words and decision to leave Sarah out of the assessment, disappointed her. She knew that if this was a hospital for humans, she would be allowed in without discussion. *What are they doing to her? Will I be able to see her beforehand, if she dies?* Sarah wondered.

The clock on the wall seemed stuck on the same time. It reminded her of the big, white, round ones in elementary school. They never worked properly. The second hand repeated its movement back and forth on the number five. Sarah stared at it and drifted.

Someone next to her in the waiting room started crying, and she snapped out of the trance. She felt pity for the poor soul who was just dealt a blow to their emotions. The experience was surreal. Some of the awaiting parents were told that there was nothing anyone could do to save their beloved dog or cat. Sarah hoped that she would not be one of them.

The clock's hand never progressed, but the sound it made was just as disruptive as a screaming child in a quiet library.

Tick.

Tick.

Tick.

Tick.

About twenty minutes later, a gentleman in a white coat burst through the emergency room doors. "Em's family?"

"That's me!"

"Come, please."

The two walked down a short hallway filled with the noise of clang-ing, stainless-steel trays, utensils, whispering voices, shouting voices, bark-ing dogs, and screaming cats. It was frightening to Sarah and all too clinical. She could only imagine what it felt like for poor Em. There was one thing she did not hear – coughing. Fear of being told Em was dead, iced Sarah's veins. Her blood pressure rose, and a panic attack gripped her chest. She stopped to catch her breath.

"Are you ok?" the doctor said.

"Yes – I'll be – fine."

The kind man pointed to his right, suggesting Sarah follow the direc-tion of his finger.

She turned the corner to find a sleeping little Em. "Oh, thank you, Doctor!" Sarah rushed over to the oxygen chamber. Em felt her mother's presence and peeled her eyes open long enough to take in her image. The furry friend then dropped her head back down to rest. Em had been pumped full of sedatives, enough for her to remain calm so that her airways could open up to a less constricted state.

"She's not the strongest little girl. She's hanging in there, but we're just not sure how much time you have left with her."

Sarah felt instantly guilty for not staying home with Em and putting her own desires, first. Her heart sank into her stomach; it ached. Her entire body tightened with stress, bracing for worse news. Em was breathing so slowly. "What can I do?" she asked.

"Make her as comfortable as possible. Her airways are irreparable. I'm sorry." The doctor tried to sound sincere, but there were other pets awaiting his care, and he had to go.

"Irreparable," Sarah said with defeat – under her breath.

"We have made her restful for now. But we're recommending she stay with us overnight until she is good enough to go home. We will give you some stronger sedatives. The prescription is at the front desk." He started for the doorway and looked over his shoulder to give Sarah one last piece of advice. "There is something you *can* do, Miss Gallus."

"What's that?" she asked.

"Pray."

Well, that's new! Sarah thought. *I've never heard a medical professional tell someone to pray. Doctors don't typically mix medicine with religion. It was bold of him to do so – and brave.* "I – I don't believe in that anymore, Doc. There is no God or Jesus. But thank you for the sentiment," Sarah said with a faked smile.

"I'm sorry you feel that way, Miss Gallus. Perhaps you will believe again." The tail end of his white lab coat was all she saw as he turned the corner and vanished.

Sarah was thankful that Em was alive, although the vet's diagnosis was not what she wanted to hear. Going through another panic episode was terrifying. She wanted so much to fix all that was wrong with her baby.

"Prayer," Sarah said doubtfully, out loud. "I have done that too many times in my life. Nothing ever comes from it." In her opinion, there was no loving God. No merciful being would have allowed this to happen to Em. Her trust had died away, along with her faith. Prayers had never saved those she had already lost. Now, it was Em's turn to suffer with no divine intervention. Sarah sat down next to the little dog's oxygen chamber and wept.

Chapter 13

EVEN IN LAUGHTER

After a day of rest, the little pooch returned home with her mommy. Sarah kept the dog's condition at bay, using the heavy medications and sedatives that the vet had prescribed. At least for the moment, the universe stopped wreaking havoc on the two of them.

As for Robbie, he had not texted or called Sarah since she left him naked in his bed. Not hearing from him was perplexing. She figured he would have at least asked her *why* she left. There was no sign of concern at all, and Sarah was not about to call him.

Laden with stress, regret, guilt, worry, and remorse, she fell into a depression. Em's life hung in the balance. Her photo jobs were sporadic. Plus, she feared that Stuart and Robbie would suddenly drop her if they believed she was acting like a whore.

A heat spell blew through Long Beach, making it hotter than usual for the time of year. Stuart was moved by the weather. The cool ocean breeze – mixed with the sun's warmth – soothed his skin – and his soul. He needed to relax and wanted to share the moment of serenity with his two friends. *Drinks, sunshine, good times. Beach this week?* he texted Robbie and Sarah.

Little did Stuart know that his invitation was the remedy Sarah needed to get out of the doldrums.

Buzz. Buzz. The rhythmic sound from several messages alerted her while she finished a load of laundry and a second bottle of wine. Sarah rushed over to her device in hopes that the notes were from one of the guys. When she looked at her screen, she noticed that there were messages from them both. Her eyes overlooked Stuart's comment and invitation and made a beeline to Robbie's reply.

Can't . . . working, read his text.

The dismissive answer struck a chord. *What? When has that ever stopped you from socializing and drinking?* It was not unusual for Stuart or Robbie to get together on a work night – or any night for that matter – and drink. Sarah tried to rationalize what on earth he might be doing that was more important than spending time with his friends. As she further over-analyzed Robbie's reply, it dawned on Sarah that this was not just a dismissal. He was manipulating the situation, again. *He knows I'm on this text, and he said nothing to me?* she questioned.

Deep down, Sarah knew she had no right to be mad. She had left him with only a note on the kitchen countertop. Even though she did not leave with any malicious intent, Sarah was just as guilty at game-playing as Robbie. Eventually, the embarrassment that she felt the morning after their interlude would deserve an explanation.

Stuart followed up with a private text to Sarah. *How 'bout just you and I do a movie together, tomorrow night?*

Yes, I'll be over! And I'll bring some wine, she texted with no hesitation.

Bring Em if you want. 7p. That way you can keep an eye on her. How is she, by the way?

She's calm. Thank you, Stuart. Be there at 7.

Great! See you then.

Sarah was thrilled that Stuart told her to bring her dog. The gesture won him brownie points. Their chemistry was much different than what she felt with Robbie. She wanted badly to tell Stuart about her disappointment in his friend, but held back the urge for now.

The next day, Sarah showed up at Stuart's apartment carrying Em in her arms, a bag of dog supplies, and a bottle of wine. The man welcomed them in and listened intently to the story of the vet clinic visit. He was such a good sport and gave Sarah his full attention, letting her vent.

After getting Em settled into her bed in the corner of the living room, Sarah and Stuart hopped on the sofa and watched a poorly made sci-fi flick over two large ham and pineapple pizzas he had ordered. They cracked open the gifted wine and soon were buzzed. The pair laughed at the bad acting in the movie and the attempt at special effects. The film was undeniably lame, but that made everything more enjoyable between the two friends.

When the show ended, Stuart suggested another one.

"Oh, I'm not sure," Sarah whined, "although, I am a bit inebriated and should probably wait awhile before driving home."

Tipsy is exactly how Stuart wanted her before enacting a plan he had thought up before she arrived. "Come on. Stay," he pleaded. "I wasn't sure if you'd be into this, but since the night is still young and we are getting bored, how about trying something fun with me?"

"I'm up for anything. Can the fun get any better?" Sarah laughed at her own sarcasm.

"Yes, it can! Have you ever tried an edible?"

The coincidence of Stuart's question and having recently found what looked like pot cookies at Robbie's apartment, freaked Sarah out. Her face went blank.

"Are you ok, Sarah?"

"Yes – and no! Yes, I am ok. No, I have not tried an edible. Have *you*?"

"No, not that I can recall."

"What is it, a chocolate-like thingy?"

"It's a cookie made of dough and has little chips," Stuart snickered.

She sneered playfully. Stuart could tell by her perplexed look that she was unsure of taking part in eating a treat laced with pot. Sarah did not know how she would feel after ingesting it. She swore to herself that she was not doing any more drugs after what happened at Robbie's apartment.

Stuart got up from the sofa and walked a quick, straight line to his bedroom down the hall to get the package, which was sitting on his bureau. Snuggling in close to her, he prepared to open the three-inch square box. It had a daisy flower printed on its top.

"That's it?" she questioned with excitement, then recoiled. Sarah realized she reacted too quickly. She did not want Stuart knowing she had seen the exact box at Robbie's place.

His curiosity was sparked. "Yeah, what's wrong?"

"Oh nothing. I was just excited to look at it. It's interesting," she recovered.

"Hmm – ok," Stuart smirked with doubt.

Sarah held out her palm to hold the familiar box and analyzed the flower on the lid. Like a scientist examining a specimen in a Petri dish, she carefully opened the top and unfolded the tissue paper inside. Everything was the same. Sarah picked up the corner of the dessert and gently shifted the box back and forth to see all sides of its interior. There was only one cookie.

"Robbie gave it to me," said Stuart.

"Why am I not surprised?"

Stuart just laughed off her sarcasm. He was too interested in starting the party and getting Sarah high. "I think it will be a hoot!" he said.

Then, Sarah realized the two men must have seen each other in the last few days to make the delivery and that Robbie kept the other cookies for himself. *Did they talk about me? Did Robbie mention our night together?*

Did Stuart tell Robbie that he wanted the cookie to share with me? She was faced with more anxiety and another temptation.

Sarah and Stuart knew only rumored information about edible pot desserts. They could have multiple levels of potency as well as effects on different body types and metabolisms. As they examined it closely, the pair had mixed feelings about ingesting it. It must have come from the same place Robbie got all his medicinal marijuana for his PTSD. Stuart trusted his friend not to give him something harmful, so he was willing to try it. Sarah, on the other hand, questioned everything. But her strength was weakening. She was losing her inhibitions.

"Let's go for it! You into it, girl?" Stuart asked.

Sarah was convinced that Stuart's sweetness meant that everything would be ok. She trusted him and knew that if anything went wrong, he would be there to help her. The decision now seemed less serious. "Ok. I'll do a tiny little smidge."

Stuart took the box back from Sarah's hands and set it on the table. "Let's put on a really funny movie before we bite into this thing. I have no idea how long it will take to kick in, but I don't want to waste its effect. You ready?"

"Sure."

Stuart popped in a comedy and poured two glasses of water. At the very least, they would get thirsty. He was excited as he snapped off a corner of the cookie and handed the first piece to Sarah.

"That's too big!" she laughed while her eyes widened to the size of golf balls. She broke the fragment in half and gave the rest back to Stuart.

"Ha ha! Do you think these little chunks are going to make a dent on us?"

"We'll find out soon enough."

They both nibbled their pieces slowly. Their eyes darted back and forth from the edibles to each other's faces. They sat perfectly still and waited for something obscure to happen. Five minutes – ten minutes – fifteen minutes passed, and they felt the same – save for a bit of tension in their muscles from the anticipation of feeling high.

A full twenty-five minutes after they swallowed their first crumb of the cookie, Sarah's thighs began to tingle. "Holy moly!"

"Is that a good 'holy moly?'" he asked. "By the way, I think I ate too much."

Sarah burst out laughing, "I can't move a single, solitary muscle, Stuart!"

"What do you mean you can't move? Apparently, your mouth didn't get the message."

"Ha ha! Very funny. I seriously can't move! I'm tingling all over. My muscles are hard as a rock."

"I wish mine were," Stuart joked.

"I take that personally."

They both chuckled uncontrollably and tears poured down their faces.

"Look. Do you believe me now?" she said, trying desperately to lift her arm.

Stuart watched it closely, despite his own dysfunctions. He was able to turn his head, but had limited strength in his hands. With what little power he could muster, he extended her arm straight out in front of her like a tree limb. It remained there, stiff as a board.

There was no measure of time for the pair. What seemed like more than two hours – was only about thirty minutes. Sarah never budged from where she sat. She felt glued to the couch. Stuart seemed to have some flexibility, but not as much as he had hoped. The two laughed and laughed.

"I'm thirsty."

"Your water is right there." Stuart gestured in slow motion to the glass on the table.

"There's no way I am going to be able to drink that. I can't reach it!"

"Just bend forward!" Stuart laughed.

"I can't!"

Stuart slowly reached for the tall glass and gripped it loosely; his hand was shaking. The water vibrated as he slowly shifted it to a point within Sarah's reach.

"Now what the hell do you expect me to do?" Sarah laughed. Her right arm was still suspended several inches off her lap and straight out where Stuart had left it.

"Open your mouth; I'll serve you."

The glass came closer to Sarah's face. She parted her sticky, dry lips and stuck out her tongue in hopes of being quenched with a light trickle of the fluid. Stuart tipped the full glass in her direction. When he realized what he was doing and saw Sarah's face, he cracked up. His explosive joy jiggled his entire body, and water went everywhere. It splashed all over Sarah's parted, parched lips and down the front of her white t-shirt.

"I think I swallowed – some," she sighed.

"Yeah, you got some, alright." Stuart gawked at her chest. He pushed her raised arm down so she could try and cover her exposed wet breasts.

The antics and humorous moments continued for a while. The short movie stopped on its own. They had not even watched it. Nothing mattered outside of themselves. They were delighting too much in the euphoric moment they were sharing with one another. The pair giggled, cracked numerous jokes, and then pretended they were barnyard animals.

"Mooove something will you?" Stuart chuckled.

"Oink – you going to help me?" Sarah snorted like a pig.

"Ha! I see what you did there. Oink you going to like what animal comes out of me next?"

Sarah had a hard time catching her breath and could not see through her watery eyes. The humorous moments kept coming, one after another.

"Cocka-do-you good!" said Stuart.

That was it for Sarah. She burst out with a bark of laughter from her gut and fell forward, dropping onto the floor. "I think I just wet my pants!"

Stuart had taken in a big gulp of water and sprayed it into the air. He got up from the couch and tried helping Sarah to her feet. His weakened arms gave way, and he flopped down, knocking Sarah completely flat. They continued to laugh.

"Um – I can't tell if I'm wet with water or something else," Sarah joked.

"I'll give you some of my clothes to change into – on one condition," Stuart spoke. "You're sleeping over."

Chapter 14

WHITE HORSE

Stuart gathered enough energy to get up from the floor. He extended his hand to help Sarah stand, as well. After steadying himself, he walked into his bedroom where he retrieved a pair of his shorts and a t-shirt to give to her. He grabbed a washcloth and large towel from the hall cabinet and brought it to his beautiful house guest. "Here. You can freshen up with these."

"Thank you, Stuart. I'll clean up."

"You can stick your clothes in my washing machine if you'd like. It's right next to the bathroom."

She shuffled to the commode and took off her soiled clothes, which she stuffed into a bag. There was no need to leave laundry at his apartment. However, his offer was appreciated. A new toothbrush and tube of toothpaste had been laid out on the countertop for her to use. She was delighted by the sweet gesture. When she was clean and dry, she slipped into Stuart's pajamas. They were soft, comfortable, and smelled like lavender and rainwater – a scent she never would have anticipated finding on *his* clothes. She giggled at the revelation.

"Are you laughing at my fabric softener?" Stuart yelled from the other room. He was aware that he had been liberal with the laundry conditioner and knew someone would tease him about it, eventually.

"Ha! Maybe? And I'm also laughing at the fact that I wet my pants, like a two-year-old."

"You can wet your pants, again. I have more shorts," he responded. "And what can I say? I like lavender." Stuart snickered as he walked down the hall.

When Sarah emerged from the bathroom, she noticed he was shutting off lights in the kitchen. She limped her slightly bruised body toward the couch, where she had planned to sleep.

"What are you doing out here?" Stuart inquired.

"I was going to set up camp."

They both knew what could transpire if she made a detour to his bedroom. She was not about to head that way uninvited.

"You're sleeping with me!"

Well, well. I was waiting for that, Sarah thought. "Hey, I'm not numb anymore! But I do need to stretch out. I feel a little banged up from the fall on your floor."

"Do you need me to carry you? I already put Em and her blanket at the foot of my bed. You probably didn't even notice."

"Oh! I totally forgot she was here," Sarah embarrassingly admitted. "She's been so quiet. Thank you. And no, I think I can make it on my own."

"Right side, please."

Stuart observed Sarah walk to the opposite side of his bed and admired the way she wore his boxer shorts. She had to roll down the waistband to keep them from falling off her tiny hips. As he tried not to stare, he moved his eyes up to the blonde hair flowing around her chest. He clumsily pulled at the sheets on his side of the bed and watched her raise her legs to climb in. "I think my muscles are hard now."

"See? Sometimes you get what you wish for," said Sarah.

They both laughed. Stuart turned out the lights and plucked the stereo remote off the nightstand. He slithered into bed, snuggling into Sarah's side. A series of buttons on the controller were pressed and instrumental music began to play.

"I feel like I'm in a bachelor pad. Bow-chicka-bow-bow."

"This is how I get the girls."

"Well, if they make it this far, I guess it will be your charm that lures them all the way in. It definitely won't be this porn music."

"Ahh – you're too funny. I'm so glad you hung out with me tonight."

They both smiled and realized they needed rest. The room was warm, and the glow of the surrounding condo lights illuminated parts of the bed. They were soothed.

The music prevented Sarah from falling asleep too deeply. She drifted in and out of consciousness. "Stuart –" Sarah whispered, "I'm having a vision."

Her intrigued friend was perfectly still as he listened to what she might say next. The laughter had ceased, and the mood turned serious. There was vivid imagery playing out in her mind, and all were paying attention.

"What do you see?"

Sarah was desperately hoping the music would be soporific. But the vision she was having was quite lucid, and she could not make it go away. "I see a horse – a white horse. It's standing in a field of tall grass and bright yellow wildflowers. It's grazing – and the flowers are swaying in the breeze."

"Go on," Stuart whispered. He closed *his* eyes, too, and tried to envision the hungry equine and the overgrown field.

The music playing in the bedroom suddenly changed. It was dark yet enlightening to a degree. It had a consistent undertone that gave it forward momentum.

Sarah kept her eyes shut and searched the vision for anything mean-ingful. For the moment, she could only see the horse. She let her mind go. "Now, I see a church. I feel pensive," she said.

Stuart imagined – in his own vision – a version of the church, com-plete with steeple.

"I am walking toward the church, very slowly," she continued – then hesitated. "Wait, there's a child. She's wearing a faded floral dress at the doorway of the sanctuary."

Stuart's eyes were now wide open in the mostly darkened room. Only the light from the window lit up parts of Sarah's face. She reminded him of a teenager telling a ghost story with a flashlight under her chin. Her eyes remained closed, but she was very coherent.

"I think I am that child. I'm all the way inside the church now. I'm walking down the aisle to the podium, where a pastor would stand. But there's no one there. It's just me."

Stuart's eyes suddenly shut on their own, as if something caused them to close against his will. There was a force in the room that wanted him to see the same vision as his bedmate. He attempted to open his eyes, but could not. Unfamiliar emotions entered. His breathing grew heavy.

Tears welled up in Sarah's eyes. An intense feeling of sadness and insecurity came over her – and Stuart. The mood of the music escalated. Its rich sound penetrated the room, and the two embraced.

"Keep going," Stuart demanded softly. His body trembled while he channeled Sarah's emotions through his entire being.

"I'm walking out of the church, through a wooden side door. Now, I'm back in the field." Her eyes darted about as she explored the wildflowers and tall grass for more surprise clues. And then – she saw it again. "It's the white horse! I'm by myself with the horse, now, Stuart. But I feel so alone yet content." Sarah peeled open one eyelid to find her head on Stuart's chest. She sobbed. The tears gushed down her cheeks and onto his bare skin.

"Well, that was totally awesome – and wild, Sarah!" The experience frightened him, somewhat. But he quickly manned up and dismissed any fear that was creeping into his head. He was ready to be strong for himself and for his friend. "What do you think is the significance of the white horse? All of your vision, for that matter?"

Sarah wiped her swollen eyes with the top of the bed sheet. She quietly apologized for getting it wet. Before she answered him, she tried to return to the scene. But it was gone. Just like a dream, it vanished into the caverns of her memory. "Love. I feel that the white horse was purity – and love."

"Wow! That was weird. I felt you, Sarah. All of my energy has been drained," Stuart began to cry, as well. "Why did it feel so dark and scary? There was nothing bad in your vision – a church, a little girl, a white horse and some wildflowers."

She looked up at Stuart's face, which was barely visible. The bottom of his chin was all she could see. Sarah could tell that he was genuinely connected, plugged in to her mind and her body. "Not sure. Good question, though. The journey back to the white horse did feel disturbing," she agreed, "but it didn't end that way."

The two were quiet for several minutes and stared at the darkened ceiling. Their minds raced to make sense of what had just happened. Was it a premonition? Was it symbolic in some way?

"That has never happened – to me before," Stuart's voice slowed. He was confused. The experience had taken a toll on him.

"What do you mean?"

"I'll try to describe it. All I can say is that my heart was pounding. I felt as if we were one, intertwined spiritually. Like *your* soul was feeding off of *my* soul."

Both of their bodies trembled.

"I'm sorry Stuart. I didn't mean to do that to you. It doesn't sound like it was a good thing."

"No! It was awesome! Just a little weird, that's all. We don't have to talk about it anymore, if you prefer."

"Thank you, Stuart. I'm tired."

If all the things Sarah had envisioned were trying to tell them both something, he wanted to know. But he respected tabling the subject until she was ready to bring it up again.

The stereo timer started to dwindle down and the dramatic music gradually faded out. There was a small *click* sound, and the room fell silent. Stuart kissed the top of Sarah's head, and they exchanged *good nights*. The pair pulled the covers up under their faces and clung tighter to each other. Stuart hummed a comforting, random tune with each breath, and Sarah slowly drifted off to sleep. He followed shortly thereafter.

As they slept, the room became devoid of any light, and a chill blew through the walls. Grinning and hovering high above the bed – was a satisfied spirit.

Chapter 15

CASTLE DOME LANDING

The darkness and the spirit had dissipated – but both were bound to return.

Although she was somewhat surprised that nothing had happened in Stuart's bed, Sarah was oddly pleased when morning arrived. In her opinion, he was a very sex-driven man and quite fit. To spend several hours with a woman lying in a horizontal position – without trying to sneak in a little playtime – shocked her. She would not have turned him away if he had tried anything. His restraint was incredibly endearing. She had no desire to leave *his* bed; however, there were other things she had to do. Sarah kissed Stuart *goodbye*, scooped Em up in her arms, and promised to return his boxers, clean. Still favoring her sore body, she hobbled out of his apartment to her car.

"Beach, later? I have the day off!" Stuart yelled.

"Maybe!" Sarah shouted back. She would give him a definite answer later, after she had time to digest everything that had happened at his apartment. She thought about the vision. The white horse, the little girl, and the church swirled around her head, like a dance of dares. She felt challenged to piece the symbols together for a greater picture. *Am I the little girl? Did the church represent truth? Was the horse a messenger of that truth?* Sarah blamed the confusing vision on the pot cookie and regretted eating it. There was no denying that snuggling and laughing uncontrollably with Stuart was enjoyable. If she would have known about the effects of the sweet treat – or that it would leave her feeling uneasy – she never would have ingested it. *I think my vision is a premonition.* Sarah thought. *What is coming?* She filed the worry away for the moment.

After Sarah left the apartment, Stuart texted his absent friend about driving to the ocean. *Dude, take off work and join us. Beach! It's almost the weekend.*

Robbie received the update. He noticed the word *us* in Stuart's text and assumed part of it – referred to Sarah. If he did not go, Stuart would gain momentum in the pursuit of her. Even though he had already taken her to bed, the idea of steering Sarah away from his friend, boosted his ego. *Alright, but I have to take care of a few things at work, first. I'll leave early and pick you guys up around 1,* Robbie texted.

The weather was supposed to be stellar – a cool yet pleasant seventy degrees. It was an unusual temperature for that time of year. Perfect for hitting the beach. After numerous awkward moments over the last few days, they all needed some time to soak up the sun.

The minute Sarah returned home from Stuart's apartment, her phone rang from the bottom of her purse. She carefully set the dog down with the rest of her things and reached into the abyss to locate the device. "Hello!" she spoke loudly, before the phone reached her face.

"Hey, Sarah!" said a familiar sounding woman. "It's me, Amy! Stuart's friend from Valentine's Day."

Sarah was caught off guard. "Hi Amy! What's up?"

The bubbly woman was a party planner. She loved a good gathering, whether for Christmas, a birthday, or for no reason at all. However, there was one event that took precedence over the rest. "It's almost river time! Are you joining us at Castle Dome this summer?"

Basically, the event consisted of about a dozen friends getting together for a drinking-fest. Amy spearheaded the entire thing, from getting the vacation rental to preparing enough food for everyone. According to her, more guests meant more alcohol and more fun.

"Castle D . . . ?"

"Castle Dome Landing," Amy interrupted. "It's a little ghost town along the Colorado River inside Roka Valley. A bunch of us party at a camp in that area. Robbie and Stuart always come. It's a blast! We'll take the big raft and Mark's jet skis. There's lots of booze. You'll love it! Are you in?"

Sarah did not know what to say, but the woman needed a head count. She tried to make sense of the overload of information Amy relayed in her quickly-spoken sentences. It was Sarah's first time ever hearing of the outing. *The river? The desert? With strangers?* Sarah pondered Amy's request.

Since the guys did not do the inviting – or even mention it – Sarah was hesitant to answer. It might get awkward for her to be at Castle Dome if neither Robbie nor Stuart wanted her there. Sarah threw out a response just to move the conversation along, "Sure, Amy. I – guess I could go."

"Perfect! I'll fill you in on all the details, later – like what you need to bring, camping gear, etcetera. The boys will probably bring liquor. They always do."

"Ok, I appreciate that," Sarah giggled. She added her farewell and then hung up.

The Colorado River bordered California and Arizona and wound around five other states, like an unrecognizable signature. Sarah had never been there before. She was willing to give it a go. Maybe she could get some amazing pictures of the scenery and sell them to clients.

After organizing her trade tools with what she thought she might need for the trip, Sarah plopped down on the sofa with her laptop and started searching the web for information on Castle Dome Landing. She found a bunch of websites dedicated to the little mining town. It had quite an interesting history – abandoned, re-opened, and back-and-forth prosperity. Anything about the desert and the Old West inspired her. She thought about the chance to see saloons, old-timey jails, or horse corrals from a bygone era. The sites stated that Castle Dome Landing was, in fact, a ghost town. Amy was right.

Sarah thought it was cool that ghost towns even existed. She grew more excited when several images of the area popped up on her screen. The place looked haunted and scared her a little. It was comforting to know that she would be with the guys. *If Robbie talks to me again, maybe this can be a nice getaway for us,* she pondered. She imagined the campsite in the middle of nowhere, coyotes howling in the distance, the warm desert air – and Stuart, joining them in bed. Sarah laughed to herself.

Buzz. Buzz. A group text came through on her phone. It was from her two male friends. *Let's go. The sun is going to warm things up today, girl. We want you!* read the first message.

"What? We? *We* want you?" At first, Sarah was so excited that she did not care which man sent the text. She ran to her room to prepare a beach bag. Upon closer observation – once she calmed down – she noticed that the text was from Stuart.

Robbie followed up with even more surprising words. *Yeah, get over here and bring that cute little ass with you.* There was no other explanation for his pleasant and playful demeanor, other than having the attention span of a gnat, or he just did not care.

So, you left work? Ok. It sounds like you've forgiven me for leaving your apartment? Sarah thought to herself. She felt like she was in an alternate reality. There was no longer the need to give him an excuse for escaping his bed. She could just melt right into the present. *I'm on my way,* she texted back.

Both Robbie and Stuart enjoyed Sarah's company. She was a ball they could bounce between each other. Until they knew that one prevailed in winning her heart, they would keep playing the game. Little did either of them realize – it was a game each of them had already won.

"Hurry! I gotta jump in the ocean," Stuart texted.

Sarah followed up with her message, *What time?*

Stuart's place in twenty minutes. I'll drive.

Chapter 16

DEMONS ON THE BEACH

Sarah arrived at Stuart's apartment late. Robbie was already there. The two men were chatting in the kitchen when she walked through the open door without knocking. She did not know which one to look at first, so she awkwardly stared inside her purse and fumbled with her keys.

"Well, look who's here," Stuart said.

"Hey, guys. How's it going?"

The fragrant smell of pineapple and coconut drifted past Robbie's nose. "Sweet! Did you pre-apply suntan lotion all over that gorgeous body of yours?"

"I did, but I'm sure I'll need more, once I get to the beach."

Another layer of ice was broken, and their flirtatious pursuit was back on. Sarah bashfully glanced at the island countertop, where Stuart had prepared shots of tequila.

"Cheers!" he said.

"Cheers!"

"Cheers!" Robbie winked at Sarah, and they all downed their drinks.

No one brought up their nights together. Stuart tried to avoid showing much interest in whether or not Sarah and Robbie were getting it on.

His biggest concern – at that moment – was that everyone was getting buzzed.

I'm just going to be myself and flirt with both men, Sarah thought. *There's no use wasting this precious opportunity.*

"Ready?" Stuart said gleefully.

"Like you wouldn't believe," Sarah grinned.

They set down their shot glasses and bolted out the door. They wanted to hurry out of the apartment with hopes of getting a good parking spot close to the sand.

"Cute little number you're wearing, Sarah."

"Thank you, Robbie." Sarah was floating on cloud nine.

They walked down the sidewalk outside of Stuart's apartment and headed for Robbie's jeep. She admired her thin, white, beach cover-up and climbed into the front passenger seat. Stuart jumped over the roll bar and sat in the back. He held tight to a metal container filled with alcohol.

"What's that?" Sarah said as the sun's rays, reflecting off the vessel, hit her in the eyes.

"Oh, ya know, just one of my many gifts for you."

"Pass whatever it is around," Robbie yelled over the starting of the engine.

After taking a swig of the homemade, fruity, vodka concoction, Stuart handed it to Sarah, who then shared it with Robbie. Each took their turn guzzling the potent contents until the vessel was dry and tossed on the vehicle's floor. Stuart also brought a small cooler with mini wine bottles for them to share later.

The weather was beautiful. There were many people out enjoying the day. In spite of the crowds, the three friends were able to find a convenient place to park. After unloading their stuff, they headed for the sand. They wove around sunbathers, found a clearing, and rolled out their towels.

Sarah plunked down in the middle of the two men. She took off the white cotton sundress that had been covering a baby pink bikini. As she knelt to adjust her towel, both men watched lustfully. She carefully organized her place between them. Using a few nearby rocks, she anchored the material at all four corners. The sun was strong, but a light breeze cooled their skin. It blew strands of Sarah's hair across her glossy lips.

"Can I get those for you?" Robbie asked.

Sarah only smiled in return and tugged the wisps away while she reached into her bag for sunscreen.

"Here. Let me cover you before you burn," Robbie boldly offered, snatching the bottle from her hands.

Sarah kept quiet. She positioned herself on the towel and stretched out onto her belly. Stuart – who was mildly distracted by several brunettes passing by – pretended to ignore Robbie's hands all over Sarah.

Robbie applied the warm cream to her shoulders and then swept down her spine to the small of her back. His touch was gentle, yet she felt the power of his whole body, as he pressed firmly with every motion. "You look awesome, today," he remarked.

Sarah closed her eyes and reminisced of their night together. She pictured him leaning over her fragile body, scanning her entire form. "I do?" she said innocently. "Thank you, Robbie."

Stuart could smell Sarah's tropical sunscreen and it reminded him of Hawaii, where he and Richard had gone one summer. She turned to see him wiping a tear from his eye. He was unaware of her observance. Richard had left him alone with their friendship, and he was worried that Sarah would do the same. He was revealing his softer side.

"Are you ok, Stuey?"

"Yeah, just thinking of my buddy. I should have been there."

"He loved you a lot. I'm sure he knew you were there in spirit."

"Some days are harder than others. I miss my friend. I try to keep my mind off of him, by staying active. Thanks for being a shoulder. I told you I'd need it someday."

"Any time. I miss him, too."

Stuart picked up his can of suntan oil and sprayed his muscles. He took pride in the results of his daily exercise regimen and flexed for Sarah's benefit.

"Looking good, dude!" she said, admiring her friend's hard work.

His feelings for Sarah were growing, but if she and Robbie were sleeping together, the entire triangle would be weird. Even though he was not looking for a commitment, Stuart felt jealous at the thought of sharing the woman with his best friend. He propped himself up on both elbows and stared at the ocean. It was majestic with its vast, endless beauty. He appreciated *it* – and the surfers trying to catch its powerful waves.

It was Robbie's turn to spray his arms and legs with sunblock. He snatched the can from Stuart's towel and applied it like bug repellant, swaying his arm in broad, rounded motions. Only a few droplets landed on his skin. The majority rained down on Sarah's legs.

"Hey! I thought you already lubed me up!" Sarah's sarcasm embarrassed Robbie. Instead of ogling his brawny physique as he expected, she buried her eyes in a fashion magazine and continued to giggle under her breath.

Feeling spiteful, Robbie bent down to pick up a football he had brought with him and invited Stuart to a game of toss. "Let's go Stu!" he shouted.

"You got it, Rob! Sarah, grab a wine for yourself, and get one ready for me, too!"

"Sure!"

Stuart enjoyed spending quality moments with his friend. They made him feel manly. The two guys played well, throwing spiral passes to each other and never dropping the ball.

Sarah flipped over, downed some wine, and tanned the other side of her body. She peered above the upper rim of her sunglasses to watch the men toss the ball. It was fun to see them together. They were busy, so it was the perfect opportunity to work on her side project. She reached into her big beach bag for a notebook and pen and began to write. Shortly after she had written a few pages, Sarah felt a spray of sand on her legs, accompanied by a sinister laugh.

"What the hell, Robbie?"

He had thrown the football at his towel, nearly hitting her. "Oops!"

"That's all you have to say?"

Sand was everywhere. Frustrated, she attempted to brush off the grains that had gotten stuck on her sticky legs and within the folds of her notebook. Robbie did not know how to handle an upset Sarah. He decided to ignore her expectation of an apology and remained standing while looking elsewhere.

"What are you writing?" Stuart interjected.

"A memoir – about a female photographer who travels the world. I've been on many adventures – Fiji, Venice, Guadalupe."

Robbie interrupted, "You haven't taken my picture yet. I could be your greatest adventure." He snatched Sarah's phone and opened the camera app.

"Hey, gimme that! You're all sandy!" Sarah shouted.

"How convenient. It's not locked," Robbie laughed and knelt down to snap a selfie of the threesome. "Say cheese!"

Sarah was annoyed. To avoid a picture she would regret seeing later, she tossed her hair to one side, flung her arms around their shoulders, and forced a smile. Robbie took the shot and threw her phone back in the bag.

He ran off toward the shoreline, leaving his friends baffled by his aloof behavior.

"I wonder where he's off to, now?" Stuart mused.

Sarah picked up her phone to show him some of her work. She stopped to admire the photo Robbie had just taken.

"Aww – cute," Stuart commented.

"We look good together."

Although her photographs were always taken with professional camera equipment, Sarah had uploaded a few favorites to her phone – just in case she needed to show samples to prospective clients. She continued to swipe through her pictures.

"These are awesome! I think it's a great idea that you want to write about your experiences. You should get it done."

Sarah loved hearing words of encouragement. She smiled with appreciation and peered off at the ocean.

Stuart surmised that she was in deep thought about something – most likely Robbie. "I hope you don't let him get to you. I don't think he can handle being snubbed or scolded. He goes off in some weird place in his head."

"I'll try and remember that." Sarah handed him a small bottle of opened wine. She put the notebook and pen in her bag, leaned back on her towel, and closed her eyes.

The wine was refreshing to Stuart's over-heated body. He remained by her side and sipped his beverage. Together, they listened to the distant sound of children's laughter, combined with the roar of the sea.

Thirty minutes later, Robbie returned and needed to dry off. He had a good swim. As he plucked his towel off the ground, more grains of sand were sent flying into the air and onto Stuart and Sarah. The two sat up quickly in reaction to his rude move and had to spit out particles that landed in their mouths.

"Are you ever considerate, dude?" Stuart yelled. "That's like the second time you've done that!"

Robbie only laughed nervously, spread the towel down next to Sarah, and dropped like a lead weight onto his stomach. He turned his head away. She glanced at Stuart and rolled her eyes in disgust.

"I gotta get outta here before I punch somebody," Stuart barked. "Do you wanna come with me on a walk, Sarah?" Apparently, Stuart had trouble taking his own advice about not letting Robbie be so bothersome. He sprayed more sunscreen on his body and prepared to leave.

"Thanks Stuart, but I may go back to writing. I just want to relax."

With a nod and wink, Stuart left.

The competition had been cleared away. Robbie took the opportunity to open up to Sarah, who had gone back to reading her magazine. "I have demons," he told her.

"No kidding," she responded while her eyes roved the pages.

"I'm serious, Sarah. Listen to me. I – have – demons."

At that moment, the sun grew dim.

Sarah was astounded and realized Robbie was not joking. She lifted her head to stare at the sea and felt a heavy weight on her chest. "What kind of demons?" she asked quietly, keeping her eyes fixed on the water.

"Demon, demons. I believe there's only one kind," Robbie said sarcastically.

"Tell me more." There was no ignoring his statement now. Having been raised in a Christian household, when someone said they *had demons*, she figured they were struggling with pretty dark things or they were tormented with the opposite of what was good, moral, or honest.

"I'll tell you more sometime," Robbie teased again.

"Is that it? You're going to leave that carrot dangling?"

Robbie smirked and looked to the ocean. He was not sure she could handle his troubles. At the same time, he wanted to make her think – and make her run. His words were not meant to draw Sarah in. Winning her affection was his intent, but he did not want her to fall in love with him. Yet the more he tossed out mysterious, cryptic phrases and actions, the more curious she became. Nearly twenty minutes of silence passed. Sarah waited for his explanation, but it never arrived.

Finally, Stuart returned. "What did I miss?"

Sarah awkwardly shuffled her feet on her towel.

"Not much," Robbie responded. "Ready to go?"

Are you kidding me? Sarah thought. *He's going to throw out something like 'demons' and not follow up to it?* She was left hanging over the edge of a relationship cliff.

"Seems like a good night for a movie. Let's get pizza!" Robbie suggested. It was clear, he was not willing to further the discussion. His mention of demons was buried in the sand.

The three agreed to leave the beach, pick up food on their way back, and return to Stuart's apartment to eat.

Sarah shook out her towel far enough away from everyone. "You see how that's done, Robbie?" She was not happy with the way he ended the conversation and was feeling spiteful. She folded the towel into a neat square and packed it in her bag.

He ignored her, and Stuart snickered to himself. They grabbed the rest of their belongings and headed toward the car. As they walked off the beach, they passed a group of young girls who gawked at Sarah.

Robbie took note. "They're admiring how a real woman carries herself with two men at her side."

Boy, you are a charmer, or was that sarcasm, again? Is that a dig at my poise, or are you complimenting yourself *in some back-handed way?* The questions swirled through her head, making a knotted mess. She just snickered in acknowledgment and then smiled at the girls. Robbie did not deserve a verbal response.

The three departed the beach and washed their feet off under the outdoor shower. The water was also a refreshing cleanse for their minds. All conversations were left behind, including the one about demons – or so Sarah thought.

Chapter 17

FOOLS DESPISE WISDOM

It was the day that Robbie mentioned having *demons* that would mark the beginning of many afternoon outings at the beach, followed by pizza dinners at Stuart's apartment. The threesome had made amends and the laughter had returned to their twisted friendship.

Sarah and Robbie spent some steamy nights at his apartment; however, they shared very few deep conversations anymore. Despite his ongoing, nonchalant approach to their affair – along with his strange attitude – Sarah still held out hope for some kind of commitment. She had her doubts that he could love her fully, but she was reeled in – and thrown back – over and over again.

On a Sunday in May, after spending time at the beach, they came together at Stuart's to relax over beers, pizza, and a good comedy. Laughter continued for hours as they downed alcohol and cracked jokes at the acting.

Things were going too well, which meant Robbie had to put on the breaks. "Stuart, remember when that twenty-something chick from the other side of your complex used to hang out with us like this?"

"Oh, yeah!" Stuart recalled. "What was her name?"

"No clue, but she smelled good. Great body, too."

Both men laughed arrogantly at not remembering the woman's name. Sarah fell for the bait. *Am I the replacement?* she wondered.

The guys were her friends, but at that moment, she felt insignificant. Her skin crawled and her gut hurt.

"She was a sweet blast," Stuart joked, clueless to Robbie's game. "I recall she liked the porn."

At that, Sarah wanted to get up and leave. Every word they said pricked her heart. What was she supposed to do? She stared at the television screen, but paid no attention to the movie. A devious grin drew across Robbie's face when he looked at her profile, trying to catch her reaction to his rude behavior.

The tension was building within her, as she read between their lines. *How many women have come before me? Why did Robbie even mention this person?* Sarah could no longer keep her thoughts quiet. As the men delighted in the memory of this other woman, she felt like a pawn in a twisted game. "Where is she now?" Sarah blurted out.

Robbie grinned, like a Cheshire cat. He reveled in Sarah's displeasure, which he could read all over her face. "Oh, I'm sure she's around," he chuckled.

"I don't know what happened to her. I haven't seen her in years," Stuart added innocently.

Sarah shuddered, immediately jumped out of her seat, and walked briskly to the kitchen to get some water. *What was that?* she wondered. *Why did my body tingle?* The atmosphere felt strange to her. She tried to shake it off. *Is our entire friendship some lewd pursuit?*

Hanging out with both men and then having sex with just Robbie was a regimen she had come to accept. However, the once, fun routine now felt dirty and regretful. These men were unattainable, but she had hoped they would change. Upon hearing the night's conversation about the mystery woman, her feelings were beginning to wane.

"Hey, are you alright out there?" Stuart called.

"Yeah, just waiting for the water to get as cold as possible."

The two men looked at each other and shrugged their shoulders. Meanwhile, Robbie knew that he had triggered her emotions. He wanted Sarah to feel uncomfortable.

Sarah swigged down a full glass of water and then filled it up again. She lingered in the kitchen for several minutes before returning to the living room. One surprise after another was driving Sarah crazy. She could not concentrate on the movie. She wanted things between the three of them to be smooth and easy – and fun. Yet Sarah's longing to make their entanglement a deeper one was bashed at every attempt. "Well, you guys, I'm tired. I think I'll head home."

"Are you sure, Sarah?" asked Robbie. "We were going to watch another movie."

A forced smile drew across her full lips, and she quickly slipped into her flip-flops. "The sun drained me, today. I'm about to fall asleep. Next time, I promise." She bent down to give Stuart a kiss on his head. "Thank you for always opening your home to us, Stu."

"Of course, honey," he said as he searched Sarah's eyes.

"Text me when the next gathering takes place."

"What about *my* kiss?" Robbie asked.

"I'm too tired to walk over to you," she said, in a low, soft voice.

Out the door she went. Robbie's plan had succeeded.

On the way back to her apartment, Sarah's brain spun a spiderweb of thoughts. She wanted to believe that their intentions were always good. She trusted the men to a certain degree, as far as being there for her. But this night was weird. *Did they do something terrible to that girl? Would they hurt me?* Sarah knew those were big accusations to make, but something was amiss.

It was late by the time she snuck into her apartment. She hoped not to disturb Em. But there was no chance of getting past the pup. Out came her bark. "Oh, Emmy, I'm home now. It's ok."

She opened the slider to the small yard and let the pup out to pee. Sarah was always cautious when the dog was outside, especially at night. It was not unusual to see urban coyotes, bobcats, or owls in her area. Little Em would be a darling appetizer for any one of those predators. She brought her inside, quickly, put food down, and checked her phone for any missed messages.

An unknown number appeared on the display; she clicked on it. *Hey love! It's Jenny. Got your number from Stuart. Aerobics class this Friday morning with me and some friends? I'm in town for a few. New gym on the corner of West Camino. If you can make it – see you at 9. Cheers!*

Sarah was excited – another companion. However, unbeknownst to her, Jenny's real motives were to get a kickback from the gym for bringing in new members and to hear the latest scoop on Robbie and Stuart.

Love to! I'll see you then, Sarah texted back.

She showered off the sand from earlier and got into bed. Temperatures hovered in the mid-70s again. That was warm for nighttime. The heat made Em pant. "Are you a *hot dog*?" Sarah joked. Em seemed to smile. "I'll set up a fan for you, honey."

The turning blades forced tepid air across Em's tummy. Her fur fluttered back and forth, like leaves on a Ficus tree – frail and delicate. The breeze was relaxing and allowed them both to drift off to sleep.

Chapter 18

VIRGO WITH SCORPIO RISING

Without realizing it, Sarah was being escorted down a tunnel of sin. She was living within a dimension she could not see or touch. If all that surrounded her in the spiritual realm was visible, it would have terrorized her. Instead, the experience, at times, smelled like the forest and desert wildflowers – and exhilarated her like cool rain. Sarah could not see the dangerous edges of what she thought was good. Her gut questioned things, but she still walked into the fire. With its sweet taste, a dark dimension was slowly luring her away from the light.

Buzz. Buzz. Sarah's eyes flew open like window shades at the sound of her vibrating phone. *Can I come over, tonight?* Robbie's text read.

"Oh wow!" Sarah said out loud. "He's never been here."

Sarah's addiction to Robbie was overwhelming. What happened to the anger she felt when they were at Stuart's? Sarah just kept coming back for more potential upsets. Robbie was a poison she wanted to ingest, despite the potent effects. *Why don't you ever call me?* she wrote back.

He immediately picked up on the harsh tone and responded with the same. *What's up your butt? I don't like disturbing you. This is safe.*

Exactly! Sarah texted. *It's safe.*

It was accurate for her to assume that Robbie did not want to pay her a visit just for a game of checkers. He wanted his ego stroked – and possibly more. He might have thought she was losing interest and that would mean losing the sex. Meanwhile, she did not want to be free for the taking.

Leave the attitude behind. Do you want me to come over or not? he texted.

Yes, you can come over. Are you bringing food?

Sure. Is Chinese ok again?

Perfect. Beef and Broccoli for me.

Ok, I'll be over around 5.

Sarah's body was awakened by the over-production of endorphins. The substance went right to her libido. She was living some weird reality, drawn in by every twisted moment. Her world was filled with excitement and seduction – yet puzzlement, pain, and risk. "This is so oddly hot although confusing! Whatever he does – good or bad – I keep taking him in!" Sarah was determined to pull Robbie's secrets out into the light and willing to enter the unknown to do it. She hated herself for not walking away from this toxic man.

There were files of photos in Sarah's computer that needed client approval. She planned to be done in time to prepare for her house guest. Emails were sent and answered and pictures were deleted or stored. It pleased her that she was able to complete many of the outstanding projects. She glanced at the time. "Aargh! I gotta get ready!"

After her shower, Sarah decided on a pair of silky, soft white pants and a loose, light-weight sweater. She felt naturally beautiful, sensuous, and sexy. It was perfect for lounging around the apartment and for cuddling.

Robbie decided to take his motorcycle to Sarah's apartment. He had been riding since he was a kid and could whip around town and down the highway, like a stunt man. He loved the freedom it gave him. The masculine, leather, riding outfit he wore over his white t-shirt and jeans was meant to impress. After picking up dinner, he set off to Sarah's place.

When he arrived, Robbie revved his engine then dismounted his bike. Sarah peeked through a tiny window on the side of the front door and watched him pull off his helmet. He appeared strong and sexy while retrieving the food from his saddle bag. She saw him approaching and hid out of sight.

"Anyone home? I have sustenance!"

Smelling like plumeria and coconut, Sarah slowly opened the door and posed. She was a sweet vision. "Hello, there!" she greeted.

Robbie absorbed her beauty for a few seconds. He placed his helmet and the food atop a small wooden bench on her porch. He snaked his arm around her waist and kissed her soft lips. "Hey, how've ya been?" he said in his cool demeanor and brushed past her.

Sarah mentally added another brick to the wall of protection she was building after his aloof entrance. The aroma of Chinese food wafted past her nose as he swayed into her living room. Em ran up to sniff his boots – and growled.

"Nice place you got here. Cute pup."

"Thanks. I like both."

"Let's eat. Food's getting cold." As they devoured their Asian cuisine, Robbie made small talk and attempted to be playful. "So how much do you know about the signs?"

"What signs?"

"Astrology, silly."

"Oh, yeah! You're a Scorpio. I know a little."

"I follow everything," Robbie boasted.

"I've been waiting for you to bring up the subject. I assumed you wanted to know if we were going to get along."

"Oh, I'm well read – especially of Virgo," he smiled. "I told you we'd be in trouble. Was I not right?"

"No, I guess you were."

"I haven't talked about it prior to now because I take it seriously. If I didn't take *you* seriously, I would not have brought it up tonight."

Sarah was sugar-coated – and weak as hell. She fell for that line, like a kitten to catnip. How tangled it sounded. Rather than question how important she was prior to tonight, Sarah decided to move on. "I've been reading a book about the compatibility of the signs. Do you want to see it?"

Robbie took his last bite of food and nodded in agreement. He was very excited that Sarah was educating herself on the subject. This meant they had something in common, which meant he could walk a straighter line to her bed.

"It is spot-on in describing me. I think you'll like it," she stated proudly when she returned with the book.

"Oh, I've not only read that one, but I have about eight other astrology books."

"I should have guessed."

"It's been a while since I opened this one though. Let's read it together. Sign compatibility is a must for a good friendship."

Friendship? Well, I guess that's better than just a fling, she thought.

"Do you mind if we read it in your bed?" he coaxed. "I need to lie down after that huge meal."

Sarah was not fooled by the suggestion to get between her sheets. She wished that Robbie was not in such a hurry. "Sure – second door on the left, down the hall."

No guy she had ever dated was interested in the stars or thought that celestial-worshiping carried any weight. Since Robbie expressed his devout reliance on it, she became elated at the potential for further connection.

She followed behind and made a detour into her bathroom, where she freshened up. The image staring back at her had changed over the last few months. Her eyes looked lost. Her mouth slightly drooped at the edges from being over-tired. *Brush it off, girl. An anxious Robbie is waiting.*

When Sarah entered the room – there he was, wearing only his boxer shorts. *Sign to Sign* was in his hands. Sarah felt a wave of uncertainty again. He was being awfully presumptuous. "More comfortable in just your underwear, I see," Sarah joked.

"Yes, comfort. You should try it, too."

She stalled. "I think this is a great time to take your picture – like you wanted."

Before he could answer, Sarah ran down the hall to get camera equipment from her office. She returned rapidly, flinging the strap around her neck and snapping one or two candid shots while he prepared himself for posed photos.

"Not really what I had in mind for tonight, but I guess we can take a few quick pics," Robbie shrugged. "Maybe I can read to you about Scorpio as you click away." He was such a narcissist, posing between sentences as he read aloud, "Scorpios are great in bed."

"So, I've heard," Sarah mocked sweetly.

Robbie absorbed her response, like dehydrated dirt. He bent his right knee upward and shifted onto his left elbow for the next photo. "It also helps that my chakras are open and healed."

"What do you mean, chakras?"

"We all have several energy centers within our bodies, each representing specific areas. I devoutly meditate on them. Clear them out, so I don't have stress, ya know?"

"I'm learning more and more about you every day."

"But I focus on my sexual energy the most."

"I bet," she said. Sarah was interested in hearing about what Robbie was practicing. Since she had denied God, she did not feel at liberty to judge him for *his* practices. But instinctively, Sarah believed that what he was describing was not of the Biblical God, and for some reason, it made her feel uneasy.

"I leave my body a lot, too. It's amazing what I see."

Sarah snapped more photos. Her gut twinged. "What do you mean?"

"I concentrate really hard and have actually left my body while on my bed. I have – spiritually – gone to someone's house and seen them inside. Can't communicate with them, but I see them."

"Wow! That's not right, is it? You dabble in a lot of mysterious stuff that opens you up to unknown forces, no?"

Robbie was slightly miffed at her dismissive statements and reference to his practices as mere *stuff*. He was careful not to show his frustration too much, otherwise he would not get any action. "It's over your head, little girl. Let's focus on your picture-taking skills."

Sarah swallowed his patronizing statement, hard. But she continued to snap photos.

Robbie hammed it up for the camera with and without his boxers on. The action of removing his shorts – while peering into the lens and Sarah's eyes – was stimulating to both the subject and photographer. He glanced back down at the pages of *Sign to Sign* and came across the term *power of persuasion* regarding Scorpio. At that moment, he closed the book and threw it on the floor. "Come here, baby."

That did it for Sarah. In an instant, she was convinced it was alright to continue with the night and forget the things that exited Robbie's mouth. She set her camera on the dresser and crawled into bed. "We never read about Virgo."

BEFORE THE ROOSTER CROWS TWICE

He drew her sweater over her head and tossed it next to the astrology book. "I know all about you," Robbie growled quietly, "and I'm about to know more."

Chapter 19

HE SENT FIRE

It was Friday morning, seven o'clock; Sarah thumbed through the pages of *Sign to Sign* looking for more insight into her friendship with Robbie. She was stepping, carelessly, into a deceptive realm. The information seduced her senses, but it was giving false hope for a deep and meaningful relationship.

A mug of hot, sweetened tea – and being curled up with Em at her side – was a perfect start to Sarah's morning. Content that she had read enough to map out her future with Robbie, she set the book down and pondered about other things he mentioned. He talked about leaving his body, or *astral flight*, and it disturbed her. Mentally and spiritually going to another place to spy on people – was creepy. It did not seem natural. *Has he visited me?* she wondered. *Maybe that's the reason Em growled at him.*

She and the dog jumped in the air when the alarm on her phone suddenly went off, alerting her to the workout with Jenny. "Ugg, I totally forgot! Can I change my mind, Emmy?" Sarah giggled. "I'm happier right here."

The air flowing through an open window felt unusually warm. Sarah checked the weather app on her phone. To her astonishment, there were record highs predicted for the day, with temperatures reaching a whopping ninety degrees. "Yikes, Em! This is horrendous! Was Jenny nuts to think we should exercise in this heat? I hope the gym has the AC turned on."

Despite the weather, Sarah got ready. She gave Jenny her word. Besides, her body needed some strengthening, and the invitation made her feel like *one of the gang.*

Sarah bent down to kiss the little dog on the forehead while she put together a workout bag. "It's going to be very hot for you, my love. Would you like me to leave a fan running?" The dog's ears perked up, and she cocked her head to one side to show her mommy approval of the suggestion. Sarah smiled and prepared a spot on the tile entryway. The dog pressed her belly on the cool floor, sprawled her legs out behind her, and enjoyed the breeze from the turning metal blades.

Sarah texted Jenny to tell her she would be heading to the gym soon. There was a short window of time to make a smoothie and toast. She got down on the floor and stroked her furry friend's back while she ate and drank. When the last gulp was down, Sarah left for the gym.

It was just past rush hour, but for some reason traffic was heavy. As she approached the first of only three stop lights on her way, a fire engine – blaring its siren – flew past her. A multitude of cars waited at the intersection. Soon it became clear, what all the ruckus was about. In the sky to her right was an enormous black cloud of billowing smoke. Flames could be seen in the distance. The fire was too close for comfort. Sarah turned on the radio to find any news of the incident. The only thing coming out of the console was music and long-winded commercials. Since Sarah had not heard back from her workout buddy, she assumed Jenny might not know about the fire. *Maybe it will be put out quickly,* she thought.

Sarah was ready to go. When the light turned green, all of the drivers looked in the direction of the blaze, then at each other. It was as if they were waiting for someone to tell them that they should *carry on.* She finally tapped the gas pedal and headed south, away from the incident. A nagging feeling urged her to turn around and go back home, or at least drive by to see what was on fire. She dismissed the thought, knowing that she would only be at the gym a short time. *What could happen in an hour?* she wondered.

Sarah reached her destination. She got out of her car and looked to the sky in the direction of the fire. Not much change. She shrugged her shoulders, trusted the fire department to do its job, and proceeded to enter the building.

"Ready to work out?" Jenny rallied.

"Hi, Jenny! Great to see you! Thanks for the invite."

"Meet my two friends, Mary and Lana."

"Hi!" Sarah acknowledged the other gorgeous females who were dressed up in name-brand workout gear and wore heavy makeup. "Did you see the fire? Isn't this heat scorching?"

"No and yes," Jenny responded. "You didn't have to come if you didn't want to."

Sarah was surprised by her curt response. She clearly misinterpreted the attempt at making conversation with the strangers. Jenny was there to enjoy the morning, not worry about a little fire and heat. These topics were dampers that had no place for discussion at the gym. *Kind of bitchy,* Sarah thought. *Did she not hear what I said? There is a fire!*

Jenny quickly changed the subject and her demeanor, "Grab a mat, Sarah, the class is about to get started. You can sign up later."

The slender woman found a spongy exercise platform on the other side of the aerobics room and positioned herself in front of the many mirrors. "I guess these are here to remind us of how badly we need to work out," Sarah giggled, referring to their reflections. Not one word was uttered in response. The four ladies formed a line, lifting their legs in tandem to the beat of electric dance music, like a synchronized swim team on speed. Sarah tried to keep her ears open to the instruction of the director. The endless leg and arm reps were tiring. Nevertheless, she gave it her all. The class lasted about forty-five minutes. When they were finished, the mats were folded and returned to a stack in the corner of the room.

"So, what have you been up to?" Jenny inquired.

"Oh, not much. Hanging out, working, normal stuff." Sarah was afraid to reveal that she had shared *time* with Stuart and Robbie – let alone their beds.

There was probably a good reason why Stuart had not invited Jenny to recent events. She probably cramped his style, or maybe it was because he was truly interested in Sarah.

Jenny might be jealous and upset if she found out the boys were partying without her. "Let me know if you guys do anything this weekend. I'm staying at Lana's and can come out and join the three of you."

How does she know the 'three' of us get together? Sarah wondered. *Was she once a threesome with the guys, too – or did she just assume I was?* "Ok, I can do that," Sarah said. "I'm not sure when there will be a get-together, though." She downplayed their meetups. The last thing she wanted was a jealous woman on her back.

Jenny and Stuart still talked on a regular basis. He had mentioned, in passing, that he and Sarah were hanging out from time to time. But that was it. He did not want a jealous woman on *his* back, either.

"So – did you like the workout? Don't you want to sign up?" asked Jenny.

Just then, Sarah's eyes opened as big as golf balls while she looked past the woman.

"What is it?"

The sky was filled entirely with smoke!

"I've got to go, Jenny. My apartment is up there," Sarah said, pointing north. "I need to check on my dog. Hopefully the flames haven't spread to the hills."

"Wow! I guess you were right!" Jenny, along with her two friends, looked up and saw only grey and black. The first thing she thought of was to call Stuart. She reached into her bag for her phone.

Sarah bolted to her car and zoomed out of the parking lot with only one thing in mind – Em. Driving toward her apartment, she could smell the smoke. Ash particles were getting whipped around in the breeze. Some of them started to collect at the top edges of her wiper blades. She rolled up the windows and turned on the air conditioner to ensure there was circulation inside the vehicle. The smoke drifted in the direction of the hills. "Oh, Em. I hope you're alright!" Sarah panicked.

Very few cars were traveling in her direction, so there was no traffic to slow her down. Although, it may have only been a four-minute drive; it seemed like an hour.

"Please, let Em be alright!"

Who was Sarah hoping would help her? Whenever things got out of control, she merely spoke out loud to no one. At other times, she attempted to handle issues on her own. She had been a fair-weather friend to God in the past, and He took notice.

Sarah pulled up to her apartment and rushed inside. The little dog was panting with excitement to see her mommy. "Oh Baby! Are you ok?" She grabbed Em and held her close. "We have to figure out what we're doing. We've got to get out of here."

Sarah set the dog down and ran out the front door to the neighbor's, making sure not to let any ash particles inside. Ben Knobes was washing his car and paid no attention to the smoke. "Ben!" Sarah shouted. "Are you getting out of here, soon? I don't know what to do."

Ben was a salesman and typically high-strung; however, this time he appeared calm and collected. He held the hose over the hood of his sports car, letting the water dribble around the edges. "What's the frenzy about, girl?"

"I just came from the direction of the fire. It's headed this way."

"No need to get excited. Nobody's evacuating."

"Dude! They will have us out of here for sure. Don't you see the ash in the air?"

"Eh. It will be under control in a bit."

"If you're not going to evacuate, at least get inside and don't breathe this. I really think you should leave. Can't you stay with family somewhere?"

Her words fell on deaf ears. Ben waved – implying that Sarah was over-reacting – and continued washing his car.

She threw her arms up and ran back to her apartment, covering her mouth with the neckline of her shirt. There was no time to waste. Loud sirens blared from all directions. Once inside, Sarah frantically sped from one room to another, trying to decide which valuables to take with her. She grabbed Em's food and medicine, photography equipment, laptop, clothing for a few days, Richard's ring, and some family heirlooms. Everything, except the camera bags, was packed into three pillow cases.

She sent Robbie a text. *There's a fire by my apartment. It's coming this way, and I think I should evacuate. Can I stay at your place until they contain it?*

Twenty minutes went by – no answer from Robbie. She put together a toiletry bag and filled up a small cooler while she waited.

Buzz. Buzz. A text came through from Amy. *I just heard from Stuart, who talked with Jenny about the fire in your area. You can come stay with us if you need!*

Sarah texted back, *Thanks, Amy. That is so kind of you. I think I am going to leave in a little bit. I will let you know what I do and where I go.*

Sarah thought about asking Amy if Robbie was working with her today, but instead she tried calling him. Only his voicemail answered, so she hung up. Forty minutes had now lapsed since her first message to him. *Robbie had better be dead, because there's no other excuse to abandon me like this.*

Her phone rang. It was Stuart. She answered breathlessly, "Stuart – this is crazy! I'm so scared."

"Hey, girl. Looks like you've gotta get out of there. You and Em can come stay with me if you want."

It was as if Heaven opened and delivered an angel, donning scruffy facial hair and designer shoes. Once again, Stuart had come to her rescue. "You are a godsend, Stuart. But aren't you affected by the fire, too?"

"By some miracle – and probably since I'm coastal – we've got a strong wind blowing the smoke in the opposite direction. There's occasional ash in the air, but it's hardly noticeable."

"I'm seeing tons of ash and I can tell that the smoke is getting stronger by the minute. I'm worried about my neighbor, though."

"Don't worry about him. He'll take care of himself. I'm home – so grab a few things and head over."

Chapter 20

SOJOURNER

Horns blared, and middle fingers were raised, as frantic drivers struggled to get out of Sarah's neighborhood. They were revealing their true colors under the duress. Ash in the air was getting into Em's lungs, and the stress was bringing on a coughing fit. Sarah had no choice but to take her out into the carbon-monoxide-filled atmosphere. The little pup's health issues were exacerbated.

The fire was rapidly spreading toward Sarah's home. As she drove away from all of her belongings – except what she could fit into the pillow cases – Sarah worried about Ben and other over-confident residents at her complex. They were convinced that the fire would not reach them, and there was no need to get out. She knew she was doing the right thing by leaving.

Sarah viewed going to Stuart's place as a silver lining, a chance for her to bond with her friend again. She was grateful and relieved that he had offered up his home without hesitation, despite any tension that may have developed when she was there, before. There were more pressing things to worry about. Now Stuart was her savior, and that was all that mattered.

Em continued coughing. Sarah tried to be calm and keep the dog relaxed. The last thing she wanted was a detour to the veterinary hospital again. There was no telling whether it was even open, since it was in the same neighborhood as her apartment. For all she knew, the vet clinic staff may have evacuated, too. She rummaged through one of the pillow cases for Em's medication while keeping one hand on the steering wheel. The bottle had fallen to the bottom of the bag. "Not now!" Sarah said nervously. "Please stop coughing, my love."

There was too much going on. She was keeping an eye on the road, worrying about Robbie, and dealing with Em's hacking. Finally, Sarah's hand grasped the small vessel containing the suppressant. She pulled over to the side of the road to relieve the poor dog. "We should have done this before we left the apartment, Em!" Sarah said with frustration. All the events of the day were getting on her nerves.

Sarah administered the medication and the pup downed it like a champ.

Taking a moment to compose herself, Sarah stepped out of the car and got a good look at the sky over her apartment. It reminded her of a bad bruise. Previously charcoal-colored clouds had now turned to light grey with putrid yellow edges. The atmosphere felt like death. There was no sunlight; it looked like the remnants of war. As she paused to take in the weight of the situation, Sarah reflected on the last hour. Her material possessions suddenly had no value. Anything left behind did not matter anymore. "I thought this only happened to other people. It's just you and me, Emmy. We'll get through this."

Robbie popped into her mind. She checked her phone for any missed calls or texts. Still no note from the man with whom she had shared her bed only a few days before. His lack of concern for her during this whole ordeal could not be dismissed. He had made a big mistake. *Are we not lovers, for crying out loud?* Sarah questioned in her head. *Your absence just might be a deal-breaker, Robbie. But that's probably what you want, isn't it?*

Sarah got back into her car. She started the engine and slithered into the line of traffic that inched its way onto the freeway. Each driver was like a drop in a sea of despair, collectively searching for an island to call *safety*. She felt grateful that the fire had not engulfed them all. There would have been no escape. Too many people were trying to leave the area, and the roads were jammed up.

It took two grueling hours to reach Stuart's apartment because of the heavy traffic. When Sarah finally parked at his complex, she sat in her car for five minutes and cried. A handsome Stuart met her at her vehicle, with a welcoming, cold margarita. "Greetings and salutations, my friend. Come and make yourself at home." For that moment, all Sarah's worries washed away. He served the drink in a pretty, blue and green, salt-rimmed glass that glistened with condensation. It was a delightful sight and sparkled in her eyes. The beautiful cocktail was exactly what she needed to calm her nerves and cool her soul.

"Good ol' Stuart," Sarah remarked. "You do know how to save the day!"

"Alcohol solves your problems," Stuart chuckled. "And since we are not going out dancing tonight, I presume, you may as well put your hollow leg on. I have more where that came from."

Sarah laughed at his comment and set Em down to take the offering. The little dog immediately got reacquainted with her semi-permanent surroundings. She was doing better in the cleaner environment. Stuart loved having Em visit and was attentive to her needs. A bowl of cool water was already on the kitchen floor for his new four-legged roommate.

He helped Sarah in with her things and they both dropped on the couch to relax. "I smell the smoke on you and your stuff."

"Oh, great! I'm so sorry Stuart. I can take a shower if you want."

"Well! If a woman offers to take a shower – accompanied with an apology – that is any man's dream. Kick back and drink up."

Sarah laughed and shook her head in disbelief at his corny quip. The pair ended up chatting for hours. When night began to fall, Stuart heated up some leftover chicken pasta. They ate at the coffee table and watched an update of the news. The margaritas kept flowing.

"I can't believe how severe the fire is. I watched the news before you got here and one of the reports said it was purposely set."

"Are you kidding me? All of this chaos because of some jerk?" Sarah's head and body fell limp against the back of the couch. She faced the ceiling, trying to gain some strength. Footage of the fire appeared on the local news station. She started to lift her head off the cushions to see the television when a text came through on her phone.

Hey. Sorry. Got tied up at work. Robbie wrote. *There's no way I can get there. Is there any place you can stay?*

Sarah hesitated before she responded. Her gut had been delivered another relentless blow. It was easy for her to read between the lines. Robbie wanted no part in helping the damsel out, especially by providing room and board. She was dying inside. His icy response carried enough insensitivity to harden her heart. *Do you know how long it's been since I texted you?* she wrote. *I would have perished already if I had waited for you to 'get there.' Btw, I'm at Stuart's!*

Sarah had been *too* nice to Robbie. He deserved nothing from her, neither her time, nor worry. His lame excuse made her feel tense and nervous again. She hid her emotions from Stuart. Putting him in a bad mood with her negativity was the last thing she wanted to do.

Just when things could not get any worse, Robbie sent another message. *Awesome! Stuart will be a great host.* And just like that, he was off the hook. He offered no help of any kind and never even asked Sarah if she and Em were ok.

Her gut ached. "I'll have another!" she cried and raised her decorative glass for Stuart to refill and relieve her pain.

"So, let me guess," he inquired while he poured from a large pitcher. "Was that our friend Robbie texting you with discouraging words?" Stuart read her well and seemed to be aware of her involvement.

Whoops! I guess the cat is out of the bag, Sarah thought. She did not want to purposefully gossip about Robbie, but who else could she talk to about the head games he was playing? Perhaps Stuart could offer her some insight into the man.

"He's an odd duck, ya know? Not sure I really like him, anymore. I used to feel bad for the guy. He never had too many friends. But I know he must hurt you."

Sarah stared right through Stuart, in deep thought. With her lips to the glass, she slowly slurped up the little granules of ice floating at the top of her margarita. She pulled them onto her tongue, one by one, and swirled them around her mouth until they melted. Was she supposed to be upset, sympathetic, vengeful, or just forget about Robbie altogether? "What do you mean by 'odd duck', Stuart?"

Fortunately for Sarah, the alcohol that Stuart had consumed worked like a truth serum. "Ok, if you must know. He always says things that are off-putting, and people don't like it. Jenny can't stand him – and I have often considered whether I should stop hanging out with him. The way he acts is just not normal or cool."

Sarah was glued to his every word.

"His dad messed him up, big time; I know that much. Abused him, or some crazy ass stuff like that. Don't fall in love with him, Sarah. You will regret it."

"Oh," was all she could say.

"That girl he brought up the other night at my house? She fell for Robbie, and he dropped her like a hat. I have no clue where she is now. He treated her like crap."

Sarah listened and stared at the wall. The things Stuart was saying were tough to hear, but they confirmed what she already sensed about Robbie. She remembered their awkward conversations and the mention of demons that day at the beach. *Is he afraid of Robbie?* she wondered. There was no way she could stay friends with someone she did not trust.

Stuart did the exact opposite. He kept Robbie around because it was seemingly safer to be friends with him. But safe from what?

Sarah now questioned her role in this triangle. There was a conflict of whether to expose Robbie for being hurtful or help him to be better. She saw a sad, damaged boy inside the shell of a very proud, macho man. But she was in no position to be his therapist. The timing was all wrong. Hidden in the dark side of her life was a scared and struggling girl in need of her own repair. He was the last thing she needed for *her* mental health.

A little sleepy and inebriated, Sarah pulled her bare feet up on the cushions and snuggled into the throw pillows behind her back. Stuart studied her face as she rested. The age lines on her cheeks were prominent when her muscles relaxed. They were endearing. He was content with her being there and had no expectation of her departure any time soon.

Buzz. Buzz. Sarah's phone startled her. She read his text. "What is this?" she shouted, her mood instantly changing. "Call me sometime?" Sarah could not contain herself any longer. She was visibly upset.

Stuart rolled his eyes. Despite understanding what she was going through with Robbie, he had hoped for a quiet, drama-free night with his lady friend. He got up from his cushy seat and headed to the bathroom. It was not Sarah he was upset at, but rather Robbie, who was ruining everything – intentionally.

"You should call ME, you jerk!" Sarah yelled at the phone and then threw it on the coffee table, nearly breaking it. No longer did this strong, virile man seem attractive. Robbie was a pompous jackass. The once sweet taste in her mouth had now soured. The bright glory days of dancing and drinking were grossly clouding up with dissension and discord.

Stuart was caught in the middle. He knew what Sarah was getting into; he had seen it before. It was a rabbit hole he did not want her falling down. His hands were tied. Robbie was his so-called friend, yet so was she. He watched as Sarah reached for her phone. "Are you sure you want to do that?" Stuart questioned from across the room in a low, almost authoritative voice.

Sarah ignored him and phoned Robbie. The alcohol took control.

"Hey, babe," Robbie answered smugly. "I didn't think I would hear from you so soon."

"How could you not respond to me earlier? There was a fire raging near my home, and I had to evacuate. I needed your help!"

"I told you I was working, " Robbie defended himself, "and I can't have your dog here with my roommates."

"Is that why you didn't call me? Because of my dog?"

"You'll be fine at Stuart's," he said patronizingly. "Maybe I'll come over and visit. Goodbye."

"Don't bother!" she yelled, before the phone disconnected.

Robbie felt berated. He knew he was guilty of avoiding Sarah. There was no excuse for his lack of compassion. Even though he deserved to be scolded, he was not going to stay on the phone and take it.

"We should have never moved here, Em," Sarah cried and looked at her beloved pooch.

There was now a wedge driven between all three of them. In some form or another, they were each to blame for the demise of the fun they once had together.

"Come, lie down with me," Stuart interrupted her fury. "I don't want you to be alone out here." He had no plans to take advantage of Sarah. He genuinely wanted to give her comfort – the comfort of a true friend.

"Ok, Stuart. I will take you up on that. I'd rather not stay on this couch, anyway."

He gently pulled her up off the cushions and nudged her to the bathroom to get ready for bed. Everything was laid out for her again – a toothbrush, toothpaste, shower gel, wash cloth, facial cleanser, cotton balls, and a freshly washed pair of boxer shorts, paired with a t-shirt. She thanked him and showered, quickly.

When she exited the bathroom, all the lights in the apartment had been turned off. However, Stuart placed several timed, battery-operated candles in each room to illuminate her way to his bed.

"Are you in here?" she giggled and walked to the right side.

"Right here."

"Ok, good. I'm getting in."

"I'm waiting."

Sarah slid between the sheets and slowly reached out to find his warm body. He gently pulled her in close, wrapping his arms and legs around her, to lock her in place. His protection was what she needed. She cried silently. Tears dribbled onto his chest. She felt around for the waistband of his shorts and slowly tugged them off his hips. Stuart was stunned! He was the one who made the moves, not the other way around. But he let her continue. She turned her head to look at his face in the candle-lit room. His eyes pierced hers as he bent down to kiss her and remove her t-shirt.

Chapter 21

A WALK THROUGH THE VALLEY

Emergency personnel from as far away as San Francisco came down to fight the blaze until it was contained. The fire destroyed several homes and businesses. It had been blown primarily to the east. Sarah called the city to see if it was safe to go back to her apartment and if her complex was even standing. They told her she could return, but if she noticed any ember flare-ups or if the air was difficult to breathe, she should leave.

Sarah reflected: *Oh, how one decision can create a ripple effect. A person decides to light a fire and the world comes crashing down for masses of people. There's an evacuation, lives are threatened, homes and businesses are lost, I fight with Robbie, I impose on a friend, my dog's health is affected – all for what? I hope the man or woman who caused this disaster goes to jail for a very long time. However, If I had to find the silver lining, I would have to say that I finally saw the light.*

Part of Sarah wanted to stay at Stuart's. He was a voice of reason and a shoulder of comfort. She dreaded going back to her apartment and having to deal with the aftermath. Nevertheless, after staying three days it was time to leave. She and Stuart both agreed that the sex they shared was a one-time thing and to not make it a regular event. It would be too confusing and complicated right now. "Thank you for being so understanding with everything. I am so grateful for you, Stuart," she said, giving him a bear hug. "Things are a mess. I need to fix a lot."

"It was nice to have you and Em here. And whatever happened between us, will *stay* just between us. Let me know if you need help at your apartment."

On her way home, the strong stench of stale, burnt wood and metal filtered into Sarah's car. It was sickening. A milky, yellow haze covered everything as far as she could see. She rolled up the windows and covered her nose and mouth with a t-shirt from one of her bags. Many structures in the area had been charred. Thankfully, Sarah's building was spared. She could see that Ben's car was not parked out front where he usually kept it. Perhaps he had heeded her advice and evacuated.

Em was taken out of the car and into the apartment as quickly as possible. She was tired. Her pathetic stare into her mother's eyes was telling. This whole ordeal had weakened the little baby. Her panting increased. It was getting more difficult for Sarah to watch the light in her companion's eyes dissipate. The dog's organs were sensitive enough due to her terminal illness, so the slightest bit of carcinogen she inhaled was detrimental to her health.

There was no escaping the odor. It had permeated throughout the interior, including the attached garage. Sarah assessed the damage and began the cleaning process. She opened all the windows, ran the fans, and attempted to clear out the smell – and the memory – of smoke. Frustrated at life, Sarah yanked the sheets off the bed and brought one of the pillowcases up to her nose. The smell of Robbie's shampoo was still detectable through the smokey fabric. She drew in a heavy sniff and then threw everything on the floor in a huff.

Next, she tackled the bedroom closet. Sarah pulled skirts and dresses off the rods and stuffed them into garbage bags to give away. She knew that eventually the stench would wear off – with someone else's time and washing. For Sarah, many of the clothes carried memories of the moments she had spent with Robbie. The purge was liberating. She kept and laundered a set of sheets and a few casual garments just so she had something to use and wear until she could go shopping.

The night came quickly after Sarah's day of hard work around the apartment. Her head pounded with fatigue. Delirious and a little out of sorts, she decided to send a text. *Hi, Robbie. Are you available to chat?* Robbie's treatment of Sarah would not go unchecked.

While she waited for his response, she heard an odd sound outside her bedroom window and tiptoed closer. The ominous and repetitious hoots of a night owl alerted Sarah to its eerie presence. The haunting call sent shivers down her spine. Although she closed the window, the noise still made its way through the walls. She peeked through the glass to see where the bird was perched, but could not find it. Folklore, told to her while on a photo assignment in the deciduous forests of Ontario, Canada, popped into her memory. The legend was: whenever an owl hooted outside a home, the occupant would suffer a loss or death. Sarah's entire body shook, as if ice had been dumped down her back. Her jaw clenched. She looked down at Em for comfort, when suddenly, the phone rang loudly. She picked it up. "Hey."

"What's happening? I just got out of the shower and saw that you had texted."

"Um. I'm going to cut to the chase. Why the hell didn't you offer up your place to me? I was basically on the street. We're sleeping together! Do I mean anything to you or am I just a bed buddy?"

Robbie bristled at Sarah's verbal attack, but remained on the phone.

"I told you already. I was working. I heard people had offered their homes to you. You didn't need me. It seemed like Stuart had it all figured out just fine."

Sarah sensed sarcasm in his tone. A sincere apology and attempt at making up to her for his lack of chivalry was all she wanted. It did not come. "That doesn't mean you couldn't have offered to help, at least to pretend you cared! You are my guy!"

"Ahh – no, I'm not! Just because we have sex doesn't mean we are married, or committed in any way."

"What? I have to be married or committed for you to give a damn? Oh, but you are 'committed' – committed to tormenting me. You're an ass. And it's *had* sex, by the way! I wasn't asking for marriage, just consideration." Sarah felt tears well up and was about to conjure a few chosen expletives when Em started coughing. "I gotta go! This is getting nowhere. You were in the wrong – period." She hung up and threw her phone down.

The dog was on the floor gasping for air. "Hang in there, Emmy. Mommy will help you!" With trembling hands, Sarah filled the dog's medicine syringe. As often as she had gone through these stressful times, it was never easy. She picked up Em's head and tried to squirt the liquid on the inside of her cheek. Em coughed again. Red fluid went all over the sheets and on both sides of her little face. Sarah tried again. This time, she only administered a third of the necessary dose. She did not want to cause the dog to choke. A pause between Em's coughing spells allowed Sarah to depress the plunger and finally send the rest of the liquid down her throat. The effects of the medication usually took about five minutes to kick in. Eight minutes passed – then ten. No change.

Sarah ran to the kitchen for a sedative that the veterinarian prescribed. She froze for two seconds and stared at the bottle. She knew Em's condition had escalated to a dangerous level. Panic got the best of her, and she struggled to remove the childproof cap. Then *pop!* About a dozen pills flew out of the container and onto the countertop. Frantically, Sarah scooped them all in her hand, leaving one out and shoving the rest in the pocket of her jeans. She reached for a cutting board and grabbed a sharp knife from the drawer. Nearly slicing her fingers, she nervously cut the pill in half, leaving the remainder on the wood. They were strong pills, and because of Em's size, it did not take much to relax her. If Sarah gave the dog more than what was prescribed, Em could go into cardiac arrest. Sarah hid the pill inside a tiny chewy treat and bolted back to the bedroom.

"I'm here, my baby!" She waived the food in front of Em's nose. The dog paused for only a second, and the morsel was gobbled down – along with the pill. Sarah was relieved that the sedative was ingested. But Em's coughing and anxiety was overworking her organs and that meant the medication may not take effect. By now, the poor animal was hoarse. "That's it, Em. I'm taking you to the ER," Sarah cried out, slipping into a pair of flip flops while grabbing her car keys.

Sarah hoped that her driving would get the pair to the clinic in one piece and that Em would not pass out from lack of oxygen. It was night, so there were very few cars on the roads. She carefully and cautiously drove through any red lights without getting caught. The way to the veterinary hospital was now familiar. And thankfully it had not burned down. The nervous mother hurried through the front doors and breathlessly pleaded to the receptionist, "Help my baby! She can't breathe."

The young woman at the check-in desk smiled calmly and asked Sarah for a list of medications Em had been given. A pair of technicians appeared out of nowhere and quickly took the little creature through the two swinging doors. The aids recognized Em and Sarah and rushed the dog to the examination room, immediately placing her in an oxygen chamber.

"You need to save her! I need to be there!"

"Please, be calm ma'am. Your dog is in good hands. I will need some information while we assess your little baby."

"We've been here before! You have our information already. My name is Sarah Gallus and my pup is Em!"

"I'm aware. We just need to verify."

"This is ridiculous!"

The medical staff in the examining room was cautious to give Em any additional sedatives, but it was crucial to stop her coughing fits. The pup was not getting any air into her lungs. They made the decision to inject her with a dose of Acepromazine. After a few minutes, Em began to slow her breathing – only slightly. As Sarah stared at the school clock on the wall, one of the physicians emerged from the back to talk with her. "We need to monitor your dog for a while, Miss Gallus. It would be best if you went home."

"Why do I have to leave?" she said softly, but firmly. "Em needs me. She's scared."

"If she sees you, it will only excite her and cause her to cough more. Please, go home and get some rest. There's nothing you can do for her right now."

Sarah had heard the same rehearsed spiel before. It was robotic, and she hated it. She felt horrible leaving Em in the care of less-concerned individuals. After all, it was not *their* dog that was dying. Her eyes felt weighted down from tears and stress, and she could barely think straight. She hung her head, turned her back on the emergency room staff, and left. "Who are these people anyway and why do I have no say?" Sarah muttered under her breath and walked back to her car. "This is *my* baby."

She sat for nearly fifteen minutes, waiting for someone to come out to get her and tell her she could take Em home – that everything would be alright. But no one came. She started up the engine and drove back to her place.

"Are we being punished?!" she shouted. "Why is this happening? If there is a god, please save her, she is dying." Sarah's words were merely tossed out of her mouth with no level of faith behind them. There was no answer. The sound of her voice fell flat, as if she spoke into a paper cup. It was lonely.

She imagined her life without Em. It was a devastating thought to be walking into a wilderness with an infinite view. No dog. No God.

Dragging herself back into the empty apartment was difficult. It was quiet, except for the owl – still perched on the tree – hooting outside her bedroom window. "Shut up!" Sarah screamed. "I know you're trying to scare me. Now, go away!" The hoots continued and so did the deafening memories of Em, gasping for breath. In her mind, Sarah heard the slamming of cabinet doors or the scolding from a doctor who did not want her to stay and comfort her little baby. The faint smell of smoke lingered from the fire. All of it was overwhelming. She closed her eyes, fell to her knees, and wept. The apartment floor was to be Sarah's bed for the night. There she was, still dressed in all her street clothes – a tired woman who had reached her mental and physical limit.

She was able to get about two hours' sleep when her cell phone rang. Thinking it might be Robbie or Stuart checking up on her, Sarah jolted upright to answer the call. To her surprise, the person on the other end was not one of the guys. "Miss Gallus? This is Doctor Banes at the veterinary hospital."

"Yes?"

"I'm sorry, but we have done all we can. Em is not responding long enough to the strong sedative. We've had her in the chamber all this time, and although she is getting *some* oxygen, her airways are becoming more restricted."

"But it's only been two hours. I thought you were going to keep her all night so she could relax?"

"Her body is fighting the sedative. She cannot relax. The only thing we can try is to put a stent in her trachea and open her up. But the surgeon who performs that procedure won't be in until nine in the morning. Right now, it's two o'clock, and we don't think she'll last until he arrives."

"A stent? Is that major?"

"The cost of the surgery is over five thousand dollars. There's no guarantee that it will work. She most likely will still have breathing difficulties. You may want to let her go." The doctor's words were surreal, as if Em was nothing more than a wild salmon caught on a fishing line, needing to be set free.

Sarah was stunned and silent. Em was her best friend and more, not something to just release with no thought.

"Are you there?" asked the doctor. "You should come down."

"Of course," Sarah finally spoke through her flood of tears. "I'll be right there." She quietly hung up and propped herself against the edge of the sofa. This time, the issue hit her soul much deeper than a fire evacuation or the loss of a lover. Em was like her child, and the grief was a feeling only she, as her mother, would experience. She was inconsolable.

When Sarah arrived at the animal hospital, she checked in with the same young girl who had greeted her before. Now calmed and somber, Sarah was gently guided through the swinging doors. She saw several dogs and cats in the treatment area, some in oxygen chambers, others being bandaged. All of them had melancholy expressions on their tiny faces. She approached Em. The poor dog was breathing heavily and coughing every five seconds. The hacking was farther apart than when Sarah initially brought her in. "Look! Isn't she getting better? Can't you do something?"

"I'm sorry," replied the vet. "She is suffering."

Sarah was *also* suffering and would never be the same. But the fits would continue, and she could not bear to see her baby die slowly and painfully in front of her eyes. The little dog started to get up in hopes of being taken home in her mother's arms. "Hi, my love – mommy loves you so much." *Why do we think we have the power to take the lives of our pets?* Sarah thought. *It's a power I do not want or deserve.*

"Miss Gallus?" the doctor spoke. "We are ready."

"I just can't do this. I don't want to do this," she said as the staff looked on. Sarah wanted Em's departure to be natural, not something she controlled. It was too confusing for her to decide whether to allow the dog to suffer for hours while waiting for the surgeon, or put her down and relieve her pain. Adding to her stress, Sarah did not have five thousand dollars to pay. If the surgery had a low success rate, it would be for nothing.

Em looked at her mommy with unconditional love. Sarah would have traded places if she could. The pain was too much to bear. She gripped herself and nodded with acceptance for the staff to proceed with euthanizing. *Euthanize means a good death in Greek,* she remembered from college. It was a pleasing thought in the moment, but it did not ease her agony.

A doctor with no bedside manner asked Sarah to step back into the waiting room while they administered the lethal injection. He was not the veterinarian who had told her to pray the last time she was in. "It's better that way, ma'am," he said.

"No way! Take her out of that cage and let me hold her!" Sarah demanded.

"We do not want to take the dog out of the oxygen chamber. It will only excite her more, and her airways will constrict completely."

"Really? She's going to die anyway! I am going to hold her in my arms or I bring her home! She needs to feel my love. Take her out of there and give her to me, now!"

Em seemed to grin from ear to ear as a nurse pulled her weakened body from the chamber and placed her in the arms of her mother. Her excited spirit filled Sarah's entire being in a bath of pure love. Sarah felt every convulsion of Em's body each time she coughed from desperately trying to inhale. The nurses allowed the pair less than a minute of time together before suggesting they proceed with the injection. Em was suffocating.

Sarah could not breathe from sobbing so hard. The lights of the treatment room became diffused – like raindrops through a bedroom window on a stormy night. Nothing existed at that moment – no doctors, nurses, or clanging of medical utensils on cold steel tabletops – just Em and the heartbreaking feeling of loss.

A faceless nurse gestured that she would inject Em's leg with a dose of pentobarbital after she first administered an extremely strong dose of sedative to put her to sleep. "It will be very quick," she said.

Sarah stood staring at the vinyl floor with her nose buried in Em's fur. And then – the coughing ceased. The nurse had injected the dog's leg once and then again with the lethal dose. There was no turning back. Sarah could not swallow. Her swollen eyes could not focus, and she felt like fainting. Em's body was still. "I do not want to let her go. I need to sit with her."

Staff gently guided Sarah to a grieving room with couches and a water dispenser. "Take all the time you want, Miss Gallus," the doctor whispered.

Sarah clutched Em's body – as if it were her bed pillow – and continued sobbing. She gently lowered herself onto the cold sofa and reflected on the short span of time in which Em had graced her life. As she cradled the baby in her right arm, Sarah reached into her left pants pocket in hopes of finding a tissue to blot her eyes. Instead, she felt Em's sedatives that she had shoved in there earlier. They rolled around in her hand. She thought about taking all of them as she glanced at the water jug standing in the corner of the room. Sarah was at a tipping point, with no relief in sight. There was no one to come home to now – no one to snuggle with in bed. She was all alone. "I could be with you right now, my little Emmy."

The room was chilly. Em's white fur blew back and forth with the cold current flowing out of the air conditioner vent above their heads. It was soothing in a way. The breeze dried up the tears that had made salty tracks down Sarah's reddened cheeks.

A whispered voice suggested to let go of the medication. Its source was unknown, yet Sarah did not question it.

The pills began to dissolve in her sweaty palm. She released them into her pocket and wiped the residue on the outside of her pants. "I'm wrong, Em. I don't think taking my life is the right thing to do. I will see you – someday. Wait for me."

Chapter 22

WITH EVERY SECRET THING

In the days that crept by after Em's passing, Sarah grew angrier. Denial and isolation ran their courses through her grieving process. She had not talked to anyone and took time off from work. In a way, she became a recluse, experiencing a temporary bout of madness. She was harboring a feeling of wrath, but it was not targeted toward Robbie, Stuart, the fire, or Em's untimely death. Sarah's fury was aimed directly at God.

It was early in the morning, and no one was at the beach. She headed in that direction and brought her camera along. There was a host of emotions to unload, and she intended to do it through the lens. The pent-up pressure inside her heart was about to explode. She grabbed an old towel from her car and found a secluded area on the sand. After she settled into her spot, she stared longingly at the sea. Wave after powerful wave banged against the shoreline, tossing splatters of salty water into the air. The smell of brine was hypnotic.

A squawking seagull flew overhead, breaking her trance. She aimed her camera and snapped a shot of its underbelly. Exposing her face to the sunlight, Sarah began to sob. Screams scored the lining of her throat as she took to her knees and shook her fist at the sky. "Why? she shouted. "Why have You caused all this sorrow in my life? Do You not want me to love? Do You not want me to be happy?" Sarah's teeth clenched. "And worst of all? You took my only friend – my unconditional love," the accusations continued. Sarah let loose on God.

The sea raged. The waves crashed louder – and the sky darkened.

"Let Your bolts of lightning strike me dead!" she screamed. "I cannot take it anymore! I don't feel loved by You. I'm constantly let down," she spoke in a softer voice. "My relationships fail. You set fire to my neighborhood, and You took Richard and my parents. What more do You want?" Her body trembled.

Sarah was living a hell on Earth.

A sharp pain in her abdomen caused her body to double over. Her limp figure slumped down onto the sandy towel. She muttered a final blow which trickled out of her weakened mouth, like the last few drops in a soldier's water canteen. "I will never have faith. You do not exist."

Stillness filled the air. The atmosphere had no substance. No gulls cried. No cars could be heard driving along the beach road, and even the ocean's thunderous roar was silent. It felt like nothing was living – including Sarah.

However – God was listening and watching.

Sarah was exhausted. She curled up on the earth beneath her and imagined Richard. The thought of him infuriated her. It was because of him that she had gotten involved with Stuart and Robbie. She felt cursed – cursed for not resuming their love affair when he begged her to come back to him, even though it would have been a mistake. *Are you getting revenge on me from the grave?* she wondered. *Are you conspiring with God, up there, Richard – if He's up there? I hope you're happy now.* All of her muscles suddenly relaxed.

The sunshine returned and the sound of the waves grew louder. Sarah pulled her camera to her eye and aimed at the ocean. She desperately wanted her mind on something else. The spray from the waves reached several feet into the air. Slowing down the shutter speed on her device, she shot at the scene – capturing the tiny, individual water droplets that flew upward with each wave. A pod of pelicans entered her line of vision from the north and surfed the wind over the water. Their undulating rises and descents over the swell were fascinating. It was peaceful to witness the group, which she was able to get entirely in the frame.

The beautiful moment was interrupted by a text message from Robbie. *What's up?*

Sarah was annoyed by the distraction and snickered with contempt. Her texted reaction was abrupt, but genuine. *My dog is dead. That's what's up.*

I'm sorry, Robbie replied. *Come over. I'll make you dinner.* There was no sincerity in his words, nor his intentions. Sarah sensed the power he held over her. Once again, he offered nice gestures, but they were always to his benefit.

You want ME to drive to YOU? she texted.

Yes, I've got to stay home and get some laundry done. Apparently, he did not sense her frustration, and the response was a virtual slug to Sarah's gut.

Is this an attempt at sex, and is he using Em's death as a reason? she thought. Despite knowing how cold and emotionless Robbie could be, Sarah still engaged in a dialogue. With every new encounter, she hoped he would change for the better. Her fingers frantically typed a response filled with bitterness, *Shouldn't YOU come to ME, given the situation?* But all was lost through the delivery of tiny letters on a white digital screen. At that point, the texting ceased for both parties.

Sarah closed her eyes and dreamt about walking into the water to drown herself. Fading away and being forgotten would be her only relief. But she snapped out of the dangerous daydream when she heard tourists and locals filtering into the area where she sat. They began to pop up tents and umbrellas. It was time for Sarah to leave – now that her solitude was invaded. Shaking the sand off her towel, she gathered her belongings and drove home. She had said her peace.

As Sarah pulled her car into the garage, her memory lapsed. She got out and quickly shut the overhead door before entering the attached hallway. "Mommy's home, Emmy!" she shouted into the empty apartment. There was no barking and no coughing – no pitter-patter of claws on the entryway tile. She soon realized that Em was not there.

The faucet knob in the bathroom was her only support as she leaned over the sink to weep and wash her face. Cupping her left hand, she gathered a pool of the cold, rushing water and splashed her salty cheeks. The sensation felt refreshing, yet it shocked her system when it made contact with her flushed, warm skin. Sarah peered into the mirror. There in the glass, once again, was an unrecognizable face. The once bright, jade flecks in her eyes were now dull and faded.

Ding! Ding! Ding! Ding! The front doorbell sounded off, like a warning alarm on a sinking ship. Sarah whipped the towel off the bar and wiped her eyes firmly. *I'm not expecting anyone,* she thought. *Who could it be?* As she ran for the door, she plucked a brush from the countertop and ripped through her wavy strands of hair. She hoped to look somewhat presentable for whomever was waiting on the other side. Her stomach knotted instantly when she looked through the window and slowly pulled the door open.

Standing there – with a stuffed animal in his clutch – was Robbie. "I'm here! And I brought food!" Robbie's right leg lunged forward over the threshold and inside the apartment. The stuffed toy shot out from under his arm, like a cannonball in a cheesy carnival act. "This is for you. I'm sorry you lost your pooch. Hopefully, it will cheer you up." In his other hand, a couple of sandwiches from the local deli.

Sarah was perplexed. "Um – thank you." Tears welled in her eyes as she squeezed the toy's furry sides and bent in to kiss its head. The smell of plush, synthetic material was no match for the sweet, warm scent of her beloved Em. Sarah turned her face away from Robbie and sobbed by the front door.

He walked into the living room and hardly noticed that she had not followed behind him. Plopping himself down on the couch, he pushed papers and mail to one side of the coffee table. The bag of food was unfurled. "Come eat!" he demanded.

Sarah wiped the tears away with her shirt sleeve and shut the front door. She said nothing and walked to her bedroom, placing the stuffed animal on her dresser top. It was a light brown, roly-poly dog with long floppy ears and a little pink tongue that hung out of its mouth. She stared at it for a moment, then returned to the living room. "He's really cute," she remarked.

"I thought you would like it," Robbie said. "I tried to find a white one, but there wasn't much time."

Sarah smiled. The aroma of ham and cheese on fresh, baked bread filled the room. She thought it might boost her appetite. The bites would be slow going down, but she needed to eat something to keep up her strength. She ate what she could, but soon her thoughts weakened her hunger. Robbie devoured his sandwich quickly. When he was done, he leaned toward Sarah to show some affection by kissing her neck. She tried to chew and swallow a small bite of her food, but he made it difficult.

"I don't know what's going on," said Sarah.

Robbie's kisses stopped. He sat back in place on the couch. "What are you referring to, darling?"

"I'm confused. Do we have a relationship – or not? You're interested, you're not interested – hot and cold. I'm in a spin."

"Let's go to bed."

Not again with the diversion of sex! Why can't you answer questions? Sarah thought. She had hoped he would say something worthwhile – something about *them,* or even about the loss of Em. Her energy was drained and she was in no mood to have a meaningless romp. She knew if she said anything more, he would get upset.

Sarah stood up and quietly lifted the dishes off the table and took them to the sink. Robbie followed behind her, throwing away their garbage. They found themselves toe to toe in the middle of the small kitchen. He studied her face, looking for any kind of response to his *bed* suggestion. Sarah's mouth remained shut. Her body was rigid. She did not want him there, but his control over her was too strong. He rolled his hand around her small waist and bent in to kiss her again. The experience rendered no passion for Sarah, but she allowed it to happen. She was led out of the kitchen and down the hallway, all the while resenting every step she took closer to her bed.

The room was dark. She opened the drawn curtains to the white and yellow glow of the midday sun. Forces beyond her control enticed her to keep going. She was stuck in the moment and lacked the strength to turn back.

Robbie removed his shirt and slithered into her bed to face the ceiling. Sarah remained clothed and got under the sheet. There was no movement from Robbie's body – aside from his mouth. "I'm going to take my nephew out hunting next weekend," he said randomly. "We are going to look for birds."

"You're hunting birds? What kind?"

"Doves," Robbie answered, in a chilly, matter-of-fact tone.

Sarah was quiet as the pair lied face up. Her mind raced with all kinds of questions. She remembered him mentioning doves the first night they met at the restaurant. "Do you eat them?" Sarah asked softly. "Why would you kill something so lovely as a dove?"

Robbie's body was stiff, and his words were almost robotic. "Some people eat them. But I want my nephew to know what it means to lose love," he said then turned to face Sarah. "Doves mate for life."

"Yes, you told me that," she replied and became even more confused. A strange sensation passed through her body. It was not necessarily a feeling of fear, but it was eerie. It was like Robbie had changed to someone else – a dark *someone else* who wanted Sarah to know what he was really like. "What are you trying to teach him?" she asked.

Robbie turned his head to look back at the ceiling. "I want him to kill a dove's mate, so he can witness how the surviving bird reacts to the loss. It's important for him to know what it feels like to lose something precious." The words he spoke were concerning and so was the emotionless tone in which he delivered them.

Sarah was silent – and revolted. *Is he trying to be manly?* she wondered. *Had he lost someone dear to him and wanted to prepare the boy for a similar life-blow? Or is he just trying to scare me away?* His theory was so bizarre that she could not find any words to follow up to it. She felt mentally abused.

Clouds moved over the sun and the room darkened. Robbie turned on his right side – away from Sarah – to show her that he wanted comfort. Instinctively, she reached for his bare back and began to slowly rub his tanned skin.

"That feels good," said Robbie. "My grandmother used to stroke me like that."

Huh? What the heck did he mean by that? she wondered.

Robbie seemed to be getting creepier. Sarah then realized he had turned the focus onto him. His visit should have been about comforting *her. Why would he tell his lover that his grandmother used to stroke him in the same way? And why would his grandmother touch him like that? Was it intimately or lovingly?* *Was he abused?* Sarah silently questioned. *Maybe that* is the reason he said he hated old people.

They both faced the mirrored closet doors. As she continued to touch his skin, she was able to look past Robbie's head at their reflection in the glass. He was looking right at her with cold, dark eyes. She quickly released her hand from his back and turned away. Sarah wanted to jump off the mattress, but she remained calm. There was no telling what he might do. A nonchalant kiss on his shoulder gave him the impression that she felt no fear. She rolled over to face the other side of the room and Robbie fell asleep.

Sarah tried to rest while her mind raced. *What kind of past has he had?* she wondered. *I think I've met his demons.* She opened her eyes and scanned the dimly lit room. The stuffed toy she had placed on the dresser caught her attention. A beam of light from the window cast a glow on the dog's face. She felt an icy chill run through her veins. The animal – was staring back.

Chapter 23

FESTIVAL OF HORNS

Killing doves, killing enemies, his grandmother touching him – it was not just *what* Robbie said to Sarah that creeped her out; it was the *way* he told these stories that sent a shiver through her spine. The tone in his voice was always low and contemplative. She was convinced these were the demons he spoke about that day at the beach. Things were getting too weird for Sarah, and she wanted nothing more than a friendship with Robbie now. Despite her physical attraction, she no longer desired him. She feared to turn any more pages in his untold story, but out of curiosity, she was compelled to read the next chapter.

Not much was said on the morning after their day of submarine sandwiches and spooky stares. The pair parted with kisses on each other's cheeks and the exchange of smug smiles. No texts. No calls. Weeks passed with no dance-club outings or movie nights at Stuart's. Altogether, activities ceased.

Sarah thought about the getaway to Castle Dome and how awkward it could potentially be with the guys. The three had lived like a layered cookie – sweet, but separable. Her gut was telling her the adventure to the desert might not be the best idea. It was a long way to go just to hang out with people she barely knew – or even liked.

In the past, Sarah never worried much when she traveled to faraway places for her job. Sometimes clients hired her to take pictures of people in third world countries or sharks at remote islands in the Pacific. She loved putting herself out there in the face of diversity or danger. However, the thought of being in the middle of nowhere with Robbie, scared her. But despite her apprehension, she convinced herself to plan on the trip.

Saturday arrived and Sarah had nothing to do. She figured Robbie and Stuart had been getting together on their own without her. There was no expectation to hear from them. Not even Stuart followed up with a text or call after her sojourn at his apartment. The stack of mail that Robbie had pushed to the side of the coffee table – weeks ago – had not moved. Sarah decided to sift through the pile. Piece by piece, she separated the junk from the bills. A colorful one-page flyer advertising *Festival of Horns* stood out. The event was a free, three-day affair that took place annually in Seal Beach. It attracted a large crowd with several bands lined up to play the entire weekend. Given that it was so close to her home, Sarah considered attending. She read further and noticed it was happening – now. *Well, this sounds fun!* she thought. *It should definitely get my mind off of things.*

Sarah sprung off the couch, ran to her bedroom, and threw on a new sundress and pair of sandals. She was ready to be distracted – and cheered up. The combination of music, drinking, new people, and sunshine was a perfect remedy. Out the door she went.

While at a stop light, Sarah applied sunscreen. The smell of coconut filled her car, reminding her of those beach days with Robbie and Stuart. A smile drew across her face, but only briefly. "No Robbie. Not today," she said out loud, and sped down the highway.

The booze corral, inside *Festival of Horns*, was outlined with bright orange barricades and filled with shirtless, tanned men and bikini-clad women. Sarah felt slightly overdressed and a little nervous to be there alone. Maybe no one would notice, since the crowd was so thick. People were sandwiched in so tightly, but the anonymity was comforting. She shimmied in line to get a cup of cheap wine and prepared to find an observation spot to watch the bands.

"Sarah!" a voice suddenly rang out amidst the chatter of all the drunks.

She looked in the direction of the voice. Baseball caps, floppy hats, and raised, red cups were all she could see.

"Sarah!" the voice sounded off again. "Over here!"

Still, she could not find the source. Then, a set of wet fingers that had been clutching a cold beer, grabbed her arm from behind. They felt familiar with their slightly calloused tips. She laughed – having faced the wrong direction – and turned to see to whom the voice belonged.

"Sarah, what are you doing here?" It was Stuart, donning an ear-to-ear grin. "Did you come by yourself?"

"Yeah," she replied shyly.

"Well, glad you came out. I thought about asking you, but Robbie told me that Em died, so I left you alone to grieve. Are you ok?"

"Yes, I'm fine, but it would've been nice to hear from you, Stuart. It's been several weeks." *What else had Robbie told him?* she wondered.

"I'm so sorry. I've been busy. But *you* could've called *me*, you know!"

"I see," she whimpered.

Stuart had always been there for her when it came to Em. Something had changed in him. Maybe he was hanging out with other friends – or women. He was not alone. His entourage appeared. Introductions to his unfamiliar acquaintances happened so fast that she had no time to be upset. A shorter man with glasses and a thin mustache stood at Stuart's left side. He held a red cup filled to the rim with frothy beer. "Meet a friend of mine," Stuart gestured.

"Hi," Sarah said, offering her hand.

"Hey, how's it going? Nice to meet you, Sarah, I'm Wesley. I work with Mark."

They shook hands, and Stuart proceeded to introduce her to two other guys he had met recently. They were more interested in the bikini-wearing barmaids than they were in meeting Sarah. Both nodded to acknowledge her while staring at the girls. She was fine with it. Her curiosity was on Wesley, anyway. They continued their small talk, and Stuart ran off with the newbies to get more beer.

"How do you know Stuart, Wesley?"

"Oh, I met him a few times when he came over to Mark and Amy's house to visit. I've been doing carpentry work with Mark – over the last year, I'd say." Wesley was not particularly handsome, and his face was scarred from sun damage. His receding hairline aged him, but his sweet and comforting disposition was attractive. "That's a pretty dress, Sarah," he said.

"Thanks, I only found out about this event this morning. I'm glad I decided to come."

"Well, then our meeting was meant to be. Hey, did you know your mouth curls up when you smile?" he said playfully. "It's cute."

Sarah giggled and bashfully looked down at her feet. It was refreshing to hear wholesome, genuine compliments – without sarcasm. Wesley was a pleasant distraction from thoughts of Robbie. His kind words delighted her. Anyone observing the two in conversation could tell he was smitten. He had no trouble making her beautiful smile appear again and again.

After several minutes, Stuart finally returned with the others. Each of them carried two beers. They enjoyed their brews while observing the crowd, which ebbed and flowed like the ocean. Jazz bands rotated, taking turns on the stage. The many bodies – within the corral – watched and listened. Some were too intoxicated to notice the music and continued to be mesmerized by the flow of alcohol.

Then, like a slow-motion video, everything around Sarah barely moved. The atmosphere changed with the impending storm. Among the faceless drinkers, appeared the man she had gone there to forget. Robbie had arrived. "Oh, God. Did he have to ruin my day?" she muttered under her breath.

Wesley noticed that Sarah's smile turned into a frown. He followed her eyes to the encroaching mood-killer. It took him a few seconds to study the man. He could size up a *bad boy* when he saw one. Wesley pegged Robbie as just that – bad news.

Robbie locked eyes on Sarah for only three seconds – until he saw Stuart. However, he did not fail to notice she had been engaging in a conversation with another man. Just like the first day they had met, Robbie's chest puffed up – like a pigeon's – at the sight of her. "Stuey!" Robbie yelled with amusement.

"Hey, bud," Stuart said.

Robbie was elated to see his pal. He nodded to Stuart and the other two men, since he could not shake their beer-filled hands. "Hi, I'm Rob, Stuey's friend." He smiled and approached Sarah, bending over to kiss her cheek. "Hey, I saw your car down the street. What brought you out of your lair? Did you come with someone? I see you're drinking already." His interrogation was meant to put Wesley on edge, but instead, exuded with jealousy.

Sarah uncomfortably delighted in the attention. "I just wanted to get out and have some fun. And, no, I came alone. But I have now met new friends, right Wesley?"

"Your name is Nesley?" asked Robbie. "I'm surprised we've never met?"

"No. It's *Wesley*," Sarah sparked. "He works with Mark."

Robbie offered his hand to Sarah's new friend. "Hey Wes, how's it going?"

"Great! Can I buy you a beer?"

"No dude, I can get my own brew. But thanks, man." Robbie's machismo was on overdrive.

Wesley was no fool. He sensed the two shared something together at one time, but he was determined not to give up on Sarah. "Would you like more wine, love?"

"Absolutely! Thank you, Wesley."

Robbie seized the opportunity to pounce on Sarah while Wesley was at the bar. Seeing her with other men challenged his ego. The flirtatious play to conquer the woman – was back on. "You look sexy as hell. I would have gotten you something, but your Neanderthal butler beat me to it.

"Do you have anything nice to say about anyone?" Sarah chirped.

"Yes – you."

Sarah ignored Robbie and tapped her foot to the beat. She was buzzed and did not want to engage anymore with him. She looked over her shoulder every minute for Wesley to return. He was taking a while. The band played. She tried to push the past out of her head with the distraction of the music, but the dizzying present kept spinning around her.

"Maybe your new friend met someone at the bar," he joked.

"Are you jealous that I'm talking with another guy, Robbie?"

"Bah ha ha ha – me? Jealous? You can talk and drink with whomever you like, my dear. But you don't seriously have the hots for this guy, do you?"

Sarah only shook her head and grinned. It was obvious to her that Robbie was worried. He had not even started drinking, and he was already bouncing from the adrenaline rush of seeing her.

"Here we go, darling," Wesley interrupted the pair.

"We can talk later, honey," Robbie said and turned to join Stuart, standing six feet away.

Wesley could read Robbie well. He was a wise and intuitive man who knew exactly what the *bad boy* was up to. And he could see that Sarah wanted nothing more of her old flame. She thanked Wesley for the wine and continued her chit-chat. It was a refreshing change to have someone desire to be with her and interested in what she had to say.

Meanwhile, Stuart peered over his cup and observed the scene. "Looks like Sarah has found a new *boo*," he poked at his friend.

Robbie sneered, furrowed his brow, and became increasingly agitated. Both men watched Sarah with concern. She could see out of the corner of her eye that the two men were staring at her. There was obvious contempt for the intruder; it was written on their faces. It pleased her to know that the guys were worried about losing their playmate to another man.

"You coming with us to Castle Dome, Wesley?" Stuart pierced the air with the impromptu invitation.

Robbie gave Stuart a look of disgust. His eyes bugged open with an expression meant to stop any more words from exiting Stuart's mouth. He did not want Wesley cramping his style. The less competitive men joining in on their vacation, the better. Stuart just laughed at Robbie.

"Yes, Mark asked me to go, so I think I will. Should be fun," Wesley shouted back.

A big smile stretched across Sarah's face. Robbie winced when he realized her grin was meant for Wesley. He elbowed his way over to inquire about the trip.

"Did you know about Castle Dome, Sarah?" Stuart interrupted.

"Yes, from Amy. Seems like I wasn't going to get an invitation from either of *you*."

"We just hadn't thought of it yet," he said.

"You're probably not into desert camping, are you – on Friday the thirteenth?" Robbie asked.

"Very into it, but I wasn't aware it was going to be Friday the thirteenth," Sarah responded. "Oh, well – should be fun." Any prior doubt she had of going to Castle Dome was gone – now that she had Wesley to play with and Robbie to make squirm.

At that moment, all three men reacted to the single woman's answer, differently. Wesley was excited. His eyebrows raised, and a crooked smile creased his cratered face. Stuart was relieved and content. He was happy to have the company to share laughs. Robbie was Robbie. It might be exciting to have Sarah along, but he was not sure the desert was the right place for her on such a superstitious weekend.

Robbie chugged his beer while he watched Wesley, then contemplated his next move with Sarah. "I think you should drive me and Stuart out to the desert in your convertible," he insisted. "We'll pitch in for gas."

Wesley shook his head and snickered at being left out of Robbie's transportation plans. They all stared at Sarah, awaiting her response.

"Sure. I'm ok with that," she said innocently and sipped her wine.

Everyone pondered the desert trip. The vastness of the uninhabited land they would travel across beckoned Sarah to expand her mind. It would be an adventure. She was a curious cat entering the unknown to hang out with several men that found her attractive. There was little resistance; an unstoppable force was pulling her.

Chapter 24

INTO THE WILDERNESS

Time had flown by since Sarah hung out at the festival with all the guys. She was proud of herself for leaving – alone. Now that the travel day had finally arrived, the focus was on the road. She was thrilled that Robbie had volunteered her to be the driver to Castle Dome Landing in Roka Valley. It was better for her to be in control of the transportation.

Sarah's attention shifted to Robbie's advances. She tried to remain stoic. She was not about to cozy up to him in the car. He still desired her in some twisted way; getting her to drive was his way of keeping tabs on her. He was not going to allow anyone else to slither into his place, especially while he was still around.

He squeezed her thigh twice and said, "Thankfully, Wesley drove his own vehicle. There is no room in this car for another man. That moose behind us is folded up as it is."

Sarah giggled at his analogy of Stuart, who was sleeping in the back seat.

"We're almost there, babe," Robbie whispered. "Can't wait to get you wet on the jet skis."

Sarah gently smiled and stared at the road. Signs for Castle Dome started popping up. Robbie loved visiting the place with his friends. He always had fun on the trips, but his emotions were never put to a test – like this adventure would do.

"So, what's up with that Wesley guy, anyway? Have you been seeing him?"

Sarah was caught off guard. She suddenly felt uncomfortable, as if she were being accused of cheating on a man with whom she had no involvement anymore. "Why do you ask?"

"I just think you like him, that's all."

Stuart woke up just in time to hear Sarah's response.

"Robbie, I haven't talked with him since *Festival of Horns*. That was weeks ago. And why is it your business?"

"Hmm – you both were quite cozy in the beer corral," Robbie continued.

"Oh, so now you care when another man shows me attention? Classic."

Stuart realized the pair must have been talking about Wesley. He quietly kept his head down and continued to eavesdrop on the conversation.

"Listen, I just think you could do better. You're out of his league."

"You're playing head games with me, Robbie. I've had enough."

"I need a drink!" Robbie huffed and turned to gander at the view out his window.

They had entered Roka Valley. They took a turn onto a dirt road after seeing a sign that read, *Castle Dome Landing – Up Ahead*. Old, wooden structures appeared along their path.

"Look at that saloon!" she shouted. "The sign says, *Museum*. I'd love to go there."

Robbie ignored Sarah's plea and directed her to turn. "Make a left at that sign that says, *River Access*."

The camp was getting closer. Another dirt road led them away from the ghost town and toward their destination.

Stuart pretended to awaken. "Good morning, sunshines! Did someone say *saloooon?*"

"Ha, Stuart! That means *al-kee-hol*. But since that one is now a museum, it's sure to be dry as a bone," laughed Robbie.

"If it's a ghost town, this whole place is a valley of dry bones," Stuart snickered.

"Ok, you guys, we don't have to visit the saloon – but focus. Tell me where I'm going."

"Hold on a sec. I'll get the address." Stuart wiped his eyes and fumbled through his wallet in search of a scrap piece of paper with a handwritten description of the camp.

Sarah saw several clusters of mailboxes come into view. "Is there a number or something we should be looking for?"

"We are staying at a different house this time, so I'm not sure exactly where it is," Robbie piped up.

There were several homes along the river's edge. None had house numbers. However, the mailboxes did. "This place is so far off the main road," Sarah added. "What mail carrier would travel way out here just to make a delivery? It's kind-of scary."

"It says on my note to look for the group of mailboxes with number seven," said Stuart. "The house is beige with Mexican tiles on the roof, and it has a gravel driveway. There's a patinaed copper star on the front, above the doorway. Do you see that anywhere?"

"No, but I found mailbox number seven!" shouted Sarah. Throughout Roka Valley, there was a mixture of vacation rentals, residences, and rickety shacks with outhouses. Judging by Stuart's description, it sounded like a regular stick-built home. Sarah hoped.

"Maybe we just count them," Stuart suggested.

"Yeah! I think I get it," Sarah's eyebrows raised. "It must be the seventh house in from that particular cluster of mailboxes."

The camps were spaced very far apart. It took thirty seconds at a slow pace to pass just one of the homes. Sarah looked ahead and counted to seven on her right, pointing to each structure along the way. They kept their necks stretched and their eyes peeled. She sped up.

"There's the star!" shouted Robbie. "I guess we could've just looked for that."

Sarah giggled to cover up a rush of nervousness. His announcement meant that their experience at the desert had begun. She pulled into the rocky driveway and observed everything that was taking place on the grounds. No humans were in sight yet. She parked, shut off the engine, and popped the trunk.

"Let me out!" Robbie said excitedly.

"Yes! I think arthritis has set in to my joints back here," joked Stuart.

The two men jumped out and grabbed their bags – some from the trunk – and walked briskly toward the sound of revelers. Sarah hung back, taking time to roll up the windows and tidy up the car's interior.

"Find us when you're done, Sarah!" Stuart shouted over his shoulder.

"Yeah, thanks – a lot." Her sarcasm, implying that they wait for her, went unnoticed. She cocked her head to one side and peered up at the house through her front windshield.

The older, two-story home looked like a cool place to stay. It seemed clean and well kept, but it had a spooky vibe. There were tall, saguaro cactuses along the outside walls and large boulders guarding each side of the entrance. It was not a fancy house, but it was not a shack, either. The home was humble.

Sarah got out of the car, stretched, and gathered up her bags and cooler. The air was dry and still. She walked around one side of the house to look for her companions. They were nowhere in sight. The path to the backyard twisted and turned around several large succulents. She heard voices. The conversations changed to laughter and blended with the sloshing sound of water. A wake from passing boats created a violent flow of ripples that knocked against a boat landing. Everything started to come into view; she had reached the river.

"Ahh! Sarah, so glad you made it !" Amy greeted. "Welcome to Roka Valley and Castle Dome Landing. Wasn't the scenery awesome driving in here?"

"Yeah, it's far out," she laughed sarcastically.

"Hey, you're here! Hungry?" Mark added as he continued to cook a batch of hamburger patties and hotdogs.

"Very!" Sarah gave Mark a big hug and then backed away from the grill. She looked around for the guys. As the white, smoky cloud temporarily blew in the opposite direction, Stuart and Robbie came into sight – along with a group of teenagers. Two of the kids were Mark and Amy's sons. They both brought their girlfriends. Strangely, the idea of younger people at the camp made Sarah feel safe. "I think we smelled your burgers cooking on our way here, Mark."

"You haven't tasted a piece of Heaven until you eat my meat," he said. "Oh, that came out wrong."

Everyone laughed awkwardly and lined up to get their share.

"I'm starving!" exclaimed Stuart. "I'm downing a couple of dogs; then I'm hitting the water!"

"That's what we'll *all* be doing. Do you see that boat over there?" Mark pointed. "That's my new baby."

"Nice one!" said Stuart as he looked over his shoulder to the dock. "That will get us around faster than that dinghy you used to have."

"Sure will!"

"Congrats! Can't wait to get in it," said Robbie.

Mark finished charring the food and distributed the offerings to the group. Meanwhile, Amy passed out small cups of a refreshingly strong, spiked punch.

Suddenly, a loud slam from the door of a truck perked up their ears. About fifteen seconds later, a familiar, gruffy voice boomed from inside the house and traveled out through the open kitchen. "Hey, I'm here!" the voice announced. "Anybody home? Must be – I smell Mark's cooking!"

Sarah lit up when she saw Wesley waltzing out of the sliding glass door with a six pack of canned beer and a large bag of potato chips. She knew nothing about this man, yet she felt at home in his presence and relieved that he was going to be hanging out with them the entire weekend.

"You're right on time," Stuart piped up and handed Wesley a hotdog. "Welcome to *the river*."

Stuart was always so cordial. Although he felt uneasy about the competitor hopping onto the scene, he knew it was best to keep things friendly rather than show any kind of jealousy. And knowing that Wesley was the topic of Sarah and Robbie's quarrel in the car, he wanted no tension, especially so soon – on *his* vacation.

"Thanks, man," Wesley grinned and nodded a greeting to the rest of the group, stopping at Sarah. "Hi Sarah, nice to see you again."

She smiled and raised her drink to welcome him.

Stuart's peace offering stunned an unsuspecting Robbie, who was devouring a burger by the water's edge. He gestured a greeting to Wesley with a tilt of his head. "Friday the thirteenth, Stu," Robbie mumbled while he walked toward his friend. "Mercury in retrograde is going to wreak havoc this weekend. I can tell already."

Stuart rolled his eyes at Robbie and brushed off his comment. His attention was on the incoming guests. The beer and chips were not all that Wesley had brought to the party.

"Hi everybody!" came a high-pitched, shrill voice from the direction of the kitchen.

"Who the hell is that?" Sarah whispered to herself, as a petite, scrawny, redheaded female poked her face out of the sliding glass door and skipped onto the patio. Sarah's happy mood was immediately squelched. The young woman was not terribly beautiful, but she had a dizzy, carefree demeanor that was inviting to the men.

"Everyone, meet Steffi," Wesley said. "She's an old friend."

Steffi bounced from person to person, giggling and shaking their hands. At the mention of the word *friend,* Sarah concluded that there was – most likely – nothing going on between the two of them. She shook the girl's hand and guzzled her punch.

Out of the shadows, came a rapidly approaching Robbie. "Hi, I'm Rob!"

"Well, hi there, handsome," Steffi flirted. "I think this is going to be a fun weekend!"

"That it is!" said Robbie, ogling the new girl.

You have got to be kidding me. Sarah thought and gulped down the rest of her punch. *He is going to seduce her right here.*

Robbie's behavior was ridiculously playful. He was not at all arrogant and tough like he acted when he first met Sarah. Steffi batted her eyes at the tall, dark-haired man as the rest of the group looked on. How quickly he had changed from being flirtatious with Sarah to overtly and grotesquely coquettish with Steffi. He was so blatantly obvious with his instant interest in the woman, that even Stuart thought it was odd and a little annoying.

"Another drink, Sarah?"

"Yes! Thanks Stuart."

Stuart smiled genuinely and fetched her a cold bottle of beer from a nearby cooler. He handed it off, along with a gentle nod. "Stick with me, honey. We're going to have a blast."

Sarah smiled in appreciation and chugged.

After all appetites were satisfied with enough grilled food, Mark instructed everyone to find a life jacket and get into the boat. Those who were not already in their bathing suits took a moment to change.

"I think I'll get on one of the jet skis," Robbie declared. "Steffi! Ride with me!"

Sarah was shocked. *What a jerk. He told me he wanted to ride on the jet ski with* me*!* She had been replaced.

Robbie ran inside to throw on his trunks. On his way out, he put on a vest – leaving it unbuckled – and motioned for Steffi to get on board. "Sit your little ass behind me cutie and let's ride."

Steffi grabbed onto Robbie's arm to balance herself while she threw one leg across the seat and pressed her body against his. The redhead tossed her hair over one shoulder, hitting him in the face. They both laughed when he reached his arm around her butt to make sure she was seated securely. The pair took off and left the others behind.

Everyone, but the teens, boarded the twenty-foot boat. The two boys and their girlfriends paired up and took off on the other jet skis behind Robbie.

"We are ready to rock and roll, Mark!" Stuart called out in an effort to get the boat started. The sooner they reached their destination, the sooner he and Sarah could drink more alcohol.

Mark revved up the engine and slowly motored out of the narrow passageway.

"Wesley, are you ok with Steffi going on the jet ski?" Sarah asked.

"Sure, why not? She's a big girl. It looks like she's in good hands."

"Well, it's just that – Robbie is kind of a daredevil." Sarah tried to come across as concerned for Steffi.

He knew where Sarah was going with her question. If his friend wanted to *get it on* with some guy, he had no say in the matter. But if Sarah was going to be jealous, Wesley's pursuit would be in vain. "Sarah, where's that smile I love?" he said, changing the subject.

Sarah knew as well that her inquiry was leading. She squinted her eyes in the afternoon sunshine and smiled for him. "Do you play Frisbee, Wesley?"

"I do! Let's play later," he said.

"Man, have I missed *Aye Aye*!" exclaimed Stuart.

Mark raised his fist in the air and laughed under his breath at his friend's nickname of their destination. "Me, too!"

"What's *Aye Aye?*" Sarah asked.

"Ha! A couple of years ago, Mark appropriately named the island we are going to, *Indulgence Island*. Now we refer to it as just *Aye Aye*, because we say *yes* to everything. Right, Captain?"

"I'm your captain, yeah, yeah, yeah, yeah!" sang Mark.

"Off to *Aye Aye*, then!" Sarah raised her beer. She glanced at the wake the boat was creating behind them and marveled at the sunlight dancing on the waves. It was a beautiful day.

Robbie and his plaything – along with the teens – had arrived moments before the boat. The jet skis were tethered to poles, already in place.

Mark was talented at operating the vessel. He idled about ten feet away from the incline of the sandbar and anchored. "Overboard, everyone!" he shouted. "Get out and indulge!"

The group jumped into the three-foot deep water and made their way to shore. Indulging was exactly what everyone wanted to do. A tall and wide tent had been pitched in the wet sand, along with a banquet table covered in more food, plastic cups, coolers of beer, and barrels filled with spiked punch, water, and wine. Sarah's eyes flitted from object to object – person to person. There was a lot to observe.

"A toast," Amy proclaimed and handed everyone shots of tequila, "to *Indulgence Island*!"

"*Aye Aye, cheers!*" they all shouted.

"Sarah! Frisbee?" boomed Stuart.

"You're on!" she said and motioned to Wesley to join them.

"I'm going to drink with Mark, first. I'll be there in a bit," said Wesley.

Sarah nodded. She and Stuart ran off, kicking up wet granules behind their legs. They were both good at the game and could fling the disk far and high. They played for about thirty minutes when Robbie and Steffi ran towards them – holding hands. Their giggles echoed across the surrounding water.

Seriously? This has got to be a joke, Sarah angrily wondered.

Steffi's breasts bounced up and down in her tiny bikini top with every leap she made. "We want to join!" she shouted.

Before Sarah had a chance to take in what was unfolding, Stuart gleefully invited them to play. "Sure!" he responded, and the group exchanged the disk back and forth.

It was apparent that Steffi had never played the game before. With each throw, the disk landed flat in the sand about six feet in front of her. She laughed obnoxiously and Robbie ran to her aid. He moved in behind her, wrapping his hand on the outside of hers to instruct the woman on how to throw. Cradling her arm, he pulled the disk in toward her chest and then pushed it out in slow-motion. He peered at Sarah over his shoulder. She watched them intently. With every demonstration, Robbie roved Steffi's heaving breasts with his eyes. She was so inebriated that she fell limp in his arms. The two gut-laughed together, which caused them both to fall in the sand.

"I'm getting more punch!" Sarah said with disgust. She had seen enough and motioned to Stuart that she wanted him to come with her to the tent for moral support.

"Bring me one, too – or a beer!" Stuart shouted back. He was okay with being Sarah's sounding board or shoulder to cry on – just not when it came to Robbie anymore. He wanted her to get over him.

Sarah was used to being rebuffed, but she never thought Stuart would reject her invitation to get more alcohol. She walked off and said nothing.

The minute Sarah was out of sight, Robbie ended the bantering with Steffi, and the laughter ceased. He picked himself up and brushed off the wet sand. The Frisbee was thrown to Stuart. Steffi was too drunk to notice that she had been tossed aside, as well.

A bit slighted and annoyed, Sarah thought twice about returning to Stuart with a drink. She wanted to appear strong. No man was going to make her feel uncomfortable in front of other people. Instead, she struck up a conversation with Wesley and Mark, who were filling one of the large coolers with booze.

Once Stuart realized that Sarah was not coming back to their game, he stomped off to get a beverage on his own. Robbie and Steffi were left to themselves. "Toss me a beer, will ya, Mark?" Stuart interrupted, sloughing off his frustration and flashing a fake smile to Sarah. He was not about to let *her* mood kill *his*.

Sarah took notice. "Sorry, Stuart. I will try not to blubber about Robbie."

He winked and gulped his beer.

"Sarah, grab a hat and come sit with me in the sunshine," Amy suggested. In a plastic bin, under the table, there were several types of head coverings, including visors and bonnets. Amy thought of everything necessary to keep her friends comfortable. Sarah took out a floppy, wide-brimmed, yellow hat and put it on for fun.

"Cute!" Wesley reacted. He looked Sarah over and smiled. He continued his chat with Mark, but his attention was diverted again when she took off her cover-up. She looked like a dish of rainbow sherbet in her pastel, magenta and peach bikini and over-sized, yellow hat. Wesley wanted a bite. "Sarah, can I get you a drink? You look great," said Wesley.

She blushed at the compliment. "Thanks! Yes, I'll take another punch. Make it a tall one."

"Coming right up!"

"So how do you like the island so far?"

"It's definitely an interesting place – where anything can happen," he winked.

The two flirted until Robbie and his playmate returned to the tent. Steffi immediately began slinging more shots of tequila. While Sarah observed her rival, Robbie assessed the tete-a-tete between her and Wesley. And Stuart watched everyone.

The day of entertainment finished out quickly with the setting sun. Sarah tried to remain mature about what she was witnessing with Robbie and Steffi. There was no way that she was going to let him bring her down with his behavior, inattention, and arrogance. She went to the river to forget him and her troubles, but they were following her whether she liked it or not. If there was one method that would work best to deal with Robbie – it was drinking.

Chapter 25

INDULGENCE ISLAND

Everyone had an exhausting, fun-filled Friday at *Aye Aye*. But it was a new day, and a few aspirins would soon cure their hangovers so they would be ready to start partying again. Nothing could stop the group from taking full advantage of the gorgeous weekend.

Mark got in the shower while Amy prepared a smorgasbord for the groggy house guests. The two were great hosts, making sure everyone was safe, fed, and liquored up. The sound and aroma of sizzling bacon and frying eggs woke the majority, like a glaring yet pleasant alarm clock.

Sarah, who had been sleeping on her blow-up mattress in the game room, was slow to rise. She turned over on her back to extend her entire body when she felt someone beside her. "Good grief! How did you get in my bed, Robbie? And *when* did you get here?"

"Mmmm – good morning, sweetheart." He stretched his arms and let out a big yawn.

Robbie was not there when she went to bed only a few hours before. At that time, she remembered seeing each person head to their respective resting places. Stuart crawled into his sleeping bag under the pool table in the game room. Mark and Amy went to the master bedroom upstairs, and

Wesley went to the spare. Steffi curled up in a downstairs recliner, and the teens sprawled out on the pit sofa in the living room. Robbie was on the patio lounge chair listening to the desert sounds while drinking a beer and smoking a joint.

"I watched you sleep for a bit. Then around three in the morning I realized there was no place to lie down. You had the most space available," he explained.

"How convenient that you forgot to bring a bed."

Robbie smiled devilishly, closed his eyes, and slithered his arm around her back, drawing her closer to his chest.

Normally she would have responded with a delighted and aroused moan of contentment. But the duplicity of Robbie's nature caused her to bristle. "I'm getting up," Sarah muttered. She rolled off the mattress and onto the floor, nearly landing on Stuart's head. He was lying perpendicular to her bed. The lion-like purr – escaping from his throat – reassured her that he was still sleeping.

Robbie reached behind him to retrieve his backpack and pulled out his cellphone and charger, which he plugged into a nearby wall outlet. "No service. I guess we're all off the grid out here – in the middle of nowhere."

Sarah heard him, but ignored his words. Instead, she was off to the bathroom to shower and prepare herself for another day of fun in the sun.

Robbie got up and offered help to Amy. He retrieved two small juice glasses from the cabinet and set them out. Platters filled with scrambled eggs, toast, meats and cheeses lined the kitchen countertops. Amy took pride in the display. One by one, the campers filtered into the big, open dining area and feasted. Robbie lingered around the carafe of juice before filling both glasses – one for himself. The other cup was left on the countertop.

Looking a bit disheveled with his messy hair and crooked eyeglasses, Wesley strolled into the kitchen to greet everyone. The two men laid eyes on each other.

"Good morning, dude," said Robbie, handing Wesley the other glass of juice.

"Thanks man. I need coffee, too."

"You're on your own for that. I don't drink the stuff and don't know how to make it well."

"No problem. I'll find my way around," he smiled. "Thanks for the juice, Rob."

"Yeah, you got it."

Wesley filled his plate and sat down to eat. He watched Robbie get out more glasses from the cabinet. "Another day of Steffi-groping, huh, Robbie?" he mocked under his breath. He knew Steffi could make her own decisions, but he was slightly concerned about Robbie hurting her. He peered at the *player* over his glass and guzzled down the contents.

After getting cleaned up from a nice, warm shower, Sarah joined the group for breakfast. "Morning, Wesley," she spoke softly.

"Good day, Sarah. Ready for another fun one?"

"I'm not sure," she giggled. "Yesterday was a lot to handle. But I'm hoping today is awesome."

"Things should only get better, right?" Wesley remarked.

Robbie exited the kitchen and purposefully turned his back to Sarah. She rolled her eyes and prepared her plate. Still a little hungover and not too loquacious, she ate her breakfast, quickly, and excused herself from the room.

There was beautiful scenery at the back of the camp waiting to be captured by her camera. Sarah climbed to the top of a dune behind the house with the star. It allowed her to view the desert for miles. The town of Castle Dome could be seen in the distance. She considered backtracking to check out the saloon, but did not want to disengage from her friends. However, it *was* the draw of their camping destination. She felt like it would be a shame to miss it. None of the others seemed interested in going, though. "Maybe tomorrow," she mumbled and snapped a few photographs. The scene – although empty and vast – was strangely active. Sarah could sense creatures hiding behind cactuses and under the sand. On the surface, the area seemed dead, but Sarah knew it was filled with so much life.

She went back inside and prepared for the river. Each of the campers, including Stuart, filled their bellies and made small chatter. When they were finished, they marched to the boat in an assembly-line fashion for transportation to *Aye Aye*. They had all taken their painkillers.

Everyone – except the teens, Robbie, and Steffi – found a secure spot on Mark's boat. It was like a repeat of the day before. Robbie helped Steffi with her life vest and perched her onto the jet ski amidst giggles and butt-pinching. The teens hopped on the other crafts and took off toward the sandbar.

The remaining campers were just about ready to head out, when Wesley forgot his sunglasses and jumped off the boat to fetch them from the house. "I'll catch up with you guys," Wesley yelled to the group. "I'll take the fourth ski."

"Ok, see you in a bit," Mark responded and started up the engine.

Sarah missed nothing. Her observation may have been hidden from the group, but she took in every bit of the action happening around her. She and Stuart exchanged glances in acknowledgment of what might be coming down the pike with regards to Robbie and Steffi. She also did not like leaving Wesley alone. The boat puttered out of the marshy distributary and into the main thoroughfare. Mark gunned the engine and sped toward the island.

It was another hot day. The tide receded, exposing more of the river-bed surrounding the sandbar. It stretched for about half a mile, welcoming hundreds of visitors. Mark anchored and each person jumped off. Sarah grabbed a football and helped Amy with a bag of plastic cups and plates. She kept a discreet watchful eye on Robbie, who was tying up the jet ski.

As expected, Robbie picked Steffi up off the seat and let her down gently into the warm water. The muddy river bottom was slimy and slippery. Steffi lost her footing and slid on her rear into the murk. An embarrassed Robbie was dragged down with her as she fell. He noticed Sarah snickering at the entire incident and bent down to kiss Steffi on the mouth. The two made out for only a few seconds, but it was long enough to infuriate Sarah.

She turned away and threw the football in Stuart's direction. "Stuart! Catch!" He quickly reacted and caught her perfect spiral toss.

The other islanders saw their impressive exchange. "Whoa! Way to go, Sarah," they all shouted. "Nice throw!"

"Thanks, guys. I don't think I've ever done that before." She was proud of her toss and loved the compliments, but part of her attention was on her ex.

Robbie perked up at the group's praise of Sarah and let up on his grip of the redhead, who slipped back into the shallow water.

"Hey! What'd ya do that for?" Steffi cried out.

The look on Steffi's face was enough for Sarah to feel slightly vindicated. She smirked and turned to Stuart just in time to catch another slow toss of the football. Robbie paid no attention to the redhead. His eyes were on the game that his friends were playing. He walked farther out onto the sandbar, leaving Steffi behind to get up on her own. The threesome played ball until more of the group joined in.

The morning passed by quickly, and soon it was after noon. Football, Frisbee games, swimming, and drinking kept the partyers very entertained.

Sarah was downing a lot of alcohol. Food would help tomorrow's hangover. She visited the tent to get something to munch on. Surprisingly, no one was there. All of the goodies that Amy and Mark had brought over on the boat were hers for the taking. "Well, this is nice! Wouldn't Wesley just love this smorgasbord?" she said out loud, hoping he would hear. Sarah glanced around. "Oh, no! Where *is* Wesley?"

His jet ski was nowhere to be seen. Wesley had never made it to the island.

Stuart was about twenty yards away, chatting with some girl, when Sarah ran up with the news. "Stuart!" she said breathlessly. "I'm concerned about Wesley. He should've gotten here by now. It's been hours."

"Hey, maybe we can catch up later," Stuart told the stranger and turned to help Sarah. "Let's go talk to Mark and see if he knows anything. Maybe we can take the boat back to the house. Did you look around the area really well?"

"Yes, but do you think he would have gone away from our group? Why would he do that? Plus, I don't see the fourth jet ski."

"I don't know. Maybe he met someone."

Sarah shook her head in disagreement. The two ran to Mark, who was downing another beer and chatting with Amy near the boat. They told them the timeline of when Wesley was last seen.

"I'm sure he's fine, but Stuart, take a ski, and retrace the path to the camp house," Mark advised.

"I'm going, too!" Sarah demanded while Stuart started the engine. She threw on a life jacket, got on the back, and wrapped her arms around him.

"Hang on, sistah!" he said.

Robbie – who had resumed flirting with Steffi – caught a glimpse of his two friends riding out of sight. He approached Mark and Amy. "Where the hell are they going?"

"They were concerned about Wesley not showing up, so they went to look for him."

Robbie snarled with disgust, "Wesley's a big boy. He's fine."

Mark was not impressed by Robbie's lack of compassion for his friend. He turned his back to the man, guzzled his beer, and tended to the boat's dock lines. "Don't like the guy?" he asked over his shoulder.

"I have no opinion. He's hanging all over Sarah, that's all. I think he could back off a bit."

"You mean the same way you're hanging all over his friend, Steffi?" Mark whispered under his breath.

"Come again?" said Robbie.

"Oh, nothing. Wesley hasn't even been around here today, Rob. Not sure how he could be 'hanging all over Sarah'. Do you happen to know why he's not here?"

"No clue!"

Mark nodded and continued talking with his wife.

Meanwhile, Stuart and Sarah investigated the marshy riverbanks on their way back to the camp. There was no sign of Wesley. They slowed down as they entered the narrow passageway and scanned the water for any debris. When they reached the house, they spotted the fourth jet ski. It was resting on its side in the sand and reeds – along the river's edge.

"Oh, Stuart! That doesn't look good."

"Let's not think the worst," he said and tied a guide rope to the dock.

Sarah unbuckled her lifejacket and dropped it on the ground. She ran inside to look for their friend. "Wes! Wes!" she cried out.

There was no answer. They checked the recliner, sofa, and even Sarah's bed in the pool room. Venturing upstairs was next.

"I'm in – here," cracked a voice from the spare room.

Stuart ran up the curved staircase with Sarah on his heels. He pushed open the door and found Wesley lying on the bed, doubled over in pain. "Dude, what happened?"

"Are you alright?" said Sarah.

"I – am not sure how I got sick," Wesley explained. "I was about to head out to you guys, but my jet ski lost throttle and veered off into the river weeds. The ski dumped me. I couldn't get it started again, so I had to swim back to the house. I got really nauseous. I'm not sure if it was the water I swallowed or something I ate for breakfast. I've been puking for the last two hours."

"Why didn't you text us?" Stuart asked.

"There's no cell service, so I couldn't get in touch with anyone. Besides, I noticed that most everyone left their phones here – on their chargers."

"Oh, yeah – good point."

"We thought you were dead," Sarah partially jested as she touched Wesley's forehead to check for a fever. He was hot.

"Thanks for your concern, Mom, but I'll be alright. I just need to rest."

Sarah offered to stay with him and nurse him back to good health. She rushed off to the nearby bathroom sink to prepare a cool, wet wash-cloth. Wesley insisted they return to *Indulgence Island* and enjoy them-selves. Sarah was not so sure she should leave. She felt guilty for having fun while her friend was suffering.

"Drink a ton of water," Stuart insisted. "You gotta stay hydrated."

"I'll try – if I can keep it down. Those dry heaves are doozies."

"We'll go back if you don't want us around, but please get some rest," Stuart smiled and patted Wesley on the legs.

"Maybe I should stay," Sarah glanced at Stuart.

"No!" Wesley shouted with what little energy he had left. "No way, are you going to nurse me. This is your vacation time to have fun. I'm an adult with an upset stomach." He coughed a few times and turned on his other side.

"Are you sure, Wes?"

"Go! Please," he insisted. "I'll be fine."

The pair smiled pitifully at the sick man. "Ok, we will try and come back early," said Sarah.

"Grr . . . ," Wesley grumbled and drifted off to sleep.

Stuart and Sarah tiptoed out of the room. "I hope he'll be ok. I wonder what made him so sick," she said.

"Well, the water out here isn't the clearest, ya know. Maybe he got a bug. He'll be fine."

Sarah snatched a bottle of opened wine from the kitchen. Stuart retrieved the broken-down craft by tethering it to the other jet ski and towing it to the dock. They both mounted the working jet ski and prepared to return to the island. Sarah downed a few swigs of wine, while Stuart glanced over his shoulder and smiled. The pair zoomed off, satisfied that they had found their friend – and thankful he was alive. The day was about to see its second beginning.

Chapter 26

RIVERS OF FLOWING WATER

The pair reached *Indulgence Island* and rejoined their acquaintances, who were either prepping for more fun or getting drunker than ever. Mark and Amy were busy dealing with an issue on the boat while the teens played volleyball. Steffi was passed out in a beach chair that had sunk into the wet sand a few inches and was tipping to one side. She was slumped over, and no one seemed to care – as long as she was breathing. Robbie had lost interest, since the *toy* had become inoperable. Plus, without Sarah there to make jealous, there was no point in his pursuit.

But the excitement returned when Sarah showed up at the sandbar. Her former lover lit up, like a spotlight. "Where'd you two go?" Robbie clamored.

Sarah gestured to Stuart to tell the story of their adventure back to the camp house while she took off her life vest. He filled Robbie in about the broken jet ski and the state in which they had found Wesley, doubled over in bed.

As Sarah listened to Stuart, she grew a bit suspicious. "Isn't it strange that Wesley mentioned possibly getting sick on something he ingested? I thought we all ate the same food. No one else got sick."

"How the hell should I know?" Robbie barked.

"Well, you know a lot about food, right? It's just really odd that it happened and he wasn't able to hang out with us," she continued.

"You think I had something to do with his issues?"

"No, I'm not accusing you," said Sarah. "You sure are getting defensive, though."

"You must admit that when only one person in a group gets sick and everyone else has eaten the same thing, it's cause for concern," Stuart reiterated.

"Maybe he ate something before he got to Castle Dome. Maybe he caught a bug. Why don't you two have some more wine."

Sarah did not want to have negative thoughts about Robbie, nor assume he had bad intentions, but she wondered if he had something to do with Wesley's illness. Lately, Robbie had left such a sour taste in her mouth, and she trusted him less and less. The woman shook her head from side to side and walked away from the guys. She entered the tent, poured herself some wine from the open bottle she had taken from the house, and stared into the drink. Her mind raced with concern as she squinted with every gulp.

Just then, Mark and Amy ran around pinching everyone's rear ends and shouting, "Let's go!" They continued back to the boat, which now had a giant, blow-up device attached to its stern. "Tubing, you guys?" Mark yelled with excitement. "Put your vests back on and hop in. You're gonna love it!"

Stuart buckled his jacket back together and motioned to his friend. "Come with me, Sarah! Let's go have some fun!"

Robbie was miffed. Not only was his plaything out of commission, but he was being dissed by Mark and his best friend, Stuart. He was also failing miserably at trying to make Sarah jealous.

Stuart and Sarah ran over to the big rubber raft, which only held two adults and maybe a smaller, thin person. One of the teen girls volunteered to join them. Sarah had no idea what to expect from the ride, having never been tubing before. She assumed the inflatable circle would be dragged at high speeds down the river.

"It will be a blast!" Stuart encouraged both ladies. He flexed his muscles and stepped onto the middle of the raft for balance. "Here, grab these attached wooden handles."

"I'm scared, Stuart!" Sarah exclaimed and nervously giggled with the teen. "This is nuts!"

When Stuart heard the engine start, he suddenly became terrified of flying off the tube. "Actually, maybe I should wait this one out," he said with a devilish grin.

"Ha! That's ironic," said Sarah. "Not a chance! You're not leaving me on this thing. If I die, you're going down with me!" With a boost of excitement, Sarah slapped Stuart's belly and said, "Hold on to your britches, cowboy."

Robbie, wearing a bitter expression, took large, deliberate steps through the water to reach the boat. Running his hands along the body of the fiberglass vessel, he gripped and applied pressure to its interior as he hopped on board. Amy was already seated at the bow, so he joined her there. He looked at the tubing group through the windshield in front of Mark's steering wheel – with envy.

Mark revved the engine and shouted to the tubers, "Everybody ready to fly?"

Stuart's eyes bugged out. The look of fear on his face was humorous.

"Ha ha! I think we're all good back here!" Sarah glanced at her raft mates and gave Mark a *thumbs-up* with her right hand.

The teen gestured a confident *ok* sign and smiled. Stuart double-checked his life vest buckle and reluctantly raised his right fist in agreement.

Mark gave the boat a boost of throttle, and all three were thrust backwards. "Oops! Just checking to see if you're awake back there," he chuckled.

"What the f - - - ?" Stuart cried out.

"You're too much, Stuey!" Sarah laughed. "You better prepare yourself for another teaser from our driver." The wine had eased most of the fear in her; she was having fun.

The boat slowly accelerated to a steady pace and then quickly gained speed, pulling the tubers behind it. A heavy mist from the wake sprayed their faces. Soon, they were soaked. Mark went faster. Screams of laughter – combined with fright – echoed down the waterway. The three thrill-seekers sounded like tortured cartoon cats. It was a funny sight, even for somber Robbie. He enjoyed watching them ride the waves in a terrified frenzy. Mark gave more gas and twisted the boat around the intertwining passageways of the Colorado River.

"Aargh – slow down!" shouted Stuart.

"Faster!" yelled Sarah and the teen.

Mark could not hear them. Their commands were drowned out by the engine's loud roar and the sloshing waves. Despite Stuart's genuine fear, his mood and reactions made Sarah laugh – non-stop. She tried to get a good look at him while the tube bounced up and down. It was difficult to keep her head straight and focused. Stuart's petrified facial expressions – caught in the corner of her eye – were hilarious. She continued cackling, uncontrollably, while their bodies jostled – like limp ragdolls – with each forceful pull of the boat.

"Whoa! Look out for this big one!" yelled Mark.

The tube caught the crest of a taller wave formed by the wake of a passing vessel and flew upward. The trio was thrown about eight feet into the air.

"Oh, my God!" screamed Sarah.

"Help me, Mother!" Stuart yelled.

Sarah laughed and screeched at the same time. She did not know whether to close her eyes tight or take in the birds-eye view while airborne. The teen, who was more limber than her mates, held on without being fazed. They landed with a loud *whack,* and all three burst into laughter.

Mark made sure everyone was intact, and the boat continued down the river. "Had enough?" he said, quieting the engine to a rumble.

Sarah's vision was blurred from both the river water and tears of joy. "I guess so!" she shouted back.

"Yeah, I think we're good – but whatever," Stuart said coyly. He did not want to give the impression that he was terrified of another treacherous ride. A gentle withdrawal from the idea of nearly dying, suited him just fine.

Sarah snickered, recalling Stuart's earlier screams as the water splashed them all. She closed her eyes and wiped her face with her hands. It was over now. Mark found an alcove and shut the engine off. He jumped in the water to cool down. The boat floated in one spot while the wet tubers pulled themselves on board to dry.

"Stuart, you idiot!" Robbie joked. "You should have let go of the handles and nosedived into the river on that last wave. You flew, buddy."

"Yep. That's all I need – to blow out an eardrum – or DIE! Be my guest if you'd like to try that, my foolish friend," Stuart mocked.

"I'm all set."

Sarah continued wiping herself with a towel. She was quiet as she listened to the two exchange playful insults. Robbie ignored her, never once praising her for staying on the raft, even though her body had flip-flopped out of control. She sat at the stern with the teen.

Mark got on board and took the group back to *Indulgence Island*. They checked on Steffi and the other teenagers. They were gone, including the jet skis. Amy suggested packing up the food and booze and returning to the house. The sun would soon be setting behind the desert mountains, turning the sky into a hazy kaleidoscope of colors. Sarah daydreamed about her surroundings.

When they arrived at the camp, Sarah checked on Wesley, who was fast asleep. There was an empty glass and plate full of toast crumbs on the nightstand. She was relieved that he had tried to eat something and hoped he was able to keep it down. The door to his bedroom was shut quietly, and everyone was asked to keep their voices low to allow him rest.

The tubers needed to clean up before dinner. Someone was using the downstairs bathroom so Amy offered up her en suite for Sarah to use. The master bedroom was beautiful – complete with wood flooring, a marble-tiled shower, roman bathtub, and dual closets. Sarah wondered if the owner had lived in the house permanently at one time. Its humble exterior held secret, its interior grandeur.

Sarah tugged at her damp clothes and shed them, like a serpent changing its skin. The warm, evening breeze of the desert blew through the sliding, balcony door that had been left open. Still, she shivered. She stepped onto the cold, stone tile and turned on the water. The pulsating stream massaged away any tension. Memories of Stuart's fearful screams while they bounced on the tube caused her to chuckle involuntarily. "Oh Stuart," she whispered aloud, "you were so funny."

She finished up and dried off in front of the vanity. A beckoning sunset could be seen in the mirror. The stream of gold and orange hues was like tantalizing fingertips, motioning her to walk toward it. She stepped onto the stucco balcony, which measured half the length of the bedroom. No other houses obstructed her vision. The picturesque scene was so overwhelmingly tranquil.

"Dinner!" Amy's faint call from downstairs pierced her bubble of serenity.

Sarah drank in the view, once more. The sun had dropped below the horizon, leaving a stack of colors in its wake. First, muted red, then orange, yellow, and every color of the rainbow – until an expanded stripe of pale violet filled the sky. "So incredibly breathtaking," she said, slipping into a pair of pajama pants and a t-shirt. She slowly gathered up her belongings and joined the group.

Everyone was doing their own thing. Wesley was up and about, stuffing his face with greasy potato chips and Mark and Amy were milling around in the kitchen, putting out the food. Sarah placed her damp clothes in a plastic bag by her other belongings and made a beeline to Wesley. He seemed to be feeling a lot better, and his skin was not so pale, anymore.

"Take it easy, there, dude," Sarah advised.

"Hey. I don't know what came over me. I thought I was going to die, Sarah. What did I eat?"

"I don't know. Did anyone give you anything weird?"

Wesley tried to recall the last several hours. Most of his recollection was that of retching in the bathroom. "No. Not that I can think of," he said. "Well, wait. Robbie poured me a glass of orange juice."

"Really?"

"Yeah, but you don't think . . . ?" he laughed before finishing his sentence.

"Well, I am so thankful that you are feeling better," Sarah said. She quickly thought about the repercussions of accusing Robbie of doing something harmful to Wesley. They were in a remote location with no police nearby. If he had done anything to intentionally hurt Wesley, there was no telling what he might do if she pointed a finger at him.

Sarah scanned the room for her ex-bed buddy, who she found bobbing back and forth in a light conversation with Stuart and Mark.

Apparently, Robbie had smoothed things over with the other guys. He noticed that she was talking with Wesley and began his next plan to distract her. But he was not the only one conjuring.

Chapter 27

EAT, DRINK, BE MERRY

The sun had fully set, and the grounds surrounding the camp would soon be lit by the full moon. As Sarah sat with Wesley, she looked around the room, enchanted by the situation in which she had found herself. There were friends she was getting to know, men she wished she knew better, and the desert – vast and lonely in its own right. It mystified her.

Robbie chugged a beer and walked past the pair, sitting on the sofa. "It's warm in here, ain't it? You must be roasting."

"I feel perfect," Sarah responded, moving closer to Wesley.

Robbie sneered. As he sauntered around the big room, he glanced at Steffi, sleeping on a chair. Unfortunately for him, she was unavailable. She was able to shower and get into some comfy clothes earlier, but it was right back to sleep for her worn out body.

In a way, Sarah felt sorry for Steffi. She could see the drunkard had been used. It was not the poor girl's fault that she was a pawn in Robbie's game of making Sarah jealous. On the flip side, she enjoyed the affection, just like Sarah had. *Maybe Steffi being here is a good thing,* Sarah thought. *A test. A drawing salve, that is pulling the real Robbie out and into the light.*

Wesley felt stronger, despite the residual weakness from his morning affliction. He liked Sarah. She was responsible, beautiful, classy, and sexy. Even though Steffi was his friend, he had no interest in her romantically. Robbie could have her.

"Anyone up for a game of Charades?" boomed Mark's voice from the kitchen.

"Yes!" Sarah and Wesley answered simultaneously.

The others followed suit, except for Robbie. He opened another bottle of beer. The golden liquid poured smoothly into his glass. He was too proud to play a game that he felt was meant for children. While the rest gathered around the coffee table, eager to look like fools, Robbie paced about.

The campers played for more than two hours – making hand and body gestures. They tried to get their respective team to guess the right movie, book, person, or thing they non-verbally described. Barks of right and wrong answers were occasionally interrupted by laughter. Deep down, Robbie wanted to participate. He felt the urge to help the failing teams, but instead he remained quiet and merely observed from across the room.

Finally, the players slapped hands and congratulated each other on a good time. The friends separated, either to find something else to do or retreat to their awaiting beds. The house became quieter.

Mark and Amy meandered upstairs to their big bedroom. "Good night, all," they shouted from the staircase.

"Good night, you two!" said the others.

Meanwhile, Stuart and Wesley rummaged in the kitchen for something to satisfy their cravings. Robbie was not tired either and joined them. The night was young, and they were not finished drinking. Grabbing two short, rounded glasses from the cabinet, Robbie brushed past the other men and prepared a workspace on the countertop. Several unopened bottles of expensive wine sat by the sink. He uncorked a red with finesse and filled the cups like he was on a mission. On his way out, he smirked in Wesley's direction. It went unnoticed.

Sarah was intrigued by the moonlight streaming into the open patio sliders. She stood in the lonely doorway and gazed out into the night. The full moon illuminated the grounds almost as beautifully as the sunset had done hours before. Distant howls of coyotes echoed across the river, electrifying her spine; the pack had made a kill. The sound faded – along with the chill – and she focused on the breeze. It was light at first, but then blew past her, as if it were searching for something beyond where she stood. Suddenly, a glass of red wine appeared at her face.

"Add this to that view you are admiring," Robbie broke the silence.

"Thanks."

"What do you see?"

"Nothing." Sarah gently grasped the glass and brushed past Robbie. She was lying, of course. There was much to see, but there was no way she was going to share a romantic, intimate moment with Robbie after the way he had treated her.

He tossed his head back and rolled his eyes. He knew full well that he deserved Sarah's reaction. But he was not bothered. There was someone else he could count on for small talk. "Hey, Stuey!" Robbie said. "You up for a game of pool?"

"You're on!" Sarah answered for Stuart. She clinked glasses with her blonde-haired friend and sarcastically said, "I'm his partner. Who will *you* play with, Robbie?"

He laughed while looking around the room at bags of opened potato chips, empty wine and beer bottles, and bodies dripping over the arms of furniture, like melted marshmallows. There was only one person left standing. "Wesley! Play a little pool, buddy? You and me against these two?"

Wesley was not about to back down at the request. "Definitely. I'm in!"

"Awesome! How well do you play, man?"

"I'm not sure if I'll be a help or hindrance, but I can play."

"No worries, Wes. I've got something that will shoot your game right up through the roof." Robbie reached into his backpack, lying by the pool table and plucked out a tiny box with that same hand-drawn 70s flower on the lid. He opened it, revealing a brown lump of what appeared to be chocolate.

"Is that an edible?" Wesley asked. "It's so small."

"Yeah," Robbie confirmed, "but potent as hell! Here – take a smidge." He sliced into a corner of the one-inch square of chocolate with a pocket-knife, paring off less than a quarter of it. The chunk remained stuck to the end of the metal, which he showed to Wesley.

The man hesitated, but held out an open palm. He thought about his sensitive stomach and if he should add anything like a drug to its already weakened state. Wesley glanced at Sarah, who had noticed the flowered box. They exchanged looks of concern as Robbie impatiently plopped the small morsel into Wesley's hand – with a smile – and casually walked back into the kitchen.

Sarah followed. "What the hell did you bring?"

"I get it with my medical marijuana card. It's harmless. I'm just trying to relax everyone and boost their natural abilities. What's wrong with that?"

"People lose control on that stuff, Robbie." Sarah stared at his dead-pan eyes. She could not decide if she should continue to scold him or just throw up her hands and join the recklessness.

"Try a little piece," Robbie beckoned her, like a witch with a poisoned apple. He hunched over the box and cut off a small chunk of the edible, about the size of a snake's eyeball. "You probably won't even feel it; it's so minute, Sarah." His shoulders straightened out, extending his height two inches, which he had lost from slumping. His left eyebrow rose. The corners of his mouth unfurled – yielding a devious grin – and he placed the sliver of chocolate into her hand.

She looked at the glossy brown particle and was perplexed. *Should I? What could happen? It's only a little, right? Where's Stuart?* The strong red wine was abetting her. Without further ado, she sucked the little clump off her skin and quickly chewed it up.

Just as the sweet made its way down the back of Sarah's throat, Stuart entered the kitchen. "What's everybody doing?"

"Here ya go, bud," Robbie said, handing him a slightly larger piece.

Stuart gladly swallowed it down without protest or hesitation. "Come on partner. You breaking?" he asked Sarah. He pulled her out to the game room, and the others followed.

Sarah was quickly distracted from her concern of ingesting cannabis. There was no time to ask Stuart his thoughts. With a cue stick in one hand and a drug in the belly, each of the three players looked on as Robbie grabbed the triangle and prepared to rack the balls. The game was about to begin.

Chapter 28

SHADOW OF DEATH

A large, overhead light illuminated the green felt of the pool table. While the rest of the house guests slept, three men and Sarah were awake and ready to battle each other in a game of billiards. It would not be long before they started to feel the mind-altering effects of the chocolate edible. Sarah did not know what to expect. She guessed it would be similar to the feeling she had with Stuart that night in his apartment when she had her vision – a little muscle atrophy, but a lot of laughter.

Robbie racked the balls, rolling the triangle back and forth over the surface of the table. He positioned the group of hard, resin globes perfectly on the dot at the lower quadrant. The one-ball was right at the apex. As he bent his body, he admired his mastery and peered up at Sarah. "Would you like to break?" Robbie felt confident she would not have the strength to sink anything.

"No, I'm good. I think I'll let Stuart do the honors." Sarah picked up the little square of blue, pool cue chalk and gently rubbed it on the end of her stick. It would help her hit the ball accurately when it was her turn. Bits of cobalt dust formed a small cloud. It was reminiscent of a slow trail of smoke from a lit cigarette. She gently blew it away and handed the cube to Stuart.

Suddenly, the temperature dropped in the room. The four adjusted their shirts to accommodate for the quick yet temporary change.

"Brr...," Wesley remarked, "I thought this was the desert. Maybe we should close a window."

"It can get a little chilly at night. Not sure what that was, though," Robbie responded. "Maybe it's wind from a stampede of coyotes and rattlers."

"You wouldn't catch me out there at night," Wesley said.

"Me neither! I wouldn't go out this late." Robbie refocused on the game. "Break 'em!"

"You sound like a couple of grannies," Stuart joked.

Robbie raised his eyebrow in response.

After hearing both men whine about the desert, Stuart felt like he was the most manly one out of the bunch. He was ready to play. He flexed his hard muscles for Sarah's benefit and shot the cue ball at the triangular cluster. He was a good pool player and known to commence bar games in his younger years. Although he was less cocky than his friend Robbie, his skills had won him some money, at least.

On the other hand, Robbie was good at everything – in Robbie's opinion. If he could not figure something out, he would fake it, or at least convince others in believing he could.

Sarah was no slouch either. Trained by her grandfather when she was only six years old, she could certainly sink a ball or two. Her good looks deceived the *old-school* boys into thinking a pretty girl could not play well. With careful aim and alignment of the stick, Sarah could eye a straight shot into the hole.

Crack! In what sounded like a clap of thunder, the spheres broke apart and trickled across the felt tabletop, like ripples on a pond. Narrowly missing the eight-ball, the three-ball sped across the table, landing in the corner hole – farthest from where they stood.

"Nice one, partnah!"

"Thanks, partnah!" said Stuart playfully.

Sarah snickered and walked over to the windowsill, where she had placed her glass of red wine. It tasted delightful. The merlot had been slightly chilled by the cool desert air, which blew strands of her golden hair across her moistened lips. She smiled, knowing that it would not be long before the combination of the spirit and the drug took hold of her senses.

Stuart failed to sink a second ball.

It was Robbie's turn, now. He lined up his sight while keeping a watchful eye on Sarah. She was sipping her wine. Her delicate placement of the glass back on the sill, intrigued him. For a moment, he shook off the urge to stare and tried to concentrate on the game. But as he pulled the stick back, her sensual moves distracted him once again, and he popped the cue up in the air. Robbie missed getting anything in the hole.

Sarah prepared for *her* chance at the table. She wiped her perspiring hands on her pink and white striped pajama pants. Perched on a side table was a talc cone, which she used to coat her dried palms. The shaft of the pool stick could now slide smoothly between her fingers.

Robbie stroked the soft green cloth that was wrapped around the edge of the table. He observed Sarah rolling the wooden stick between her delicate hands. He noticed that the alabaster substance had gotten on her face after she brushed the strands of hair away. Snapshots of their sexual encounters popped into his mind – they flashed behind his eyes, like a strobe light on a nightclub dance floor. *Nonsense*, he thought. Robbie tried to suppress the visions. Those times where he might have felt close to Sarah had no place in his life – or his head. Still, they persisted. He swigged another drink.

"Solids," confirmed Sarah. The stick slid slowly back and forth between her left-hand fingers. She closed one eye to get perfect aim on the seven-ball and thrust the stick forward to hit the cue. It traveled across the felt and made contact with the sphere, pushing it delicately into the corner pocket.

"Hurray, Sarah!" Stuart shouted. "I wasn't sure you had it in you."

"Never underestimate me, my friend – or the mystery of a woman."

"Oh, I won't!"

Sarah had no luck on her next try, and the play turned over to Wesley. He eyed number fourteen. Focusing was not on his side at the moment. He concentrated for thirty seconds before he hit the cue and missed a colored ball. He was getting tired and just wanted to go to bed. The drug had zapped him of his energy.

The game was back in Stuart's control. He pulled the wood between his rough hands and thrust it hard, sending the white sphere into the side of the table. It ricocheted, hitting the six-ball away from any pocket. All of a sudden, he felt a jolt at the center of his brain. Stuart was no longer in control. A wave of fogginess rapidly overcame his vision, and his mouth closed tight with tension. The drug had kicked in. Stuart was silent.

"No worries, Stuey!" Sarah shouted. "We'll win this!" She had no clue what had just happened to him. He looked perfectly normal from her perspective. Then – just as she motioned for Robbie to take *his* turn – *her* eyes began to feel heavy. Sarah was gripped with momentary paralysis. She could hear Robbie hit the cue ball; however, only a part of her mind comprehended any movement. All she could see were lines of white with bands of color mixed in. The balls rolled at seemingly half their normal speed. "Hey everybody, a slow-moving sunset is on the pool table!"

The men just dismissed her comment as goofiness and studied the balls.

After mustering up several ounces of energy to turn her head, Sarah noticed that Stuart's torso was stiffened, yet he was swaying back and forth, like a tall palm tree caught in a tropical storm. He stood at the edge of the table, anticipating a need for support. Sarah's head started to feel thick and numb. She parted her feet to distribute her weight evenly and keep from falling. Gripping the cue stick with both hands – stacked one above the other – Sarah planted the rod on the floor. She teetered on her two legs while she held onto the wooden pole, creating an unstable tripod.

"Is something wrong, you guys?" asked Robbie. His voice was low and muffled. He sounded further away than where he was actually standing.

The crisp, night air had vanished, and Sarah's body became overwhelmingly warm. All thoughts grew increasingly vivid. She was living in her head, yet any movement or noise seemed to come from another dimension.

Wesley interrupted, "Well, you three, I'm off to bed. This stuff is making me tired. Carry on without me."

The man's voice was heard and processed in a foreign area of Sarah's mind. She felt some uneasiness at the thought of being left alone with Robbie and Stuart. The previously enjoyable environment had changed to one of unfamiliarity and fear. "But it's your turn, Wessy!" Sarah tried to get him to stay.

"Play without me, hun. I'm out." The drug affected Wesley in a different way. He appeared to be only sleepy.

Suddenly, nothing made sense to Sarah. She squinted in confusion and stared at the rug beneath her sock-covered feet. Every fiber became magnified as if it were right under her nose, being viewed through a microscope. Lint balls – gathered along its surface – were like tumbleweeds, frozen in time.

Wesley could not tell that Sarah was having trouble focusing. It was late, and all he cared about was getting into bed to rest his battered body.

"Good night, Sarah. See you tomorrow, you guys." He disappeared into the darkened, upstairs hallway.

Sarah regained some mobility and was able to tiptoe around the table, observing the sticks, balls, walls, windows – and Robbie. Plucking her glass of wine from the sill, she slowly brought the rim to her lips. Her eyes were drawn to the ruby-red swirl of color flowing to her mouth. A distorted reflection of herself stared back in caricature-like fashion. She pulled the glass away from her face with dread.

Stuart hobbled to meet up with Sarah on one end of the pool table. He wanted to laugh at the whole situation, but at that moment, he was confused.

Sarah slowly set the wine glass back and proceeded to speak. It was difficult for her to form any words without the corners of her mouth turning sharply downwards. It was like they were being pulled by strings attached to the floor. It pained her to talk. "Look at my face, you guys. I'm frowning with every word."

Robbie observed the unfolding scene from the other side of the room, expressionless, awaiting his turn to play again. He was pleased that Wesley had retired to the upstairs bedroom. He did not need the competition or any potential one-upmanship. Now, he had the impaired duo all to himself. Robbie's eyes darted back and forth between his two friends. "I don't see it," he said to Sarah. "I don't see the frown. I'm going to take over for Wesley." He aimed at one of the striped balls, but missed.

Sarah and Stuart started to laugh, upsetting Robbie. But it was not because of him that they were so amused. The two teammates were laughing at Sarah's facial plight. They did not even notice that Robbie had taken his turn.

Pulling at her skin, Sarah tried forcing the corners of her mouth upward. She struggled to tell her teammate it was still his turn. "Quit – holding up – the game. Go, already!" she stammered.

"I don't know – if I can," Stuart gagged.

"Do you need the bridge?"

The two chuckled even harder. Sarah dropped to her knees to hold in a laughter-induced rush of urine trying to escape her body.

"No, I don't need the bridge, you numb-skull. It's *your* turn!"

"Oh," she giggled. "The only thing – I could hit – is the floor. Take my turn!"

Stuart's feet felt like he was wearing weighted boots. He walked around the table to position himself in front of the cue ball. Taking aim, he noticed all the black and blue marks as well as each nick on its acrylic shell. He drew an imaginary dotted line from the cue to the one-ball, with his mind. Its solid yellow color reminded him of the sunrises he witnessed from his balcony back in Long Beach. He daydreamed and closed his eyes. Stuart had drifted away from any semblance of sharp focus.

"Shooooot already," Sarah slurred with more laughter.

Robbie was quiet, still witnessing the unfolding of his friends' euphoric states. The idea that he was responsible for their experiences made him feel elated and arrogant. He leaned back against the wall and observed them. It was like watching a slap-stick comedy.

Stuart looked at Sarah, who was rubbing her cheeks, still trying to loosen their tension. He observed her mannerisms before taking a shot at the ball.

Sarah rotated her jaw back and forth, squinting with each circular motion. The powder from her hands coated most of her face now. She looked at her white palms with grave confusion and screamed, "Aaah!"

Robbie quickly came to her defense. "It's just chalk, darling. Your face isn't falling off."

Sarah cocked her head at Robbie and giggled.

Anger was taking over Stuart's emotional state, due to his lack of coherency. He knew he was experiencing more than just the normal high effects of marijuana. "What did you put in this stuff?" he queried.

"What are you talking about?" Robbie answered, gripping his pool stick tightly. "It's just pot."

"No. This is a crazy and seriously, messed-up drug."

Robbie was silent, awaiting another accusation. The chocolate edible was much stronger than the cookie he had given Stuart before – and Stuart knew it. The effects were frightening him. He tried to shake off his dizziness and then took his shot. He missed. The one-ball went rolling off to the side of the table, knocking a few others out of its way.

The room – once brightly lit by the light above the billiards table – grew eerily quiet, and slightly dimmer. It was ten o'clock. The time had passed quickly, yet it felt as though it was creeping.

The sand and brush surrounding the house was lit up. The clouds had parted, revealing more lunar light. Wavy stripes and flecks of white shimmered off the river water. All else was still. Visitors in nearby homes were fast asleep, exhausted from an active day at the island. Upstairs, Amy, Mark, and Wesley slept peacefully. Downstairs in the living room, the teens and Steffi were also out cold. No one was awakened by the staccato sound of clacking balls.

They continued. Stuart's play left a clear shot for his opponent to sink the fourteen-ball.

Robbie glanced toward his friend with each stroke of the stick, checking for any change in his behavior. *Success!* Robbie got number fourteen in the pocket. The balls then seemed to line up to his advantage. He took aim at the fifteen. He struck the cue, hitting the stripe of choice. The burgundy band of color turned like a clock's gear as it rolled across the table. But the ball drifted off course at the last minute and knocked the eight-ball into a side pocket. Down it went – the game was over.

"Yay! We won!" Sarah cheered.

"Play again!" Robbie demanded. His ego was bruised, and he hoped a rematch would heal it.

Stuart was not sure if he could play another round. He sat down on a small hassock at one end of the pool table. His head spun, and he thought he might pass out.

"Are you ok, Stuart?" Sarah asked.

"This drug is weird. My skin feels six inches thick. My whole body is responding at a snail's pace."

"This doesn't feel right."

"Yeah, I've never experienced anything like this, Sarah."

"Really?" she exclaimed. "If *you* have never felt anything like this, then there must be something very wrong." She was scared.

The focus was now on Robbie, who was gathering all the balls from the pockets and lining them up along the back side of the table.

"There's a hallucinogenic in this, isn't there?" Sarah accused him.

"What? No. Why and how would I do that? I purchased it from a dispensary."

"And you brought it here to use on us?" Sarah pushed.

"There's something in this, dude," said Stuart. "I'm feeling messed up."

"You're both just paranoid," Robbie defended himself. "There's nothing in it, but pot."

By now, Robbie had gathered all the spheres at his end of the table. To Sarah, they seemed like hard, colorful cannon balls, shinier and more polished than they appeared before. Their hues were vibrant – red, orange, yellow, green, blue, violet, maroon – and black. They decorated the felt-covered table, like bobbles on a Christmas tree.

"If you didn't put something in this, then maybe the dispensary did," Sarah suggested. "But why would you bring it here, exposing us to this garbage?"

"You didn't have to take it. I believe you have free will to decide," replied Robbie.

"We have been drinking!" Sarah raised her voice. "We were impaired."

Robbie leaned into the table – pressing his hips against its wooden edge – and listened intently to Sarah and Stuart reprimand him. He felt attacked. Suddenly, his eyes glossed over and his face lost all expression. One by one, he took each ball in his hand and slowly rolled them toward the pair – first the yellow one-ball, then the two. They ricocheted off the opposite side of the table, directly returning to Robbie. His moves were sinister – in a way. Methodical. Intentional.

Sarah's body suddenly felt taut and her eyes tensed up. She felt something take control of her mouth as she spoke to Robbie, "You're a bad – bad – man."

Instantly, the mood of the room changed. It was dead silent. A shadow of fear fell over the entire house, encapsulating it in a prism of evil thoughts and accusations.

Right as Sarah spoke, Stuart threw both hands over his face. He did not speak, or budge from the footstool. She was worried that he was upset by her saying something hurtful about his friend. Immediately, she felt insecure and singled-out. There was no comradery from her pool *partnah*, anymore. "Stuart, are you alright? What's wrong?" Sarah whispered.

Still, nothing from Stuart. His hands remained pressed firmly over every inch of his face.

She turned back to Robbie in fear. Robbie was not the same. There was a void in his eyes, a change in his face, and a strange aura around his entire being. Something had been awakened inside the room and inside them all. Fright filled Sarah's body, and she began to shake and sweat. She wanted to flee. As everyone else in the house slept, she felt like a lone rabbit facing a pack of wolves. If she ran, they would be provoked to get her – for sure.

"Did you feel that?" Robbie said. "Something evil just descended on us."

Sarah was petrified. Her body shuddered when he mentioned the evil presence. The thought of something unseen hovering over them was more than she could take. Sarah fought back the urge to weep. Doing so would only make her appear weak. Something supernatural *had* occurred. It was necessary to sober up from their high. She tried very hard to think clearly, but the fight was tough. Sarah knew she had ticked off both men, but getting out of the situation would call for a strategic plan.

She toughened up and slowly approached Robbie to hug him. "I'm s-sorry for what I said, Robbie. I didn't mean *you* were bad. I just thought having the pot here was a bad idea."

Robbie did not feel the need to embrace Sarah's sorrowful attempt to make amends. He knew she meant what she said, but he allowed the hug, anyway. "Your words reminded me of my father, a man who I have tried to forget all my life," he spoke in an eerie tone.

A chill ran down Sarah's spine, and her heart rate increased. She felt the presence of evil within Robbie's proximity. More demons had been released. Sarah slowly backed up a step, fearing he might strike her. She tried not to make eye contact and hoped he would not say anything more. But there *was* more.

"My father abused my dog, Jack, and then turned around and blamed me for it. He hit me." Robbie's voice was deep and monotone, now. "He hated me and always found fault. He hurt me by punishing my dog. My father killed Jack in front of me."

Sarah was stunned to hear his story. Was he making a comparison between his father's actions and her words? Surely, what Sarah said was not on the same level as killing his beloved dog – as his father had done. She was puzzled. But knowing that she had awakened painful memories of his father was enough for Sarah to feel uneasy about what he might do in retaliation. She retreated and went back to Stuart, whose face was still buried in his sweaty palms.

Terror is what she felt. Sarah knelt by Stuart's side. Her eyes darted around the room, scanning her surroundings for any way out of the situation. She looked at the men, the door, the staircase to her left, and the grouping of billiard balls under Robbie's hands at the end of the pool table. How hard they must be – and how deadly. Sarah's mind raced. She thought of Stuart attacking her for insulting his friend. She imagined Robbie hitting her over the head with one or several of the balls. Might Sarah have unleashed a bottled-up monster? Years of turmoil had been suppressed – until this night. *That's why he used medical marijuana,* she thought. *That's why he hid things he didn't want me to know. Maybe that was the true source of his PTSD.*

Suddenly, Robbie's voice changed. He spoke directly and deliberately to Sarah. His tone was emotionless and calculating. "Why – don't we go for a walk – outside?"

A huge rush of fear gushed through Sarah, like a raging river. She recalled Robbie telling Wesley that he would not go outside at night. Why would he suggest to go out, now? She envisioned the area around the house.

Desolate.

Dark.

Dangerous.

No one – other than the fellow campers – knew she was in the desert. If she went missing, it would be a long time before anyone noticed.

He spoke again, "Getting out in the fresh air – will do us all – some good. Let's –take – a walk."

Sarah shivered. *They're going to kill me, and then once they dump me outside, they'll come back and do the same to everybody else.*

Stuart was still stone stiff.

It seemed to her that Robbie was trying to manipulate the air she breathed and control her thoughts. She fought the urge to follow his commands. *Is he having the same effect on Stuart?* Sarah thought Robbie might be trying to manipulate Stuart, or silently conspire with him to hurt her. The atmosphere was unpredictable.

Who was the man standing at the opposite end of the pool table? Was it an entity – entirely separate from Robbie – peering at Sarah through his eyes? She felt impending death so strongly, not only for herself, but for everyone sleeping in the house. There was a chance that someone upstairs might hear her call out for help. But if they did not respond, then she was fair game. Sarah needed to appear in control.

More dark thoughts entered her mind. She envisioned the heavy reeds and brush that lined the riverbank behind the house. *That's where they'll probably put my body – buried in the sand.* She saw Robbie pummeling her skull and leaving her limp body to be dragged off by coyotes. Stuart's silence scared her just as much as Robbie's weirdness. She imagined him helping Robbie with the task. Sarah dared not blink for fear of finding either of them standing over her.

Without a thought, she knelt on the floor next to Stuart. She put her hands together in a prayer position and shoved them between her shaking knees. The involuntary response showed submission and communicated to Robbie that she and Stuart were not a threat. But the phrase "you're a bad, bad man" took up residency inside their heads.

"Fresh air would do you good. Why don't we go outside?" Robbie startled her again with a deadpan stare.

Sarah bowed her head and focused on the floor, trying to avoid Robbie's glare. If she looked up at him in that moment, there was no telling what fury might be unleashed. She did not know how to answer him.

"What's the matter with you two?" Robbie asked slowly. "I really think – we should all go take a walk – by the river – where it's cooler."

His frightening tone sent another chill through her entire body.

Time was of the essence. Fighting her paralyzed muscles, Sarah forced herself to reach out with her right hand to touch Stuart's leg. When she finally was able to move it, she gently squeezed his calf to reassure him of her presence and their need to stay strong together. He showed no response to her touch. Sarah swallowed hard, got up enough courage to lift her head, and looked directly at Robbie's face. "We're not going anywhere," Sarah said sternly.

Robbie's hands still toyed with the billiard balls, twisting and turning them.

Sarah locked eyes with his. If her attention moved to his weaponry, she feared he would attack her. *What should I do?* she thought. *What is going to happen – to me?*

Robbie just stared.

If Sarah stayed in one place, she was certain Robbie would bolt over to her side of the pool table. He might drag her outside. There was only one thing that could help her, only one hopeful way out of the situation.

God.

She had to call on God. But how could she redeem herself after her tirade toward Him at the beach? If His forgiveness was true, she hoped it would come through for her, now. There was no other way for her to turn. He had to help, or otherwise she would die at the hands of her friends.

Sarah needed to get out of that room. She lowered her head to the floor again and studied her legs – the left, then the right. They were cemented in their folded positions. She tried to move them, but her brain was unable to send them messages. The drug – or something else – was still in control. It was like her legs were disconnected. She squinted hard for a few seconds. In that short moment, she silently asked God to give strength – and the ability to move – to her limbs.

Nothing happened.

She concentrated hard and said firmly inside her head, *God help me move. God help me move. Move my legs, please, Father.*

Robbie and Stuart seemed frozen while Sarah fought internally to get out of her own skin. She thought of the winding staircase to her left. It must have been twelve feet across the room, a far walk in her condition. She had to try and make it there and grab hold of the railing. If she could get upstairs to wake Mark and Amy for help, she might survive.

Dark thoughts crept in, again. She envisioned the entire house of people being slaughtered by the two men in her midst. Robbie was sinister in his demeanor and Stuart was a wildcard. The once, mild-mannered friend was no longer there for her. Stuart sat there in silence, covering his face.

How did Sarah get to this frightening place? Everything had been perfect – in a way. They were all having fun only hours before.

Am I the bad one, here? she wondered. What drove her to tell Robbie that he was a *bad man*? From what place had her words come? Maybe it was a feeling she harbored after everything he put her through. Sarah snapped back to the present. There was no time for second-guessing herself. She needed to move – now. *Father God! I love You and I need You! I believe in You. Please help me, now!* she silently screamed – one last time.

Then, as if a bolt of lightning struck her body – her legs were set free. The relief was overwhelming. She was able to pull her left foot out from underneath her, stand up, and walk slowly to the staircase. Sarah had to figure out how she would get upstairs without Robbie stopping her – so she pretended to cry.

Remorse and sadness were what she hoped Robbie would see. She continued walking slowly to the stairs and reached for the railing. Step by step, her legs lifted her higher toward the second floor. Sarah cautiously glanced across the room. Robbie stared. Stuart was still a statue and appeared asleep. But the dark and evil presence was wide awake.

Chapter 29

HE PROWLS

Escape the game room: that was Sarah's mission. She was uncertain she could do so and held tightly to the railing of the staircase. To her surprise, no one chased her. But she was not out of the woods yet. Robbie and Stuart were very strong – and fast. There was just not enough space between her and them for Sarah to feel safe.

Each riser in the staircase seemed like a mountain to climb. When Sarah reached the top, she ran toward the master bedroom. The journey down the hallway was long, but she was determined to make it – despite having tremendous fear to look back over her shoulder. When she reached Mark and Amy's bedroom, she found the door wide open. They were asleep. Sarah rushed in and rattled Mark's shoulder. "Wake up, you two. Something's wrong!"

"Aah!" Amy gasped and bolted upright in bed.

Mark was jolted out of a deep slumber and barked out to the figure standing by his bedside, "What? Who's there? What's wrong?"

"It's me, Sarah," she whispered. "I think Robbie is going to hurt us."

The couple was confused. They tried to collect their thoughts and make sense of Sarah's claims. They were in disbelief that she would barge into their room with crazy accusations about Robbie. Mark rubbed his eyes and turned on the bedside light, illuminating Sarah's powdery white face. It startled him. "What the hell is all over you? What happened, Sarah?"

"We were playing pool. It's just chalk. You have to listen to me! He is going to do something – something bad. Maybe Stuart is, too!"

"What do you mean?" asked Mark.

"Are you high?" Amy interrupted.

"No! Well – I ate a sliver of an edible Robbie brought, but this has nothing to do with that. I'm perfectly sober."

"Oh, Sarah. It must be the drug. Robbie is definitely a strange person, but I can't see him – or Stuart for that matter – hurting anyone. They're our friends," Amy sighed.

Sarah tried to convince them – and herself – that she was not experiencing a hallucination. She was frustrated that they did not believe her. The time was ticking. The men could make their way upstairs to attack her and the rest of the group at any moment. "Please, you have to come down and help us. Stuart is not functioning right. He's not moving! I left him alone with Robbie, and I'm afraid something terrible is going to happen."

"Stuart is not functioning or moving?" questioned Mark.

"Sarah, go to bed. You're just feeling a little paranoid from the drug," said Amy.

"You've got to believe me. I'm not imagining things." Sarah turned to Mark and pleaded, "Mark, help. The guys are not in their right minds."

"What do you want me to do, Sarah?"

"Go down and check things out. I am not sleeping down there. Please, let me stay in your room," she implored.

Mark silently communicated to Amy with his eyes that he was concerned about Sarah's allegations. He nodded and pulled the sheets aside to ready himself for a trip downstairs. "I'll be right back, honey," Mark reassured his wife. "I have to find out what this is all about." He slipped a pair of pajama pants over his boxers and guided the frightened woman back to the staircase. "Let's go see what's up, Sarah."

"Oh, thank you, Mark," she sighed. "Can we grab my bed and pillow, too?"

Mark did not respond to her request as he approached the steps. He was less than thrilled to be awakened from a deep sleep and even more annoyed that she wanted to take over his bedroom for the rest of the night. But he would oblige to keep her safe – and happy.

They could see the entire game room from atop the stairs. It was still lit. Robbie now stood over Stuart, who remained seated on the hassock with his hands over his face – the same way Sarah had left him.

"Huh!" she gasped at the sight. "What is he doing to him?" she feared.

Robbie had an opened energy drink in his hand and was offering it to Stuart. Mark went down the staircase ahead of Sarah, who stayed a few steps behind.

"Don't drink it, Stuart!" Sarah yelled. "What did you put in that, Robbie?"

"I put nothing in it," he replied, glancing up the stairs. "I'm just giving him something to drink. Chill out."

"Why did you have to open it?" she inquired.

Robbie did not answer her, but instead looked puzzled at why Mark was downstairs. He stood off to the side, holding the drink.

"Stu, you ok, man?" Mark said, placing his hand on Stuart's back. "Stuart, can you hear me?"

There was no reply. No one was able to reach him. Stuart seemed to be in a trance.

"Sarah, run to the bathroom and get a wet washcloth," Mark ordered.

Not wanting to leave Mark alone with the two men, she hesitated. When she did not obey, he pointed to the bathroom with a forceful gesture and snapped his finger. She finally did what he asked and quickly returned with the wet towel.

Mark placed the compress over Stuart's hands, hoping he would open them and use the cloth on his own to wipe his face. He bent down to listen for any breathing. Finally, he saw Stuart's chest rise and fall. But there was no other movement from his friend. "Are you ok, buddy?" Mark rubbed the wet cloth over the back of Stuart's neck. He looked at the others, who were watching his moves – like a hawk. "What the hell happened down here? You all should've gone to bed."

Like two guilty children being scolded, neither Robbie nor Sarah said a word.

Mark walked away in a huff and headed toward the other side of the house to look for Sarah's mattress. He had to travel through the darkened kitchen to reach the living room where it was being stored. Steffi and the teens were still fast asleep there.

Robbie followed. "I'll help you, my friend," he murmured under his breath.

Sarah's nerves shot up as soon as Robbie slithered behind Mark. She ran toward the kitchen, hoping to warn him of his presence. She knew that Mark did not need any help with an inflatable mattress. It must have only weighed a few pounds. From her perspective, Robbie's intention was to hurt, not help. Mark was entering a cave with an encroaching dragon blocking the only way out. As Sarah approached the kitchen doorway, Robbie made an abrupt U-turn to face her. She jumped!

"What's the matter, Sarah?" Robbie said, eerily. "Where are you going?"

"Mark!" Sarah yelled into the dark room.

There was no response.

"Sarah, let me help you," Robbie motioned with outstretched arms.

"Get away from me!" she shrieked and threw her hands up defensively.

"What is wrong with you? I want to help you."

"Help me with what? I don't need any help."

Within a minute, Mark returned, carrying the bulky blowup bed and Sarah's pillow. He struggled to shimmy the mattress out of the small kitchen doorway. It slid, uneasily, against the wooden framework and sounded like the rubbing of an oversized balloon. Sarah helped, by pulling one end through. They carried the bed to the staircase.

"I'm going with you, Mark!" Sarah backed up the steps behind her security guard, keeping a watchful eye on both her pursuer and the man on the hassock. *Is Stuart going to sit there all night, shut off from what is taking place around him?* she wondered. *Is he building up anger, ready to explode?*

The scene was ominous from the top of the stairs. Sarah's bird's eye view above the lights gave her greater power over the situation, yet she did not feel completely safe from the threat of danger. Mark had continued down the hallway with her mattress. "What are we doing about Stuart – and Robbie?" Sarah asked.

"Stuart will be ok, Sarah. Just give him some time to snap out of it," Mark consoled her. "I'll check on him later. I didn't feel any threat from Robbie. Go to bed and get some rest."

"Ok, thank you, Mark. And thank you for letting me stay in your room."

Mark set the mattress down at the foot of his bed. He grabbed some sheets from the linen closet in the bathroom and quickly prepared her resting place. "Good night, Sarah," he said.

"I'm so sorry, Mark. Good night."

"Everything's ok. Now rest."

Sarah crumpled to her knees and crawled onto the mattress, trying to be as quiet as possible. It shifted back and forth, like a river raft, squeaking with every move. Amy was not asleep. She peered with one eye over the top of the covers while Sarah's head disappeared below the edge of the bed.

Mark and Amy were too tired from being awakened to say anything more. They would have no trouble falling back to sleep. For Sarah – it would be the opposite.

She stared at the sliding glass door. The warm and comforting feeling she had experienced earlier while admiring the view from the balcony – had now vanished, completely. The light from the moon forced its way through partitions in the curtains and cast strange shadows about the bedroom.

Things were all quiet from an outsider's perspective, but there was a war raging in Sarah's head. It was a battle of right and wrong – good and evil. Sounds of knives sharpening, curdling screams, and elevated arguments went off in her mind. The nagging fear that someone – or something – was coming up the staircase, vexed her. Sarah would not be sleeping anytime soon. She prepared herself for the fight of her life.

Chapter 30

ANGELS AND DEMONS

Sarah stared at the ceiling, motionless. The atmosphere in the entire house was placid. Yet the noise in her head was deafening. She was determined to stay awake and vigilant, despite the drowsiness she felt after ingesting the marijuana and wine. *What is happening downstairs?* she wondered. *Is Robbie killing Stuart? Or are they conspiring? Are the teens and Steffi alright?* Her mind raced.

Fatigue fought against her will to stay up. She experienced in-between states of awareness and lack of consciousness. It was when her body started to drift further into a sleep-state that she imagined hearing frightening noises: screams, choking – even gunshots. "Get out!" she whispered strongly under her breath. "Get out of my brain!"

Sarah was so frightened that she started to shake. The only thing to do was change her perspective and her attitude. She remembered a line of scripture from her church-going days and her father's readings. Back then, they seemed to be only thoughts on paper. The passage was in the book of *Ephesians, 6:11.* She whispered to herself, " 'Put on the whole armor of God, that you may be able to stand against the wiles of the devil.' " With all the strength she could muster, she demanded that the evil spirits invading her mind be cast out – in the name of Jesus.

The sounds stopped – temporarily.

Demons were tormenting her and they would not give up their fight, easily. They tempted her to give in and not call on God for help. The sounds returned every time she drifted to sleep – when she was caught off guard and vulnerable. She tried as hard as she could to put her faith and trust in God, but she still struggled with doubt. *Am I going to die, tonight? Is everyone going to die?* she wondered.

The universe was swirling behind the plaster of the ceiling and the roof's Mexican tile shingles. There was a virtual storm of darkness and what seemed to be impending danger looming above her. The ticking of a small wall clock started to lull her to sleep.

She snapped back to lucidity and prayed. Yes, Sarah prayed. "Father, please forgive me for all that I have done. Forgive me for yelling at You and all the times I used Your name in vain. Forgive me for wanting two men and for my promiscuity. Forgive me for neglecting Em when she needed me around. Forgive me for things that have not found favor in Your eyes. Please, save me and all these people in the house." Her words were barely audible, in fear of waking Mark and Amy. Quiet tears rained down her cheeks. She continued to beg God to protect her. "Send Your angels into this entire home, Father – downstairs, upstairs. Fill this place with Your Holy Spirit. Help Stuart and Ro . . . ." Her words trailed off as she drifted.

Then, there was a diabolical chuckle, the sound of a knife being forcefully driven into flesh and bone, and the distant voices of men verbally fighting. Sarah shook herself awake and pinched her thigh to remain alert. She pictured Robbie doing terrible things to Stuart. Sarah wanted to believe that it was all in her imagination. *My mind is playing tricks on me,* she thought. *I must be the only one hearing this disturbing interference.*

Mark and Amy were not awakened by the sounds Sarah was hearing. Their presence brought little, if no relief. *Why isn't Mark checking on Stuart, like he promised?* she wondered.

Sarah wanted to go downstairs, but she realized it would be a big mistake. Praying and being positive were the only things to do. She painted a vision in her mind of all whom she thought were good or comforting – her parents, little Em, the white horse, and even Richard.

Meanwhile, the thin streams of moonlight peeking through the cracks in the curtains danced around the room. But this night, Sarah did not need windows of light for clarity. She could see through the walls. The universe continued to stir above her, like a hurricane. Sarah was its eye. She stared upwards, hoping the sky would open and reveal the answers she was looking for – answers to everything that had taken place. She thought, again, about her family and the feeling of love surrounding her. Her greatest need was to be rescued from the storm.

But the true Savior – had not shown up yet. Sarah called upon Jesus. His light and grace were needed to cast away her fears and pull her to safety. She tried to picture Him standing in the room – all in white – but she fell asleep, then awakened. Had He arrived while she slipped out of consciousness? Possibly, briefly. Then vanished? With all her mental strength, Sarah tried to pull Him in to stay. His spirit could be felt somewhere around the room, but she could not see Him. He was just outside her grasp. It was perplexing and she feared abandonment.

Jesus! Where are You? Please lay Your hands upon us and keep us alive, she screamed inside her head. "I know You died for me. I know You love me. I'm so sorry I pushed You away. Please come back. I want and need You," she whispered.

Suddenly, the air in the room turned cool. He had arrived. Jesus had stepped into the fray of the devil's invasion of Sarah's life. He had been there all along – watching and waiting – allowing her to fall just far enough to be brought back with a deeper understanding of who He is. Sarah cried, uncontrollably, at the feeling of relief. She meditated on His presence. "Thank You, Father. Thank You, Jesus. Please, don't ever leave me."

Then, Sarah was shown a series of visions – visions that did not make sense to her, at first. They were random scenes of people – crowds of people. Dark water. Screams in the fire. Animals running free. Lights in the sky. They just kept coming, rapidly. Everything was spinning above her in a dark, clouded backdrop. Her observation of the churning universe felt so overwhelmingly clear. She believed that what was happening to *her* was happening to the whole world! Sarah was being shown the details. Her involvement with Robbie and Stuart was a trigger to this final culmination. *This is a trifecta! Is it ordained?* she wondered. The experience must have been a trilogy of three, vastly different stories. That is what she believed God was telling her. *But why? Why are You putting me through this, Lord?*

God was not finished.

Pop! A synapse of information suddenly ran across her brain, like a desert rat on the run from impending danger. She saw a vision of Richard's accident and funeral.

What was that? a startled Sarah thought. She focused intently on the ceiling where she could still see through to the outside world.

Pop! Pop! More and more flashes were being shown to her in rapid succession. They seemed to be Sarah's experiences or discussions over the last several months – all centered around Robbie and Stuart.

Pop! The lust for two men.

Pop! The lure of sex.

Pop! The Devil Inside perfume.

Pop! The hatred of old people.

Pop! The killing of enemies.

Pop! The Astrology.

Pop! The out-of-body experiences.

Pop! The pot-laced edibles.

Pop! The demons mentioned at the beach.

Pop! The fire and the evacuation.

Pop! The vision of the white horse.

Pop! The death of Em.

Pop! The stuffed animal.

Pop! The creepy grandmother.

Pop! The need to kill doves.

Pop! The abusive father.

Pop! And, finally, the portal that was opened at the pool table.

Everything plugged together. Each moment had a meaning and was relived as quickly as a dream. Any other pathway Sarah tried to take her thoughts, kept leading her back to the former months with Robbie and Stuart. *This is too much!* she thought. *Are You trying to tell me that I've been with demons? What do I do with all this, God?* Sarah had picked up on the signs over the last few months, but their meanings were clearer now. They were not just signs – they were warnings.

The spinning universe, beyond the ceiling, was a vision of the world being lured into sin and away from God. She could see scenes of so many people surrounded by demons, yet they had no clue of it. They were dismissing God and Jesus, just as Sarah had done. They were inviting evil into their lives – in so many different ways – yet carrying on as if nothing mattered. The world was growing darker and darker. Sarah wept for them and herself. It was frightening to watch. But then – it stopped.

Sarah's heart raced. She was out of breath and felt faint. God had more for her to piece together. She feared sleep and longed for Sunday's sun to rise, but she needed to rest. Daybreak would be safe. *Things are always better in the light,* she hoped – and drifted off.

The hands on the wall clock spun from one hour to the next. Then, three o'clock hit, and her body started to change. An uneasy feeling developed in her bowels and awakened her; it was the urge to release all toxins from her body. She dared not get up and walk across the room to the toilet. The flush would be heard downstairs, potentially awakening the fiends. The pain increased. Her system needed to purge.

Arching her head backwards, Sarah looked upside down at the slightly partitioned door behind her. She wished it had been shut tightly. Maybe Mark had purposefully left it open so he could hear any sounds that the guys would make downstairs. She scanned the room, detailing the furnishings, dancing light, and dark shadows surrounding her. Mark and Amy were fast asleep and snoring simultaneously.

"Protect me, Father," she said and rolled softly off the mattress, onto the wooden floor. Her knees crackled as they unfolded. She stood still to prevent any noise before tiptoeing her way to the bathroom. Remarkably, the floorboards kept quiet.

Emptying her system of the night's edible and alcohol was a necessary cleansing. When she finished, the atmosphere changed. She felt safer. At least in her mind, there was no threat. "I don't know what just happened, but You work in mysterious ways, Lord," Sarah whispered and giggled to herself. "Thank You, Father. Is it over?"

The fear in Sarah may have subsided, but her journey in search of the purpose was *not* over. There were several hours to go before the rest of the household would be awake and preparing for their return home. Sarah lied down quietly in her bed and covered her face with the sheet. She planned on never seeing Robbie or Stuart again. As far as she was concerned, they both wanted her dead.

Chapter 31

DAYBREAK

The aroma of roasted coffee and sizzling bacon drifted up the staircase and into the bedroom where Sarah was sleeping. The scent trickled past her nose. It could not have been a more awakening and welcoming fragrance. Amy and Mark must have gotten up and started cooking for their friends. Things seemed back to normal.

Sarah rubbed her face and stared up at the solid ceiling. She could no longer see the chaotic universe beyond the plaster. The dancing moonlight that had come through splits in the curtains had changed to sunlight and it filled the room. A muffled din of conversations and clanging dishes was heard downstairs.

"Sarah, time to get up and eat. Breakfast awaits you, my dear," a softened male voice whispered through the opening in the door.

"Morning, Wesley. I'll be right there," Sarah whispered quickly before the sound of his sandaled footsteps faded down the hallway.

The tired woman rolled off her mattress, stood up straight, and stretched her arms above her head. She closed her eyes and took a moment to thank God that she was alive. "You saved my life, Father. In the name of Jesus, thank You for protecting me."

Sarah hoped that in the coming weeks, God's purpose for her life would become clearer. She trusted Him more than ever. There were too many questions to be answered, but she would have to be patient. For now, the main thing on her mind was getting home to her peaceful sanctuary.

After washing her face and dressing in some comfortable driving clothes, Sarah stopped to look at her image in the bathroom mirror. A few wrinkles seemed to have developed overnight. She was cautious to gaze too long. Given the events that had just taken place, there was a feeling of uncertainty that someone or some *thing* might appear alongside her reflection. Her body shuddered, and she dashed out of the bathroom to begin packing her belongings. The airbed was easy to deflate. Sarah folded it into a heap, which she carried downstairs with the rest of her things. Snippets of the evening flashed through her mind as she anticipated bumping into Robbie or Stuart.

The staircase spit her out right at the pool table. The balls that Robbie had lined up earlier – as weapons – were neatly tucked into the triangle. Suddenly, her nerves tensed up. *I wonder who did that.* She turned to see if Stuart was still seated on the hassock. It was empty; no one was in the game room. *Where is he?* A handful of house guests came into view. Sarah felt uncomfortable making eye contact with anyone. She was not sure if they knew of the night's craziness. They minded their own business and fixed their breakfast plates. Finally, she found Stuart – standing at the kitchen sink, washing his hands. They were no longer pasted to his face. He moved about as if he had never been stone cold and lifeless; he was perfectly normal.

Am I in another dimension? Sarah wondered. The atmosphere felt odd to her. Rightfully, so. There were entities still in her midst. She scanned each adjoining room, looking side to side and over her shoulders for Robbie. She started to approach Stuart from behind to find out how he was doing when suddenly, out of nowhere, Robbie crossed her path – blocking her attempt to reach him.

"How are you feeling this morning?" he blurted.

"Aah!" Sarah gasped, jumping in place. Clutching her chest to slow her sudden, rapid heartrate, she breathlessly responded with sarcasm, "I – *was* – ok."

Upon hearing their short verbal exchange, Stuart came away from the sink. He snatched a dish towel from the counter and hastily dried his wet hands. Neither Robbie nor Sarah had ever witnessed the anger Stuart was about to display. The man clenched his teeth and with a low, but stern voice, displayed his ire, "Let's go talk alone, because I need to know what the hell happened!"

"Ok, dude. Calm down. Come with me," Robbie said.

They walked out of the kitchen and into the game room. Flashbacks zipped through Sarah's mind. The balls, the green felt of the table, and the wicked aura haunted her.

As Robbie began to speak, the memories pierced Sarah's brain, like knives. "I believe something evil entered this room last night," he began. "I've never felt anything like that before in my life."

Stuart and Sarah looked at each other first, then at Robbie, whose skin was pale. His tone was serious. He seemed frightened. Sarah was baffled, since *he* was the one both of them had been afraid of.

"I was pretty messed up," said Stuart. "Something was definitely in my head."

Sarah listened intently to their words. She was reluctant to talk too much about the experience. They were still in a remote location, and she did not want to create another evil episode by rehashing the night. Home was a long drive away, and the guys were not trustworthy anymore. But she needed to respond somehow. After all, they were her words that started everything. "So, you think it was an evil spirit, Robbie?"

"Definitely! Don't you? If it wasn't a poltergeist or something like that, then what was it?"

"I want to know what was in that stuff you fed us?" Stuart interrupted. "We didn't experience the effects of just THC. It was hallucinogenic. You need to explain it, now!"

"I swear, you guys," Robbie pleaded, "I bought it from the dispensary that I always go to for my medical pot. I had the same amount as you and I felt normal. *I* was not hallucinating. Maybe your bodies just reacted to it differently."

"Clearly, our bodies reacted differently!" Stuart shouted. "I was not myself. I was someone I did not recognize – and having some pretty wicked visions."

"I thought you were going to hurt us, Robbie," Sarah blurted out, but quickly recoiled. *He can't know,* she thought.

"I would never hurt you guys! You're my friends. Are you kidding?"

Sarah searched Robbie's eyes for genuineness and legitimacy. She wanted more of his side of the story. But now was not the time. The guys were back to their normal, argumentative, old selves again. She could not quite put her finger on it, but a heightened perception of something odd within her surroundings had not completely dissipated. "I don't know what catapulted the night into a dark abyss. But I do think whatever it was – it was trying to tell us something," she said.

Stuart listened and looked around the room, then fixated on the hassock. Even mighty Stuart felt some sense of terror at reliving those moments. He turned back to Robbie. "Dude, you were controlling my thoughts. There was something about you that changed. You were not the person I know."

Robbie was not surprised to hear those words. He knew some entity or force had either entered him or was awakened within him. But he would never admit it. That would mean that a possession had taken place. He wanted to blame the occurrence on an entity that was only in *the room*, not within *him*.

Sarah knew Robbie was not being completely truthful when he said nothing to address Stuart's concerns about thought-control. That raised a red flag. "I don't know what to tell you, Robbie. All I know is that the room filled with a dark, demonic presence and negativity. It was not cool," she said. *Does he know what came over him? Does he not want to admit to anything for fear of being judged or accused of something?* she wondered.

They were all distracted when Amy entered the room, carrying a plate of scrambled eggs and a glass of orange juice. "Sorry to interrupt your little soiree, but I noticed you never ate, Sarah. You, my dear, need energy for the ride home. Here."

"We can talk later," Sarah told the men. She thanked Amy graciously and carried her breakfast plate to the kitchen bar. A mixture of thoughts and worries weighed on her brain. Sarah hungrily shoveled the eggs into her mouth. She could barely taste and enjoy her meal, pondering the desolate drive home alone with the guys.

In the other room, Robbie left Stuart's side without saying a word and gathered up his things. Stuart shook his head in disbelief and walked to the kitchen. He had more to say about last night's drug-induced horror show. "Sarah, finish up quickly and let's go outside," he demanded. "We need to talk more about this."

"Ok, ok," she said between chewing.

On his way to the patio, Stuart grabbed a lighter and one of Mark's stogies that was left on the counter. Mark puffed on them only when he camped at the river. Stuart was in need. He was determined to get resolution and not just brush off the strange experience. He was the partier – the happy-go-lucky guy who always had a smile on his face and a drink in each hand. But this time, he was different. His eyes were bloodshot and watery – and his demeanor – somber. Something strange was happening in his head. He felt an immediate distrust for the other house guests and was plagued with paranoia.

Sarah gobbled up her breakfast, quickly. She was anxious to hear whatever it was Stuart had to say that could not be expressed in front of Robbie. Glancing over her shoulder at the room with the pool table, she could see that Robbie was busy packing up his things and conversing with Steffi. It was the perfect moment to slip outside.

Sarah met up with Stuart who was sitting on a lounge chair – puffing away. "Since when do you smoke cigars, honey?"

"Since right now."

"Ha! Funny." A warm breeze blew past Sarah's nose, picking up a pleasing aroma of burnt tobacco leaves in its path. She slowly seated herself on a chair while watching a pair of mating dragonflies flit off the reeds at the side of the riverbank. Her thoughts flashed to earlier, when Robbie asked her to go outside and when she imagined him laying her dead body among those same reeds. She shook off the horrid vision.

"Sarah. What happened last night? I was being manipulated by an evil Robbie."

"Your guess is as good as mine. I was scared out of my pants. I saw an evil Robbie, too!"

"So, we felt the same thing?"

"I guess so!" she nodded in agreement. "Stuart, I have to know. Why did you have your hands over your face for so long?"

"I was fighting really bad thoughts in my head – and I was afraid that if I opened my eyes, those thoughts would become reality. I was confident that I would carry out the actions."

"What kind of bad thoughts, Stuart? What kind of actions?"

"Not sure I want to get into that part, now. I don't want Robbie overhearing our conversation."

Sarah grew frustrated. *I thought talking about the night was why he asked me out here,* she wondered. The event was too serious to ignore. Sarah was afraid of what the men were really thinking. It was crucial for her to have confirmation that what she experienced was not imagined. There was definitely more to share, like her encounter with God. But it would have to wait.

She gently plucked the cigar from Stuart's fingers and took a shallow puff, gazing into his crystal blue eyes. A thin trail of white smoke escaped her lips and floated above her, giving the appearance of an upward-flowing waterfall. Stuart smiled sensually at the sight.

"I do want to know one other thing," he inquired. His body trembled slightly, and his eyes bugged out. "When you look at each person in this house, can you see inside their soul?"

Sarah's ears perked up. She handed the cigar back to her friend. "Explain."

"I mean, is your brain analyzing them? Do you see the good or evil in each one, as if they're wearing a sign stating so?"

A shiver ran up Sarah's backbone, rattling her entire body. She closed her eyes and shook off the chill. She knew exactly what he meant. "Yes! I wondered if you were having the same insight."

"It's bizarre. This whole place is creeping me out," Stuart said and snuffed out the end of his cigar, but not before puffing on it six more times. "I've never felt this freaked out at the river. Maybe it's this house." The last bit of smoke from the earthy tobacco left his mouth and curled around Sarah's nose.

She breathed in the sweet smell. It calmed her nerves – then disappeared before she spoke, "Amy is bad. Mark is good. The twins and their girlfriends are bad. Steffi is good – well sort of – in a weird way. Robbie is bad," Sarah listed each one. "Is that what you mean?"

"Wesley, good," Stuart added. "Yes, that's exactly what I mean."

"What is happening to us?"

"Don't know. But this is unbelievably strange, Sarah. I'm looking right through to their insides, and I see their transparencies – their truths, their intentions."

"H-h-how do you see me, Stuart?"

He hesitated suspensefully. Searching Sarah's entire face was like navigating a winding road. Stuart smiled softly with his eyes and answered, "Good."

"I see you as good, too, my friend," Sarah smiled back. Even though she feared what he might have done to her, she did not see him as evil now. "Stuart, I must tell you about last night. The weirdest thing happened after I went upstairs. I couldn't sleep. I worried about you, but I was also afraid *of* you. My mind played tricks on me. I kept hearing you get murdered downstairs."

Stuart twitched his eyebrows up and down quickly in a surprised gesture. "Thanks for coming to my rescue," he joked. "How many times did I get killed?"

"I'm sorry about that," she giggled. "I wanted to trust that it was only in my imagination."

"I stayed on that hard hassock all night. To the best of my knowledge, Robbie went to bed in my sleeping bag."

"There's got to be an explanation for all this. I just want to go home, Stuart. But honestly, I'm scared to be in the car with him."

"It will be fine. If he was, in fact, possessed last night, he doesn't seem possessed anymore. By the way, I'm trained in martial arts. He won't touch us. But you will have to tell me later – when we have more time – why you were afraid of *me*!"

Sarah started to speak, but Stuart got up and walked back into the house. There were more questions to ask and details to tell him about her night upstairs. Could she trust him? After all, she had feared him. She stared out at the river. The jet skis and the boat were docked. The water showed no activity or wake, like earlier in the weekend. And the fun moments they had shared seemed so far away. She was ready to return to Long Beach. It was up to her when they would leave the house, since she had the car keys. The desert scenery was admired for its beauty one last time, before Sarah blew a kiss at the sky and walked back inside to get her things.

People were rushing around the house, getting ready to leave. There was a lot that had to be organized and packed up. Sarah was careful not to gawk at any one person too long. She was compelled to feel the strangeness from them, but she fought off the urge. The twins, along with their friends, whizzed by to get the boat and skis up on their parents' trailers at the launch.

Sarah searched the house looking for Mark and Amy to thank them and tell them *goodbye*. She was hoping to catch them before they got too busy with all the water crafts. While she peered around corners, she bumped into Wesley. "Hey, I hope you feel better. Let's get together when we get back to LB," she promised.

"Are you gonna be alright? I heard you guys had an odd night after I went to bed. But yeah, let's have dinner when we all get back home from this crazy weekend."

"I'll be fine, Wesley. It's a long story for another time. Thank you for caring." The two stretched out their arms and hugged. "Hey, would you mind following behind me on the drive back home?" she asked.

"Yeah, no problem. But I'll be taking a different route at the highway split, so I won't be able to follow you for the second half of your journey."

"Oh!"

"I have to take Steffi home, first. She lives in the opposite direction of my house."

"Ok, I guess there will be some sort of civilization at the split, right?"

"Maybe? If there is, I never noticed it. Why do you need an escort, Sarah? Are you afraid of something?"

"It's the desert, you know – desolate place. It's just best to travel in numbers, that's all. Ok, I'll catch up with you before you leave. I have to find Mark and Amy."

Wesley rushed off. He was ready to leave the campsite and get home to other friends who did not share the same type of *fun* that the current weekend had brought forth.

Sarah hoped there were some businesses along her path in case she needed to find someone for help. However, she remembered it was Sunday, and they were most likely closed. She would have to accept whatever amount of security she could get from Wesley.

She found Mark and Amy cleaning up the house and getting ready to head outside to help the teens. "Hey you guys! Thanks for setting this whole thing up. It was fun. And I'm sorry about inconveniencing you last night by sleeping in your bedroom," said Sarah.

"Oh, my goodness! We have no hard feelings at all, honey," said Mark. "We just hope you are alright and can put last night behind you." They were children of the sixties, so they were quite knowledgeable about marijuana and the effects of hallucinogens. The couple was convinced that drugs were to blame for the scary night.

Sarah changed the subject. "Do you need any help cleaning up?" She figured they were not getting much aid from Robbie or Stuart who were practically in the car already.

"We're all set," Amy said. "Thanks for coming out to Castle Dome. I hope you don't let what happened ruin the opportunity to come here again."

"I'll have to think about it, Amy."

"Ok, then. Maybe next time we'll get a chance to visit the actual ghost town and the saloon. I've been told it's truly haunted!"

"... by cowboys, outlaws, and fast women?" Sarah joked.

"Sounds like a good time to me! You had a lot of fun this weekend, right, Sarah?" Something in Amy's tone was off.

"Yes, of course – for the most part." Sarah's nerves shot up with apprehension. She tried to dismiss the idea that Amy and several of the other house guests were *bad* as she and Stuart had discussed. But the thought of it kept invading her head. Amy did not believe in God. She dabbled in fortune telling and horoscopes, just like Robbie. She was fascinated with the occult. The skull and horned hand hanging around her neck conveyed to Sarah that there was darkness surrounding her life. Sarah was fine with not returning to the river. The group hugged and parted.

The closer everyone was to leaving, the more anxious Sarah felt. *What if Robbie pulls a gun out of his bag in the car and holds me and Stuart hostage or just flat out pops us off? Perhaps Stuart is in cahoots with Robbie.* Sarah was in the midst of an anxiety attack, worrying about what could be. She vacillated about taking the men in her car. Even though they could figure out a way to get back on their own, she could not bring herself to leave them there. She prayed, "Father, please get me home alive. Cast all evil out of my car and out of Robbie and Stuart. Protect us from harm. Stay with me."

God had pulled her out of the storm she weathered overnight. She needed to have faith that He would get her home safely, as well. Doubt crept into her mind – doubt that she might not be fully protected. What about all the other times in her life He had let her down? What made this time any different? The choice to trust was hers to make, alone. *If something happens to me, so be it! It will be God's will,* she thought.

Suddenly, the sound of a truck's engine revving could be heard from the driveway. Wesley and Steffi were about to leave.

"Come on, guys, we gotta go!" Sarah shouted to Robbie and Stuart.

"Bye, Steffi!" Robbie yelled to the pickup.

There would be no rest for Sarah if she had to travel back the same desolate way without anyone trailing. She could not let Robbie know about her fear and what she had asked of Wesley. If Robbie was a demoniac, there was no telling what might happen on the road – in the lonely desert.

Chapter 32

THE AWAKENING

The small trunk on Sarah's car popped open and the trio threw most of their bags inside. Other items made their way to the back seat with Stuart. They all climbed into the little convertible and got as comfortable as possible – as they had done before. Sarah started the engine and backed out; then Wesley and Steffi took off. That was not the plan. *Wait, Wesley! You were supposed to follow me!* she screamed inside her head. A sudden rush of panic gripped Sarah. She threw the car into *drive* and stepped on the gas in an attempt to catch up to his truck.

"What's the hurry, darlin'?" Robbie inquired.

"No reason. I just want to get home."

Wesley noticed Sarah and stuck his left hand out the window in acknowledgement of her presence.

Back inside her car, Robbie and Stuart were preparing for the journey. Despite having to share the back seat with a cooler, Stuart was content with the arrangement as usual. There was a compelling need for each of them to talk about the night; yet the unspoken consensus was not to relive the last twelve hours – at least in such tight quarters.

Sarah glanced in her side view mirror and noticed the camp house in its reflection. At the same time, she tried to navigate off the dirt roads that led to the main highway. The image of the house remained imprinted on the glass as if it were following them home. Sarah was so focused on the camp, that she forgot about watching Wesley's truck. He was getting farther and farther away. She sped up when she realized how far back she had fallen. *Slow down, Wesley. Did you forget me?* she wondered. *Don't panic, girl. Demonic spirits love it when you panic.* She stepped on the gas pedal.

Poor Wesley had a momentary lapse in memory and judgement. He noticed her approaching his truck and blinked his brake lights when she got closer. It would be an additional ninety minutes that the cars would have to travel before reaching the split in the road. Sarah was determined to keep him in her sight. However, Wesley just wanted to get home.

Inside the little car there was no music and no conversation. The warm, desert air intruded on the trio's quiet time. It whispered in their ears and aroused their past desires for one another. But the feelings did not last long. Sarah knew that she needed to steer clear of wanting two men. There would be no turning back to what they once had. Sarah blinked hard to get the thought out of her mind.

Stuart pondered the uncanny insight he had regarding all his friends. It disturbed him. He tried to feel some joy from his past experiences with Sarah – since she was one of the *good* ones – but his emotions were too difficult to reach in the cavern of his memories. Maybe once this weekend blew over, the feelings would return. For now, he just wanted to sleep.

The time it took to reach the split in the road went by like a flash. For the rest of the way, Sarah would have to go it alone, without Wesley. She felt a chill when he turned off the main highway. The road he took headed toward San Diego where Steffi lived. Wesley planned on dropping her off and then going straight home to his own bed. He waved *goodbye* to Sarah, gave her a *thumbs up,* and vanished out of sight. Hoping that Robbie would not notice Wesley's departure from their path, Sarah nervously fidgeted with her hair to distract him.

But Robbie did notice. "Bye, bye, Wesley," he snickered.

A rush of fear ran through her body upon hearing Robbie's creepy and glib farewell. She fought the anxiety and thought of something, quickly, to change the strange mood inside the vehicle. "I'm craving pizza. You interested in getting one on the way home, Robbie?" Sarah said with feigned excitement.

"You do realize that we have several hours to go before we get back, right?" he asked. "So the answer is no."

"Yeah, I know. And I have some snacks in the car that can tie me over until then. I just thought you might look forward to getting a pizza, later." Sarah's eyes darted back and forth in an effort to think up something else to say. It was a relief that he turned down her offer to get pizza, but now what? She had no choice but to continue driving in awkward silence.

They would be approaching the Salton Sea and then heading up through Palm Desert. It would take at least three grueling hours before they were home, safe and sound, and away from each other. All of a sudden, Robbie started fumbling through a small, black bag he pulled out of his backpack, which was stored at his feet.

What is he doing? Sarah wondered with fear. She watched his hands out of the corner of her eye and tried not to appear shaken. He continued rummaging through his bag. Sarah glanced in her rearview mirror to see if Stuart was awake to witness Robbie's every move. No luck. He was snoring. *What good are his martial-arts skills if he's asleep?* Sarah wondered. She stared straight ahead with bugged out eyes. Adrenaline pumped through her veins. Sweaty palms gripped the leather steering wheel. It squeaked underneath her nervous fingers.

Robbie had barely stirred for the last hour. Now he was moving around and causing a change in the atmosphere of the car by digging through his bag.

How many things could be in there? Sarah wondered. *Is he preparing a switchblade? Is he cocking a gun?* Sarah could feel a looming, evil presence. She knew what was to come if she started shivering and fearing for her life, again. *Get out!* she screamed inside her mind. *Get out, Satan!*

She needed God's power. She prayed for herself and the men. *Father, please cast away these demons. I resist them, now, in the name of Your Son, Jesus.* Sarah was not well read of the Bible, but she knew many of its messages. She was fully aware of the supernatural powers of Jesus and that He called on His disciples to cast out unclean spirits from people. She could pray them away in His name, too. She sensed a strong force around her.

Finally, Robbie's hands immerged from the bag with the unknown item. It was a package of chewing gum. A sigh of relief escaped Sarah's mouth and her heart slowed its pace as Robbie leaned back in his seat to unwrap one piece. If she did not have to keep her eyes on the road, she would have shut them and sobbed. Instead, she blinked hard and inhaled a deep breath. The fear of Robbie hurting her, subsided – temporarily.

"Are you ok, Sarah?" Robbie questioned.

"I'm ok. Are you ok?

"You just seem – a little nervous."

Sarah rolled up the windows and turned on the air conditioner.

"That's fine," Robbie approved.

"Oh!" she responded. "Sorry, are you sure it's ok to shut them?"

"Hopefully, the car won't overheat with the AC being on, that's all. I'd hate to be stuck out here in the desert with a broken-down car," he said.

Panic hit her again. She thought Robbie was subliminally trying to frighten her and make her worry about being stranded. Her heart raced.

She imagined the scene – no one around and no one to rescue her. No Mark. No Wesley.

She had to trust in God.

"I'll make sure to keep an eye on my temperature gauge," she said, faking confidence.

God had pulled her from the hands of those who wanted her dead. He was in control. His will was His will and Sarah had to accept it no matter what it ended up being. She silently meditated. Words of revelation were made clear in her mind. What she experienced was some sort of an awakening to God's purpose for her. The reason behind the mysterious occurrences of the weekend would soon be realized – she hoped. But there was still more to unravel. Her thoughts became poetic in nature.

If the feeling is hidden, it will show itself,
For all things hidden must someday see the light.
Darkness breeds grief
And grief never smiles.
It wades in black water
And is blind to its surroundings.
But sunshine breeds joy.
And misty rainbows fill the sky
As if to announce the beginning of life.
Why be a part of a world so full of uncertainty and dismay?
Let the rays beam down upon your weary eyes
That are so heavy now with sand.
Find what you are looking for
And do not be afraid of what's around the corner.
For it may just be – a rainbow.

The words brought her comfort. The poem repeated in her head while Robbie stared out the window. Turning on the radio might break the ice, so she tried finding a strong L.A. station. "Do you mind if I . . . ?"

"Not at all, play whatever you want, Sarah," Robbie interrupted, his eyes fixed on the desert sand.

"Thanks."

Robbie was preoccupied. He was a contemplator and an analyzer. The event that had happened to the group over the weekend dominated every thinking cell in his brain. He had now become afraid of himself and whatever had possessed him during their billiards game. "Mercury in retrograde," he mumbled, "full moon, Friday the thirteenth."

Sarah and Stuart had forgotten about the highly superstitious events taking place that weekend. They were too busy having fun – until the incident. But after going through hell and back, Sarah was beginning to think that Robbie was onto something. It was not just because he followed his astrological chart, it was because he invited dark spirits into his life that used divination to entertain and deceive.

Sarah could hear Robbie's eerie ramblings. She desperately wanted to ask him about what he was thinking, but she remained quiet. She kept the music low, so as not to wake Stuart or offend Robbie if a sappy song played on the radio. The background noise was an attempt to remove the need for conversation.

Robbie dove into his bag again. Sarah perked up. This time, he noticed. "Why are you so tense, Sarah?"

She was caught off guard and the serious tone in Robbie's voice took her back to the pool table. Her body tightened and trembled. A glance in the rearview mirror yielded no sense of security. Stuart was still passed out cold.

"Nope, not tense," she lied confidently. "Just a little chilly from the AC."

"Shut it off, then."

"I'll just turn it on low," she said. Sarah tried to remain calm. She silently prayed for strength and peacefulness, which Robbie interrupted.

"I know we are trying to avoid talking about the weekend, but don't you think that the full moon, Friday the thirteenth, and Mercury in retrograde had something to do with what we experienced? I mean, when you put all of those things together, it's pretty uncanny, don't you agree?"

What do I say? What do I say? Sarah thought frantically to herself. *God, give me the words.* Sarah was quiet for several seconds. Their scary night together was darker than superstitions, but Sarah did not want to engage Robbie in discussing evil spirits right now. Talking about them might conjure up their existence. Goosebumps formed on her arms. One hand remained on the steering wheel while the other one rubbed them away. "I'm really not sure, Robbie. I think we all need to go home and get a lot of rest. Maybe we can get together later this week and talk about it with clearer heads. Would you be ok with that?"

"No worries. Namaste."

Namaste? Where did the need to quote Sanskrit suddenly come from? Sarah wondered. She knew very little about Hinduism, but she had heard of the term he used and its sentiment of honoring *the god within* the person to whom one says it. Bowing to someone other than God of the Bible, however, made her uncomfortable. Robbie cherry-picked portions of different practices, never really devoting much of his true heart to any one thing. Sarah started to think that the mixture of beliefs was causing some of his inner turmoil. Maybe he picked it up somewhere and said it without thinking.

Robbie retrieved a rolled-up t-shirt from the black bag. He shoved it under his head, which he leaned against the passenger door window. Feeling more restful, the man quickly drifted off to sleep. Sarah relaxed her muscles to the best of her ability while the two men napped. Reflecting on her surroundings, she realized there were no fights over which CD to play, no passing around of the booze bottle that Stuart had always prepared, and no sharing of peanuts. Their fun had faded. For some strange reason, she was fine with it.

The time passed by surprisingly quickly and soon her little car carried them into the outskirts of Long Beach. It was still daylight when they arrived at the city. There was no doubt in Sarah's mind that the next few hours would be filled with more soul-searching. She would not get much rest. The little vehicle stopped and rolled and stopped and rolled while it made its way through city traffic. The change in the car's rhythm awakened Robbie and Stuart.

"Are we home yet?" Stuart asked, like a child.

"Almost, honey," a motherly Sarah responded.

"Drop me off, first," Robbie piped in.

Outwardly, Sarah tried to remain unfazed at Robbie's request. Inwardly, she could not wait to oust him. The sun was setting. Reds and oranges painted the sky to the west and baby blue and pink swathed the east. Sarah believed it was God's way of coloring her world with the promise of peace. She smiled to herself and repeated her poem in her head. *If the feeling is hidden, it will show itself....*

They soon approached Robbie's complex. Sarah parked along the sidewalk, and he quickly stepped out onto the curb with his bag. She popped open the trunk for him to grab other belongings and motioned Stuart to take the front seat. He got out from the back and stretched.

Meanwhile, Robbie stood on the curb, staring at the interior of Sarah's vehicle. He anticipated a *goodbye* hug from someone, but his lingering made Sarah feel uncomfortable. She remained in the driver's seat and waved. Embracing him after all that had transpired would seem weird. Getting home before the sun fully set was the only thing on her mind. Stuart fist-bumped his friend and took the front seat next to Sarah.

"I'll give you a call tomorrow, dude. I'm beat," Stuart told Robbie.

"Yeah, chat soon," he responded in a solemn voice. Robbie's face lacked expression. There was sadness in his eyes. His mouth was straight, and his head tilted toward the ground. The backpack and other bags were tossed over his shoulders as he headed toward his apartment. He knew that he had possibly lost his friends' trust, and that meant he might not see them again.

Sarah and Stuart wanted to know what happened at the river just as much as Robbie did. Deciding how they would remain in contact, if at all, would take some time to figure out. She knew they would have to embark on their own journeys for now. The dynamics of their friendship had changed. Wickedness had revealed itself in the poisoned apple that each one of them had eaten.

Chapter 33

INTO THE LIGHT

Sarah felt safe being just in Stuart's presence. She still believed the man had a gentle spirit. There was some hope that he would tell her that his changed demeanor the night before was not his true self, no matter what happened to him in the game room. "Let's get that pizza! Want to come over?" he asked.

"Um . . . ," Sarah hesitated.

"I thought I heard you were having a craving, right before I crashed."

"Sure. I guess I could do that." *Am I walking into a fire again?* she wondered. *But I need answers. And so does Stuart.*

He turned the volume down on the radio and called the pizza restaurant near his apartment. "Let's pick it up on the way to my house, and then we can relax. Sound good?"

"Sounds good."

"I have many questions, but I need something in my stomach first, like food and lots of wine."

"Ugg – wine," Sarah grumbled to herself. Alcohol was the last thing she wanted to ingest.

It only took thirty minutes to get to the pizza joint, pay, and drive to Stuart's apartment. When they finally got there, they flopped down on the sofa to rest until the feeling of riding in the car for several hours subsided. Stuart dropped the box on a set of books that were stacked on his coffee table and breathed heavily. After a few minutes, he jumped up and poured their drinks. Sarah soon followed, grabbing napkins from the kitchen. When she got back to the living room, she thought of Robbie's advances – on that same sofa. Once again, she was tormented with the memory of the threesome's good times together, but the thought was quickly extinguished when Stuart returned with a glass of vintage cabernet in each hand.

Sarah smiled. "Thank you, Stuart, although I'm not sure I can finish it," she said. "I want to be as coherent as possible and frankly would not care to see another bottle of wine again."

"This is my favorite cab so if you don't drink it – I will. Just thought you needed to relax."

Sarah set the glass down to the side. She lifted the cardboard box off of the books and magazines so that the heat from the pizza would not cause their paper covers to stick. As she placed a few napkins underneath, she noticed the publications were of religious orientation. She was very curious as to why Stuart was reading about different faiths. There were topics on Christianity, Hinduism, Buddhism, Existentialism, New Age, and a few obscure practices Sarah had never heard of.

Stuart noticed her looking intently at the books. "I've been reading up on a variety of ancient and new religions, as you can see. I'm not sure which one holds all the keys. I'd like to discuss what *you* believe, Sarah."

"I – I believe in God and that Jesus was His Son," she stuttered and smiled, "and He came here to die for our sins." Her voice became more confident as she explained. "But I have fallen away – if you hadn't noticed."

Stuart snickered and said, "Quite a change from only a few days ago when you told us you didn't believe in Jesus anymore. What makes you so sure of what you say now?"

Sarah swallowed hard and said with assurance, "Because He saved my life at the river, that's why, Stuart. Also, Jesus is righteous and good and perfect. And the Bible is prophetic. It is God's word. The universe – and everything in it – runs like clockwork. It is divine so it must have had a divine creator. And I don't think we evolved. If that was the case, animals would be talking, right?"

"Wow! Something did change you over the weekend. And you've made a good point. I definitely want to hear more about what happened to you, sometime," Stuart said. "Would you like to know what I've always thought?"

"Sure! Tell me," Sarah answered.

"I'd like to think what we do in this life advances us to another life in another dimension – a better life."

"Everything you do – even how you treat others?" she questioned his theory.

"Especially how you treat others. And death plays a large part. For example, if we were to take the life of someone else, we would either fall back or advance, depending on the value of the life we took."

"You mean if you took the life of a criminal, you would advance to the next universal level?"

"Something like that," he responded.

"That's a scary way to live if you are on the receiving end of your judgement. The Bible teaches us *not* to judge and to definitely *not* consider ourselves a god. Only God will judge."

"It doesn't mean I'm out there being a justice warrior and killing people."

"Yeah, but – what if you're wrong in your assessment of someone?"

"Then I get it wrong. I don't advance. I fall back."

"No. You go to jail!" Sarah exclaimed.

"Ha – yes," Stuart replied, "but keep in mind, anything that I would ever do would be in self-defense. I'm not some vigilante looking for bad guys to take down."

"I'm confused. When you said 'depending on the value of the life' who is determining the life's value? Are you believing in a god higher than yourself? And, what if . . . ?"

"Let's talk about this at another time," he politely interrupted. "Right now, I'm starving."

Sarah did not like being cut off, but she could sense that he was getting uncomfortable with her questioning. Maybe he himself was confused on how to answer her. According to his theory, whether she lived or died depended on the way *he* envisioned her and if he trusted Sarah to be of good heart. Sarah was not sure whether to take him seriously or if what he was saying was a joke. *No wonder I thought he was going to possibly hurt me at the river if what I said to Robbie made him upset. But he must have sensed my true self; that's why he held back,* she pondered. His statements still made her nervous.

Stuart threw open the box of pizza, and the two devoured the hot food. They had no problem with being sloppy eaters to get their meal down as quickly as possible. Questions about last night loomed.

"Let's get right to it. What the hell happened to you?" Sarah inquired between bites of pizza.

Stuart looked at Sarah dead in the eyes and answered, "I have to start by saying – that was the strangest thing that has ever happened to me. I cannot explain *why* it happened, but I can tell you what I was feeling."

"Start with the drug, then."

Stuart shook his head in disbelief. "I don't think it was simple pot, Sarah. It felt like a hallucinogen – for sure. And it didn't feel the same as when you and I ate that cookie here at my place. My body was just numb that time; we laughed and had fun."

"I totally agree with you! That candy Robbie brought had something else in it. Go on."

Stuart took another bite of pizza and spoke as he chewed, "When I walked over to the end of the pool table and sat down on that footstool – I got really light-headed. When you started accusing Robbie – something strange happened inside of me."

"I definitely felt something change in you. I was scared," she said. It was apparent that the words Sarah spoke last night were provocative. In a way, she blamed herself for the situation. Her heart began pounding. She knew whatever Stuart said next was going to mirror her exact recollection.

"I saw evil in Robbie the minute you told him he was a *bad man*."

Sarah's body shook as his words trickled through her veins with horror. She visualized everyone in the game room staring at one another. "Yes, yes, go on," she pushed.

"Sarah. I could *not* think on my own. Robbie was manipulating my thoughts, telling me to do things I didn't want to do."

"What kind of things?"

Stuart stared across the room. A few framed photos of the past hung on the wall – pictures of Robbie and Stuart at parties with other friends. He looked at them with fondness.

"Stuart! What kind of things?" Sarah demanded.

He just glared at the photos, studying Robbie's face in each one and reminiscing about the experiences. The river trip confused him. There was something not quite right about the man who had latched onto his life and considered himself a *good friend*. Stuart rubbed his unshaven face with both hands, hoping to relieve the pressure that was squeezing the muscles behind his eyes. "I fought against a voice," he eerily whispered.

His words were like demon fingers tickling Sarah's ears, but they were not shocking to hear. "Robbie's voice, you mean? What was it saying?"

"Yes, Robbie's voice, but amplified in some weird way. It was layered, as if two voices were speaking at the same time. I physically and mentally – as if my brain had hands – pushed against the commands to do these things. I tried like hell to resist." Stuart was silent, again. He continued staring at the pictures on the wall.

"What things, Stuart? Just say it!" Sarah's anger and frustration increased.

He turned away from the photos and looked at her delicate face. After a long pause, he said, "Bad things."

Suddenly, the terror returned. Now Sarah was certain that something awful could have happened in that house. She had not just imagined it all as Mark and Amy had accused. There were moments when she second-guessed what she had experienced, blaming it all on a bad batch of pot and paranoia. Not anymore. No. It was real. Very real. And Stuart had more to tell.

"What bad things, Stuart? Please, tell me. I need to know. Why are you making me hang on like this? What are you afraid to say?"

Stuart's brain was hurting. He breathed heavily and swallowed another bite of pizza. "I could hear my own voice yelling back at Robbie's perceived demands. I kept saying 'no – no, you don't belong here. Get out of my head. Get out of my body.'"

Sarah was mesmerized. Her hands grew cold.

He continued, "I was slipping away from myself." Marinara sauce dribbled out of the corner of his mouth as he became more animated. "Evil Robbie was trying to take over my thoughts. It scared the crap out of me, Sarah. I felt like he wanted me to steal, rape, destroy the house, and hurt everyone in their beds."

Goosebumps formed on Sarah's skin, again, covering her entire body. Her attention was more focused than ever. *Rape?* She could not imagine Stuart doing such a thing to anyone, especially his friends. *Did Stuart want to rape me?* she feared.

"Sarah, I am not afraid of much in this crazy world. I am trained in several different forms of martial arts. I'm pretty confident no one can hurt me. But that night, I feared for my life and the lives of everyone in that house."

Sarah's body trembled. She was sitting on the same couch with a man who was admitting some terrible things. And the haunting vision of them all around the pool table could not be erased. "Why would Robbie want to cause any of us harm, Stuart? And why would he want to command you to do these awful things under his control?"

"I do not know, Sarah. I do not know."

Sarah looked at Stuart – just sitting there – chewing the doughy pizza. Her brow furrowed as she tried to make sense of it all. *Why did God help me and Stuart?* she pondered. *If anyone deserved His abandonment, it was me. I have sinned against Him. I have blasphemed. I have lusted. Been promiscuous, unforgiving. Lied.* Sarah started to cry. She tried to piece together all that God had showed her last night with the conversation she was having with Stuart.

"Are you alright?" he asked.

"I'm not sure," she said. "You see – I felt that you were going to hurt me. You confirming what I already believed, is scary." She paused. "What stopped you?"

"I don't know," admitted Stuart. "Maybe something divine?"

"Yes, Stuart. Maybe."

"I need to ask you something very important," Sarah said as her voice quavered. "Tell me honestly, I must know."

"What is it?"

She gulped hard, anticipating an answer that would be difficult to handle. "Stuart – did you want to kill me?"

His eyes glossed over and he stopped chewing. He absorbed the magnitude of her question as he looked down at the coffee table to search his thoughts. How could he respond to such a life-altering question?

No one should ever have to ask that of a friend, Sarah thought, *and a friend should never need to answer it.*

Stuart swallowed all that remained in his mouth, took a large gulp of wine, and said nothing. Sarah grew frustrated by the amount of time he was taking to answer. This was her friend.

Her palms grew sweaty. She leaned toward him, nearly falling off the couch. Her lips were pursed, but quickly parted – baring her white teeth. "Did – you – want – to – kill – me?" she spoke slowly and deliberately.

Wiping his mouth with a napkin, Stuart looked at Sarah and answered with no expression on his face, "Yes."

Chapter 34

THEY LURK, THEY WATCH

Sarah dragged herself through the front door of her apartment and collapsed onto the sofa. The words exchanged between her and Stuart, the memories of the weekend, and fears she had felt in the presence of friends, started to consume her sanity. To think that her life may have ended less than twenty-four hours prior, left Sarah depleted. Leaving Stuart's apartment immediately after he addressed her biggest concern was the only thing she could do. There were no other questions for him. He had said enough.

Stuart's shocking confirmation stunned her, but it set her on a path of seeking answers to some serious questions of God. *Why is this happening? And why is it happening to me?*

Inside her home, things did not feel quite right. Her senses were heightened. She heard every sound and smelled every scent, acutely. The revving and honking from cars down the street sounded like they were right inside the walls. There was a deafening rustle of palm fronds and maple tree leaves. "God! What is going on?" she prayed out loud, still questioning everything. "What are You trying to tell me? Yes, I believe in You now. Was this all for me to realize that?"

Her silky, blonde hair fell gently over her face as she reclined on the sofa cushions; her tears wet the soft material. She felt somewhat safe, knowing that Robbie and Stuart could not invade her sanctuary. But even though she was behind locked doors, something gnawed at her spirit. Sarah was not alone.

She jumped up from the couch and ran to her office to search for answers. Booting up her computer took a few seconds. While she waited, she looked at the papers in disarray on her desk. It would all have to wait. None of it mattered. When the computer was ready, she placed her delicate fingertips on the keyboard and tapped out the first subject to research. "Laced marijuana and its effects," Sarah spoke the words as she typed. Page after page loaded with pictures, news reports, and magazine articles. Sarah read story after story about potent or laced pot and how it could impact a person's body and thinking. Depressants, stimulants, and hallucinogens were common additives, she learned. They were used to enhance a person's *high*. Several articles warned about the dangers of such lacings. Brain damage, hospitalization, tripping, and even death were some of the side effects mentioned.

Publications and testimonials were not hard to find. Apparently, many people had experienced severe ordeals. She came across an article of intrigue and clicked on it. The headline read: *Dangers of Laced Weed.* Sarah stopped and stared at the screen. Her fingers froze, and her heart sank as she read the information. It was written by a victim advocacy group, warning people of what they might be getting into if they partook in smoking or ingesting – seemingly – harmless drugs. There was also a forum on the website. Several folks had commented to one another about their experiences with using laced pot.

For example, there were cases involving *wet weed,* which led to people committing crimes, doing crazy things, or even committing murder and/ or suicide. *Wet weed,* she read, *means the pot is laced with PCP. It brings on psychosis, paranoia, and delusions.* Some of the victims heard voices telling them to do *bad stuff.* Oddly, a few who had followed through with these actions had no recollection of doing so. Sarah was dumbfounded at what she was reading; the information was too similar to her own experience. What the article failed to mention was the intrusion of supernatural forces. The victims did not attribute the occurrences to evil entities. Either they were not in tune to sensing when something was from another dimension or they did not want to admit it. *What else could it be?* Sarah wondered. *Something had to either enhance a darkness within that person already, or the drug was a catalyst to opening a portal for evil forces to enter the third dimension more strongly.*

There was never any mention of God's intervention. Knowing that Sarah could have ended up like the victims in these stories was frightening. But she believed God was the factor in pulling her out alive. She started crying – not out of sadness – but out of gratitude for having escaped such a close brush with death.

Night had approached. She felt a weirdness surround her again. Whatever demonic forces that had been with her at the river were still fighting to stay relevant. They were not giving up their diabolical plan to diminish her faith in God. Their goal was to pull her back to her recent ways of living.

Sarah turned away from the computer screen that she had been sitting at far too long and peered around the room. She looked out the window at the moon. It reminded her of the scene last night at the river, but this time it beamed toward her, like Heaven's spotlight. Sarah was on display. She got up and turned on an overhead light. Light was good, but still the evil spirits tried to come at her. Sarah caught a glimpse of her bare feet. Something was not normal; she focused on them more intently. Each foot appeared to be melting into the carpet beneath her. Her veins filled with an icy chill as she experienced the vision. Screaming *was* an option, but losing control might provoke another spiritual attack. Instead, she tightened her body and rejected any incoming fear.

Something followed me home, she thought. *There's no way I can still be high.* She sensed a strong presence of demons and immediately called on God, "Father be with me. Don me with Your armor of protection. Now. Please!" The demons were slithering beings and dark shadows that encompassed the space around her, barely visible in another dimension. Their presence felt heavy, threatening, and creepy. Her chill changed to sweat. A rush of heat zoomed through her body; it traveled down her arms and legs and throbbed her fingers and toes. Then another frigid chill followed, causing her entire body to tremble. She continued her request to God, "Father, please protect me. Cast all evil away from me in the name of Your Son, Jesus."

Sarah thought about getting out of the apartment, but if the presence she sensed was truly demonic, it would follow no matter where she went. *Just keep the light on,* she told herself. *Control your thoughts, Sarah. With God, nothing can come against you.*

If Sarah let the spirits frighten her, they might enter her dimension of existence. They could manifest into something tangible and more viewable. She continued pushing the fear away. Now she understood what Stuart had described feeling, when he held his hands over his face at the river. *Why are they here – with me?* she wondered. *There should be no entities left. God saved me at Castle Dome. Something must be holding them. Are these new demons?*

Light! I need light! Sarah walked swiftly through the apartment, turning on all the lamps in each room. As she did this, Biblical scripture popped into her head. John 1:5. " 'The light shines in the darkness, and the darkness has not overcome it,' " she recited.

Sarah kept her Bible in her nightstand. She had not seen it since she unpacked the pillowcases of important belongings that made their way over to Stuart's during the fire. The family heirloom was not read in years. Growing up, she never understood why her parents held the tradition of keeping one by the bed – until now. She reached in to the table drawer.

There came another chill; this time in just her arms. She brushed them with opposite hands in an attempt to rid her body of evil spirits. She knew she could defeat anything that was not of the Lord. That is what she had learned growing up. It would take strong faith to believe it and change her way of thinking. Otherwise, she would fall back into her old habits and allow the world to influence her – and seduce her away from God, again.

Sarah sat slowly on the edge of her bed and looked at the old book. The soft, brown vinyl cover had protected the pages from years of abuse, being tossed from one storage place to another. She unzipped it. Holding the book tightly to her chest, she bowed her head.

Her mind drifted back to the desert. She pictured Robbie standing at the pool table and Stuart at her right side on the hassock. His confession of wanting to kill her replayed in her head. Despite the fear that tried to envelop her, there was more work to be done.

Bible in hand, she walked back to her office – chanting in a low tone, "God be with me. God be with me."

Chapter 35

KNOWLEDGE OF GOOD AND EVIL

Sarah had not slept much over the last forty-eight hours. However, she was compelled to understand the source of the evil presence. Topics on Sarah's internet search list included: *out-of-body experiences*, *demonic spirits*, and *astrology*. She hoped to find all the information she needed to prove that the trio's strange event was supernatural. She already knew it to be true in her heart, but reading about others' experiences gave her comfort in her conviction. Sarah searched for answers, risking any fear. She peered into the windows of knowledge that had previously been a mystery to her.

It was clear why Robbie may have been chosen to host an evil spirit. The drugs altered his mind and state of consciousness, opening him up to a spiritual realm. Plus, his following of fortune-tellers and astrological charts was against the God of the Bible. His *demons,* his cryptic way of interacting, his bizarre thoughts, his haunted past, and his lack of commitment added to the entire picture. It was the culmination of everything that was stirring a melting pot of darkness. Sarah was not so innocent, either. Her promiscuity, lust, and lack of regard for following God's will had made her vulnerable to demonic strongholds.

She squinted at the computer screen. Her fingers rapped vigorously on the keyboard and typed out the next subjects: *o-u-t o-f b-o-d-y e-x-p-e-r-i-e-n-c-e-s a-n-d a-s-t-r-a-l f-l-i-g-h-t.* What she was about to discover was even more captivating than what she learned of laced pot. During out-of-body experiences, participants said they would meditate to the point of achieving a dream-like state of mind. They would lie on their bed or sofa and actually leave their bodies to *travel* to the home of a person they knew. They could look back and see themselves asleep. The next step would be to concentrate on being in the room of their subject. They said they could observe that person for long periods of time by holding their own attention on the experience and not on the uncertainty of attaining it. Otherwise, they might lose their focus and wake up. Now, whether or not these accounts were true, or if the traveler was only perceiving other people – it was up for discussion.

When Robbie was *traveling*, he may have knowingly – or unknowingly – contacted entities. Having the ability to exit his body and go elsewhere meant that he was entering into a dimension of the unknown. He was not guided by an angel or taken against his will, but rather chose to satisfy his own desires and carry out the act on his own.

Sarah glanced at her Bible. She knew Robbie was dabbling in something not of God. As she clicked on site after site, she mentally took notes of the dangers in practicing these *alternative* beliefs. It was peculiar that one subject linked to another. They seemed to fall under the umbrella of *demonic spirits* and how those spirits could enter one's life.

Click. Click. Click. Her fingers tapped the keys to spell out the next subject: *d-e-m-o-n-i-c s-p-i-r-i-t-s.* Thousands of people online had posted their individual stories about how they believed in evil spirits, were able to conjure them into human awareness, or had executed a full-blown manifestation.

One woman wrote a blog that was solely dedicated to an encounter she believed was with Satan, himself. It read: *During an affair I was having on my husband, I felt the devil's presence when I was in bed with my lover. While he slept, Satan crept between the two of us. I knew it was him by the way my stomach, heart, and brain reacted. My body shuddered. Sheer fear filled me, and I wanted to vomit from fright. Never once did I turn around. Satan was behind me! I prayed to Jesus that He would fill my room with the Holy Spirit, forgive me of my sins, and rebuke the devil's presence. Satan vanished when I dissolved the affair and went back to my husband.*

Sarah had experienced the same heavy, dark, and spine-tingling chill the woman had described. "Oh, dear! How horrifying," she exclaimed. "There's a lot to read here," Sarah continued, "so many connected topics."

Astrology was next. She searched online for a Bible concordance and then looked up the word *mediums.* The Bible warned of not turning to mediums for counsel in the books of Leviticus, Deuteronomy, and Isaiah. It was considered witchcraft. Sarah remembered when she and Robbie compared their *sign* traits. He told her that he lived by his astrological chart and felt every occurrence in his life was related to it. He consulted mediums to foretell his future. It was a practice that she had once thought innocuous, but now her mind had changed.

Hours passed by like minutes and Sarah realized it was one o'clock in the morning. Her eyes were in pain. But she needed to know more. *Robbie is playing a game with his soul. The demons are just pouring in through his meditations and drug use. I was playing, too,* Sarah concluded.

She thought of the religious publications on Stuart's coffee table. Sarah never suspected *him* to be at the core of their supernatural event. But his interest in several beliefs may have welcomed entry for a deceptive spirit, as well. He was lukewarm in what he followed, as he vacillated between the major religions. Sarah believed that both men had created gateways for creatures in other dimensions to cross over into this one.

After much research, Sarah understood that this occurrence in their lives was bigger than what it seemed. It had major significance. Each of the three friends represented those who either back-slid from their belief in God, did not know what to believe, or refused to believe at all. This was an orchestrated awakening that Sarah, Stuart, and Robbie were destined to experience.

The phone rang. It startled her; after all, it was the middle of the night. "Hello?"

"Hey, Cuz! It's Michael!"

"Oh, my goodness, Michael! How are you? And what are you doing up so late?"

"Good question! I'm not sure. I just woke up in a panic. I got the weirdest feeling that something was wrong with you."

"I'm ok, now! Your timing is perfect. You, of all people, can help me figure things out. I have *got* to tell you what happened to me this past weekend."

Michael was Sarah's cousin from her dad's side of the family. He was a bit younger than her, but despite the age difference, they were very compatible and had ruminated about life since they were kids. If anyone could clue her in on the secrets of pot, laced edibles, or evil entities– it was Michael. The man had hit some rough patches about a decade prior. He had lived a troubled life as a youth, after getting mixed up with the wrong crowd of people. Oftentimes, he took part in cultic rituals and exercises that involved drug use and conjuring up the dead. The family had become concerned for him and hosted an *intervention*. After that, it was a long journey for Michael to escape the hole he had fallen into. As far as Sarah knew, he was clean and clear-headed, now. He had rededicated his life to Christ. His transition was remarkable – a miracle. She could not have been more thrilled to hear from him.

"I wasn't sure if I should call, because of the time difference. I'm in Texas now. But it looks like you are still up, so spill! What's going on?" he asked.

"It's a long story, but I'll try to be brief. Where do I begin?"

Chapter 36

MICHAEL

Michael's deep, smooth, and calming voice was the comfort Sarah craved. She no longer felt alone in dealing with her scary situation. He was a gift – at just the right time.

"Prepare yourself. This is a doozy," Sarah warned.

"I'm thrilled to hear it. Please, do tell," said Michael.

"My friends almost killed me this weekend, and I think you can help me understand why. You see, we all met . . . ."

"Stop. Wait. What?" Michael interrupted. "Was that 'friends-almost-killed-me' part, a joke?"

"No. But let me explain . . . ."

"Before you continue – are you safe? Are you alright?"

"Yes, I'm fine. A little shaken up, but I'll be ok."

Sarah told Michael her entire story, starting with how she met and lusted after Robbie and Stuart and how she ended up in Roka Valley – as well as the drugs, Richard's funeral, losing Em, the fire, and the evil presence at the river. "Now, I've been combing through the Internet looking up all the things that Robbie was messing with."

"Wow, girl! I can't believe you went through all that. You got yourself into a pickle. It must have been God that led me to call you. Let me start by telling you this," Michael hesitated as he swallowed and gathered his next words. "Walk away, Sarah."

Neither of the cousins said a word for nearly thirty seconds. The only thing that could be heard was air flowing through the line. Sarah got very nervous.

"Hello? Are you there?" Michael finally spoke.

"Yes, you just sounded so serious."

"I am serious!" he raised his voice. "I don't know what this Robbie guy is all about, but it sounds like he is involved with the occult, and you need to get as far away from him as possible. You don't want to mess with demonic strongholds. You need Jesus at your back. Whatever Robbie is practicing, it sounds like he is opening himself up to exploring the dark side of the spiritual world."

The tiny hairs on Sarah's arms stood up. She shivered. "I survived, Michael. Jesus is in my life and saved me. But something is still hanging around me, for some reason. Like, it followed me home. Does that make sense to you? Can that happen?" She looked down at her feet. They were tingling.

"Nothing *followed* you home, Sarah. This is the universe we're talking about," Michael warned her. "Good and evil spirits are everywhere. They were already around you. You just brought them – or unknowingly allowed them – into your life."

"Dear Lord!" Sarah cried.

"They exist in a dimension we cannot see – *most* of the time. I've seen them. We can feel them. They can see *us*."

"You're scaring me, Michael."

"I hope you are scared! You need to know what is happening. And keep this in mind. We must be very careful of what we say out loud and how we think. It sounds like good and evil are going at it with each other – over you – in spiritual warfare."

"What makes you so certain?"

"Everything you're telling me, Sarah," Michael assured her. "I did a lot of drugs – as you know. But it was during the sober moments that they were visible, especially in my room at night. And I felt them all around me."

"What did you see? What did you feel?"

"Darkness. Devils. Their hunger."

"How do you know you weren't just hallucinating?"

"They were *not* hallucinations, Sarah! They were clear as day. Like I said, I was sober when I saw them. Every sin I committed made me more vulnerable to a demonic effort to pull me away from God. Evil spirits flooded in. I was – without my knowledge – welcoming them into my life and allowing them to influence it. But enough about me."

"No!" Sarah barked. "I want to know what happened to you."

Michael took a long, deep breath and paused. "Do me and yourself a favor. Get out your concordance and look up *devils* and *evil.* Or just go online and do a search. They are mentioned all throughout your Bible. That may give you better clarity if you see it written in God's words."

"I remember hearing pastors preaching about that stuff when we were kids. I ignored it back then," she admitted.

"Do not ignore it now. You need to know how Satan works. He disguises himself to deceive. Because of all the things Robbie was doing, he may have opened himself up to be a portal for evil. Whatever he said to you was probably not Robbie talking at all. It was most likely a spirit talking through him and sending thoughts to Stuart."

"Go on."

"The Bible says to beware of false prophets, too. There are people who speak good out of their mouths, but believe and practice the opposite. Their words are slightly off from the truth and meant to lead one astray."

Sarah's ears were glued to her phone. She listened intently, not wanting to miss a single word from Michael's lips.

"I was obsessed with drugs and alcohol. They were killing me, Sarah. I was deceived by those things. I thought I was more confident while on them – more productive. In reality, that wasn't happening at all. It was only what I perceived. Satan tore me down by lying to me and I fell for it. And the worst part? I had pushed God so far away. I fell right into the devil's trap. He got exactly what he wanted – *me*."

Sarah got goosebumps. Everything Michael was telling her sounded like her own story.

"But the evil spirits, Sarah – they were real. There came a point during my downward spiral that I began to see them, like I said before. They were clear as the wall in front of me – images, apparitions – and some, partly transparent. The only way I can describe them more in detail is to say they brought with them a heavy darkness full of fear."

The atmosphere in Sarah's room turned uncomfortable and cold. She wrapped a sweater over her shoulders.

"Remember, Sarah, Satan works harder to get people who have a foundation with God. Yes, you believe in God, but you have fallen away. You were weak and ripe for the devil to enter your life and entice you away from Jesus. Satan owns non-believers – those who have given their lives to the world of greed, money, and sex. But you? You were on the fence. People like you challenge the devil, and he will do whatever it takes to pull you to his side. He tempted you with Robbie. He tempted you with Stuart. And he played on your emotions when you lost Uncle Martin and Aunt Liz – and Richard and Em. My thought? He saw God fighting for you and stepped into the ring."

"You are right, Michael. I have been struggling with my faith. I could not understand why God allowed me to be hurt. I yelled at Him and said bad things."

"Oh no, Sarah! I'm convinced this was a spiritual attack on you. It's so clear to me. You were hand-picked. The lusty desire of having two men who wanted you at the same time is not of God, however fun it may have felt. You have fallen into a trap. The alcohol, pot, and partying were the carrots dangling in front of you. Those temptations made the desire more exciting and kept you unfocused. Dissing on God delighted the devil, I'm sure. You were broken and exposed."

"How do I break out of the stronghold? How did you do it, Michael?"

"Prayer and our family. When everyone was crying for me at the intervention – that's when it hit me. I saw the look on their faces and I heard the sincerity in their prayers. I started to look at myself from *their* perspective. And it scared me."

Sarah burst into tears. Had she not prayed to God sincerely enough.

Michael continued, "I started praying to God on my own. It was a release I had never felt before when I was on my knees begging for forgiveness and asking to be saved."

"Praise the Lord," Sarah cried. "I have done the same."

"You'll be alright as long as you make sure your prayers are from your heart and not empty words said only to get God to save you in the moments. Trust Him with all your being! There are some things you must do now. First, stop all contact with Robbie and Stuart. Second, purge attachments and connections of all kinds." Michael's tone changed. "Did either of them give you anything?"

Sarah looked around her office for items the guys would have given her. Still holding the phone to her ear, she got up from her desk and walked around the apartment, checking tabletops for gifts or remnants. "Why would inanimate objects be an issue, Michael?"

"I believe, things can hold onto evil spirits," he explained. "If the person that gave it to you carried that spirit, it could be filled with – what one might call – *bad juju*."

Sarah shuddered again. The last thing she wanted in her possession was anything that had *bad juju*. She laughed nervously at the term Michael used and thought it seemed ridiculous that material items could carry negative energy. In her opinion, an object was nothing more than a keeper of memories. She walked into her bedroom and scanned the walls and furniture. Her eyes stopped on her dresser. Perched on top was a gift from Robbie. "I found something!" she exclaimed.

"What is it?"

"It's a stuffed dog that Robbie gave me when Emmy passed away. Do you really think I need to toss it? Can't I just cast away its strongholds?"

"You can. But when you look at it, does it remind you of your time with Robbie?"

"Yes."

"Then, get rid of it!"

"But it's so cute," she giggled.

"Cute schmute. Cute won't save you. Now, chuck it!"

Pinching the animal's ear, she carried the toy at arm's length to the attached garage and tossed it in the trash bin. The slam of the lid was heard through the phone.

"Done?" Michael asked.

"Done," Sarah answered. "But it's still here in my home, even if it is in the garage – *bad juju*. What if I wake up tomorrow morning and that creepy dog is sitting back on my dresser?"

"Then we will have to call in an exorcist," Michael laughed. "You'll be beyond *my* help."

"Don't even joke about that, Michael. That scares me. In the name of Jesus, I rebuke any evil in my household!"

"Good. I'm glad it scared you – right into the arms of the Lord. Your salvation is real and should not be taken lightly. I'm sorry to hear about Em, by the way. I remember when you rescued her."

For a few more minutes, the two made small talk. Sarah asked Michael about new things going on in his life. As she kept him in conversation, she walked around the rest of the apartment, checking for more items that may have had attachments to Robbie – or Stuart – for that matter. "Michael, I found something else!"

"What is it?"

"A bottle of perfume Robbie bought for me."

"Dump it! Do I dare ask what it's called?"

"Ha! *The Devil Inside.*"

"Oh, my dear Lord, please guide Sarah to go bury it in the dumpster!"

Sarah laughed and took the bottle to the trash. She tossed it on top of the stuffed animal, which peered up from the barrel. The lid was quickly slammed shut, and she ran back into the apartment. "That thing was looking at me!"

"The stuffed dog?"

"Yes. Thank goodness it's pick-up day for the garbage, tomorrow. Can you stay with me on the phone while I take the barrel out to the curb?"

"Yes, go do it!" Michael laughed, but turned the conversation back to her situation. He knew that if Sarah slipped and did not stand firm in her belief in God, she could fall fast to the dark side. She had touched it already. "How are you feeling, now, Sarah?"

"I think I'm ok."

"Just ok? You think?"

Sarah looked down at her feet again. Her eyes followed the wall-to-wall carpeting out of her office, down the hall, and toward the living room. Suddenly, it seemed to be moving. She rubbed her eyes to rid them of the blurriness caused by her tears. "Snakes!" Sarah exclaimed. "There are snakes at my feet, Michael!" She was scared.

Silence filled the line between them. There was no air. No buzz. No static. Just pure silence. Michael's spine tingled. He was familiar with the feeling. It brought him back to his days of darkness, rehab, and counseling sessions with pastors. But he wanted Sarah to explain. "What do you mean – there are 'snakes' at your feet?"

"Just like it sounds, Michael. There are snakes at my feet! Hundreds of them!" she continued in a panicked tone. "They are writhing and wriggling everywhere underneath me!"

"Is that what you see or is that what you feel?" Michael tried to remain calm for her.

"I'm not sure. I don't see them physically, but I know they are there. It's like my brain is comprehending their existence, but my eyes cannot witness them." Sarah was frightened, but she was not fully weakened. While Michael was still on the phone, she felt safe.

"What else do you sense?"

Sarah closed her eyes and spoke, "If I could actually see through to the dimension in which they live, I would say they are swimming in black water or in the upper portion of nothingness. Does that sound crazy to you?"

"No. Pray, Cousin," Michael whispered. "You must dive into your Bible more than ever before. Do you have a *devotional Bible*?" He knew from experience that Sarah had demons all around her. If she succumbed to the fear, the days ahead would be terrifying.

"Yes, I have *The Daily Devotional Bible,* why?"

"Go get it. But first, let's pray." They both closed their eyes and bowed their heads on either ends of the phone line. Michael led the prayer. "Father, I pray for my cousin, Your dear daughter, Sarah, that You fill her with Your Holy Spirit and shelter her from all evil. I pray that You cast all demons, the snakes, and Satan away from her. Please allow her to find peace. Don her with Your armor of love and protection. It is in the name of Your Son, Jesus Christ of Nazareth, that we pray and ask for all these things. Amen."

"Amen," said Sarah.

"Read your *devotional* for this past Saturday's date. I'll check back in with you in a couple of days. I've got to get some sleep before work. Keep praying. Call on the Lord."

"Do you have to go, Michael?"

He paused for a moment. "You'll be fine. And Sarah . . . ?"

"Yes?"

". . . run from Robbie and Stuart. They are keeping the bad spirits around. I mean it. I love you."

"Yes, Cuz," Sarah smiled. "Sweet dreams, and thank you for everything. I love you, too."

She waited on the line until Michael disconnected. Sarah was on her own, now. She teetered between holding onto God's invisible hand or falling into an apparent dimension of serpents.

Chapter 37

LIGHT IN THE DARKNESS

The light from the lamps in Sarah's apartment would have to make up for the absence of Michael's comforting voice if she wanted to get any sleep. The last time she drifted off was in the camp house, so she was reluctant to do it again – knowing that dark spirits were waiting to intrude and attack. Sarah pictured the face of Jesus in hopes to rid the snakes from her mind. They were still slithering around her in an invisible dimension. She cleansed her face. It was refreshing and necessary. The next step was diving into her *Daily Devotional* at the advice of Michael. She finished up in the bathroom and got into bed.

The *devotional* was a complete *New King James Version* that divided each day of the year with a portion of *The Old Testament* and *The New Testament*, *Psalms* and *Proverbs*, and a brief summary. Its fragile papers were thin and crinkly and rustled loudly with the turn of each page.

"June eleventh, June twelfth – ahh, here it is," she said, skipping to Saturday's date, "June fourteenth!" The passages for that day started off with *2 Kings 15:1-16:20.* The chapter was about sinful men who had killed for power – good and bad kings who fulfilled God's word or sinned against Him. *That's a coincidence,* she thought.

What really caught her attention were the scriptures that followed. *Psalm 73:21-22* came next. " 'Thus, my heart was grieved, And I was vexed in my mind. I was so foolish and ignorant; I was like a beast before You.' " Sarah skipped forward to *verse 28*. " 'But it is good for me to draw near to God; I have put my trust in the Lord God, That I may declare all Your works.' " The room warmed up, and the tension in her muscles relaxed.

Sarah moved on to the next entry, *Proverbs 18:20-21*. She read, " 'A man's stomach shall be satisfied from the fruit of his mouth, from the pro-duce of his lips, he shall be filled. Death and life are in the power of the tongue. And those who love it will eat its fruit.' " The meaning was clear. The power of Sarah's dooming words she had spoken to Robbie yielded a darkness that had been waiting to come out. "Oh, Father, what have I done?"

The pieces of the puzzle were slowly coming together. There was still much to learn about the scope of her sins and their impact on her life – and the lives of those around her. Sarah continued in *The New Testament, John 21:1-25*. In the verses, Jesus appeared to His disciples at the Sea of Tiberias, after being raised from the dead. He told them to cast their nets, after a long day of coming up empty-handed. They did not know it was really Jesus they saw. Once they did as He instructed, their nets were filled with fish. Jesus sat and ate breakfast with them and they knew He was the Lord. At that point, they held no doubt that He had been resurrected. Sarah held no doubt either. He was being revealed, minute by minute, word by word.

She flipped the pages back to *2 Kings* and re-read about all the evil-doing the kings had done to seek control. The story caused her to think about why, with *her* situation, the supernatural visit at the camp house brought the feeling of death as its goal. "Murder is a crime rooted in lust, and lust, in part, is a sexual desire. Everything surrounding Robbie and Stuart centered on desire – for sex, attention, acceptance, euphoria, ado-ration, defiance. Death seemed like the ultimate gain," she whispered to herself. If she had died at the hands of the men, her soul would never have had the chance to repent.

"I was sinning. Disasters were bound to happen. I *felt* punished. I don't believe God punished me, per se, but I do believe He allowed me to go down the wrong path. I refused to trust Him. I knew wrong from right in my heart. I thought He had abandoned me, so I did whatever I wanted. I had nothing to lose, I thought," she said to herself. "I was wrong. I had everything to lose."

The light on her bedside table flickered. It startled Sarah. She kept very still, waiting for any other disruption. She sensed Jesus. The demonic spirits had not given up, though. Her sins had created a wormhole big enough for a dark army to enter. And that needed to be dealt with. God's power was much stronger than any evil presence could ever hope to possess. Yet the demons still tried to remain in the atmosphere. Somewhere in the back of her mind, she still doubted she could be saved. God was not there just for her comfort. He was fighting for her and battling against the spirits that were working hard to keep Him out. He was stomping on the heads of the snakes, and He was clashing against the darkness that had entered through the portal the three friends had opened. She knew God would prevail, but her soul saving would depend on how much of Him she would let in. She had to remain strong in her faith and convictions.

But the seeds of doubt had caused a blockage. The deaths of Richard, her parents, and Em reminded her of pain and suffering. The devil tormented her with these memories over and over again.

"Father, take it all away. Stop these things from entering my head. I know You are real. I know You are here. Whether or not I can see You, I have faith. Your will is Your will no matter how much it hurts – You have Your purpose for things that happen in our lives. And we must accept it. Jesus, You are my Lord and Savior and I want to walk beside You regarding everything in life – my relationships, my job, my body – which is a temple – and all my decisions. I worship You only. Amen."

Sarah felt relief. The doubt was gone. The skies opened again. The universe was swirling with light and hope encompassed her. It would always be there. But she had to hold onto it.

The Bible was about to close when an added reference scripture at the bottom of the last page of the June fourteenth entry caught her eye. The quote was from *Isaiah 55:7*. She read out loud, " 'Let the wicked forsake his way, and the unrighteous man his thoughts: let him return to the Lord, and He will have mercy on him; and to our God, for He will abundantly pardon.' " The parallel consumed her. "Are You sitting at my bedside, God?" she asked. "I sure feel You." She needed no physical proof. God spoke clearly through scripture. He was alive – and He had saved her life. She was one hundred percent certain of it.

The Bible case was zipped up and Sarah clutched it in her arms. She cried herself to sleep with the book tightly pressed against her chest. The light on the bedside table remained *on* all night, until daybreak – which came quickly.

Chapter 38

BEFORE THE ROOSTER CROWS TWICE

The warm, morning sunlight slowly awakened Sarah as it draped over her face. Its silky entrance into her room blanketed her with renewed energy. Her arms were still wrapped around her Bible, and the tears she had cried earlier had crusted over. She let go of the book for a minute to rub the remnants away from her face. Sarah was a new person. She was excited to process all that she had learned from her online research, her conversation with Michael, and the divine intervention with which her life had been blessed. Her eyes opened fully and she stared up at the ceiling. "Everything good is waiting for me," she spoke to God. "You are where the true light resides."

Sarah had a new life. The safety and comfort of her bed caressed her spirits. She turned her face to the delicate sunlight at her window and then to her Bible. There was no doubt in Sarah's mind that God was leading her back to knowing Him more than she had allowed in the past. There was once a time when she expected Him to wave a magic wand and fix all her troubles. As she learned more, she realized – that was not the way He operated. God should not have been blamed for her clouded life. The cloud formed from what Sarah allowed in and the way she responded to temptations she was dealt. Deep inside, she knew that her life might be different if she had made God a top priority. She may not have been able to control the losses, but she would have been able to react to them with a strength only achieved by a trusted faith. God did in fact wave His hand over her life, but not in the way that she had envisioned or hoped. She received a wake-up call. And that awakening – was at the river.

Sarah opened up the old book again and fanned the thin pages, hoping her fingers would lead her to whatever section God wanted her to read. A chunk of the sheets flapped over, followed by three or five at a time. She felt the urge to stop. On the page to her right was *Mark:14.* She read it swiftly, searching for a sign. Her eagerness to find a message of relevance caused her to misunderstand the words. Slowing her pace, Sarah took a deep breath and started from the beginning. The passages seemed to be highlighted on the paper. Messages flew off the sheets. She read *Mark 14:55-56* out loud, " 'Now the chief priests and all the council sought testimony against Jesus to put Him to death, but found none. For many bore false witness against Him, but their testimonies did not agree.' " Her eyes darted to *verse 65.* " 'Then some began to spit on Him, and to blindfold Him, and to beat Him, and to say to Him, 'Prophesy!' And the officers struck Him with the palms of their hands.' "

Sarah stopped reading and wept for Jesus. *How could such a true and loving man be tortured like that? He was and is good. He* is *the Son of God.*

Then, guilt gripped Sarah. She recalled the time Robbie asked her about her faith – and when Em's doctor told her to pray – and when she yelled at God on the beach. She had denied Jesus. She had rejected God. What she had done – mirrored the scriptures.

Sarah kept reading. The strongest words hit in *verse 72.* " 'A second time the rooster crowed. Then Peter called to mind the word that Jesus had said to him, 'Before the rooster crows twice, you will deny Me three times.' And when he thought about it, he wept.' " Sarah cried, "My words were not unlike Peter's. What difference did two thousand years make?" She had denied God and Jesus. Sarah felt nauseous and fell to her knees, clutching the book to her chest. "How many times has history repeated itself for those who deny Christ's existence? It has repeated itself with me." Sarah wept hard.

Buzz. Buzz. In came a text. Did she dare look to see who it was? Maybe it was Michael, offering some additional advice about how to rid her life of *bad juju*. She glanced at her phone, which was face down on the nightstand. *Buzz. Buzz.* It sounded off again. She did not like letting go of her Bible, but she placed it back inside the nightstand drawer and picked up her phone. It was Stuart. "What the heck does *he* want?"

The three of us need to meet for dinner to talk about this further, he texted.

"What!" Sarah gasped.

Stuart's message was weighty. Her safe and quiet sanctuary had been disturbed. Sarah did not want to venture out of the house so soon – and definitely not to see the guys. They all wanted closure. However, her method did not involve them. She had *her* closure. It took her a grueling night to finally rid herself of darkness. Why would she want to hang around them again? Thinking there might be malintent behind his request to meet, Sarah hesitated to respond.

Buzz. Buzz. Stuart wrote, *Robbie and I think we have an explanation of what happened, and we want to talk with you about it.*

Sarah felt belittled after reading his preposterous statement, as if *she* needed to be told what she had experienced. *This* – from the man who had his hands over his face all night. *Do they think of me as naïve and a child?* she wondered. If Stuart's confession of wanting to kill her was not enough to convince them that something evil was present, then nothing was.

Sarah now felt a rush of confidence and the need to enlighten the two men on what *she* had discovered. *Ok, I will meet with you, early. But I cannot stay long,* she texted. She refused to be out with them after the sun went down. Her gut reminded her that the night changes a person and that moods might get unpredictable once it got dark. A daytime rendezvous was more appropriate. *Can we meet for lunch, instead?* read her next message.

I have tomorrow off and would like to get this resolved. But Robbie works until 6 all this week so we can't do lunch, read his text.

Sarah was fine with meeting in the six o'clock hour, because there would still be some sunlight left. She started to respond when he texted again. *Can you meet tonight?*

Her nerves electrified and her mind raced. *Why tonight?! Why the sense of urgency?* she wondered. *Is it a trap? If it is, I'm armored up.* She and Stuart had already discussed what took place, and he admitted to feeling manipulated by a possessed Robbie. *Did he change his mind?* She texted him back, *Where and when?*

The Olive Pit – by my house. 6:30?

Sarah believed in her gut that God was calling her to go and tell her side of the story – the truth of what had happened. She had to forge ahead with fortitude. Her heart pounded. *Ok, that's fine. See you then,* she wrote.

Great, see you then!

As she waited for a hot bubble bath to fill up, Sarah messaged her cousin so he would know where she was. *Michael, they want to meet – tonight! I'm going to go. Don't worry. I'll be alright.*

Go-time would come, and Sarah wanted to be both physically and mentally prepared for their conversation. All she could think about were the looks on their faces and how they would try and intimidate her into believing something she was certain did not take place.

By late afternoon, she finally heard from Michael. *Oh, Sarah! Please reconsider. Do you really want to put yourself back in that state of mind again?*

As she stared at his message, Sarah second-guessed her decision. Was she doing the right thing? Their friendships had already ended; the three-some was dead, so there was to be no rekindling. But she needed to hear what they had to say. Sarah convinced herself that she and her faith would be safe as long as she called upon God. The security of the restaurant staff and surrounding patrons would provide additional comfort. The pizza place was well lit and the sunset was at eight o'clock; she would have plenty of daylight.

I'll text you when I get home.

Ugg. Don't do it, Michael pleaded one last time. *If you decide to go, I will be waiting on the edge of my seat to hear from you. May God be with you. I will pray.*

Sarah sent back a *smiley face* and a *thumbs-up* emoji to reassure Michael that she would consider his request. Having her cousin in the background – ready to catch her – provided her a solid and safe feeling.

The afternoon passed quickly. Before she walked out the door, she thought of her Bible. *It would be comforting to have that with me.* She reached into the nightstand drawer for the book and noticed the box holding Richard's engagement ring. She picked it up. It opened with a loud creak. She put the ring on her finger – once again – and admired its sparkle. "I guess you could say I'm married to Jesus now, Richard. I think you'd be pleased." It was returned to the drawer.

As Sarah walked to the kitchen to get a bottle of water, she passed the sofa on which she and Robbie had shared a meal. "Father, protect me as I venture into this situation with him and Stuart. Wrap Your gracious arms around me while I am in their presence. Speak through me, the words You want them to hear. Keep me safe. In Jesus' name, Amen."

Chapter 39

TWO OR MORE

It was a typical summer evening in California. The marine layer had mostly burned away as Sarah drove closer to the ocean. Beams of crystal light shone down through small, semi-transparent, white clouds. She tried to take in the view, but was distracted by her beating heart, which thumped loudly in her chest. The truth was within her and Jesus was by her side.

When she came to the first stop light, Sarah glanced at her Bible resting on the passenger seat. Placing her right hand on its cover, she was reminded that everything was going to be alright. Only a little apprehension remained. She knew it was normal, given the circumstances.

I wonder who is going to start the conversation, she thought. She anticipated Robbie and Stuart ganging up on her. The closer she got to the restaurant, the more her confidence waned. She shrugged the feeling off. "You got this, Sarah. You got this," she said.

Once she reached the parking lot, Sarah pulled into an empty spot and prayed again. Regaining her composure was the key if she was going to appear knowledgeable to the men. Sarah needed to be confident. No wishy-washy statements. She regrouped her thoughts and took a deep breath before exiting her car. When she walked toward the restaurant, Sarah noticed Stuart's vehicle was parked in a nearby space. She fidgeted with her clothes and hair before going in.

There they were. Robbie was slightly behind Stuart. Both were standing in line at the hostess stand, like two hungry lions waiting to feed. *Do I shake their hands or hug them?* she wondered anxiously. Then Sarah blurted out the first thing that came to her mind. "Hey, did you guys order?"

Both men quickly turned around. "No, we were waiting on you," said Robbie.

Stuart only smiled upon seeing her. She asked them about pizza toppings and whether they should sit inside or outside.

"We're doing pepperoni and mushroom. Is that ok?" Robbie asked. "Let's eat out on the patio."

"Cool. Here, take a ten," she said to Stuart, offering to help with the cost.

"Don't worry. I got it. I'm just going to put it on my card."

Robbie handed his friend a ten-dollar bill, also, and Stuart gladly accepted. They both smirked at each other. The three chose a table outside away from other patrons and waited for their order to be delivered. They sat down to an uncomfortable silence for several minutes.

Then Stuart broke the ice. "How are you doing?" he said, nervously adjusting his shirt and shorts.

"I'm doing better," replied Sarah. "It's been an interesting few days."

"That it has," Stuart agreed.

Robbie seated himself next to Stuart. They faced Sarah, like interrogators in a crime investigation. It was oddly similar to the night they played pool, when she thought they were both out to get her. Sarah wanted to make eye-contact with them, but it was hard. She looked down at the table and back toward the interior of the restaurant, hoping the waiter would return soon with the pizza.

"I think it was a haunting!" Robbie abruptly exclaimed. "The house we stayed in must have had something happen there in the past – something bad. Maybe a spirit was awakened while we were playing pool."

The expressions on his face were studied as he told his theory. Sarah pondered the thought of an already-haunted house, but then quickly dismissed the idea. She opened her mouth to offer her opinion, when Stuart interrupted.

"I don't believe there was something *evil* there, Sarah, like we had mentioned before. Robbie and I have been talking about this since you and I met at my apartment."

Sarah assumed Stuart would stay far away from Robbie. After all, the man had fed bad thoughts into his friend's head. The fact that they had discussed the event together – prior to their meeting – made her feel isolated. The few words they had spoken already was best summed up as a dismissal. The guys tried to make the situation out to be *no big deal.* To them, it was just an unsettled ghost that was trying to spook them all into leaving its domain. Stuart and Robbie were ready to move on. Sarah believed they were fooling themselves; they knew there was a demonic presence in the room, but they were too scared to accept it. And they did not want her thinking ill of Robbie or that he had potentially been possessed.

"No," Sarah interjected, "this was meant to happen – and it was meant to take place between the three of us."

Both men sat perfectly still and stared at Sarah. They were hinged on her words.

Robbie laughed, "Are you saying it was *ordained?*"

"I am," she quickly responded with confidence. "Robbie, you're an atheist, right?"

"Well, if *you* say so – I . . . ," he started to respond.

"And Stuart, you don't know what to believe when it comes to God, right?" Sarah interrupted.

"You don't have to put it quite like *that*," he grumbled.

The two men mumbled under their breath. They did not know how to react. They wanted to deny such allegations, but they were intrigued by her insight.

"I'm a Christian," stated Sarah. "I haven't been a good one – mind you – but I'm a believer that had backslid."

At the mention of the word *Christian*, Robbie rolled his eyes and looked over his right shoulder away from the other two. He turned his head back to face them. "I'm sorry, but you think *your God* made this happen? What are you getting at?"

Sarah's eyes widened at the man's accusation, "I think God *allowed* it to happen. We are responsible for what we do with our lives. God is just trying to save us from our own destruction."

"Wow! That's one profound theory, Sarah," Stuart mocked.

Robbie raised his voice and scoffed, "My mother is one of you *Born-Agains*. She has spent her entire life trying to convert me and persuade me into believing in some guy named Jesus. I'll have no part in that fantasy world, my dear."

There seemed to be many painful and resentful events in Robbie's history, including the stories he told of his father and grandmother. If it were true that he was abused by his family, then finding God was probably the farthest from his thoughts. But to Sarah, it was what he needed the most. She felt compassion for the man.

"This was a ghost or a grand hallucination," Robbie continued.

"Wait! Sarah stated. "You believe in ghosts, but not in God? That doesn't even make sense. God IS a spirit! Do you choose to believe in the spirit of a dead person, because it's more glamourous? And why would it be a *grand hallucination* if you didn't lace the edible with a hallucinogen?"

Robbie felt attacked and did not quite know how to answer Sarah. Suddenly, they were interrupted by the waiter when he returned with their order. The two men quickly dove into the pizza to avoid confrontation.

But Sarah had more to say. "I definitely think the pot was enhanced, but I did not imagine things. Where did you get the edible."

"I can't give you that information. The dispensary is private."

Sarah's back straightened up with a sudden onslaught of confidence. She folded her arms and placed them on the table. "Robbie, if there's a dispensary out there selling laced marijuana that makes people want to harm their friends, don't you think they should be shut down?"

"It wasn't laced. I have gotten pot from the same place for a while now, and nothing has ever happened. I'm telling you – that house was haunted."

Sarah tabled the drug subject for the moment. It was not where she wanted the conversation to go. She brought it back around to God and stared straight at Robbie. "This totally makes sense to me. You, Stuart, me – this was a coming together of a non-believer, a lukewarm believer, and a lost believer. We were the *perfect storm* – can't you see that? The devil had his hand in this – and so did God."

Sarah's notion was too far-fetched for the boys to comprehend. They would rather believe in an unhappy ghost, than admit the event could have been about them.

"Ahh, come on Sarah," Robbie doubted.

"Look. If you believe in a ghost – something you don't see – then why is it so hard to believe in *God* that you don't see? Furthermore, the type of ghost you speak of is a spirit of a former living person. It may have occupied that home at one time and never passed on; I don't know how ghosts operate. But an evil spirit or demon is totally different," she continued. "A demon is sent by Satan."

"Nonsense!" Stuart piped up. "I don't believe in evil. I believe we may have conjured up some negative forces, but . . . ."

". . . they were already in the house to begin with," Robbie completed Stuart's sentence.

"Really, Stuart? You were the one that told me you saw an 'evil Robbie' trying to manipulate your thoughts!"

"Yeah, you did say that, dude," Robbie spoke. "I don't know why you said it, because I had not changed as far as I could tell. Only the atmosphere changed." He was lying. Robbie knew something had come over him, but he was trying to save face.

"Don't you understand what happened here, guys? This was God's way of letting each one of us know that we need to believe in Him – repent and quit sinning. I think us meeting back in February was meant to be. Even though my faith was weak, I am the vessel He is using to bring us closer to Him."

"I'm outta here," Robbie spoke angrily and threw down his pizza crust. "No one is going to try and make me believe that this was God versus Satan or that I should become a Christian. Your theory just doesn't jive with me."

"I'm not forcing my faith down your throat, Robbie," Sarah fought back. "I'm asking you to consider what I so obviously see – and to just think about it."

Robbie got up from the table and stared at Sarah. He had no interest in hearing the rest of her interpretation of the event. He was so turned off by the mere mention of God, that nothing else mattered. It was a strange haunting to him – and that was that. In the moment of silence, Sarah could see all of Robbie's pain. She sensed the darkness over him – that same feeling she had at the river. It was very present and made her body shudder.

Robbie's eyes welled up with tears, and the corners of his mouth turned downward. "I'm hopeless, Sarah. Let me go."

She was shocked to hear his words. They did not sound like something he would say. Deep down, Robbie imagined that God might be trying to speak to him, but he was not about to put his pride aside and let Him in, especially in front of Stuart. He had completely abandoned hope. It was clear to Sarah that he was hiding inside a shell of demonic strongholds. She felt pity for him. He was a broken man who needed to hear the Word of God.

Stuart's mouth hung open as he observed the scene. He watched the facial expressions and body movements of each of his friends – and said nothing.

Sarah was stymied. Since the guys were not open to listening to her, she did not know what to do. Being a witness for God was not her forte – yet. Before she could work on saving Robbie and Stuart, she needed to figure out her own life, first. Sarah was at a standstill. But God took hold of her tongue, as she bowed her head. "Father, I lift up my friends to You . . . ," she started to pray under her breath.

"Stop! I'm leaving," Robbie demanded.

Stuart immediately pushed his chair out and rose to his feet.

Sarah got up as well. They all looked at each other.

Robbie stuck out his hand in a gesture of truce. There was no hug or kiss, only a firm, icy handshake. He was done. "Goodbye," he said.

"See ya, hun," Stuart interrupted and hugged Sarah. "Good luck."

Sarah was dumbfounded and speechless. The men walked away from the restaurant, leaving her standing alone. The feeling in the air was weird and empty. She felt unsettled and unfinished yet renewed.

The sun was close to setting over the ocean. The orange sky was a dramatic backdrop as Sarah drove home, thinking of their conversation and how she had been perceived. *Why did the talk fail?* she wondered. "They must have thought I was crazy. God, this is in Your hands," she spoke out loud. "I said my truth." Out of habit, Sarah glanced in her rearview mirror to check and see if anyone was following her home. No one was there. She sighed with relief and turned back to watch the road. "I can't make them love You, God. I just hope that the words I said will sink in someday and that they will take some time to reflect on their lives – and what happened to us at the river."

The twilight sky now illuminated the rest of her way. Sarah had arrived home before dark. When she got inside her apartment, she sent a quick text to Michael to let him know she was back – safe and sound. *No more snakes, Michael,* the message read. *It's done.*

Chapter 40

REJOICE

The next day, Sarah woke to a renewed life, filled with sunshine and promise. It was mid-morning; she had overslept. But it felt good. With outstretched arms, Sarah looked upward and yawned, loudly, "What do You have for me this day, Lord?"

Her energy level was high. It did not take long for her to jump out of bed, slide into a pair of fuzzy slippers, and grab a hot cup of tea with milk and honey. As she prepared her drink, she checked her phone. Michael had responded to her text letting her know he was pleased with how the night ended and that he wanted to catch up again when he was finished with his business travels. Sarah smiled and set her phone down.

She shuffled briskly to the patio and stepped out into the daylight to gaze at her surroundings. The vision was a series of pictures in time to capture and remember. She put her tea on a small, nearby table, ran into the apartment to get her camera, and returned quickly to the scenery. Perfection was in everything she laid her eyes on. The twisting branches of the trees and their multi-shaped leaves offered a beautiful sight. The hills were lush – dotted with patches of wildflowers. *Lovely,* she thought. Sarah snapped photos from several angles. Everything appeared fresh and different to her.

The beauty of nature was no longer to be captured only for clients. Sarah had a new appreciation for it all – because it was created by God. The vivid backdrop was precise and flawless. Her camera clicked rapidly.

Sarah pulled the viewfinder away from her eye and breathed in the moist air. It was all so delightful: the sights and smells, the peonies on her patio, the maple and palm trees, the chirping birds, the baby-blue sky, the distant hills – even the people walking on the sidewalk. She closed her eyes and slowly exhaled. The outdoor scent lingered in her mind. It carried with it, familiarity and happiness. She grinned.

Sarah headed back inside and hopped on her computer. There had to be something she could find to do outdoors. While online, two notices popped up on the side of the screen. One was for a discount on ferry service to Catalina from Long Beach, and the other promoted a church located in her neighborhood.

"Mom and Daddy!" she said with excitement. "This must be a sign." Sarah was determined to visit the island where her parents had perished. She clicked on the ad and looked into getting a ticket for the following weekend. Upon retrieving her credit card out of her wallet, Sarah pulled out the sepia picture of her mother and father and took both items back to her desk to continue the transaction. She was excited to spend the day touring the island on which the couple had spent their honeymoon. She knew they must still be there – in spirit, at least. A kiss was planted on the photograph and her ticket and itinerary were printed.

Once again, the promotion for the church popped up. Sarah clicked on it. The structure in the picture seemed very familiar to her. She realized she had passed it several times coming home from her outings. Growing up, there was never any excitement to attend church. It was only important on holidays. Things were viewed differently now. Her relationship with Jesus was direct – with Him and Him alone. But she understood that gathering with other believers was good for spiritual growth and to hear God's messages. The ad stated that the church was open all day – every day.

"I think I'll go," Sarah said out loud. "Yes, I want to go – right now." With no hesitation, she dressed, ate a couple slices of toast with peanut butter, and flew out the door. It would only be a ten-minute drive. She just wanted to go inside the building and look around. That was all.

When Sarah arrived, there were only a few cars in the lot. No service was going on. She parked. A flicker of light flashed on her face. She looked up to see her necklace with the cross gently twisting in the sunlight. The tiny etchings on its surface reflected the light so beautifully – it made her smile. Sarah stopped it from swaying with her hand, and took a moment to stroke the metal.

The church's doors were open. When she walked into the sanctuary, a calmness immediately washed over her. The room was lit with natural light and lofty. There were long wooden beams along the ceiling that reminded her of an old barn. She heard music in the distance. It was coming from the overhead speakers, positioned in the upper corners of the room. The sound was low enough to create a sweet ambiance. It was pleasant and sounded like Spanish guitar. She grinned.

The room was very large and appeared to accommodate about three thousand people. No one was inside at that moment, but Sarah did not feel lonely or alone. A tall, simple podium was positioned in the center of the raised stage and was lit by a tiny light. An open Bible was on top.

Sarah approached the second pew from the front and slowly eased her body down on the seat cushion. She looked around at the church's interior. The vaulted ceiling was about twenty feet above her head. An overwhelming feeling of being safe made her weep. There was no threat of evil. There was no fear of judgement or shame. She held her head in her hands and cried.

Suddenly, she heard muffled voices coming from behind the stage walls. She figured they must belong to volunteers and church staff. Then within seconds, a man appeared at her side – out of nowhere. "Hello, Miss – are you ok? Can I get you some water?"

"No," Sarah said humbly, gazing up at the stranger. "Thank you. I'm just here to pray."

The man smiled at her. "Alright, then. Stay as long as you want," he whispered. "Let me know if you need anything. My name is Pastor Ray. Would you like me to pray over you before I go?"

"Yes. Thank you, Pastor." Sarah stood up to shake his hand. "My name is Sarah. I think I experienced spiritual warfare. I almost died at the hands of my friends. But Jesus saved my life."

The man nodded gently at Sarah and reached into his pocket for a tiny vile of oil. He smeared a drop on her forehead in the shape of a cross and then placed his right hand on her left shoulder. "Dear Father in Heaven. Thank You for delivering our sweet sister, Sarah, out of darkness and into the light of Your mercy and grace. Lord Jesus, You have rescued her from the grips of Satan. We pray that You bind all evil and cast it out of her life to never return. May Your promise of love and salvation lead her down a righteous path. Fill her with Your Holy Spirit, Father. Thank You for leading her here today to repent of her sins and remind her that Your Son has paid for them all by the shedding of His blood. In the Holy name of Your Son, Jesus Christ of Nazareth, I pray and ask for all these things. Amen."

"Amen," said Sarah. "Thank you, Pastor Ray."

"God is good, Sarah – all the time," he said with a smile. "We hope to see you again." Then he walked away.

A happy Sarah sat back down on the pew. She was comforted by the pastor's kindness and consideration. There was something special about him that made her tear up. Maybe it was his genuine demeanor or his intuitive prayer. Her eyes glistened as she watched him vanish out of sight.

Sarah had more to say to God, privately. She bowed her head between her forearms, which she placed on the pew in front of her, and whispered a child-like prayer, "Father, dear Father in Heaven. Thank You for saving me, forgiving me, bringing me out of darkness, and pulling me from the pit that I had fallen into. Thank You for Pastor Ray being here to pray over me. Thank You for Michael and his encouragement. I lift up to You, Robbie and Stuart – and everyone. I pray they come to know Your mercy and Your love. Remind us to not rely on our own understanding and remind us to follow Your will. Let us look to – and live – Your Word, daily. I repent of all my sins. I deny myself, now Father. I shed my old life for a renewed one – with You. Thank You, Jesus, for dying for my sins. I want to follow You and please You every day of my life. You are there for us, always. We need only to let You in. Fill me with Your Holy Spirit. Thank You, Father God. It's in Jesus' name that I pray. Amen."

The room was peaceful. She did not want to leave. Sarah waited silently to hear His voice. Her eyes remained closed, and she breathed in deeply, allowing the glowing atmosphere to consume her. It was so serene. She doubted nothing. Tears fell upon her knees. The feeling was intense, yet gentle. Safety – love – peace; that is what she felt.

Then, cool air tickled Sarah's face and swirled around her body. It startled her a bit. First, she thought it was the pastor returning, creating a breeze as he passed by. But there was no person there. The wind made her laugh. She inhaled deeply and held her breath. She did not want to let it go. Was it God saying hello? Feelings of forgiveness and redemption filled her as she exhaled. Sarah had been saved.

When she finally walked out into the courtyard, she could not help but admire the grass at her feet. It was a beautiful blanket of green. Each blade reflected the sun's light. They crunched under her shoes, and she giggled.

All of a sudden, an unusual feeling came over her. She lifted her head to look toward the parking lot. Was she witnessing an illusion? In a matter of seconds, she had to make sense of the fact that Stuart was standing next to her vehicle; he was not empty-handed. In his arms was a tiny, grey-and-white-haired puppy.

She ran to him. "How did you know I would be here, Stuart? And who is this little baby?"

"He doesn't have a name yet," Stuart said, handing Sarah the dog. "I was on my way to deliver him to you, but when I arrived at your place, you were just pulling out of your driveway. So, I followed you."

"He's mine?!" Sarah asked, excitedly. "You've been waiting out here all this time?"

"It was no problem. I was checking out the building and playing with the pup. And yes, he's yours. I know he can never replace Em, but I thought both of you could use a friend."

"I can't believe you did this for me."

"Yeah. I hope you like him. I rescued him from the shelter. I guess he was a runaway. He's got a pretty cute disposition, that's for sure."

The little dog lapped at Sarah's face and pawed his way up to her shoulders to snuggle behind her neck. She thought of little Emmy. Tears of happiness filled her eyes as she felt his unconditional love. "He's adorable. Thank you, Stuart. I love him."

Stuart froze for a moment, looked her square in the eyes, and said, "Sarah, after leaving the restaurant last night, I went home alone and thought long and hard about our conversation. I've contemplated for a long time – the universe and our existence. Everything I've ever learned has left me feeling more confused or empty – until I met you. Your words circulated in my head all night long. And then I remembered your vision of the white horse and the church. I started to realize that there was a message there for me to learn, too. I think we were both being guided. So – I have a proposition for you."

"I'm speechless, Stuart. What is it?"

Stuart cleared his throat and bent over to kiss the puppy on its head. Then he looked directly into Sarah's eyes again. "Please – tell me more about God."

AUTHOR'S NOTE

Sarah, Robbie, Stuart and all other people or animals featured are fictional characters; however, the inspiration for this book came from a real and - some would say - supernatural occurrence that happened among friends while vacationing in the desert. It was because of the incident that one of them renewed their faith and became a devout believer in Christ. Modifications and embellishments were made to creatively tell the story without involving or describing real people and their occupations.

The Awakening

If the feeling is hidden, it will show itself,
For all things hidden must someday see the light.
Darkness breeds grief
And grief never smiles.
It wades in black water
And is blind to its surroundings.
But sunshine breeds joy.
And misty rainbows fill the sky
As if to announce the beginning of life.
Why be a part of a world so full of uncertainty and dismay?
Let the rays beam down upon your weary eyes
That are so heavy now with sand.
Find what you are looking for
And do not be afraid of what's around the corner.
For it may just be – a rainbow.

Acknowledgments

Tons of gratitude goes out to all who participated in helping me on this journey. Thank You, God; thank You, Jesus - first and foremost.

My dear friend and mentor, David Richards, stayed up late on the phone listening to me read every chapter. His gift of lobster rolls were incentives to keep plugging away when I was nearing the end. He stood by me – patiently waiting for the final draft, at which point he happily praised.

The cover scene is two photographs. The hanging cross in the car was taken by me on a quiet road in Southern California and superimposed over a 1926 photo of the Castle Dome Mountains, obtained by the U.S. Geological Survey Department of the Interior. Amazing layout work was done by Michael Campos. His expertise, along with his kind spirit, brought it all together.

Thanks to Prosperity Shoppe, David, and Mark Catheline, who all helped with editing.

The countless prayers from Bible-study friends will forever be appreciated. My own prayers go right back to them.

Thank you, Mom, for reading the final draft. She had to put it down, momentarily, to cry.

To my son – thank you for loving me and knowing how important it was to get this book written.

Thank you to the reader. I hope you enjoy *Before the Rooster Crows Twice*. This story is being told for you.

God bless you all.
C. Arden Michaels

About the Author

C. Arden Michaels is a former news director, anchor, reporter, and radio announcer, as well as published poet and magazine writer. Michaels is the winner of several journalism awards and was a board member of the Maine Association of Broadcasters. Time is spent in California and Maine with dog Bogart. *Before the Rooster Crows Twice* is C. Arden Michaels' first novel.

CArdenMichaels.com
Facebook.com/CArdenMichaelsOfficial
@CArdenMichaels

"Let us lay aside every weight,
and the sin which so easily ensnares us,
and let us run with endurance
the race that is set before us."

Hebrews 12:1